SHE'LL STEAL YOUR HEART

RACHEL LACEY

COPYRIGHT

1

The floor vibrated beneath Lauren Booker's sneakers, thumping rhythmically as the train sped along the tracks. Lauren stared out the window to her left, her gaze locked on the Manhattan skyline adorning the horizon ahead. Her arms tightened around the backpack in her lap, and butterflies danced in her stomach.

Home.

At least, it used to be. Now the sight of the familiar skyline filled her with a deep sense of yearning. After over a year in Rhode Island, one of the hardest years of her life, she missed her hometown desperately. Officially, she was here now to meet some of her online friends in person for a fun weekend get together.

Unofficially...Lauren was going to fight like hell to stay. But for that to happen, she would have to face her past and accept the consequences of her actions. She would have to turn herself in to the police.

The knowledge rested heavily on her shoulders, slowly pushing her down, and she couldn't bear the weight much longer. She had to set herself free, even if it meant going to jail. But first, a fun weekend with friends.

"Can you believe we're finally back?" she whispered to Craig. When she and her brother fled the city together over a year ago, she hadn't been sure when—or if—this moment would come.

The train plunged into a tunnel as it began its descent below Manhattan. Lauren stared into the darkness outside her window. Anticipation coiled inside her. Despite everything, she was so glad to be back in this city, *her* city. She'd missed it every single day she'd been gone.

"What do you think, Craig? Should I stop for a hot dog from Sunny's on my way to the Airbnb?" She grinned at the thought, and her stomach gave a hungry gurgle.

Her phone pinged inside her backpack, the sound of an incoming email, and she unzipped the top pocket to pull it out. The email was from Archive of Our Own—better known as AO3 in the fandom community—the website where she read and posted fan fiction. Someone had left a new comment on *Skin Deep*, the *In Her Defense* fanfic that was Lauren's pride and joy.

In Her Defense was a legal drama starring Lauren's favorite actress and celebrity crush, Piper Sheridan. Piper's character on the show, Samantha Whitaker, was a badass lawyer who seemed destined to hook up with the show's male lead, but she also had amazing chemistry with her onscreen best friend, Claire, which had prompted an online queer cult following for Sam and Claire. Their fans had dubbed Sam and Claire as #Clairantha on social media.

Reading fan fiction about Sam and Claire had been a much-needed source of joy for Lauren over the last few years, and it had sparked something in her, a long-repressed urge to write. As a child, she'd written stories on note paper and dreamed of being an author someday, but as an adult, it hadn't seemed like a practical goal. She and Craig had bounced through the foster care system until she aged out and took legal custody of him, and then she'd had to work her ass off to provide for them both.

"You drew the coolest illustrations for those stories I wrote for you when we were little," she whispered. "We made a great team."

Her arms tightened reflexively around the backpack in her lap, feeling the solid outline of the urn containing Craig's ashes inside it. Her vision blurred, and her throat ached. She sucked in a breath, determined not to cry on a crowded Amtrak train. Ever since they were kids, it had always been Lauren and Craig against the world. Who was she now without him?

Desperate for a distraction from her spiraling emotions, she clicked on the email from AO3.

SamIsMyWife left the following comment on Skin Deep: OMG you're amazing! I just binge read this whole story, and I'm crying at how beautiful it was. This is without a doubt the best Clairantha fic I've ever read.

Lauren's cheeks warmed at the compliment. She'd been terrified to post the first chapter, certain no one would read her indulgent little story, and if they did, they'd definitely laugh at her and tell her she was a terrible writer.

That hadn't happened. Instead, she got regular comments like this one, comments that filled the void where her self-esteem ought to be. She'd made online friends in the *In Her Defense* fan community, people who shared her obsession with the show and with Sam's character in particular. That community and these comments had almost single-handedly gotten her through the past year.

Her phone dinged again, this time a new message in her WhatsApp group chat. Lauren clicked on it, and a photo appeared on her screen: two smiling women who she was about to meet in person for the first time. Ashleigh's jet-black hair, pale skin, and cherry-red lipstick gave her a bit of a goth vibe. By contract, Fatima's skin was a warm golden brown, her wavy black hair pulled back in a ponytail as she grinned at the camera. They wore matching Clairantha T-shirts, the same shirt Lauren was wearing.

The caption below the photo read, "WE'RE HERE!!!" Lauren could just make out the living room of the Airbnb they'd rented for the weekend behind them. Another photo followed, this time Sarah and her girlfriend, Quinn, also in their Clairantha shirts.

Sarah: Our flight just landed! We'll be there in an hour or so. CAN'T WAIT TO SEE AND HUG YOU ALL!

Quinn: <smiley face emoji>

Ashleigh: Our Airbnb is so nice! Fatima and I are going on a grocery run. The door code is 4853 if you get here before we're back.

Lauren: I'm on Amtrak — should get there around the same time as Sarah and Quinn. Excited doesn't cover it!

Fatima: Same, girl. Same!!

Mia: Leaving the café shortly. See you all soon!

Lauren took a quick selfie in her seat and sent it to the group. The new season of *In Her Defense* would release at midnight, and she and her friends were going to hang out in their Airbnb all weekend and watch it together.

Lauren could hardly wait, both to see the new season

and to meet her friends in person. Mia was the only local and would be staying in her own apartment this weekend. She was a former lawyer who'd recently opened a cat café in Brooklyn, which Lauren totally wanted to visit now that she was back in town so she could snuggle all the cats.

Mia had been a huge help to Lauren when she was writing *Skin Deep*. She'd answered all Lauren's legal questions for the story, and she had been one of the first people to read and rave about the fic after Lauren posted it. They often messaged each other outside the group chat and had formed a friendship that Lauren cherished. Consequently, she was extra excited to meet Mia today. She hoped their online friendship would translate seamlessly into a real-life one, especially as Lauren—hopefully—reestablished herself in Brooklyn, where Mia also lived.

The train slowed as it began its approach into Penn Station. Lauren took a final glance at the messages on her phone before she tucked it inside her backpack. The train rolled to a stop, and people began crowding at both ends of the car to exit. Lauren slipped her backpack over her shoulders and stood, reaching up to retrieve her duffel bag from the overhead compartment.

Then she followed a stream of passengers out of the train and up several flights of stairs to the main part of the station. She followed signs to the subway and boarded the 3 train, which would take her to Brooklyn.

She felt a bittersweet tug of anticipation as she found an available seat, duffel bag between her feet and backpack in her lap, everything she owned crammed into a subway seat with her. It could have felt depressing, but right now, she was glad for the simplicity. Her life was portable this way, which had come in handy this past year.

And hopefully, she was here to stay. It wouldn't be easy.

She knew that. The cost of living in the city was a hurdle, not to mention her legal troubles. But she'd reserved a bed at a nearby hostel for the next two weeks and hoped she'd have something more permanent by then...assuming she wasn't in jail.

Her stomach pitched, and she tightened her arms around the backpack in her lap. No matter what happened, she'd get through it. Life rarely went the way she'd planned, and even if she didn't succeed this time, someday Brooklyn would be home again.

Thirty minutes later, Lauren exited the subway at Hoyt Street. As she stepped outside into the balmy August afternoon, her spirits soared as the familiar sights and sounds of her old neighborhood surrounded her.

She sucked in a lungful of air, laced with car exhaust and the candy-sweet scent of the bakery on the corner, feeling content in a way she hadn't since she left Brooklyn last year. This place was rooted in her soul. She hoisted her duffel bag across her shoulders and set off in the direction of the Airbnb, about three blocks away.

As she walked, Lauren became distracted watching the woman in front of her. She had on a gray Oxford shirt neatly tucked into eggplant-colored pants that perfectly cupped a shapely ass, not that Lauren was looking...except she was totally looking. The woman walked with a brisk, confident stride, and well, Lauren had always been a sucker for a smartly dressed woman.

And okay, maybe it had been a long time since she'd hooked up with anyone, long enough that she was ogling a stranger's ass, apparently. Lauren dragged her gaze up to the woman's wavy, ash-blonde hair, which was just long enough to brush her shoulders.

Idly, Lauren hoped the woman would turn around, so

she could see if she was as attractive from the front as she was from behind. As the blonde stopped to wait for the light at the crosswalk ahead to change, Lauren seized the opportunity to stand beside her and satisfy her curiosity.

She gave what she hoped was a casual glance to her left, and then her breath caught in her throat, because the woman was every bit as gorgeous from the front, but Lauren hadn't been ogling a random woman on the street.

It was Mia.

"MIA?"

Mia Solano turned at the sound of her name, recognizing Lauren easily from the many selfies she posted in their group chat. Lauren looked just like she did in her photos, with long brown hair and an earnest smile.

"Lauren!" Mia exclaimed, pulling her in for an impulsive hug.

Lauren hugged her back. "It's so good to finally meet you in person."

"You too," Mia said.

"You cut your hair. I didn't recognize you from behind."

Mia reached up to touch the ends of her newly shortened hair. "I did, just a few weeks ago. Part of the new me, I guess."

Lauren nodded. "I like it. It suits you."

"Thanks," Mia said. "We have a fun weekend ahead."

Lauren's expression brightened. "I can't wait to see everyone and watch season five."

"It couldn't possibly live up to *Skin Deep*, if you ask me."

Lauren ducked her head with a shy smile. "I'm sure *Skin Deep* was smuttier, anyway."

Mia laughed as the light changed, and they crossed the street together. "Definitely smuttier, but it's not just that. You wrote about Sam and Claire working together on a case that was just as complex and interesting as anything they've done on the actual show."

"With your help." Lauren walked beside Mia, wearing a black backpack with a duffel bag resting below it, like she was heading out on a long journey, not a weekend with friends.

She was more serious in person than Mia had expected. Online, Lauren was often exuberant and silly, a passionate fangirl for *In Her Defense* and Piper Sheridan, the actress who played Sam on the show. But then again, Lauren's brother had died last month, so that was probably the reason for the sadness lurking in her brown eyes.

"I was happy to help," Mia told her. "I love reading your work. Why so many bags?"

Lauren reached back to touch the duffel. "Oh, I'm staying here in Brooklyn after our watch party to settle a few loose ends for Craig and me."

"I'm sorry," Mia told her. "That must be really hard, and you don't have any other family around, right?"

"It was just the two of us." Lauren kept her gaze straight ahead as she walked. "Our mom died when I was fifteen and Craig was ten, and neither of us knew our dad."

Mia's life hadn't been all sunshine and rainbows, but she'd never buried anyone in her immediate family, and she was older than Lauren, who was entirely too young to have experienced so much loss, especially a younger sibling. "Does that mean you're back in Brooklyn to stay?"

Lauren gave her a small smile. "I sure hope so, but it will depend on how things play out next week. In the meantime, our fan weekend should be just the distraction I need."

"Thank goodness for that." Mia had been a little bit hesitant about this weekend, afraid she wouldn't fit in. She wouldn't exactly classify herself as a "fangirl," and she was at least ten years older than the rest of the women in their group, who all seemed to be in their twenties, but she was short on friends since the divorce.

She and Kristin had met in law school, and their social circles consisted almost entirely of fellow lawyers, so when Mia walked away from the law—and her wife—their friends had had to take sides, and unfortunately for Mia, most of them had chosen Kristin. The few times she'd gotten together with them since the divorce had been awkward.

Apparently, Mia's friends had had more in common with her career than with her as a person. So here she was, about to spend the weekend with a group of online friends who'd been her lifeline this year. Hopefully it would be fun, a new direction for her life.

She and Lauren approached the front of the building where their Airbnb was located. Mia stepped forward to enter the code Ashleigh had given them, and then she motioned Lauren ahead of her into the entrance hall.

"Looks like we're on the third floor," Lauren said, leading the way up the stairs. "Have you met anyone else from the group before?"

"No," Mia said. "You?"

Lauren shook her head. "I feel like I've been chatting with you all online forever. I can't wait to meet everyone."

"See who looks like their photos?" Mia quipped as they turned the corner at the landing and kept climbing toward the third floor.

Lauren looked over her shoulder with a smile. "I think I've seen enough selfies of everyone to have a pretty good idea, but it's still different meeting someone in person. Like, your voice is different than I was expecting...a little deeper. Isn't it funny how we've chatted for years and never knew the sound of each other's voice?"

"It is, and I've heard that before about my voice," Mia said. "I'm told it made me more intimidating in the courtroom."

"I bet you were pretty badass in court." Lauren stopped in front of the door to apartment 3B and knocked. There was no response. "Ash and Fatima must still be at the grocery store."

"Probably," Mia agreed.

Lauren entered the code for the door and let them inside. The studio apartment looked much as it had on the Airbnb listing, with dark-paneled walls, a full-sized bed in back, and a small galley kitchen. Lauren dropped her bags against the wall and wandered the space, hands in the pockets of her jeans.

Mia sat on the couch. "You're from Brooklyn, right?"

"Born and raised," Lauren confirmed.

"Well, I'm glad you're back. Why did you move to Rhode Island last year?"

Lauren flinched. "Long story."

"We've got time." Mia gestured to the empty apartment.

Lauren shook her head, her expression pinched. She almost looked...frightened. Or was it wary? "A story for another day."

"Sure." Mia sat back, startled by Lauren's response.

An uncomfortable silence spread between them. Before Mia could decide what to say, the door to the apartment swung open. Ashleigh stepped inside, followed by Fatima, both of them weighed down with brown paper shopping bags.

"Lauren!" Ashleigh put down her bags and wrapped

Lauren in a hug that lifted her feet right off the floor. (she'd released her, she turned toward Mia, hesitating just long enough to make Mia self-conscious again that she was too old, too *serious* for this crowd, before pulling her into a hug as well. "Mia, it's great to see you."

"You too, Ashleigh."

Fatima joined in for more hugs, and then Mia and Lauren helped them put away the groceries, which included a variety of alcoholic and nonalcoholic drink options for celebrating the new *In Her Defense* season. They'd barely gotten the bags unpacked before there was a knock at the door and Sarah and Quinn entered the room.

Sarah was a tall Black woman, her natural hair pulled back from her face with a red band that matched the color of the font on her Clairantha T-shirt. Quinn had fair skin, and her light brown hair was buzzed on one side, falling to her chin on the other. Together, they made a striking couple.

Sometimes, it was hard for Mia to wrap her mind around the fact that she was single again, after having been with Kristin for eighteen years. Mia had thought she was partnered for life. She and Kristin had worked for the same law firm, both so dedicated to their jobs that they rarely made time to watch television or go out after work...even for a date.

Mia had suffered constant migraines from the stress. She and Kristin fought incessantly. Mia had been *miserable*. Then she'd landed in the ER with a bleeding ulcer, where a harried doctor had told her she was working herself into an early grave.

And here she was a year later, a single woman who owned a cat café. She was in a room full of people she'd met online, strangers brought together by their love for a TV show. It was as confusing as it was thrilling. Despite her lingering feeling that she didn't quite belong, Mia was excited to watch the new season of *In Her Defense* with these women who shared her excitement for the show instead of sitting home alone with her cat.

Now that everyone was here, there were more hugs and greetings, women moving around the room to put down bags and pour drinks as they got to know each other. Eventually, they gathered around the kitchen table, where Ashleigh led a rather exuberant toast.

"To Sam Whitaker," she concluded, lifting her glass.

"And to Piper Sheridan for bringing her to life," Fatima added.

They tapped their glasses together, and Mia sipped her wine.

"I made something new to celebrate our weekend," Quinn told them as she set down her glass and walked to her bag. She pulled out her laptop and set it in the middle of the kitchen table.

"Oh my God, did you make a new fan video?" Lauren asked.

"I did," Quinn said with a proud smile. She worked in digital media at her day job and used her talent to make these really amazing videos where she paired clips from the show with music. Her videos always made Sam and Claire's relationship look more romantic than it actually was, which Mia supposed was the point.

She was surprised to find herself cheering along with the others as Quinn shared her newest video, set to a hauntingly beautiful song Mia had never heard before with lots of angsty shots of Sam and Claire gazing longingly at each other. Actually, it seemed like Sam was doing most of the gazing, and since she was played by a bisexual actress, Mia sometimes wondered if the way Sam looked at women was more Piper than Sam, but maybe that was just the cynic in her.

This led to a marathon viewing of various Clairantha fan videos. Eventually, they moved to the couch with the laptop on the table in front of them, all six women crammed together, laughing and sharing their favorite moments from the show. The new season didn't release until midnight, so this evening was a chance for them to get to know each other.

"Group selfie!" Sarah announced, holding up her phone.

"Wait. Mia, where's your Clairantha shirt?" Fatima gestured to Mia's gray button-down. "You're the only one not wearing it."

"Oh." Mia looked around and realized it was true. Earlier today, she'd felt self-conscious about working at her café wearing the shirt, and now, she felt embarrassed for being the only one *not* wearing it. "I was going to change once I got here."

"Then go change." Quinn made a shooing motion with her hands, gesturing toward the bathroom on the far side of the room.

So Mia took the T-shirt out of her bag and went into the bathroom to change, eyeing herself for a moment in the mirror. She frowned at her reflection, feeling ridiculous in a shirt that had #Clairantha printed in big red letters across the front and a sketch of Sam and Claire kissing below it. She'd never been a fan of branded tees.

But when in Rome...

After carefully folding her blouse, she went back to the living room, where she posed for a series of selfies with the other women. They ordered pizza, sharing plenty of laughs as Sarah dramatically read Clairantha fanfic to them while they ate.

"Who wants to go out for a drink before the new season drops?" Ashleigh asked after the pizza boxes had been cleared away.

"Me!" Sarah said, and the rest of the women quickly agreed.

"Mia, you're our local," Quinn said. "Know a good place?"

"There's a great little gay bar near here that has amazing drinks," Mia suggested. "The owner also runs a kitten rescue and helped me get set up with a rescue for my new cat café."

"Rescue kittens!" Fatima exclaimed. "Do we get to play with them?"

"No," Mia told her, smiling. "Josie's rescue is separate from the bar, but you can play with the rescue cats at my café if you want to visit."

"Oh please," Fatima said, nodding. "We definitely need to visit your café while we're in town."

"I agree, and the gay bar sounds perfect for a drink tonight," Sarah said, and a murmur of assent went around the room.

"Perfect," Mia said. "Let's go to Dragonfly."

"No!" Lauren said, a bit too loudly, and when Mia looked at her in surprise, Lauren was sitting rigidly on the couch, hands clenched on her knees. "I, um, I can't go there. Sorry."

2

———

"**Y**ou can't go to Dragonfly?" Mia asked. "Why on earth not?"

Lauren opened her mouth and shut it, fighting the urge to fidget beneath Mia's intense stare. Of all the bars in Brooklyn, Mia had to suggest the one that had been the scene of Lauren's fall from grace. Worse, apparently Mia and Josie were friends. What a small-world moment, and not in a good way.

Lauren would be visiting Josie and Dragonfly on her own next week to make things right, but she couldn't get into any of it with Mia, not without losing her friendship and potentially putting her in a legally awkward situation. "I have, um, history with the owner."

Mia hesitated, looking like she wanted to push the issue, but then she nodded. "Sure, no problem. There's a quiet bar a few blocks over with great whiskey and cheap beer. Does that work?"

Lauren exhaled in relief. "That sounds great, if it's okay with everyone else."

"Works for me," Quinn said, and the rest of the women agreed.

As everyone got ready to head out, Lauren used the moment to compose herself, pushing back the emotions that had risen over the last few minutes. Not that she'd intended to confess her secrets to Mia, but now that she knew Mia knew Josie, she also knew that if Mia ever learned the truth, she'd take Josie's side. She'd hate Lauren for what she'd done. Of course she would. Lauren couldn't even blame her. She hated what she'd done too.

She felt self-conscious about bringing her backpack to the bar, but there were things in it that were too valuable to be out of her sight. So she slung it over her shoulders, hoping no one would ask her about it, and luckily, no one did.

The bar Mia had suggested was indeed quiet, or it was until their group arrived. They clustered around several stools near the back, laughing and talking. Lauren settled on a stool and ordered a beer, her mood buoyed by the women around her. It had been so long since she'd been out with friends like this, and it fed her soul, as if a withered spot inside her had just bloomed for the first time in over a year.

She'd needed this night *so* much.

"Laur, I just reread *Skin Deep* for like the eighth time," Ashleigh said. "You should be writing books. I'm serious. You're that good."

Lauren smiled into her beer. "Thank you. That's actually my dream...to publish a book."

"Oh, you should," Mia said from where she stood behind Sarah and Quinn, tumbler of whiskey in hand. "You *are* that good, Lauren."

Her cheeks heated. "It felt unachievable when I was a teen writing stories in my notebooks at school, but fanfic has given me some courage, and self-publishing is an option now, so it's definitely something I've thought about."

"Have you written an original story?" Fatima asked.

Lauren nodded. "I've started too many to count, but I finished writing my first novel earlier this year."

"If there's anything you want me to look at for you, I'd be happy to," Mia offered.

"Thanks. I really appreciate that."

"Speaking of books, I just read an *amazing* sapphic romance," Quinn said. "It's called *On the Flip Side*, and both heroines are so smart and sexy. I'll send you all the link."

"Oh, I've read a few of that author's books," Lauren said, nodding. "I love her style, and I've been meaning to read that one."

From there, the conversation turned to the topic that had brought them all here this weekend: *In Her Defense*. They spent the next hour or so discussing theories and hopes for the new season. They all thought an on-screen romantic relationship between Sam and Claire was a long shot at best, but they were at least hoping for more of the semi-flirty scenes they'd gotten in season four.

Lauren rested her elbows on the bar, relaxed and happy. She'd just met these women, but already she felt comfortable with them. And then there was Mia, looking just a little bit more sophisticated than the rest of them, but every bit as enthusiastic about the show.

There was a magnetism about her, something Lauren couldn't seem to look away from. She knew what it meant. Lauren had been attracted to a friend before, and it hadn't ended well. But generally, if she ignored it, the inconvenient attraction would pass with time.

As if she'd summoned Mia with her thoughts, she slid onto the vacant stool beside Lauren, giving her another one of those intense looks. Her rich brown eyes were a striking contrast to her pale skin and blonde hair. It was darker at the roots as if she dyed it, or perhaps it lightened naturally in the sun.

"So are you going to tell me what went down between you and Josie?" Mia asked, her voice low and smoky.

Lauren had been nursing her beer since they got here, hoping to make it through the evening without ordering another one since she was pinching her pennies, but suddenly, she wished there was a *lot* more alcohol in her veins. "It's...complicated."

Mia gave her an assessing look, lips pursed as she twirled her whiskey glass idly in her left hand. "Were you and Josie an item before she married Eve?"

"Eve," Lauren repeated, her mind whirling. "Josie married Eve Marlow?"

"Yeah," Mia said slowly. "You didn't know?"

Lauren shook her head, brushing back a strand of hair. No, she hadn't known, but when she thought back on her time at Dragonfly, she remembered Josie being starry-eyed over a new woman in her life, which had been during the time that Eve was filming her TV show at Josie's bar. The idea of them being married now made Lauren smile. "I had no idea, but that's great."

"You aren't jealous?" Mia asked, still watching Lauren closely, reminding her that Mia thought she and Josie had been a thing.

"No. Josie and I weren't together. I actually used to work there," Lauren spluttered. "It ended badly...because of me, not Josie. Josie's great."

"Oh." Mia lifted her drink for a sip. After a moment, she gasped, setting the glass down so hard the bartender gave her a startled glance. "Oh my God, you're *that* Lauren? You're the Lauren who robbed the bar?"

MIA TOSSED BACK what remained of her whiskey as Lauren seemed to shrink on the stool beside her. Her new friend was a criminal. A thief. Mia hadn't known Josie at the time of the robbery, but she'd heard her tell the story. Just weeks after her bar's grand reopening, Josie had let her new bartender close for her for the first time. Lauren had made off with the contents of the cash register and some of Josie's most expensive liquor and then skipped town.

Mia *had* known Lauren then, although only from their online chats. She vaguely remembered that Lauren had disappeared from their group chat for a few weeks, later mentioning that she'd moved to Rhode Island, but Mia had never suspected Lauren was on the run from the law. Now that she knew, it felt like a betrayal.

"I can't believe this." Even Mia could hear how angry she sounded.

"I should go," Lauren said quietly. She slid off her stool and reached for the backpack she'd been carrying all evening. Her shoulders were hunched, her expression stricken. She looked like a kicked puppy, and Mia didn't like that either.

"Aren't you even going to try to explain yourself?" she asked, harshly enough for Lauren to flinch.

"Would it make a difference?" Lauren straightened to meet Mia's gaze. "You and Josie know each other. You're friends."

"We're friends," Mia confirmed. "But you're my friend too, Lauren. In fact, if you count our online friendship, I've known you longer than I've known Josie. So yes, it matters. Explain yourself, but don't give me any bullshit excuses."

Lauren sat and reached for her beer. She took a fortifying sip. "I robbed Josie's bar," she said, softly enough that only Mia could hear her. Luckily, the rest of their group was currently engaged in a lively discussion about Sam's most memorable power suit. "I take full responsibility for what I did. In fact, part of the reason I'm back in Brooklyn is to make things right, to repay her and turn myself in."

"I want to believe you." Mia had been a defense attorney for fifteen years. It had been her job to defend people like Lauren, whether they were guilty or not. But she wasn't Lauren's lawyer. She was her friend, and that felt different.

Lauren reached for her backpack again, and Mia thought she'd decided to leave after all. But she slid it into her lap and unzipped it, then removed an envelope from the top pocket. She passed it to Mia, but as she accepted the envelope, her gaze caught on a large canister taking up most of the space inside the bag. It looked like an urn.

Jesus fucking Christ.

Lauren exhaled softly, reaching out to touch it. "I'm going to scatter his ashes while I'm here too, but I didn't have a safe place to leave him in the meantime."

Mia opened the envelope Lauren had given her. Inside was a certified check for three thousand dollars, made out to Josie Swanson, which corroborated Lauren's story that she'd returned to Brooklyn to pay Josie back. In the face of that check—and the urn in Lauren's backpack—Mia felt her anger deflate like a ruptured balloon. "Why did you do it? Did you just need the money?"

Lauren shook her head as she carefully placed the check into her backpack and zipped it shut, returning it to its spot between her feet. "No, I was doing okay for once, and I loved my new job at Dragonfly. I truly did. Josie's the best, as I'm sure you know."

"Then why did you rob her blind? That really set her back—financially and emotionally—just when she was starting to turn things around for the bar."

Tears shone in Lauren's eyes, and her bottom lip shook. "I never meant to hurt her. When she left me on my own to close the bar that night, I was glad she was starting to give me more responsibility. I didn't want to let her down."

"You have a funny way of showing that," Mia muttered, gesturing to the bartender for another drink.

Lauren took a shaky sip of her beer. "My mom died of an overdose when I was fifteen. She struggled with drug addiction for most of her adult life, and so did Craig. I tried to help him, to get him clean, but he was in way over his head, both with his addiction and with the people he owed money to. Terrible people, Mia." Her voice wavered, and Mia's stomach plummeted. "He came into Dragonfly that night to ask if he could crash at my place for a few nights, and he... they'd beaten the shit out of him. He was terrified, and so was I."

Instinctively, Mia reached over and rested a hand on Lauren's against the bar top.

"He was completely strung out, and he owed *so much money*." Lauren took a slow breath. "I was afraid of what those people would do to him—or me—if he didn't pay back what he owed, and I was standing in front of a full cash register. I panicked. I told him to take the money to pay off his drug debts, but I didn't think it through, because then I was a thief. There was—and still is—a warrant for my arrest, and Craig...he did pay off his debts, but he didn't get clean."

"Jesus," Mia said. "Your heart was in the right place, but that was a really stupid thing to do."

"I know." Lauren nodded. "It was *so* stupid, and I regretted it almost immediately, but I couldn't turn myself in, not without leaving Craig all alone while he was in terrible shape. I feared for his life every day, Mia. I thought if I was there, I could keep him alive." Lauren swiped at her eyes. "So we skipped town together and started a new life in Rhode Island, such as it was, with me on the run and him still numbing his pain with opioids. Last month, he OD'd, just like our mom. After all that...I still failed him."

"I'm so sorry." Mia's hand was still on Lauren's. She couldn't relate to anything Lauren had just shared. She'd never battled addiction or known anyone who had. She'd never lost a loved one. And she'd never committed grand larceny in the name of love. "But you didn't fail him. Addiction is a disease."

"I know that," Lauren whispered. "But he was my baby brother, and I had promised him that I'd keep him safe. But it turns out, I couldn't do that, no matter how hard I tried."

"It sounds like you did your best," Mia said. "And you're here now to clear the charges against you?"

"Yes, I...I'm going to start by paying Josie back. And then I'll turn myself in and hope for the best."

"Okay, well you're not going to do *that*," Mia said. "You need a lawyer first, and you shouldn't walk into Josie's bar unannounced either."

Lauren stared at her out of wide eyes, looking confused, scared, and so damn young. "Why not?"

"I'll call Josie and see how she wants to do this, but it shouldn't be an ambush."

Lauren flinched. "I don't want to ambush her, not at all."

"I know you don't, but I'm afraid that's what it would feel

like if you just come strolling into her bar after the way you left."

Lauren nodded, eyes downcast. "You're right. I'll figure something out, but I don't want you to feel like you have to get involved just because you know us both. I'm trying to do the right thing here, not cause more trouble for anyone, least of all you."

"I don't mind making a phone call to see how Josie wants to handle this. As for the rest...you really do need a lawyer." She met Lauren's gaze. They both knew Mia was a lawyer. She could offer to represent Lauren. It would be so easy, a chance to flex her legal muscles, which, honestly, she would enjoy. But she didn't offer, at least not yet. She needed time to think, to sort out her feelings about what Lauren had done.

"I'm not asking for your help," Lauren said, lifting her chin.

"No," Mia agreed.

"I just want to make it right." Lauren traced a finger through the condensation on her glass.

Mia exhaled. "Let's talk on Monday before you go to the police."

"Oh my God," Ashleigh screeched, bouncing beside Lauren on the couch.

It was past two in the morning, and they'd just finished watching the second episode of the new season of *In Her Defense*, which had ended with Sam in the shower, crying against the tiles after losing an important case. And yeah, she looked hot with water coursing over her face and the swell of her breasts visible at the bottom of the screen.

But Lauren's heart ached for Sam. She knew what it felt like to put on a brave face for the world and save her tears to be shed later under the protective cover of the shower.

"Oh, Sam," Fatima moaned, turning to wrap her arms around Lauren. "You're breaking my heart."

Sarah paused the playback as everyone broke into conversation about what they'd just seen.

"Season five is off to an amazing start," Quinn said, pressing a hand against her chest. "So much great Sam content, and that scene with her and Claire in the board-room? I almost thought we were going to get a canon reen-actment of the conference table scene in *Skin Deep*."

"Great chemistry in that scene," Mia agreed.

Lauren had trouble meeting her gaze after their conver-sation in the bar earlier. She could hardly believe Mia knew the truth, and she hadn't turned Lauren in to the police...at least, not yet. In a way, it was a relief that she knew, that *someone* knew the truth about Lauren's past.

Her future felt inevitable now. In a few days, she would either get the charges against her dropped or she would go to jail. Either way, she would end her time on the run and start the next chapter in her life. In the meantime, she was soaking up every moment of this weekend, in case it was her last weekend of freedom.

"Anyone want to keep going and binge all night?" Fatima asked sheepishly.

"I've got to head out before I'm too tired to make it back to my apartment," Mia said, although she didn't look partic-ularly tired. She looked...softer was the best word Lauren could think of to describe this late-night version of Mia. Her posture was relaxed, her brown eyes less intense.

"I'll be a zombie tomorrow if I don't sleep soon," Ash

said with a yawn. "Let's crash and regroup in the morning. What time are you coming back, Mia?"

"Whatever time you all are up," Mia said with a shrug. "I've got staff covering for me at the café all day."

"You're sure you don't want to stay here with us?" Sarah asked, although Lauren wasn't sure where Mia would sleep if she did stay. Quinn and Sarah were sharing the bed, Fatima and Ash would sleep on the pull-out couch, and Lauren got the twin-sized air mattress.

"Tempting, but I didn't bring anything with me to sleep, and anyway, Lola would riot if I'm not there to feed her in the morning," Mia said, causing everyone to laugh, because they'd all heard stories about her diva cat.

"See you in the morning," Quinn said with a sleepy smile. "Not too early, though."

Mia stood from the couch. "I'll bring coffee and pastries from the café."

"We love you forever," Sarah told her, and they all laughed again.

"All right, ladies, have a good night, and I'll see you in the morning." Mia's gaze landed on Lauren, and her stomach clenched, a combination of her body's automatic response to being caught in Mia's stare and the knowledge that Mia knew what she'd done.

As Mia picked up her bag and let herself out of the apartment, a cynical part of Lauren's brain wondered whether she should expect the police to come knocking in a few hours. Surely Mia wouldn't do that. Would she?

Lauren forced the thought from her mind as she joined the other women in preparing for bed. Ashleigh unfolded the sofa bed while Lauren retrieved the air mattress from the closet and began to inflate it. It took almost an hour before the lights were out.

It was past three in the morning now, and she ought to be exhausted, but she lay awake in the darkened room for what felt like hours, her mind replaying her earlier conversation with Mia, the fun she'd had with her friends, and the less fun things she had to do next week.

Lauren could just make out the shape of her backpack beside the air mattress. Helplessness rose inside her as she thought of the urn inside it, of spreading Craig's ashes. Without him, she was all alone in the world. She had no home, no family, no friends left except the women in this room...and Mia.

This weekend was a splurge for Lauren, but it was a much-needed one. She'd worked extra shifts and skimped on meals all month to be able to afford her portion of the apartment rental and groceries, and it was worth every hard-earned penny.

Finally, her eyes grew heavy, and she drifted into a fitful sleep. Bits of the show incorporated themselves into her dreams. She saw Sam crying in the shower, Sam in one of her power suits defending Lauren in court. And then it was Mia standing beside her in a power suit, arguing with the judge to get the charges against Lauren dropped.

Her eyes popped open, and she rolled to her side, cringing at the squelching noise the air mattress made beneath her. It was obnoxiously loud in the room full of sleeping women. Someone was snoring, and while that sometimes annoyed her, tonight it was a welcome sound, reminding Lauren that she wasn't alone.

She'd rarely had the luxury of her own room, sharing with Craig as a child, then other foster kids in her group home, and later, roommates. But since his death last month, she'd been by herself in their apartment in Rhode Island. It was the loneliest, worst month of her life.

The next time she woke, she heard murmured voices. She smiled as she opened her eyes, so damn happy to be in a room full of friends. Blinking to clear the sleep from her eyes, she turned her head to see Ash and Fatima sitting together on the pull-out couch, looking at something on Fatima's phone.

Sarah and Quinn were still asleep, cuddled together in bed. Of all the things Lauren missed about having a girl-friend, snuggling in bed was high on the list. Sure, sex was amazing, but she liked having someone around for the mundane parts of the day too. She would have loved to have someone to hold her when Craig died, someone to stand beside her while she spread his ashes.

"Lauren," Fatima whispered, waving her over. "Come look. Piper posted some selfies from filming season five."

Lauren grinned as she scooted toward the side of the air mattress. It had semi-deflated as she slept so that the edge collapsed beneath her, dumping her unceremoniously on the floor. She stood and walked to the couch, sitting beside Fatima, who held her phone out for Lauren to see the photos on the screen.

There was an image of Piper in front of a mirror ringed with lights, smiling as someone did her hair, one of her sitting at Sam's desk, and one of her posing with Eliza Burroughs, the actress who played Claire. Piper was play-fully kissing her cheek as Eliza grinned at the camera. She'd captioned the photo "#Clairantha — kicking ass in the boardroom and out of it."

"Um, holy shit," Lauren whisper squealed. "She is such a tease, and I love her for it."

"Maybe she's not just teasing," Ash said hopefully. "Maybe we're going to get real Clairantha content this season."

"I'm not holding my breath," Fatima said. "But I thank Piper profusely for keeping the dream alive."

"What are you all whispering about over there?" Sarah mumbled from the bed.

"New selfies from Piper," Ash told her, holding up Fatima's phone. "And she's teasing us about Clairantha again."

"Oh my God, bring that over here," Sarah said.

So they all piled in bed to gush about Piper's selfies. It felt like the grown-up version of a high school slumber party, and Lauren's heart was light. There was a brisk knock at the door, and just like that, her whole body tensed. Surely it wasn't the police, but...

This was how it would be for her every moment that she remained in Brooklyn until she turned herself in. If she was going to be arrested today, she'd at least like to brush her teeth and pee first. Her heart thumped against her ribs.

Unaware of Lauren's turmoil, Fatima hopped off the bed and walked to the door. She opened it to reveal Mia standing there. *Thank God.* Lauren slumped in relief.

Mia had on black pants and a blue-patterned top, looking fresh and put together while the rest of them were sleep rumpled and still in their pajamas. Mia carried a large paper bag and a carton of insulated drinks. Her eyes met Lauren's across the room, and her heart sped for an entirely different reason.

3

"Oh no," Lauren murmured as the man onscreen pulled a gun on Sam.

Mia gripped her hand without thinking, caught up in the moment. Gunshots rang through the room, and Sam fell, causing various gasps and cries from the women sitting around Mia.

Credits rolled as episode six began to load, and Sarah hit Pause so they could process what they'd just seen. This had become their unofficial routine, pausing between episodes to chat and get refreshments before they dove into the next.

"Sam," Lauren moaned.

"Well, she can't die," Quinn said. "I mean, they can't just kill off one of the leads."

"It's been done before," Fatima argued. "Does anyone know how many seasons Piper is contracted for?"

"She's not going to die," Mia said. "Remember in the season five trailer when they showed that clip of Sam and Claire in a bar? We haven't seen that yet, so obviously Sam's going to recover."

"Mia for the win!" Lauren exclaimed, bumping her

shoulder against Mia's. "She's totally right. There's at least one scene with Sam that we haven't seen yet, so hopefully that means she's going to be okay, but ugh, I hate the thought of her being shot. Why do shows feel like they have to cause characters so much pain just for ratings?"

"I think you just gave the reason," Mia said. "Ratings."

"Well, I certainly hope Claire will be there to nurse her back to health," Sarah said.

Quinn went into the bathroom, and Mia headed for the kitchen to pour herself a glass of water. Some of the women had started drinking already, but since it was just midafternoon, Mia was sticking with water for now. Lauren joined her in the kitchen. She poured her own glass of water before grabbing one of the remaining donut holes from the box Mia had brought.

She gave Mia a hesitant smile, but when Mia tried to return it, her face didn't quite cooperate. She hated that Lauren was a thief, hated *knowing* that Lauren was a thief, hated that she would have to decide what to do about it tomorrow when the rest of the women went home. Mia wanted to believe that Lauren had only been trying to help her brother and that she was back in Brooklyn to make things right, but could she trust that Lauren had told her the truth?

"Come on, ladies," Ash called from the living room. "Get your asses back in here so we can find out what happens to Sam."

They piled back onto the couch and queued up episode six. Lauren's legal troubles aside, Mia was surprised by how much fun she was having. She'd been afraid she would feel out of place this weekend, but she was on the edge of her seat as the episode began to play.

Fatima gripped her hand as the screen filled with an

image of Sam on the floor, blood leaking from her mouth and gasping for breath. Claire dashed into the lobby and knelt beside her. She ripped open Sam's shirt and pressed her hands against the gunshot wound, blood oozing between her fingers. Eyes wide and frantic, Sam lifted a hand and grasped at Claire's blazer.

"Did she just grope Claire's breast?" Sarah demanded, jumping to her feet. "Because I swear she just grabbed Claire's boob!"

"Rewind," Quinn said. "Because I saw it too."

"Oh my God," Lauren said softly, and when Mia looked at her, her expression was a mixture of worry and wonder. "This is the hottest gunshot ever."

They replayed the scene, and everyone squealed when Sam indeed palmed Claire's breast. It was surprisingly sexy to see them with their hands on each other's chests, even if Sam was fighting for her life.

Over the next hour, they watched Sam recover from her gunshot wound—much too quickly to be realistic, according to Ashleigh, who was a nurse. After watching episodes seven and eight, they decided to break for dinner. Soon they were crowded around a table full of Chinese food and several open bottles of wine.

"Only two episodes left," Sarah said. "I have a feeling all kinds of shit's about to go down."

"Sam, Sam, Sam," Fatima said in a mock-serious voice. "Picking up random men in bars when we all know she really wants Claire."

"Or Tony. The showrunners obviously want her to end up with him," Quinn said with a shrug. "Although I almost never root for the couple that feels forced on me by the show itself. I think the best ships are the ones that happen organically from the chemistry between the actors, like Sam and Claire."

"Preach!" Sarah held her wineglass in the air. "If only the showrunners could see what we do."

The group was lively and in good spirits as they ate, and Mia felt a twinge of disappointment that the weekend was almost over. They had two more episodes to watch, and then she'd go back to her apartment. Would she see the women again tomorrow morning before they headed home?

Well, she needed to see Lauren, but that was a separate issue, one Mia hadn't decided how to handle yet. Her gaze slid to Lauren, who was sitting on the floor with a plate of lo mein in her lap, giggling as Fatima showed her something on her phone. Lauren looked so young, so innocent, but she wasn't innocent. She'd committed felony robbery.

Lauren looked up and caught Mia watching her, and the laughter faded from her lips. Her eyes lost their sparkle, as if she'd read Mia's thoughts, and Mia didn't like that either. She forced a smile, and Lauren returned it hesitantly.

Out of nowhere, Mia had the thought that Sam Whitaker would surely champion Lauren. The premise of the show was Sam and her partners defending women who'd been taken advantage of by the system, women who had nowhere else to turn. At the very least, Mia would call Josie and set up the meeting between her and Lauren.

And maybe...maybe Mia would dust off her courtroom skills and represent Lauren. She deserved a good lawyer, even if she'd lied about the motive for her crime, but Mia's gut said Lauren was a decent person who'd made a bad decision in really shitty circumstances. Her love for her brother was obvious and heartbreaking.

After dinner, they gathered in front of the TV to watch

the final two episodes of the new season. Mia sipped her wine, seated between Lauren and Sarah on the couch.

On the screen, one of Sam's clients dropped her over a decision Claire made when she was covering for Sam while she was recuperating from her gunshot wound. Sam stormed into Claire's office with the kind of fiery rage that, to Mia's eyes, could only stem from suppressed feelings, but who knew what the show's writers had intended.

"How dare you?" Sam's voice was voice low and lethal, her blue eyes snapping.

"You weren't here, Sam," Claire said, remaining seated behind her desk. "She was always going back to her husband. It didn't matter whether I included the clause or not."

"You still should have tried!" Sam slammed her knuckles against the edge of Claire's desk.

"I did try," Claire said calmly. "I talked her through all her options, but ultimately I had to do what the client wanted, even if it wasn't what I thought was best for her."

"Your best wasn't good enough." Sam spun on her heel and stormed out of Claire's office, causing several whoops from the women watching her on TV.

"Sam's hot when she's mad," Quinn said.

Mia couldn't argue with that. She didn't have a crush on Piper Sheridan the way some of the others did, maybe because she didn't generally go for younger women, but she couldn't deny that Piper was beautiful. Sam Whitaker was undeniably sexy in her power suits...especially when she was worked up about something.

Later in the episode, Claire went to Sam's apartment, and Sam apologized for snapping at her earlier in the day. The next thing Mia knew, Sam and Claire were leaning toward each other over the kitchen island like they were about to kiss. Everyone cheered, even Mia, who was so lost in the moment she forgot that screaming at the television wasn't something she did.

At the last moment, Claire pulled back and went home, sending a groan around the room.

"Calling it now. This season's going to be nothing but a tease." Ash got up in a huff to refill her drink.

Lauren reached for her glass. "At least Sam looks super-hot while she's teasing us."

"Yes, she does," Sarah agreed.

"All right, ladies. Let's do this." Quinn loaded episode ten—the last episode—and they settled in to see how the season would end.

They watched Sam win an important case and then go out for drinks with the other lawyers in the firm to celebrate. Sam got a bit too drunk, and then she had a flashback of being shot, which led to her having a panic attack in the alley behind the bar.

Lauren reached over and squeezed Mia's hand, her expression intense enough to make Mia wonder if she had a history of panic attacks. Her fingers trembled, and Mia stroked her thumb back and forth over Lauren's palm in a gesture of support. As she sat there, watching Sam hyper-ventilate on the TV with Lauren's shaking fingers clutched in hers, Mia's decision crystalized in her mind. She would help Lauren in any way she could.

On the TV, Claire left the bar, looking for Sam. "There you are," Claire said as she approached Sam in the alley. "What are you doing out here?"

Sam stared at her for a moment, breathless and slightly disheveled from her panic attack. The look she gave Claire was positively *feral*. Mia sucked in a breath. And then Sam stepped forward, pinning Claire against the brick wall, and crushed their lips together.

The room exploded with screams, and the couch bounced beneath Mia as Fatima leaped up to fist-pump the air. Mia found herself whooping along with the rest of them as Sam kissed the shit out of Claire onscreen.

Through all the noise, Mia heard an awestruck "wow," and as she turned her head, she saw Lauren sitting there with her mouth hanging open, her free hand pressed against her chest and tears shimmering in her eyes.

It was one of the most pure, unguarded, beautiful things Mia had ever seen.

LAUREN WAS CRYING. Honest-to-God tears wet her cheeks as the credits began to roll on the screen before her. Sam and Claire had kissed, and it hadn't been a hesitant peck on the lips. Sam had gone for it with everything she had. It was hot, and emotional, and just...everything Lauren had wanted.

"That was perfect," she whispered. "It was so perfect."

Mia squeezed her hand. "I can't believe they really kissed."

When Lauren glanced at her, Mia was watching her with that laser-sharp intensity, and for a moment, she wondered what it would feel like if Mia kissed her the way Sam had just kissed Claire. Lauren's heart was racing, her skin flushed, and she wasn't sure if it was from the Clairantha kiss or Mia's proximity. Maybe a combination of both.

Everyone was talking at once, sharing their thoughts on the kiss. Sarah was already backing up the episode so they could watch it again. This time, Lauren squealed when Sam's lips crashed into Claire's. She noticed the way Sam's hand landed possessively on Claire's waist and how Claire's eyes widened in surprise before sliding shut as she surrendered to the kiss.

"Hot," Sarah said.

"So hot," Quinn agreed, grinning at her girlfriend.

They watched the kiss on repeat until Lauren had lost count, swept up in the euphoric energy of the room and blissfully aware that Mia's hand was still in hers. Eventually, Ash poured shots, and they toasted the kiss with whiskey. Fatima, who didn't drink, toasted with juice.

Then Quinn opened her laptop, working her magic to turn the kiss into a gif for social media. Sam and Claire's kiss was about to take the internet by storm, if it hadn't already. They'd all agreed to stay off social media today to avoid spoilers.

"I'm really glad I got to watch this season with you all this weekend," Mia said, sounding thoughtful. "It was a lot of fun."

"Imagine if I'd been home alone when I saw that kiss?" Fatima said, eyes wide. "It was a hundred times better watching it with you ladies."

"We'll have to do this again for season six," Sarah agreed.

Lauren nodded, trying not to wonder where she'd be in a year when the next season dropped. She desperately hoped she'd be right here in Brooklyn, with a new job and a new apartment, but the reality was, she might be in jail.

"So," Mia said, turning to face her. "You're still planning to stay in Brooklyn this week?"

Lauren heard her unasked question, and her stomach clenched. "Yes. My plans haven't changed."

Mia nodded. "Stop by the café tomorrow after you leave here."

"Okay." Lauren appreciated Mia's subtlety in front of the other women, but she was desperate to know what she was thinking. What had she decided?

"Oh, I want to come," Ash said. "I'm not leaving the city until after lunch, and I totally want to see your café and play with the cats before I leave, Mia."

"Definitely come," Mia told her, sounding pleased at the idea. "In fact, I'd love for you all to stop by the café in the morning if you have time."

"Dammit, I wish our flight was later so we could come," Sarah said with a pout. "Someone take pictures of all the rescue kitties for us, okay?"

"You bet," Ash agreed.

"All right, then. I'd better get home," Mia said. "I had a lot of fun this weekend."

"It was so great to meet you, Mia. Sorry we won't get to see your café in the morning." Quinn pulled her in for a hug, followed by Sarah.

"I'll see you in the group chat," Mia said as she pulled free.

"Thank God for the group chat," Sarah agreed.

"And I'll see the rest of you tomorrow at the café." Mia looked around the room with a smile.

Lauren nodded, trying not to look as nervous as she felt. Her weekend reprieve was ending, and now it was time to face the music. "See you tomorrow."

4

L auren rounded the corner onto 9th Street, flanked by Ash and Fatima. They were all weighted down with their weekend bags, in need of caffeine, and excited to visit Mia's café, but Lauren was probably the only one whose skin was clammy with fear. This wasn't just a social visit for her.

Mia wanted to talk to her about...well, Lauren wasn't exactly sure, but it definitely had to do with her crime. If Mia wanted to call Josie and set up their meeting, Lauren wouldn't say no. That would be a huge help, and as Mia had pointed out the other night, it would be less stressful for Josie too.

Once Lauren had paid back what she'd stolen, she would turn herself in to the police. She'd been working toward this moment since she fled Brooklyn last year. She was desperate to have it behind her so she could start moving forward with her life again, but now that the time had finally come, she was terrified. That fear seemed to penetrate all the way to her bones when she imagined walking into the police station.

"Oh, I see it," Fatima said, drawing Lauren from her thoughts.

Sure enough, Lauren spotted a familiar storefront ahead, familiar because she'd seen so many photos on Mia's social media. The café had large windows overlooking the street, through which Lauren could see a cat perch, currently occupied by a black-and-white cat. Whiskers Cat Café was printed over the window in big white letters, with little whiskers coming out of the W.

"Aww." Ash waved to the cat in the window.

"You're a cutie," Fatima told the cat, who watched her out of lazy green eyes.

"I love this place already," Lauren said as she grasped the handle on the door, ignoring the tremor in her hand. She couldn't think of anything better than playing with cute adoptable cats while enjoying a hot drink, especially in a café owned by one of her friends. Well, hopefully she and Mia would still be friends when all was said and done.

Inside, the café was divided into two parts. To Lauren's right was the café counter and several tables for customers, and to the left was a glass wall, behind which were more tables in the area where the cats resided. Currently, most of the tables in the cat enclosure were occupied and an employee in a black Whiskers Cat Café T-shirt stood beside one of them, talking to a woman who was petting an orange cat.

As Lauren swept her gaze toward the café counter, she spotted Mia standing with her back to the door, talking to one of her employees. She had on a black pencil skirt and a burgundy blouse, and Lauren had to force herself not to fixate on the way that skirt hugged her curves, because this was too much like the first time Lauren had seen her, when she'd been ogling Mia's ass on the street before she realized who she was.

As if she'd felt Lauren's eyes on her, Mia turned, smiling as she beckoned Lauren, Fatima, and Ashleigh into the café.

"Morning," Mia called. "Why don't you come with me so I can show you a place to leave your bags while you're here?"

"That sounds great." Lauren's shoulders ached beneath the combined weight of her backpack and duffel bag.

Mia led them down the hall to a small room with a desk and a row of cubbies containing various purses and bags. "This is my office, but it doubles as the employee break room. No one comes in here but me and my employees, so feel free to leave anything you don't want to carry."

Lauren put her duffel bag with Ash's and Fatima's bags in the corner, but kept her backpack with her.

"Now, do you want a tour first or caffeine?" Mia asked.

"Tour," Fatima said at the same time Ashleigh said, "Caffeine." Lauren just smiled.

"How about a quick tour first, and then you can sit and hang out for as long as you like while you drink your coffee?" Mia suggested.

"I suppose cute kitties are worth delaying my coffee for a few minutes," Ash relented.

"They are pretty cute," Mia said as she led the way out of her office. "I have five cats right now. They stay in a separate area so they don't pose a health code violation for the café space. Guests pay ten dollars an hour to visit with the cats, which includes a bakery item and a donation to the rescue."

Lauren followed her into the cat enclosure, grinning as she watched a little girl roll a toy toward the black-and-white cat in the front window. Ash stood beside her as Fatima closed the door behind them.

"That's Gilbert." Mia pointed to a short-haired black cat at the top of a cat tower. "He's pretty shy. In fact, the rescue said that if he doesn't warm up to the café environment soon, they might move him into a foster home instead."

"Aww," Lauren said, looking up at Gilbert. "Poor guy."

"And this is Pearl," Mia said as a calico strolled up to them. The cat twined herself around Mia's legs before approaching Fatima, who bent to pet her, looking absolutely thrilled. "As you can see, café life suits Pearl just fine."

"She's gorgeous and so friendly," Fatima said as she rubbed Pearl. "I'm surprised no one's adopted her yet."

"She's only been here a few days, but you're right. I'm sure she'll get adopted quickly." Mia led them through the room, introducing them to the remaining cats. "Was that quick enough?" she quipped, drawing laughter from the group. "Now let me know what you'd all like to drink, and then you can find an empty table while I get you some caffeine."

Ashleigh asked for a nonfat latte, and Fatima ordered a flat white.

"I'll have a mochaccino please," Lauren said.

Mia headed toward the café counter, and Lauren followed Ash and Fatima to an empty table near the front window, where they sat and rehashed some of their favorite moments from the new *In Her Defense* season. A few minutes later, Mia brought over their drinks and a plate of pastries for them to share.

"Mm, thank you," Fatima said as she accepted her drink.

Lauren murmured her thanks, inhaling the chocolatey aroma of her drink. Once everyone had their drinks, Mia joined them with a mug for herself too.

"I can't wait to see the next fan video Quinn makes, now

that there's an actual kiss to work with," Ash said as she reached for a mini muffin.

"I'm probably going to reread *Skin Deep* on my train ride back to Philly," Fatima said, grinning at Lauren.

She smiled into her mochaccino. "I'm going to miss you guys. This weekend was amazing."

They chatted for a few more minutes, and then Ashleigh and Fatima headed out to catch their trains—Fatima to Philly and Ashleigh to New Jersey—leaving Mia and Lauren alone at the table. Lauren gripped her mug as that jittery feeling returned to her stomach.

"So," Mia said.

Lauren looked up and met her eyes. It was time to have the conversation she'd been dreading. Her mochaccino trembled in her hands. "So."

Mia wasn't sure whether to address the elephant in the room directly or inch her way toward it. The skittish glance Lauren darted in her direction made her decide on the latter. "Where are you staying tonight?" Mia asked.

"A hostel on 7th," Lauren told her. "I've got a bed there for the next two weeks while I get things sorted out."

"Ah." Mia kept her face impassive as she sipped her cappuccino. "Do you have to share a room with strangers?" The thought set her teeth on edge. She was very particular about her space and her belongings, and she didn't share either easily.

Lauren nodded. "I do, but it's fine. I've done it before. It's a cheap place to sleep, and that's all I need."

"Hm." Mia decided not to push the subject, aware that she didn't know what it was like to be in Lauren's situation.

Mia's upbringing had been comfortable, and her years as a lawyer hadn't exactly been lean. She'd never had to share a room to save money. On the contrary, her income had allowed her to buy this café and the apartment upstairs. As much as she sometimes missed her former career, that all-too-familiar ache in her stomach was a reminder of why she'd had to leave it behind.

"This weekend was really fun," Lauren said, a wistful look on her face. "It added so much to the season, watching it with a group like that."

"Yes, it did," Mia agreed. "I had never watched the show with anyone before."

"You didn't watch the early seasons with your wife?"

Mia lifted her cup and sipped. "I guess Kristin did watch a few episodes with me, but she couldn't stop critiquing all the details they got wrong."

Lauren grinned. "Occupational hazard, I'm guessing?"

"Oh, for sure, and I've definitely tapped out of legal shows before because they were too unrealistic, but *In Her Defense* does pretty well, all things considered. Sure, they screw up some of the finer points, but it's Hollywood, you know? The show has such a strong message of female empowerment, I'm willing to overlook a few things."

"But Kristin wasn't a fan?"

Mia shook her head. "We ended up arguing whenever she watched, which, honestly, is a pretty good way to summarize our whole marriage."

Lauren scrunched her nose as she ripped off a bite from her chocolate-filled croissant. "Was it always that bad?"

"No." Mia sipped her cappuccino as her mind spun back to happier times. "We were so much in love during law school. We were both driven for success and so career oriented. I thought I'd found my perfect match."

"What went wrong?"

Mia shrugged. "Maybe we were too much alike? We both graduated at the top of our class and started as first year associates at the same law firm. Our competitiveness was our downfall, I think. After a while, it started to feel like our entire relationship was based in trying to one-up each other. Who had more billable hours, the biggest office, the most high profile client, who would make partner first... It wasn't healthy."

"No, it doesn't sound like it. I'm sorry it turned out that way."

"So am I," Mia said. "I never imagined I'd be starting over as a newly divorced woman with a new business at my age, but here I am." She'd expected to spend her forties comfortably settled, maybe raising a family. Instead, she was starting from scratch, both personally and professionally.

"You're rocking it so far." Lauren tapped her mug against Mia's.

"I hope so."

"The café's doing well, isn't it?" Lauren asked.

"It is, but..." Mia paused, hesitant to admit the doubt that had begun to creep in recently. "It's been a bigger adjustment than I'd expected."

"How so?" Lauren asked.

"It's a much slower pace than I'm used to," Mia said. Last year, in the middle of her divorce, with nonstop migraines and a bleeding ulcer, she'd gotten to the point where she hated everything about being a lawyer. She'd been desperate for a reprieve from the stress, but now...now she'd give anything for a little excitement in her life.

Lauren dropped her gaze to the half-eaten pastry in front of her. "Transitions are hard."

"They are," Mia agreed. "But while we're on the topic of lawyers, I'd like to be yours. Unofficially, that is."

Lauren looked up with wide eyes. "What?"

"I'll go with you to the precinct after your meeting with Josie. You'll be treated much more fairly with a lawyer at your side, but assuming Josie doesn't want to press charges, it should just be a matter of having the warrant dismissed and setting a court date to get the charges against you dropped."

"Mia... I couldn't ask you to do that for me."

"You didn't ask," Mia reminded her. "I offered. I'll enjoy the chance to dust off my legal skills to help a friend."

Lauren gripped her mug. "I don't...I don't want to feel indebted to you. The whole purpose of moving back to Brooklyn was for me to pay off my debts and make a fresh start."

"And you're going to do that," Mia said. "But there's no reason not to let me help. I'll give Josie a call tomorrow to see how she wants to handle it. Why don't you plan to come here in the morning, and we'll take it from there?"

WHEN LAUREN LEFT THE CAFÉ, she set out for the hostel to check in and leave her things. After that, she had the rest of the day to herself, and she planned to make the most of it... just in case she went to jail tomorrow. The hostel was a twenty-minute walk from Mia's café, and Lauren's shoulders ached from the weight of her bags by the time she reached its weathered front door.

She went inside and checked in, receiving a key to one of the shared rooms. She'd booked the cheapest bed in the place, but she wasn't picky. She'd stayed in plenty of places over the years that weren't nearly as nice as this one.

She walked upstairs and knocked on the door to her room before she swiped her key card, in case anyone else was inside, but when she opened the door, it was empty. The room contained two sets of bunk beds with blankets neatly tucked. A black cabinet with four lockers took up the space between the beds, a place for guests to lock their valuables.

One of the beds had a yellow jacket tossed across it, but that was the only indication anyone else was currently using the room. Lauren placed her duffel bag on the other bottom bunk, claiming it for herself. As a girl, she'd fallen off the top bunk during a nightmare and broken her collarbone. She hadn't been able to sleep that far off the ground since.

She sat on the bed and checked her phone, finding several new messages in WhatsApp, her friends chatting happily as they traveled home. Lauren sent a message of her own and then put her phone down. Now, what to do with the rest of her afternoon? She eyed the lockers. Her duffel was too big to fit, but there was nothing inside worth stealing anyway, just her clothes and toiletries, none of which were worth much.

So she left it on the bed and brought her backpack with her as she left the hostel. Without even considering her destination, she found herself boarding the subway, headed for Prospect Park. How many afternoons had she and Craig spent sitting by the lake, hoping their mom would have passed out by the time they got home?

After their mom died and they were placed in foster care, she and Craig had carved their initials into a big oak tree that stood just off the main path. They would sneak out of their respective foster homes once a week to meet at that tree, determined not to lose each other, no matter what happened.

The backpack was heavy on her shoulders as Lauren entered Prospect Park, the weight of her failures pressing against the damp T-shirt that clung to her back. As she walked, it began to rain, a light sprinkle that had people around her reaching for jackets and umbrellas. Lauren had neither. Her only jacket was in the duffel bag at the hostel, so she just ducked her head and kept walking.

She turned onto the path that skirted the lake, moving against the flow as people headed for the exit to get out of the rain. Lauren's breath caught as she spotted their tree. She walked to it and traced her finger over its knobby bark until she found their initials, gnarled and sunken into the surface of the tree.

Tears burned her eyes as her finger traced CAB. Craig Andrew Booker. She'd teased him about his initials, but he'd loved them. For his ninth birthday, he'd asked to ride in a yellow cab to FAO Schwartz to pick out a new toy, and when their mom was too high to leave the apartment, Lauren had raided her mother's emergency cash and taken Craig herself. They'd had a magical afternoon together, one of her favorite childhood memories.

In hindsight, maybe Lauren had been a thief, even then. Always a well-intentioned one, though. Always for Craig. She sat on one of the tree's protruding roots as her tears broke free. This was where she would spread his ashes. She'd done some research on the train yesterday to make sure it was allowed before she inadvertently committed another crime, and it was perfectly legal to scatter his ashes in the park.

Since there was a chance she'd spend tomorrow night in jail and therefore wouldn't have a safe place to keep Craig's remains, logic said she should do it now. She should spread his ashes while she had this quiet moment to herself, just Lauren and Craig beneath their favorite tree.

But as she sat there in the drizzling rain, hair sticking to her cheeks where rain mixed with tears, she couldn't do it. Her arms tightened reflexively around the backpack. She wasn't ready to say goodbye.

5

Lauren lay on her bunk in the hostel later that night, blinking into the darkness. Today had been unexpected and overwhelming in so many ways. She wasn't sure what to think about Mia's offer to help get the charges against her dropped. Was she taking pity on Lauren? Did she judge her for what she'd done? Lauren judged herself plenty, but she also knew she'd mostly just been trying to help her brother, and now she was trying to make it right.

Luckily, the college students who were sharing her room had finally settled down and turned off the light, although it had taken them until almost two a.m. to stop giggling. Lauren had put in her earplugs and rolled to face the wall, and it wasn't her roommates' fault she was still awake. After spending years in various group homes, she'd learned to sleep in a room full of people, no matter how noisy they were.

No, tonight's insomnia was caused by the day ahead, an uncomfortable tightening in her stomach that wouldn't loosen no matter how hard she tried to clear her mind and meditate her way to sleep. She finally dozed off sometime in the wee hours of the morning, waking to muted sunlight filtering through the thin blinds over the window.

Her backpack was in front of her face, propped against her pillow where she could be sure no one touched it while she slept. The college students were quiet now, probably planning to sleep in after their late night, and while Lauren wished she could join them, she was too anxious to go back to sleep.

Instead, she slipped out of bed, took a few things out of her bag, and went down the hall to the bathroom. She showered and dressed, then tried to hide the shadows under her eyes with concealer, frowning at herself in the mirror. Sometimes she felt like she'd aged a decade in the last year. But hopefully, after today things would start to get better.

Lauren crept back into her room, careful not to wake the other women. She made her bed and left her duffel bag on it, then put on her backpack and headed to Mia's café. First, she stopped in the lobby for some instant coffee. Obviously, the coffee at the café was a million times better, but Lauren was on a budget.

She sipped her coffee as she walked, enjoying the brisk morning air. By the time she reached the café, she'd ditched her now-empty cup and was feeling halfway hopeful about the day ahead. It would be a huge help if Mia set up the meeting with Josie, but Lauren should probably do the rest on her own for the sake of their friendship.

The bell jingled over the door as she entered. Mia was behind the counter serving a customer, but she glanced at Lauren with a smile. She wore a sleeveless black top, her blonde hair dusting her shoulders in tousled waves, and even without seeing the rest of the outfit, Lauren was struck again by how stylish Mia looked.

It wasn't hard to imagine her in her former life as a lawyer. In fact, she didn't seem entirely at home here in her own café. Surely those chic clothes weren't practical for interacting with cats, but it seemed like Mia had staff for that. Mia's top dipped in the front, allowing Lauren a glimpse at her collarbones, and *oof*, she'd always been a sucker for collarbones. Mia's were as elegant as the rest of her.

Lauren sat at an empty table and set her backpack on the floor between her feet. While she waited for Mia, she looked at her phone, and her heart sped when she saw the new selfie Piper Sheridan had posted on Twitter.

Her auburn hair hung over her shoulders in her signature style, and she wore a colorful, floral-patterned dress. Lauren peered closer, trying to see what was in the background of the photo. Piper appeared to be standing on a patio lined with greenery, and a woman's hand was visible on her shoulder.

Lauren had heard rumors of a new girlfriend in Piper's life, and despite her celebrity crush, Lauren was thrilled that Piper had found someone who made her happy. At least, she sure looked happy in this selfie, and Lauren hoped her new girlfriend was at least partially responsible for that. The caption read "Back in Hollywood, but what am I filming? Any guesses?"

Lauren tapped her lips. She didn't think *In Her Defense* was filming its next season yet, but she remembered that Piper had a new movie role in the works. A quick Google search told her the film was called *Being Schooled*, and Piper would play a teacher.

Ever the nerdy fangirl, Lauren replied to the tweet with "Being Schooled? You look amazing, can't wait to see the new movie!" followed by several heart emojis. Yes, she knew she was a dork, but once, Piper had liked one of her tweets, and Lauren had almost died on the spot.

When she looked up, Mia was standing by the table with an amused smirk. "Declaring your undying devotion to Piper yet again?"

"Well, not exactly." Lauren's cheeks heated. "I mean, you can see she's with her girlfriend, but look! She's filming something new."

At that, Mia grinned, leaning in to see the photo on Lauren's phone. "That's exciting. Jordy came in early today to cover the counter for me. Want to come upstairs so we can chat?"

Lauren put away her phone with a quick nod. "Yeah, sure. Thank you."

"No problem." Mia beckoned for her to follow. She led the way down the back hallway and unlocked a door that let them into a narrow, white-walled stairwell.

Lauren followed her up the stairs, where Mia unlocked another door, leading the way into her apartment. It was surprisingly spacious, with a large, bright living room and a galley kitchen to the left. A pale blue couch faced a wall-mounted TV, and several windows on the far wall let in plenty of natural light. A white cat lounged on the windowsill, eyeing them lazily.

"You must be Lola," Lauren said to the cat. Mia had shared plenty of pictures of her in their group chat.

"The queen herself," Mia confirmed. "Can I get you anything? Coffee? Water?"

"Water would be great. Thanks." Lauren walked to the kitchen table and set down her bag.

"I talked to Josie this morning," Mia told her as she filled two glasses with water and brought them to the table. "She wants to meet with you today since the bar is closed on Mondays."

Lauren blew out a breath as the ball of tension in her stomach tightened. "I really appreciate you setting that up for me, but I can take it from here."

Mia narrowed her eyes as she sat across from Lauren, and Lauren had the uncomfortable feeling she'd offended her. But she had to at least offer to do this on her own. The last thing she wanted was to overstep the bounds of her fledgling friendship with Mia.

"Why are you so determined to do this on your own?" Mia asked.

Lauren dropped her gaze to her water. "Because it's my problem, and I should be the one to fix it. And because I appreciate your friendship too much to take advantage of it."

"Well, you aren't taking advantage of me, so you can let go of that excuse. I'd like to help, and honestly, you'd be foolish not to accept."

Lauren blinked. That was...harsher than she'd expected. "Okay."

Mia nodded briskly. "Then it's settled. I'll come with you to Dragonfly, and once we've squared things with Josie, we'll go to the precinct to get that warrant dropped."

"I...thank you." Lauren sipped her water, resisting the urge to fiddle with her glass. Anxious energy spiraled through her body, because this was really happening. After fifteen months, she was finally going to make things right. It was going to be a hard, awful day, but when all was said and done, she'd finally be able to move forward with her life.

"You're welcome," Mia said. "Josie's expecting us after lunch, so you can hang out here with me in the meantime if you like. I can go over with you what to expect when we get to the precinct."

Lauren nodded, ridiculously thankful for Mia's help even if she still felt guilty accepting it. "I would appreciate that. How did Josie seem when you talked to her?"

Mia rolled her lips inward, then shrugged. "She was pretty upset at first, but she's willing to hear you out. She's got a big heart, so I imagine she'll be understanding once you've given her that check and explained what happened."

"I hope so." Lauren blinked as her eyes filled with unexpected tears. "I hate that I hurt her. I really do. I've been wanting to make it right ever since it happened."

"What took you so long, then?" Mia asked, direct as ever.

"Well, for one thing, I had to save up the money. I left the city with nothing after I robbed her bar. But also, I couldn't risk turning myself in until I was sure it wouldn't affect Craig. But now..." She gestured helplessly toward her backpack, still heavy with his urn.

The decision to have him cremated had been a difficult one, but ultimately, she couldn't afford a burial. Cremation was so much cheaper, and this way, she could bring him back to Brooklyn with her. Now, his hometown would be his final resting place. She hadn't had to leave him behind in Rhode Island.

"Hey." Mia covered Lauren's hand with hers. "It's going to be okay. Truly. People do stupid shit all the time, way worse things than you did. We're going to get it sorted."

Lauren whispered her thanks, still looking at the backpack. Her heart was racing again, because she'd almost forgotten. "I have to...I have to scatter his ashes before I go to Dragonfly."

"Right now? Why?"

Lauren sucked in a shaky breath and blew it out as she

met Mia's eyes. "In case I spend tonight in jail. I don't want his remains to get lost in police lockup."

Mia sat back, pressing her palms against the table. "One, you're not spending the night in jail, not with me here to advocate for you. And two, leave your things here at my apartment. You shouldn't be carrying your brother's remains around the city in a backpack anyway."

Lauren opened her mouth to protest because she was already letting Mia do too much for her, but this would keep Craig's remains safe until Lauren was ready to say goodbye, and how could she argue with that? "Okay. Thank you."

Mia nodded. "No problem. Now, let's talk about what will happen once we get to the police station."

LAUREN'S STOMACH was in knots as she and Mia boarded the subway to take them to Josie's bar. The rest of the day was going to be *so* hard, but as Mia gave her a reassuring smile, Lauren realized it would be at least a little bit easier with Mia at her side.

She'd left her backpack at Mia's, bringing with her only a small bag that contained the check for Josie, her identification, and her phone. As the train carried them across Brooklyn, Mia was quiet, and Lauren didn't know what to say either. She was so grateful to Mia for being here, but at the same time, Lauren didn't know her well enough yet to really lean on her today.

Lauren sat with her hands in her lap, fighting an increasing sense of dread. Walking into Dragonfly was going to be one of the hardest things she'd ever had to do. She felt off balance without her backpack and the weight of Craig's urn in her lap, as morbid as that sounded. He'd been the one constant in her life, and today, she felt his absence more acutely than ever.

All too soon, she and Mia exited the subway and climbed the steps to the street. Lauren's knees shook as she walked, and her chest felt unbearably tight. Up ahead, the bar came into view. Its lavender dragonfly-shaped logo was exactly like Lauren remembered, and she smiled in spite of herself. She'd spent three wonderful weeks here, tending bar side by side with Josie.

"Ready?" Mia asked, looking over her shoulder at Lauren.

"Yes," Lauren said breathlessly. She wasn't. She would probably never be ready, but Mia had gone above and beyond to help her today, and the least Lauren could do was keep her emotions in check and get it done.

The sign over the door was dark. The placard in the window read "Closed," but Mia tapped her knuckles against the door, and it opened moments later.

Lauren gulped as cold fear gripped her stomach, but it wasn't Josie's face she saw when she stepped into the doorway. Eve Marlow stood there, and the expression on her face was downright terrifying. Lauren had always found her somewhat intimidating with her brisk, no-nonsense attitude, but she'd also been decent and fair during Lauren's time at the bar.

Today, she looked ready to wage war, and Lauren was the enemy.

"Eve, hi," Mia said calmly. "Thanks for agreeing to this."

"You have Josie to thank for that." Eve's brown eyes pierced Lauren like daggers. "If I'd had my way, we'd be having this discussion at the police station."

"Lauren and I are headed there as soon as we're finished here," Mia said.

"Then she'd better start talking." Eve crossed her arms over her chest as she continued to glare at Lauren.

"Eve, stop it. You're scaring her." Josie appeared in the doorway and rested a hand on her wife's shoulder. She gave Lauren a hesitant smile, which was probably a friendlier reception than Lauren deserved. Josie had changed her hair since the last time Lauren saw her. Today, her blonde tresses were streaked with bright red.

"Hi," Lauren managed, her throat painfully dry. Her palms, by contrast, were damp and clammy. "I, um, I'm so glad you agreed to see me so I could apologize in person."

Josie nodded. She stepped back to invite them inside, gesturing toward a table behind her. "Water?" she asked.

Lauren nodded gratefully, keeping her head down as she took a seat at the table. Mia sat to her right while Eve followed Josie to the bar. She took glasses of water as Josie filled them and brought them to the table, then sat to Lauren's left. Josie took the seat across from her, watching Lauren with an unreadable expression.

Lauren lifted the glass Eve had placed in front of her and sipped. "I don't know how much Mia told you on the phone."

"She said you wanted to apologize, and that I should hear you out." Josie's tone was even, but her posture was stiff, and while she wasn't as outwardly hostile as her wife, she didn't look very happy that Lauren was here either.

Lauren darted a glance at Mia, who gave her another reassuring smile, before returning her gaze to Josie. "First of all, I want to tell you that I'm *so* sorry. You trusted me, and I betrayed that trust. I hurt you and your business, and it has haunted me every day since."

Josie pursed her lips. "Thank you for the apology, but... why did you do it, Lauren?"

"I did it for my brother." Lauren reached for her water to swallow over the lump in her throat. "He struggled with drug addiction his whole life, and he owed money to some really bad people. He came into the bar that night to ask for my help, and they...they had beaten the shit out of him. I panicked and made the really stupid decision to clear out your cash register so he could pay off his drug debts before they hurt him any worse."

"So you gave the money to your brother?" Josie asked, her brow furrowed.

"I did."

"And did it help him, at least?" Josie asked.

Lauren nodded, blinking back tears. "Yes. He never got in debt like that again."

"You're speaking about him in the past tense," Josie said quietly.

"He overdosed last month," Lauren said, her voice hoarse. She wiped away an errant tear. "He was my only family, and I was so desperate to help him, but that doesn't excuse what I did."

"I'm sorry for your loss," Josie said, her expression kind.

"Thank you, but I'm not here for your sympathy or your forgiveness. You don't owe me anything, but I owe you a lot." Lauren reached into her bag. "And I'm here to pay you back."

Josie's eyes widened as Lauren slid the envelope across the table to her. "I wasn't expecting that."

"Sorry it took me so long," Lauren told her. "And if that's not enough, please let me know. I gave it all to Craig, so I wasn't sure how much I actually took."

Josie opened the envelope and took out the check, turning it so Eve could see it too. "To be honest, I don't remember the figure the insurance company calculated, but I think this is more than enough."

"It was just over twenty-eight hundred," Eve said, sounding gentler now.

"I've long since recovered what I lost, and there was an insurance payout too, so I'll put this check toward my kitten rescue," Josie told Lauren. "I've been hoping to invest in a couple of incubators for the newborns. Eve and I have a new litter upstairs right now."

Lauren smiled at the thought. "I was always so in awe of how you juggled the rescue and the bar."

"Well, you set me back on that front when you emptied my cash register and took off." Josie dropped her gaze to the table. "I had been trying to give myself some time off from the bar to focus on the rescue and my personal life."

"I remember," Lauren said. "And when you approached me about working that extra shift for you, I really was thrilled about it. Robbing you wasn't premeditated."

"That's good to know, actually," Josie said. "I had always wondered if you were scheming behind my back, just waiting for me to offer you enough responsibility to take advantage. Eve always tells me I'm too trusting."

Eve gave her a fond look. "Because you are."

Josie shrugged as her lips curved in a smile. "I look for the best in people."

"I wish I had lived up to your expectations." Lauren's throat was tight, and tears blurred her vision. "I'm so sorry I let you down."

"I can't say I understand why you did it," Josie said. "But I do know what it feels like to be in a desperate situation, and I believe that a sincere apology is a valuable thing. It must have taken a lot of courage to come here today, and I appreciate that. You said you weren't looking for my forgiveness, but you have it regardless." Josie extended her hand across the table.

Lauren took it, blinking back more tears. Josie's handshake was warm and firm. "Thank you. I don't deserve it, but I appreciate it...so much."

Josie nodded. "We're square as far as I'm concerned." She looked at Mia, who had been watching the conversation quietly. "So what happens next?"

"Next we go to the police station," Mia said. "I'm going to serve as Lauren's legal counsel. Josie, they'll need to know if you want to press charges against Lauren."

Josie sat back, glancing at her wife. "It's up to me?"

"To some extent, yes," Mia said. "If you decide to drop the charges, then it'll probably just be a matter of setting a court date to make it official. The district attorney could decide to press charges anyway, but in a case like this where the parties have resolved things privately, that's usually the end of it."

"I don't want you to go to jail," Josie said, looking at Lauren. "You've been through enough."

"She could be lying about her reasons for stealing," Eve said. "So don't make your decision based on that."

Josie rolled her eyes playfully. "Are you accusing me of being too trusting again?"

Eve's lips quirked, and she shrugged. "I'm just playing devil's advocate."

"I've known Lauren online for a while, and although I didn't know about the robbery, I can vouch for part of her story," Mia said. "Her brother did overdose last month. In fact, his remains are at my apartment right now for safekeeping in case Lauren has to spend the night in jail, which" —she gave Lauren a quick look—"I don't expect to happen."

"That's good enough for me," Josie said. "But I do have to come to the station with you, right?"

Mia nodded. "Yes."

"All right, then." Josie stood from the table. "Let's get this over with."

Lauren stood, tucking her bag over her shoulder. As hard as this meeting with Josie and Eve had been, the next part was going to be even harder.

Mia gave her shoulder a reassuring squeeze. "To the police station."

6

"You'll report to the courthouse on this date." The bored-looking officer jabbed his finger against the paper he'd placed on the counter in front of them. It listed Lauren's court date as September 15th, about three weeks away. "Don't leave the city in the meantime."

"Okay." Lauren darted an uncertain glance at Mia.

"We understand," Mia told the officer. This was all more or less what she'd expected. They'd successfully gotten the warrant for Lauren's arrest dropped, and now she would need to appear in court to have the charges against her officially dismissed. "Thank you, Officer Harney."

Lauren folded the court summons and placed it inside her bag, giving the officer a hesitant smile. Then she followed Mia outside into the August sunshine. Josie had left about a half hour ago after giving her statement.

"That went as well as we could have expected," Mia said.

Lauren nodded. Her fingers were clenched around her bag, but her relief was palpable. "It's not bad that I have to wait so long for my court date?"

Mia shook her head. "No, and believe me, three weeks is

actually not a long time to wait. The courts are always backed up."

"But I could still go to jail?" Lauren looked at her out of wide brown eyes.

"Technically, yes, but it's extremely unlikely. Remember, you have a lawyer now, and I'm a pretty good one, if I do say so myself." Mia nudged her elbow against Lauren's, earning a small smile.

"It was way less scary walking into the police station with you," Lauren told her. "Thank you so much for your help today. I feel like such a weight has been lifted, like I can finally start looking forward again."

"Good." Mia grasped Lauren's hand and gave her fingers a quick squeeze. "And what do you see when you look forward? What's next for you?"

"A job. An apartment. Both of those will be hard to find." A wrinkle appeared between her brows. "I still have a felony charge hanging over my head."

"You're deceptively innocent looking for a felon," Mia teased. "And I've met quite a few felons in my day."

Lauren smiled again, wider this time. "I'll stay at the hostel for now and apply for any and every job in Brooklyn. I have a lot of experience waiting tables and tending bar, and I'm not afraid to get my hands dirty and scrub toilets if it comes to that."

Mia studied her for a moment as they waited for the light to change so they could cross the street. Lauren might not be as innocent as she looked, but she'd taken responsibility for her crime. She'd made amends, and now she was trying to get her life back on track.

Mia respected that. She and Lauren had spent a lot of time together over the last four days, and Mia enjoyed her company. She didn't have many friends these days, which made her even more glad for her budding friendship with Lauren. "I could use an extra pair of hands at the café," she heard herself offer almost before she'd consciously made the decision to do so. "I mean, if you don't mind working with me, at least until you find something else."

Lauren blinked at her in surprise. "Oh, I...really?"

Mia nodded. "If you're interested, come in tomorrow for a trial day to see if it's a good fit, and we'll take it from there."

"I'm definitely interested," Lauren said.

"I can't pay as much as you'd earn in tips as a bartender, and I can only offer you a few shifts a week, but it's a place to start if you want it, and then you can use me as a job reference when you apply somewhere else."

Lauren ducked her head. "That's really kind of you, but please don't feel like you have to help me just because we're friends."

"Believe me, I'm not the type to do that. One of my regular employees needs to cut her hours for the next few weeks, so I was already looking for someone to cover her shifts. I mean, to be clear, my offer involves keeping the cat enclosure clean and scooping litter boxes. It's hardly glamorous."

"Like I told you, I'm not afraid to get my hands dirty." Lauren gave her a hesitant smile. "If you're sure, then yeah, I don't see how I could turn down an offer to work at the café. I haven't spent much time with cats, but animals in general tend to like me, and I like them, so I think it could be a good fit. I'm a hard worker."

"All right, then," Mia said. "Stop by tomorrow around ten."

"Thank you, Mia. I mean it."

"No problem."

They boarded the subway together, lapsing into silence

as they rode toward Mia's neighborhood. She needed to get back to the café. She'd checked in often over the last few days, but this was the first time since it opened six months ago that she'd let her employees manage the café without her for more than a single day.

Everything seemed to have gone smoothly in her absence, and she'd really enjoyed her weekend with her fandom friends, but she was eager to get back to her regular routine. No doubt, she had plenty of messages to catch up on. No cats had been adopted over the weekend, and she wondered why. Had Gilbert started to come out of his shell yet? There were two new cats arriving in the morning, a pair of six-month-old kittens named Chaos and Mayhem, who would need to be integrated into the space.

Mia opened the notes app on her phone and started jotting a list of things that needed her attention. Lost in her thoughts, she didn't even hear the conductor announce their stop.

"This is us," Lauren said as she stood from the seat next to Mia.

Mia followed her off the train and up to the street. "I'll see you tomorrow morning, then?"

Lauren nodded. She looked exhausted. "See you at ten."

They parted ways at the corner, and Mia strode the two blocks to the café. As she passed the building next door, she noted that the office space that had been vacant for the last few months now boasted the name of a law firm on the door. She rolled her eyes. Sometimes it felt like her former career followed her everywhere she went.

It figured that she'd have a bunch of lawyers next door now, rubbing her nose in what she'd given up. She reached for the door to the café and pulled it open. The bell tinkled as she walked inside.

"Hi, Mia," Jordy called from behind the counter.

Mia smiled as she approached the counter, resting her palms against it. "Any problems while I was out?"

"Nope," Jordy told her, reaching up to adjust their glasses. They were Mia's assistant manager and easily her most dependable employee. Without them, Mia never would have been able to take the weekend and most of today off. "Today's Lovely Bean shipment hasn't come in yet, but it's still early."

"Okay," Mia said with a nod. "I'll check the order status and make sure nothing's amiss." Every Monday, the café received a shipment from the local company that provided their coffee beans. Mia glanced toward the cat enclosure to see Wendy sitting with several guests, talking animatedly to a little girl who had Pearl in her lap. It was a relief to walk in and see everything running smoothly.

After talking to Jordy for a few minutes, Mia headed to her office, where she spent the next two hours sorting through emails, invoices, and all the other paperwork that came with owning a business. The delivery from Lovely Bean arrived at four. Once everything was put away, Mia helped Jordy at the counter until closing. The last few hours of the day were always busy as people stopped in for caffeine on their way home from work.

Promptly at seven, Jordy flipped the sign on the door to Closed while Mia finished up with their remaining customers. While Jordy wiped down tables, Mia packaged the leftover pastries for Jordy to drop off at the local shelter on their way home.

Wendy waved to her from the cat enclosure, and Mia let herself in. Wendy was a volunteer with 4 Paws Cat Rescue, which provided the adoptable cats who lived here in the café, but she also worked for Mia part-time as a cat care specialist.

"How's it going?" Mia asked.

"We received an adoption application for Pearl," Wendy told her.

"Oh good." Mia glanced at the calico cat, who was currently winding herself in figure eights around Mia's legs. She bent to scratch Pearl behind her ears. "I knew this girl wasn't going to be here long."

"Definitely not," Wendy agreed. "She's a catch. This family seems like a great match for her too. Their daughter was so smitten with Pearl, and the feeling seemed mutual."

"Wonderful," Mia said, remembering the little girl she'd seen holding Pearl earlier. "Any progress with Gilbert?"

She gestured toward the black cat, who was in his usual spot at the top of the cat tower, gazing down at her with wide yellow eyes. The foster coordinator at the rescue wanted to talk to Mia at the end of the week about moving him into a foster home, fearing the café was too hectic of an environment for him to come out of his shell.

It might be the best move. Some animals—and people— simply preferred to be left alone, but Mia's inherently competitive nature made her want to help Gilbert find his forever home while he was still under her care. She'd try to carve out some extra time to work with him this week.

"I haven't been able to get him down from his tower," Wendy said regretfully.

She helped Mia clean up the space, and then she and Jordy headed out, locking the front door behind themselves. Once the café was empty, Mia brought out several cans of cat food. She spread the contents across paper plates for the cats to enjoy. Gilbert merely watched from his perch, his eyes seeming to gleam at her in the low lighting.

"If you're still here in October, you'd make a great Halloween cat," Mia told him. The cat watched quietly as she opened the last can of food and held it toward him. "Hungry?"

He sniffed the air, watching her for a minute before he crept down to the lowest level of the tower. She held the can toward him, letting him eat from her hand. A thin purr reached her ears as he ate, and Mia smiled. He demolished most of the can before sitting back on his haunches to wash his face.

Mia extended her free hand for him to sniff before she stroked him beneath his chin. "Sorry the café's been overwhelming for you. I'm going to spend some extra time with you this week to help you feel more comfortable. What do you think?"

He leaned into her touch, purring louder. This was the most interaction she'd had with him yet, and it made her all the more determined to keep working with him so he could stay here until he was adopted. He'd be fine if he was moved to a foster home first, but she didn't want to see him shuffled around too much. The sooner he went home with a family, the better.

After a few minutes, she stood and picked up the empty plates, then carried them to the back room to throw away. She double-checked that everything was locked up and secure for the night before heading upstairs to her apartment.

A high-pitched meow greeted her as she flipped on the light in the living room. Mia set down her bag and bent to pet Lola, who had trotted over to greet her. Lola sniffed Mia's hands and looked up at her with hopeful amber eyes, meowing again.

"Do I smell like cat food?" she asked, rubbing Lola's

head. "I'll get you some in a minute. I need a shower first, and then I'll fix supper for both of us."

She walked to her bedroom and stripped out of her clothes, tossing them into the bin in the corner. This was one benefit of living alone. Not that she'd been shy around Kristin, but they'd never made a habit of walking around their home together naked. Brushing thoughts of her ex-wife out of her mind, Mia started the shower and stepped inside.

As she lathered up her skin under the hot spray, her thoughts drifted to Lauren. What was she doing this evening? Surely she wasn't hanging out at the hostel with a bunch of people she didn't know, but where else would she go? She must have other friends here in the city since she'd lived here almost her whole life, but Mia hadn't heard her mention anyone.

Mia finished her shower, wrapped herself in her favorite robe, and padded into the kitchen to peruse her dinner options, discovering that her refrigerator and pantry were depressingly empty. Sighing, she pulled out a premade meal from the freezer. She'd never been much of a cook, but cooking for one was even less fun.

Mia didn't miss Kristin, but she did miss having someone at home with her. She missed sitting across the table from someone, sharing a meal and talking about their day. She'd never lived alone before, having shared an apartment with roommates during college before she moved in with Kristin.

Toward the end of their marriage, she'd dreaded going home after work. Mia had fantasized about having her own place, no one to fight with over what to watch on TV or whose weekend plans took precedence. She'd wanted a bed to herself, and now that she had it...she was lonely.

Maybe that meant it was time to start dating. She wasn't ready for anything serious yet. She'd only been divorced for eight months. But as she sat alone at her kitchen table with a microwaved meal in front of her, she acknowledged that it might be nice—exciting, even—to go on a date. Surely there were other single women her age out there.

For now, all Mia wanted was a fun night on the town with a woman whose company she enjoyed. Maybe a night of casual sex, although it had been such a long time since she'd had casual sex, she could hardly imagine it now. God, what did dating even look like these days? Would she have to use an app on her phone?

Lola sat at her feet and meowed, reminding Mia that she hadn't fed her yet. As Mia left her own meal on the table to fetch a can of food for her cat, she decided it was time to get herself on a date before she turned into a cat lady. She unlocked her phone as she ate and typed "dating app" into the search bar.

The results were somewhat overwhelming. She'd had no idea there would be so many options. Was there an app specifically for lesbians? This was going to take some time and research.

Lauren pushed through the door of Whiskers Cat Café promptly at ten on Tuesday morning, feeling a burst of excitement to be here. She'd worked lots of odd jobs in her twenty-nine years, but she'd never worked with animals. She'd never had a pet either, but she'd always wanted one. Once she was back on her feet and had a place of her own, maybe she would get a pet. Maybe she'd adopt one of the cats from Mia's café. The thought made her smile.

"Morning," Mia called from behind the counter. Another employee stood beside her with their back to Lauren, working the espresso machine. "I'll be with you in just a minute," Mia said, gesturing to the line of customers waiting at the counter.

"Sure, no problem," Lauren said.

"You can leave your bag in the break room."

"Thanks." Lauren went down the hall to the room Mia had shown her when she visited with Ash and Fatima. She found an empty cubby and tucked her bag inside. Her backpack was still upstairs in Mia's apartment, a fact that made her vaguely uncomfortable. Or maybe uncomfortable wasn't the word. Maybe it was vulnerable.

As much as Lauren appreciated everything Mia had done for her, she didn't want to feel indebted to her. She wanted their friendship to be on equal footing, which meant she needed to find something she could offer Mia in return for the kindness she'd shown Lauren. But what did she have to offer? Not much.

With a sigh, she headed back into the café. Mia had said she needed help with the cats, so since she was still busy at the counter, Lauren let herself into the cat enclosure. She walked to the back, drawn by two small cats in a wire cage that hadn't been here the last time she visited.

"Are you Lauren?"

She turned to see a young woman of Asian descent with shoulder-length black hair and a warm smile walking toward her. Her nametag read Wendy, and Lauren smiled to see that the Whiskers nametags also included the employee's pronouns. That was a thoughtful touch.

Lauren nodded. "I am."

"I'm Wendy," she said, extending her hand. "I volunteer with 4 Paws Cat Rescue, and I also work here in the café when my schedule allows. I'm a lighting technician at the Sapphire Theater, so it usually works out for me to pick up a few hours here earlier in the day."

"Oh, that's so cool," Lauren said. "You work the stage lights?"

Wendy nodded. "I love it. You should come to a show sometime."

Lauren would *love* to attend a show. Seeing a Broadway show had always been an unattainable dream for her, something she'd fantasized about as a child, but couldn't afford. "I'd love to."

"We just ended an eight-month run for *It's in Her Kiss*, which was one of my favorites," Wendy said. "Anyway, we're about to start blocking a new show, which means I'll be working days at the theater for a few weeks while we work out all the lighting arrangements, so I won't be able to be here at the café as much as I usually am."

"Okay." Lauren was relieved to learn that Mia really did need an extra set of hands and wasn't just taking pity on her.

Wendy gave Lauren an inquiring look. "Mia said you're going to fill in for me?"

"Yeah. Well, I'm not sure if it's definite," Lauren hedged, since Mia had mentioned it kind of casually yesterday and Lauren hadn't signed any paperwork yet. "She asked me to come in today and see how it goes. I don't have much experience with cats."

"Oh." Wendy's brow wrinkled. "How much is not much?"

Lauren felt foolish all over again. "I like them. They like me?"

"Okay," Wendy said, but she didn't look as enthused about Lauren covering for her as she had a minute ago. "I'll check with Mia to see what she had in mind. In the meantime, you can spend a few minutes getting to know the cats. These two arrived this morning, so they'll be in the crate for a day or two to adjust before they come out into the room. We usually integrate new cats after the café's closed, when it's quiet."

"Makes sense." Lauren peered at the placard on the front of the crate, introducing the cats. "Chaos and Mayhem?" she asked with a giggle.

"I'm told they're aptly named." Wendy's lips twitched with a grin. "They're six-month-old kittens who were adopted a few months ago, and guess why they were returned?"

"They caused chaos and mayhem?"

"You got it. They're very energetic and playful, so we thought they might do well here in the café with lots of other cats and people to interact with," Wendy told her. "They're like teenagers right now...immature minds in nearly full-grown bodies. They'll settle down."

The employee Lauren had seen earlier working at the counter with Mia entered the cat enclosure, waving at Lauren. "Hi, I'm Jordy."

"Lauren. Nice to meet you." She noted with a quick glance to Jordy's nametag that their pronouns were they/them.

"I've got to get back behind the counter," Jordy said. "Just wanted to introduce myself."

"Thanks." Lauren gave them a grateful smile. Everyone at the café seemed so nice, which made her even more glad to be here. She knelt to peek at the two cats inside the cage. They were curled up together, fast asleep, looking deceptively sweet and innocent. Both were gray with tabby stripes, their coats long and fluffy. They were gorgeous cats.

"I see you've met our newest troublemakers."

Lauren turned at the sound of Mia's voice. "They don't look too troublesome at the moment."

"I expect they'll live up to their names once we let them out of that cage, but it's nothing we can't handle." Mia stepped closer to the crate, gazing affectionately at the cats inside.

The black-and-white cat Lauren had seen the last time she visited approached, pawing at Mia's pants to get her attention. She crouched to pet him, and Lauren watched quietly, fascinated. Mia usually seemed so cool and a little bit untouchable, but that faded when she interacted with the cats, and Lauren was a bit smitten with this softer side of her.

"Now," Mia said, straightening to face Lauren. "Let's get you started."

7

Mia flipped the sign on the door to Closed with a sigh. Her head throbbed with an impending migraine, and the Tylenol she'd taken at lunchtime hadn't done a thing to help. She avoided ibuprofen and aspirin as much as possible because they could aggravate her ulcer, but sometimes it was unavoidable, and this might be one of those nights.

She closed out the cash register and took its contents to the safe in her office while Jordy cleaned the counters and tables. Lauren had spent most of the day in the cat enclosure with Wendy, learning the ropes. When Wendy left an hour ago for her job at the theater, she'd told Mia that Lauren seemed like a hard worker, but she'd been concerned about Lauren's lack of experience with cats.

Wendy had a point, but at the same time, whenever Mia had observed Lauren today, she had seemed at ease both with the cats and with the café's customers. Mia entered the cat enclosure now to show Lauren how to get it squared away for the night. The space was empty except for Lauren, who sat cross-legged on the floor in the back corner, facing the wall.

How...odd.

"Lauren?" Mia said quietly so as not to startle her.

Lauren waved a hand over her shoulder, gesturing Mia toward her. She approached cautiously, hoping Lauren wasn't upset, but when she got closer, a most unexpected sight greeted her. Gilbert, the black cat who was so shy the rescue wanted to move him into a foster home, was curled up in Lauren's lap, eyes closed as she stroked a hand down his back.

"I didn't want to move and disturb him," Lauren said.

"When I hired you, I had no idea you were a cat whisperer." Mia sat beside her, leaning against the wall as she stretched her legs in front of herself. "That's impressive."

"I'm not a cat whisperer," Lauren said. "In fact, I think Wendy was ready to send me packing this morning when I told her I'd never worked with cats before. I just sat here and started talking to him, and the next thing I knew, he was in my lap."

"Definitely a cat whisperer, then," Mia said, "because Wendy and I have been trying to earn his trust all week. You're a natural. Here, let me document the moment, and Wendy's opinion on your suitability for the job might change."

Mia snapped a couple of quick photos of Gilbert in Lauren's lap. Lauren grinned cheekily for the photos, a lightness in her smile that hadn't been there when Mia first met her. She texted one to Wendy before sliding her phone into the back pocket of her pants. As she rested her head against the wall, she resisted the urge to flinch at her rapidly intensifying headache.

"How did the rest of the day go?" she asked Lauren.

"It was wonderful," Lauren told her, shifting slightly so her back wasn't to Mia. Gilbert lifted his head at the movement, looking up at her with those big yellow eyes. "I loved interacting with the cats and the customers too."

"You seem to be good with both humans and felines, from what I saw."

"I've done a lot of bartending and waitressing, and the customer service skills are basically the same, although people seem to be much nicer when they're here to play with cats than when I'm serving them food."

Mia laughed under her breath. "I bet. You enjoyed it, then?"

"I loved it," Lauren told her. "And Wendy was super helpful. She showed me everything I need to know for working with the cats and what's allowed and not allowed when the guests are interacting with them."

"Wendy's wonderful," Mia agreed, and speaking of Wendy, Mia's phone buzzed with an incoming text from her.

I had my doubts when I first met her, but she did great today, and this pic confirms her rapport with the cats. She has my approval!

Mia smiled. Ultimately, all staffing decisions were hers to make, but she preferred to have Wendy's approval on employees who'd be working with the cats. "Looks like it's unanimous. Gilbert and Wendy both think you're great, and I happen to agree, so if you're interested in the job, it's yours."

Apparently deciding he'd had enough attention, Gilbert hopped out of Lauren's lap and darted back to the cat tree. She turned to face Mia. "I'd love to work here," she said. "My only concern was that you were hiring me for valid reasons and not out of pity."

"I don't pity you, Lauren. To be frank, I'm not charitable

enough to hire someone if I don't think they'll do a good job."

Lauren blew out a breath. "I promise I won't let you down."

"Good, because I might not be as forgiving as Josie," she teased, nudging her shoulder against Lauren's. "Now come on. I'll show you how to prepare the cats for the night."

They stood, but the change in equilibrium intensified the pain throbbing behind Mia's eye. She winced, pressing a hand against her forehead.

"You okay?" Lauren asked.

"Migraine," Mia told her with a self-deprecating smile.

"Sorry. Why don't you sit? Just tell me what to do to finish up."

"I'm fine," Mia said reflexively. When she was a lawyer, her schedule hadn't allowed her to slow down for a migraine, and old habits died hard. She led the way to the supply closet to show Lauren how to prepare the cats' night-time meal, but when she bent to retrieve the cans of cat food from the bottom shelf, the pain behind her eye was so intense, she had to rest a hand against the shelf to steady herself.

"Sit," Lauren said as she took the cans from Mia's hand. "Let me handle this."

Reluctantly, she backtracked to the nearest chair and sat, rubbing her temples. "You'll spread that wet food across four paper plates," she told Lauren. The cats had access to water and dry food all day, but she fed them canned food before the café opened in the morning and again after clos-ing. It was a special treat for them and also an easy way to slip medication to whichever cats needed it. "One of the plates will go in the crate with Chaos and Mayhem, and the rest on the floor."

"When will Chaos and Mayhem come out of their crate?" Lauren asked as she worked.

"Tomorrow morning. I'll come down early to help them get acclimated to the other cats before the café opens. Then we can keep an eye on them all day to see how they're adjusting."

"Want a hand in the morning?" Lauren asked.

"I actually don't need you until the afternoon when Wendy leaves. I'll email you later tonight with a schedule for the week."

"Okay," Lauren agreed.

While they talked, Lauren spread food across the plates as instructed. Never one to sit still, Mia stood and freshened the cats' dry food and water bowls. By the time she'd finished, she was light-headed from the pain, so she asked Lauren to wipe down the tables, sweep, and scoop litter boxes. Mia walked to her office and fumbled through the drawers of her desk until she found a bottle of ibuprofen.

She popped two pills and leaned back in her chair, closing her eyes. Upstairs, her empty apartment waited, and even though she ought to be glad for the peace and quiet tonight, she still didn't look forward to it. She'd thought living alone would suit her, but it was becoming apparent she'd been wrong.

"Everything's all set," Lauren said quietly.

Mia opened her eyes to see her standing in the doorway. "Thank you."

"How's the head?" Lauren asked.

Mia sighed, rubbing her forehead. "I'll live."

"You should go upstairs and lie down," Lauren said. "Is there anything I can do?"

"No, but thank you, and that's exactly what I'm going to do." Mia stood. The pain had spread to her stomach now, thanks to the ulcer that stubbornly refused to go away. Nausea gripped her, and she held her breath as she waited for it to pass.

"Hey." Lauren's voice sounded closer now, and a moment later, Mia felt a warm hand on her wrist. "At least let me walk you upstairs."

"I don't need—" Mia's protest died on her lips when she realized Lauren was just trying to be a good friend. Of course, Mia could go upstairs by herself, but hadn't she just been lamenting the empty apartment that awaited her? "Thank you," she said instead, slipping her arm through the elbow Lauren had offered.

They went into the hall, and Mia locked the door to the café behind them before leading the way upstairs to her apartment. She let them inside and paused, not sure what to do now. Should she just thank Lauren and ask her to leave? She wasn't in any shape to play hostess at the moment.

"Sit," Lauren said, gesturing to the couch. "Have you taken anything for the pain?"

Mia sat, leaning into the cushions behind her as she closed her eyes. "Yes, but now my stomach's angry at me for it. Sorry, I'm a mess."

Lauren chuckled. "You're *so* not a mess, but even if you were, I'm the last person to judge. Stay there. I'll be right back."

"Okay." Mia wondered what Lauren was doing. A little voice in the back of her mind wondered if she should get up and see for herself, but no. If they were going to be friends, she had to trust that Lauren wasn't going to steal from her. She heard water run in the bathroom and then Lauren's footsteps approaching the couch.

"How's this?" Lauren asked softly as she laid a cool wet cloth over Mia's forehead.

She flinched at the unexpected sensation, and then she sighed in relief, because that felt amazing. "That's nice. Thank you."

"No problem."

Mia heard Lauren's footsteps as she crossed the room and then the whir of the blinds as they closed. Lola meowed, probably disgruntled at the disruption to her evening people watching.

"Sorry, Lola, but your mom's eyes are sensitive right now," Lauren said.

Mia smiled. She hadn't told Lauren her eyes were sensitive. She must have known someone else who suffered from migraines, or perhaps she got them herself.

"Have you eaten?" Lauren asked, and Mia assumed this question was directed at her, although Lola would no doubt appreciate the sentiment too.

"No, and unfortunately, I don't have much to offer," Mia told her. Since the divorce, she'd realized that Kristin had been the one who coordinated their grocery deliveries and cooked most nights. On her own, Mia apparently had no idea how to maintain a properly stocked kitchen.

"You should eat something," Lauren said. "Especially if the medication is irritating your stomach. Creating meals out of random ingredients is kind of my superpower. Trust me in your kitchen?"

"Sure," Mia told her, resisting the urge to move the cloth from her eyes and peek at her. Lauren sounded so completely in her element right now, and Mia wanted to see what that confidence looked like. "But don't feel bad if you fail, because my pantry is really pathetic."

Lauren laughed. "I'll make do. Want me to freshen that cloth for you before I start?"

"No, I'm fine," Mia said, and actually, she did feel better

now. Maybe the cloth had helped, or the ibuprofen was kicking in...or maybe it just felt good to let someone take care of her for a few minutes. Mia relaxed as she listened to Lauren poke through her cabinets.

"Have you ever tried prescription migraine meds?" Lauren asked. "Surely there's something out there that wouldn't irritate your stomach."

"I haven't, but I'm sure you're right. I always used to say I was too busy to look into it, but I don't have that excuse anymore," she admitted.

"You should really see your doctor and get a prescription."

"I should," Mia agreed. "I will." She'd quit practicing law in part to take better care of herself, after all.

"Good. I can't believe you don't even have pasta," Lauren said with laughter in her voice.

Mia groaned. "I tried to warn you, but in my defense, according to my dad, I'm too Italian to eat pasta from a box anyway."

Lauren's laughter intensified. "Okay, but out of curiosity, what qualifies as too Italian to eat pasta from a box?"

"He was born there. He moved to New York for college and stayed here."

"That's pretty cool. I'm guessing he makes amazing pasta from scratch, then."

"He does." Mia's lips curved in a smile. Her dad was an amazing cook.

She heard Lauren rummaging through cabinets and then the sound of something sizzling in a pan. A savory scent filled the air. What on earth had Lauren found to cook? Mia tried to think what she had in her pantry, but thinking hurt, so she just sat there, listening. Lauren murmured something, and Lola meowed in response. She really did have a way with cats.

"Dinner's ready," Lauren announced a few minutes later.

Mia removed the cloth from her face and opened her eyes, squinting against the light. Lauren was walking toward her with a plate in one hand and a glass of water in the other. The plate held some kind of grilled sandwich that looked and smelled amazing. "How did you... What did you possibly find in my pantry to make this?"

"Oh, it's just a grilled cheese," Lauren said as she handed the plate to Mia, followed by the glass. "You should drink up too. Staying hydrated will help with the headache."

"Thank you." Mia took a dutiful gulp of water before setting the glass on the table in front of her. "This is a fancy-looking grilled cheese."

"I found some French bread that looked pretty stale, but stale bread is actually perfect for toasting," Lauren said cheerfully as she sat across from her. "And you had some cheddar and gouda in the fridge."

Mia couldn't remember the last time she'd eaten a grilled cheese sandwich. If someone had asked her, she would have said they were for children, but as she took a bite, she almost groaned in appreciation. The bread was hot and crispy, and gooey cheese met her tongue in an explosion of flavor. "This is delicious."

Lauren beamed at her. "I'm glad."

"Didn't you make one for yourself?"

"No." Lauren waved a hand in front of her face. "I'm fine."

But Mia knew that Lauren had been at the café all day, so she hadn't eaten dinner either. "Well, that's just silly." Mia made a shooing motion with her hand. "Go fix yourself something to eat."

"Okay. Thanks." With a quick smile, Lauren headed toward the kitchen.

Mia made short work of her sandwich and finished the glass of water too. Truthfully, she'd forgotten lunch today and probably hadn't drunk enough water either, which had no doubt contributed to her migraine. As a side effect of the ulcer, she didn't feel as hungry these days. She'd skipped too many meals since the divorce, which certainly hadn't done her stomach any favors.

Lauren joined her a few minutes later with a grilled cheese sandwich of her own. She sat in the chair across from the couch. "Can I get you anything else?"

Mia shook her head. "I'm feeling much better, thanks to you."

Lauren's smile seemed to light up the whole room. "I'm glad."

"You're good at taking care of people."

Lauren picked up her sandwich. "I looked out for Craig a lot when we were kids."

Mia wondered what that had been like, Lauren taking care of her younger brother when she was still a child herself. Had she taken care of her mother too? Mia pictured little Lauren rummaging through the cabinets in her kitchen, looking for random ingredients she could use to make a meal for Craig, and her heart clenched.

"Well," Mia said. "That might be the best grilled cheese sandwich I ever had."

LAUREN DID the dishes and cleaned up the kitchen while Mia took a shower. She was hyperconscious of not over-staying her welcome, but at the same time, she enjoyed

Mia's company, and she was glad for the chance to help her tonight. Lauren was a caretaker by nature, and it was important to her that their friendship be as balanced as possible, that Lauren didn't take more than she gave.

She sat on the couch, and Lola hopped up beside her. She stared at Lauren with those big amber eyes and gave a plaintive meow. "I'll ask Mia if you need food when she gets out of the shower, okay?"

The cat glared at her, and Lauren grinned. If today was any indication, cats had *big* personalities in those little bodies, and she was pretty smitten with them. Once she got an apartment of her own, she definitely wanted a cat. Maybe two. They were hilarious and good company too.

The shower shut off, and then the door to Mia's bedroom closed. The bathroom had doors that opened both to the living room and the bedroom, and it was probably for the best that Lauren didn't see Mia wrapped in a towel. She distracted herself by rubbing Lola, trying not to think of Mia getting dressed on the other side of that door. Mia was her friend. End of story.

But when she came out of the bedroom in pale blue lounge pants and a gray T-shirt, her hair loose and damp around her face, Lauren's heart raced at the sight. Mia's hair was darker when it was wet, accentuating her fair complexion. She'd been alarmingly pale earlier, but some color had returned to her cheeks now.

Lola leaped down from the couch and ran toward her, meowing plaintively in her high-pitched voice.

"You're hungry, I know." Mia gave the cat a weary smile.

Lauren stood. "I'll feed her."

"Thank you," Mia said as she settled on the couch. "There are cans of food in the pantry and a blue plastic plate that I put it on for her."

"I'm on it." Lauren had seen the cat food while she was looking for something to feed Mia earlier, and she found the plate easily too. She emptied a can onto the plate as Lola danced around her feet, meowing. Lauren set it on the floor, giggling at Lola's enthusiasm as she dug in. Then she stood and faced Mia. "Anything else I can do for you before I head out?"

Mia shook her head. "She'll love you forever now."

"That was kind of the idea," Lauren said, still smiling as she rejoined Mia in the living room. She sat in the chair across from the couch.

"What will you do tonight? I can't imagine relaxing in a room with strangers."

"Oh, I'll put in my earbuds and write fic, probably," Lauren said.

"Well, now I'm intrigued. What are you working on?"

"Just a little post-season-five Clairantha scene, what might have happened after that kiss in the alley." It had been on her mind since she watched the episode last weekend.

Mia's lips curved into a slow smile. "Do I get to read it first?"

"Always," Lauren told her. Mia had become her unofficial beta reader, checking for typos and things that didn't make sense on pretty much everything Lauren had published.

Mia leaned back against the couch cushions and curled her feet beneath her, looking much more comfortable and relaxed than she had earlier, and Lauren was so glad to see it. "Where do you write?" Mia asked. "Do you have a laptop?"

Lauren shook her head. "I write on my phone. A laptop

is definitely on my wish list, though, especially if I'm going to try to publish that book I've been working on."

"Which I wholeheartedly support," Mia said. "Although I can't imagine writing anything more than a text message on my phone. I'm that old person tapping along with one finger."

Lauren grinned, picturing it. Mia was so effortlessly cool and competent at pretty much anything Lauren had seen her attempt, so the thought of her tapping at her phone with one finger was too adorable for words. "I'd hardly call you old."

"I feel that way sometimes." Mia pressed a hand to her forehead with a grimace.

"You were married a long time, right?" Lauren asked, eager to seize this chance to know more about Mia, since she didn't seem to be in a hurry for Lauren to leave.

"We were together for a long time," Mia confirmed. "Eighteen years, although we couldn't legally get married until 2011. We started dating when we were twenty-four, still in law school."

"I'm sorry it didn't work out." Lauren couldn't even imagine spending that many years with someone and then having it fall apart.

"Me too," Mia said with a sigh. "Have you ever been in love?"

"No, not even close." Lauren had spent most of her life looking out for herself and Craig. There hadn't been time for love.

"Want to?" Mia asked.

"Oh, sure." Lauren leaned back in her chair. "I love the idea of finding that person who completes me, you know? I want the whole romance novel experience."

Mia rubbed Lola, who had jumped up beside her. "Any prospects?"

Lauren shook her head. "I wish, but no. I'm going to straighten my life out this year, though, get a real job and an apartment. Then I can look for love."

"Have you ever tried online dating?" Mia asked. "I downloaded an app the other day, but I have no idea what I'm doing. The whole concept feels so impersonal to me."

"Yep," Lauren said. "I've used dating apps. Did you know Sarah and Quinn met online? I have a lot of friends who've found love that way."

"I guess I need to learn, then," Mia said. "Maybe you can give me pointers."

"Sure," Lauren agreed, even if the thought of helping Mia master online dating sent a pang of regret through her chest. She needed to get over this crush on her friend, because Mia obviously didn't feel the same way, and Lauren had to get her life together before she could think about dating anyway.

"Want to watch something with me before you head out?" Mia asked. "Or are you eager to get started on that fic?"

She was much more eager to spend time with Mia than to work on the fic, but... "I don't want to keep you up if you'd rather be sleeping off that migraine."

"I'm not ready for bed just yet. I just want to lie here on the couch and relax. Maybe we could watch the *In Her Defense* episode with the kiss for inspiration for your fic?"

Lauren grinned. She didn't have a subscription to the streaming service right now, and while the kiss itself had been uploaded to YouTube, she hadn't seen the entire episode except that day in the Airbnb. "Yeah, that sounds perfect."

"Great." Mia picked up the remote control and turned

on the TV. She queued up the episode and gestured for Lauren to sit beside her.

Lauren moved to the cushion next to Mia so she was facing the TV. She toed out of her shoes and curled her feet beneath her the way Mia had done, getting comfortable. As soon as the episode began to play, she found herself smiling. "I really love this show."

"And its leading lady?" Mia gave her a knowing look.

Lauren shrugged playfully. "I cannot deny my celebrity crush."

Mia leaned back with her head against the cushion behind her, damp strands of hair curling around her face. Lauren had never seen her like this, makeup-free in her lounge clothes, hair still damp from a shower. It was a world away from the carefully put-together appearance she presented to the world each day, and Lauren could hardly take her eyes off her.

They chatted on and off during the episode, falling quiet during the more intense scenes, especially Sam's showstopping courtroom performance. By the time Sam and Claire were at the bar near the end of the episode, Lauren was overcome with anticipation to see that scene in the alley again.

Tears rose in her eyes as she watched Sam battle her panic attack. The fear on her face was so visceral, Lauren could hardly breathe. She'd had enough panic attacks of her own over the years to know that Piper's portrayal was spot-on.

Lauren leaned forward, arms clasped around her knees, so caught up in the show, she almost forgot she was on Mia's couch. When Sam and Claire finally kissed, Lauren felt a tingle in the pit of her stomach, a gut punch of emotion for these two characters she was so invested in.

She'd spent years hoping for this moment. These characters had reinvigorated her love of writing, had inspired her to write a book-length fan fiction about their love for each other. And now their attraction was canon on the show itself.

"I still can't quite believe that happened." She sighed happily as the credits began to roll.

When Mia didn't respond, Lauren glanced at her. Mia was curled on her side with her eyes closed, her face relaxed and peaceful in sleep.

Oh.

Lauren's heart squeezed at the sight. And *oof*, there was that tingle in her belly again, but this time, it was for the woman on the couch beside her. Mia looked impossibly beautiful, fast asleep with her hair in her face and a cat curled over her feet. Lauren reached for the remote control and turned off the TV. Then she took the throw blanket that had been neatly folded over the back of the couch and draped it across Mia's legs, careful not to disturb her.

Quietly, Lauren stood and put on her shoes. She picked up her bag and let herself out of Mia's apartment, turning the button on the doorknob so that it locked behind her. And then she headed back to the hostel to write smutty fan fiction on her phone. Anything to keep from fantasizing about the woman whose apartment she'd just left.

8

Mia's head was still sore as she opened the café on Wednesday morning. She'd woken in the dark hours of the night, disoriented to find herself on the couch with a blanket tucked carefully around her. And then she'd felt embarrassed that she'd passed out and left Lauren to fend for herself in Mia's apartment.

But Lauren had locked the door behind herself on her way out, and by the time Mia made it downstairs to the café this morning, she had a link to a Google doc in her inbox, the new Clairantha scene that Lauren had told her about. Mia was still boggled that anyone could write on their phone, let alone write as well as Lauren did. She hadn't had a chance to read the new fic yet, but she couldn't wait to dive in on her lunch break.

Just as she was about to duck out to eat at her desk, she saw Josie coming through the front door of the café. Mia waved her over. Josie sometimes stopped in before the bar opened, and Mia had expected she'd be in today to check on Chaos and Mayhem, who had originally been her foster kittens.

"Your usual?" she asked Josie.

"I can't believe I'm going to say this, but make it a decaf," Josie told her.

"Blasphemy," Mia teased as she grabbed a cup to make Josie's latte. "Cutting back on caffeine?"

"Mm," Josie said with a somewhat wistful expression. "How are my troublesome duo doing so far?"

"No problems at all." Mia gestured toward the cat enclosure. "I think the couple who adopted them just didn't realize what they were signing up for. They seem like perfectly normal kittens to me, maybe a little more energetic than average."

"I suspect you're right," Josie said. "But at least their adopters abided by the contract and returned them to me instead of taking them to the shelter. I'm sure we'll have them adopted again in no time, and in the meantime, they'll probably enjoy all the attention here."

"They certainly seem to be enjoying it so far," Mia said as she frothed Josie's latte. "Sticking around for a bit? I was about to take lunch."

Josie nodded, handing Mia her credit card to pay for her drink. "I'd love to sit with you while you eat."

"Want anything to go with that latte? I was going to snag one of these biscotti for myself."

"Yes, please," Josie said with a smile.

Mia put two biscotti on a plate and led the way to her office, where she settled behind her desk. Josie sat in the guest chair, sipping her latte. They hadn't seen each other since Mia brought Lauren to Dragonfly, and she hoped things wouldn't be awkward between them because of it.

"Lauren's working here part time now," she said, just to get it out of the way.

Josie took another sip. "That's fine. I'm glad she's doing better. You're a good friend."

Mia shrugged. "I believe her when she says she did it for her brother, that she'd never do anything like that again. Hopefully, I'm not wrong about her."

"I believe her too." Josie sighed, settling in her chair. "And I respect the way she's taking responsibility for her crime. She deserves a second chance, and I'm glad you're giving her one."

Mia nodded as she reached into her desk to pull out a protein bar. She took a dutiful bite, even though she wasn't particularly hungry, and then she bit back a grimace because it was dry and flavorless. She really needed to get better at meal planning.

"That good, huh?" Josie asked with a smirk.

"Someday, I'll learn to grocery shop for myself." Mia took another unenthusiastic bite. "So what's new with you and Eve?"

"Well," Josie said. "Let's just say...kittens may not be the only reason we're up for middle-of-the-night feedings soon."

"Oh." Mia sat up straight, blinking at Josie in surprise. "You two are having a baby? Wait..." She glanced at the decaf latte in Josie's hands. "Are you pregnant?"

Josie was practically bouncing in her seat, her excitement palpable. "Well, we're trying. I don't know if I'm pregnant yet, but I thought I should start weaning myself off caffeine just in case."

"That's amazing news," Mia told her. "When will you know?"

"Another week or so," Josie said. "And it's probably too much to hope for it to happen on the first try, right? But I'm already driving myself crazy trying to imagine if I *feel* pregnant." Her eyes sparkled as she touched her stomach. "Which is so weird, you know? I guess straight and bi women go through this all the time, but I've never in my life had to wonder if I was pregnant. Never even thought about it."

"Me either." Mia had never been with a man, so that was one thing she'd never worried about when she had sex. She'd wanted a family, though. It was probably for the best that she and Kristin had never gotten around to starting one, given how things ended. "Well, I'm crossing my fingers for you. I hope it happens quickly."

"Thank you." Josie took another sip. "Eve's been pretty emotional about it. She lost her first wife and their unborn daughter in a car crash about seven years ago."

Mia felt the breath rush from her lungs. "I had no idea."

"It's been hard for her, deciding to try again for a family. I just hope everything goes smoothly, for both of our sakes, but for her especially."

"I hope so too," Mia told her. "You're trying insemination?"

Josie nodded, then grinned. "And Adam is our donor." Adam was one of Josie's best friends and the new manager of Dragonfly. He was a great guy, from what Mia knew of him.

"Oh, that's wonderful."

"He'll be Uncle Adam. He's excited." Josie sipped her latte. "So am I...like *ridiculously* excited."

"I bet. I'm so happy for you," Mia said. "And definitely count me in for babysitting duty when the time comes."

"Really?" Josie asked, still smiling. "You?"

Mia scoffed. "Admittedly, I don't have much experience, but I love being around my friends' kids."

They chatted for a few more minutes while Josie finished her latte and Mia ate her lunch. Then they checked on Mayhem and Chaos, who were currently wrestling at the top of the cat tree while Gilbert watched from the cubby below.

"They seem to be doing just fine," Josie said as she reached up to pet Chaos.

"Agreed," Mia said as Josie made her way around the cat enclosure, greeting each of the adoptable cats with the gentle enthusiasm that never failed to reassure even the most skittish foster cat. Josie had been an invaluable resource to Mia as she was getting her café up and running.

Mia smiled as she watched Josie cradle Mayhem in her arms, cooing at him like he was a human baby while he batted at her fingers. Josie would be an amazing mom. Mia felt a tug of longing in her chest. She hadn't thought much about babies lately, having assumed she'd missed her chance, but suddenly, she found herself hoping for a second chance at love and a family too.

LAUREN HURRIED down the sidewalk toward Whiskers Cat Café. She'd been delayed on the subway, and now she was dangerously close to running late, which was not at all the impression she wanted to make. She'd spent the morning chasing job and apartment leads all over Brooklyn, only to come up empty on both fronts. No one, it seemed, wanted to hire or rent to a felon.

Since pending charges would show up on a background check, she'd been upfront about it when filling out applications to avoid wasting anyone's time. Although she hadn't been convicted and probably wouldn't be, this felony charge was a huge mark against her.

And even if she overcame that hurdle, many of the

rooms she'd applied for required deposits that exceeded the meager contents of her bank account. Building a new life for herself in Brooklyn wasn't going to be easy, but she refused to give up on her dream.

It was too soon to panic, but already her money was running short. The hostel was expensive. Even thirty dollars a night added up when she didn't have a steady source of income. This part-time job at the café was a good start, though, and she wasn't going to screw it up. She glanced at her phone. She still had ten minutes, and she was only two blocks away.

"Lauren?"

She looked up to see Josie walking toward her, and her stomach clenched uncomfortably. Things had gone reasonably well when Lauren met with her to pay her back, but still, she was probably the last person Josie wanted to see this afternoon. "Hi, Josie."

To her surprise, Josie gave her a warm smile. "On your way to the café? I just came from there myself, and Mia mentioned you were working for her part time."

Lauren nodded. "Yeah. I'm working with the cats. It's pretty great so far."

Josie's smile widened. "I'm glad. Hey, I just wanted you to know that we're good, okay? I don't want things to be awkward, especially since we're both friends with Mia. As far as I'm concerned, the slate between us is wiped clean."

"That's awfully generous of you," Lauren said, ducking her head as heat pricked her cheeks.

"Everyone deserves a second chance, Lauren." Josie's lips twisted to the side. "Well, not *everyone*, but most people do."

"Thank you," Lauren told her.

"Anyway, I'm sure I'll see you around. And if you ever want to stop by Dragonfly for a drink, it's okay. You probably won't even see me. I've finally got a full-time bartending staff, so I'm only filling in shifts here and there."

Lauren couldn't contain her smile. "I'm so glad. I know that was your goal."

"Yep." There was no mistaking the look on Josie's face as anything but euphoric. "This was my dream, and I've finally achieved it. Now I can focus on my kitten rescue...and my wife."

"Congrats about that, by the way," Lauren said. "It was Eve who had you all starry-eyed when I worked for you, right? That's why you wouldn't tell me her name?"

"It was Eve," Josie confirmed. "We had to keep things under wraps for a while because of our contract for her show."

"You hid it well. I had no idea, not until Mia told me you were married. I'm really happy for you both."

"Thanks." Josie's phone rang in her pocket, and she pulled it out. "Speak of the devil, that's Eve now. Well, I'll see you around." With a wave, she connected the call and headed down the sidewalk.

Lauren started speed-walking toward the café, feeling lighter on her feet than she had since...well, probably since she robbed Josie's bar. She'd never dared to hope for Josie's forgiveness, and now that she'd received it, she felt like she'd regained a bit of herself that she'd lost that night.

She was panting for breath by the time she yanked open the café's front door, but the clock on the wall read 1:58, so she wasn't late. Thank God.

Mia looked up from the drink she was mixing, waving over her shoulder at Lauren.

"Hi," Lauren said. "Sorry for cutting it so close. I bumped into Josie on my way here."

"She just left the café," Mia said.

"Yes, she mentioned that."

"All good?" Mia raised her eyebrows.

"Yep. She's been incredibly great about this whole thing."

Mia nodded. "I'm glad it all worked out."

"How are you feeling today?" Lauren asked.

"Much better, thanks," Mia said with a quick smile, returning to the drink she was making.

"I'm glad." Lauren hurried down the hall to leave her bag in the break room and then went into the cat enclosure, where Wendy was waiting for her. She gave Lauren a quick rundown on the new kittens, who'd been integrated into the room that morning, before heading to her job at the theater, leaving Lauren on her own with the cats.

Two tables near the front were occupied with customers, sipping drinks and sharing conversation as they watched Chaos and Mayhem scamper over the cat tower in the window. A single woman about Mia's age sat at a table in the corner, working on a laptop.

Lauren went into the alcove in back to check on the cats' food, water, and litter. She swept the space to clear away crumbs and cat hair, and then she made her way around the room, introducing herself to each group in case they had any questions about the cats.

"Also, please let me know if I can bring you anything from the café," she said after she'd introduced herself to the woman with the laptop.

"I'll take another coffee, please."

"Sure," Lauren said. "What's your name?"

"Beth Pfeiffer."

"Got it, Beth." Lauren let herself out of the cat enclosure and walked to the counter. Mia kept a tab open for customers while they visited with the cats, and it seemed to be a good idea if yesterday was any indication. Lauren had brought a steady supply of drinks and pastries to customers in the cat enclosure.

"Coffee for Beth Pfeiffer," she told Mia.

Mia nodded. "I'll bring it over when it's ready."

That was different. Lauren had provided all the table service herself yesterday, but maybe this woman was a friend of Mia's or something. "Sure."

She went back into the cat enclosure. Chaos darted over to greet her, and she bent to pet him. "How's your first day in the café going?" she asked. She didn't really know how to talk to cats, so she just talked to them like they were people, and it seemed to be working.

Chaos sank the claws of his front paws into her jeans and looked up at her with wild eyes. His tail twitched, and then he lunged, attempting to climb her like a tree.

"Don't get any ideas, big guy," she said, putting a hand in front of his paws to block him. In response, he bit her finger. "Ouch." She managed to free herself from him, thankful he hadn't bitten hard enough to draw blood, and walked to the back wall to pick up a toy he could play with instead. He leaped into the air to chase the feather on the end of the stick, and she laughed.

"He's an energetic one," a man at a nearby table commented. "How old is he?"

"Six months," Lauren told him. "Still full of kitten energy."

"I can tell," the man agreed. "May I?" He gestured to the toy she held.

Lauren handed it to him. "Chaos and his brother Mayhem are available to adopt together if you're looking for a pair."

"Great names," the man said as he waved the toy. Chaos

did a somersault in the air, grabbed the feather, and then rubbed his head against the man's legs, purring. "Although they sound like a handful. I'm Darius, by the way."

"Lauren," she introduced herself.

Darius wore a white button-down shirt and gray slacks, as if he'd come here from the office. He had dark brown skin, close cropped hair, and an easy smile. "I'm not sure Chaos here is the right cat for me, but I am looking to adopt. My daughter visits on the weekends, and she loves animals. I thought a cat might be a nice surprise for her."

"I'm sure she'd love that," Lauren said. "I would have been over the moon if someone had given me a kitten when I was a little girl."

"I think Kelsey will be too. I come here once a week or so to enjoy the coffee and visit the cats. Kind of getting myself used to the idea, I guess."

"Sounds like a great approach to me." Lauren looked up to see Mia walk over to the woman with the laptop and set a mug of coffee on her table. They exchanged a smile, and Mia fiddled with her hair. Her expression was one that Lauren hadn't seen before, one that made Lauren's stomach sink. Mia was flirting, and judging by the warm smile on the other woman's face, her interest seemed to be reciprocated.

And that was...fine. Mia had told Lauren just last night that she was ready to start dating.

"If you see a calm, easygoing cat who's good with kids, let me know."

Lauren redirected her attention to Darius, who was still twirling the toy for Chaos. "I sure will."

∾

MIA WAS EXHAUSTED by the time the café closed that night. It was a good kind of exhausted, the kind that followed a long and satisfying day of work, but beneath that, she was drained from yesterday's migraine.

"You look tired," Lauren commented as she swept the floor.

"I am," Mia admitted. "Probably going to be an early night."

Lauren kept sweeping. "I've got another exciting night of filling out rental applications ahead of me."

"Any leads?" Mia asked.

"Not yet, but there are a lot of people in Brooklyn looking for an extra roommate. I'm sure I'll find something soon."

Mia rolled her lips inward. She didn't like the idea of Lauren rooming with strangers, but she supposed people did it all the time. God knew it was expensive to rent in this city. "Fingers crossed. You don't have any friends you could crash with, at least for a little while?"

Lauren flinched. "I had to disable all my accounts— except my anonymous fandom Twitter—when I left town. I've tried to get back in touch with my local friends now that I can be online as myself again, but...no one has replied to me. And I wasn't even asking for favors. I was just trying to explain where I'd been."

"I'm sorry," Mia said. "I lost a lot of friends after the divorce too. People can be disturbingly fickle sometimes."

"Yeah, unfortunately." Lauren pushed one of the tables to the side before sweeping beneath it. "So did you get her number?"

"What?" Mia paused as she wiped down the table in front of her. "Who?"

"Beth Pfeiffer, the pretty businesswoman with the laptop?" Lauren gave her a knowing smile.

Oh Lord. She'd noticed Mia's pathetic attempts at flirting? Well, that was embarrassing. "No. I...no."

"She seemed into you," Lauren offered.

"Did she?" Mia couldn't help asking.

Lauren nodded. "I bet she'd give you her number if you asked."

"I don't know." She gave her head a quick shake. Her cheeks were uncomfortably warm, and she didn't even know why. "I did think about asking her out, but I'm just... I'm horribly out of practice."

Lauren grinned. "Mia, you're gorgeous, you're successful, and you're good company too. I'm sure she'd be thrilled to go out with you."

"I haven't been on a first date in eighteen years. The whole concept is completely intimidating, to be honest," she admitted.

"I can imagine," Lauren said.

"I need to dip my toes back in the water, though, but do you think I should start with someone from a dating app instead of a regular from the café?"

"Either-or," Lauren said. "I bet it'll be easier than you think."

"I hope so."

They fell to lighter topics as they finished cleaning up. Lauren headed out, and Mia went upstairs. She needed to go to the gym. Generally, she went every morning before work, but she'd skipped yesterday because of her migraine and again this morning because she'd needed to be at the café early to work with Chaos and Mayhem.

With a sigh, she rubbed her forehead. She was too tired to go tonight. She'd make up for it tomorrow. Instead, she stared morosely at her empty kitchen. Dammit. She really should have gone shopping before she came upstairs. Lola trotted over, meowing, and at least there were still a few cans of cat food in the pantry.

Mia fed her, poured herself a glass of water, and then went into the bedroom to change. Once she was dressed in lounge pants and a comfortable T-shirt, she settled on the couch and picked up her phone. The Google doc Lauren had sent her last night was still there, waiting for Mia to read it. A smile touched her lips as she saw the title.

Kiss Me Slowly

Mia curled her feet underneath herself as she began to read. The fic picked up right where the season finale left off, with Sam and Claire kissing passionately in the alley behind the bar, although they quickly came to their senses. Sam was still rattled from her panic attack, so Claire offered to drive her home, and then she insisted on seeing Sam inside.

I stumble toward the kitchen for a glass of water, my pulse beating like a wild thing in my ears. I kissed Claire. I kissed Claire, and it was one of the hottest kisses of my life. Even now, my body feels alive, electricity snapping through my veins, sparking under my skin, a live wire waiting to be touched.

And Claire does. She touches my shoulder, a touch that seems to reach all the way to my soul. I turn, and my mouth crashes into Claire's, tasting her, claiming her, devouring her. I've never felt so wild, so overwhelmed with need for another person. Claire's hand slides beneath my shirt, skating over my bare skin and drawing a moan from my throat.

Mia gasped when Claire pushed up Sam's skirt right there in the kitchen. Holy shit, that was hot. A warm ache grew between Mia's thighs as she read, and she shifted in her seat. Sam and Claire ended up on the floor, claiming each other in one of the sexiest scenes Mia had ever read. She was so turned on just reading it that she was seriously considering going into the bedroom for her vibrator.

But...in the back of her mind, she saw Lauren writing those words, the words that had turned Mia on. And now she felt more uncomfortable than aroused. This was the first time she'd read something Lauren had written since they'd met in person. Maybe that was the difference? Or maybe Mia just really, *really* needed to get laid. Probably, it was a combination of the two.

Irritated with herself, Mia's instinct was to put down her phone and change the subject in her sex-starved brain all together, but she'd promised to send Lauren notes on the fic. Mia reached under the coffee table for her laptop and booted it up. She could type so much faster on a real keyboard. Hopefully, if she read through the fic with a clinical eye, looking for typos and awkward sentences, she wouldn't get as caught up in the emotion of it this time.

Even as she was critiquing Lauren's words, Mia was blown away by the quality of her writing. Lauren really did have talent, and Mia hoped she was able to realize her dream of becoming a published author. It was beyond impressive that she'd written this entire fic on her phone last night after she left Mia's apartment.

Mia entered her notes and then sent Lauren a quick message to let her know how much she'd enjoyed the fic. Of course, the minute she'd sent the text, she was second-guessing her wording. Obviously, Lauren would have no idea just what kind of enjoyment Mia had gotten out of it, but good God, she needed to get a grip!

Huffing in frustration, she stood and went into the kitchen, hoping there was another prepackaged meal in her freezer. She tried not to let herself remember how nice it had been when Lauren was here last night, that grilled cheese she'd made out of the pathetic contents of Mia's pantry. Nope. She wasn't going to think about Lauren again tonight, not in any context.

9

For the next few weeks, Lauren threw herself full force into getting her life back on track. She worked several afternoons a week at the café, mostly helping out in the cat enclosure, but sometimes Mia put her to work behind the counter too. And Lauren got another part-time job, stocking shelves at a market not far from the café. That job came with a very convenient employee discount, which was the best perk a girl on a budget could hope for.

Lauren's main concern now was housing. The hostel on 7th didn't allow people to stay for more than two weeks at a time, so she'd moved into a different hostel, but this one was a little bit more expensive and a whole lot louder. She wasn't sleeping well, and her bank account was dwindling, but she still hadn't been able to find anyone willing to rent to her with a felony charge hanging over her head.

She was increasingly anxious about her court date, which was only two days away. As much as she couldn't wait to get it over with, she was so scared something would go wrong and she'd wind up in jail after all. She took full responsibility for her crime, and she was willing to accept whatever happened, but she was finally getting back on her feet, dammit. Going to jail would be a huge setback. Thank God Mia would be there with her in court.

She and Mia were spending more time together than ever. Their friendship was strengthening, and so was Lauren's infatuation, but she was determined to push it to the back of her mind. She'd been attracted to friends before, and with time, it would pass. Lauren couldn't even think about getting involved with anyone until she'd found an apartment. Right now, she was essentially homeless, bouncing between hostels.

Not to mention, Mia didn't seem to return Lauren's interest. Mia had flirted with Beth a few more times when she came into the café, but so far, nothing had come of it. Overall, Mia seemed flustered and uncertain when it came to dating.

As Lauren pushed through the café's front door that afternoon, she was so lost in her thoughts, she almost ran straight into Mia, who was standing just inside the door with a strand of orange lights shaped like leaves in her hands.

"Sorry," Lauren said as she dodged to the side. "Halloween decorations already?" It was only mid-September, but she'd already started to see pumpkins on doorsteps.

Mia smiled. "I prefer fall to Halloween, but yes, I like to decorate."

"Those lights are super cute," Lauren told her. "Let me know if you need a hand."

"I will. What's in the bag?" Mia gestured to the insulated shopping bag Lauren carried. She'd just come from the market, where she'd stocked up on groceries from the clearance shelf, a habit that was sustaining her until her finances improved.

"I grabbed a package of fresh-made raviolis and some sauce if you want me to work my weird magic later in your kitchen?" Lauren asked hopefully. Without access to a kitchen of her own, she'd been eating a lot of granola bars since she couldn't afford to go out, but Mia seemed to like it when Lauren came over to cook her random clearance finds, something she'd done several times now.

"Sure," Mia agreed. "Just don't tell my father you've fed me store-bought raviolis."

"Says the woman who never cooks for herself," Lauren teased. "You're such a hypocritical Italian, Mia."

Mia laughed, waving her off so she could get back to work with the fall lights.

Lauren went down the hall to leave her bags in the break room. After changing into her Whiskers Cat Café staff shirt, she headed for the cat enclosure. All the cats who'd been here when she first started had been adopted now, except Gilbert. Chaos and Mayhem had been adopted together last week and were thriving in their new home. Gilbert was making progress, though. Lauren spent extra time with him during all her shifts, helping him come out of his shell.

She began her now-familiar routine, interacting with the cats and customers. Their newest arrival, an orange tabby named Pumpkin, was already a favorite. Everyone in the café was talking about him while he basked in the attention, purring loudly. Lauren had already processed two adoption applications for him by the time she took her first break.

"Hi, Lauren."

She turned to see Darius settling into his usual seat with a cup of coffee. "Hey, Darius. How are you?"

"Enjoying this fall weather, that's for sure."

"Same," she told him.

"Any new cats you think might be a good fit?" He'd been visiting the café regularly over the last few weeks, looking for the right cat for him and his daughter.

"Well, Pumpkin would be perfect, but we've already had a few applications come in for him."

He followed her gaze to the orange cat in the front window, currently being petted by a little girl who looked completely smitten. "Damn. Does that mean I'm too late?"

"You could still put in an application. Sometimes things fall through, but yeah, it's probably too late. Actually, I had another idea I wanted to run past you. Is your daughter more quiet or rambunctious?"

"Quiet," Darius told her. "She loves to read and play with her dolls, and she has a very gentle touch with animals."

Lauren smiled. "I wonder if Gilbert might be a good fit for you and Kelsey."

"Gilbert?" Darius gave her a blank look.

She pointed to the black cat in his usual spot at the top of the cat tower. "He's been here a little while. He's shy and slow to warm up to people, but he's really come out of his shell with me recently, and I watched him bond with a little girl about Kelsey's age earlier this week."

"Hm." Darius gave the cat a skeptical look. "He doesn't seem very friendly."

"He finds the café a little overwhelming. The rescue thinks a quiet home would be best for him. We were thinking that meant no kids, but if you could have seen him with the little girl earlier this week...well, I just think it's something to consider."

"Maybe," Darius said, but he didn't look convinced.

"Let's see if I can get his attention so you two can meet."

Lauren sat beside the cat tower, talking quietly to Gilbert

and clucking her tongue. She did this with him every day, and about half the time, he would come down to say hi. Hopefully, he was feeling social today since they had an audience. Sure enough, Gilbert hopped down and rubbed himself against her legs, purring contentedly.

"See?" she said softly. "He's very friendly once you get to know him."

She petted him for a few minutes, feeding him a couple of the cat treats she'd started keeping in her pockets for this purpose. Gilbert curled up beside her, paws tucked underneath himself like a cat loaf. "If you come over quietly, I think he'd let you pet him," she told Darius.

"All right." Darius got up from his table and came to join them, extending a hand toward Gilbert so the cat could sniff him. Gilbert gave him a wary look but didn't move away.

"Excuse me."

Lauren looked up to see a woman at a nearby table waving to get her attention. She turned to Darius. "I'll leave you two to get to know each other." She stood and walked over to the woman.

"I have a couple of questions about this guy," she said, and Lauren saw that a gray tabby named Jasper had curled up in the chair next to her.

Lauren answered the woman's questions and then made a loop around the café to see if anyone else needed her assistance. Darius left a few minutes later with a promise to come back and visit Gilbert again soon, and Lauren smiled, hopeful she'd found a match.

She saw a bit of herself in the shy black cat. When she first entered the foster care system at fifteen, she'd naively hoped a loving family would walk through the door of her group home and choose her. Then she would convince them to adopt Craig too, and they'd be a family again.

It hadn't worked out that way, but it brought her joy to see these abandoned cats getting the second chance she hadn't. Older children and teenagers were hard to find homes for, but that didn't seem to be the case for adoptable cats. She might cry when Gilbert finally got adopted, and now that the idea had taken root, she was really hoping he might find a home with Darius and Kelsey.

Two women had sat at a table by the window, so Lauren headed over to greet them. "Welcome to Whiskers Cat Café. Have you visited us before?"

"We have, and before you ask...we're not interested in adopting," one of the women told her.

"Yet," the other woman added with a playful smile.

"We're friends of Josie Swanson," the first woman said. "I'm Sophie, and this is Jules."

"Oh, hi." Lauren reminded herself she didn't need to flinch at the mention of Josie's name. "It's so nice to meet you. I'm Lauren."

"I adopted two kittens from Josie last year," Jules told her. "But Sophie and I share a studio apartment, so we aren't ready to expand the family yet, so to speak."

"Two women and two cats in a studio is plenty, trust me," Sophie said with a laugh.

"I'm sure," Lauren agreed.

"Anyway, we're hoping to move to a bigger place next year," Jules said. She had glossy brown hair and a camera-ready smile. "And Soph promised me another cat once we have room."

"I said *maybe*." Sophie rolled her eyes, then gave Jules an affectionate look.

"We both work on Broadway, and with our crazy sched-ules, we won't be having kids any time soon or even a dog," Jules said with a shrug. "So...cats."

"Oh wow…Broadway?" Lauren felt suddenly starstruck, even though she didn't know Jules's and Sophie's last names. Here she was, casually chatting with two actresses without realizing it. Were they famous? Should she have recognized them?

Jules gave her a megawatt smile. "Yes, we both perform on Broadway. We actually met while we were auditioning for the same role."

"She got the part," Sophie said. "And here we are, talking your ear off when we aren't even here to adopt a cat. Sorry."

Lauren laughed. "No worries. A lot of people come in to play with the cats when they aren't interested in adopting. We're happy to have you. Now, tell me where I can see you perform?"

"I'm playing Gloria Estefan in the new production of *On Your Feet*," Jules said, pride dripping from her words. "It's the honor of my life to play one of my idols and a fellow Cuban American."

"Wow…Gloria Estefan. That's amazing," Lauren gushed.

"And I'm between shows at the moment," Sophie told her, "but I'll be joining the cast of *Six* after the new year."

"Okay, jotting this down because I definitely want to go see both of you." Lauren pulled out her phone. "Last names, ladies?"

"Julia Vega and Sophie Rindell," Jules told her.

Lauren saved their information in her phone and brought them coffee and pastries before getting back to work. Jules and Sophie seemed so happy together. Lauren wanted that for herself, once she was settled in her own apartment. And she wanted to see them both perform. Wendy had told her about an app that offered last-minute discounted tickets to Broadway shows, and she'd been meaning to check it out.

Maybe Mia would want to go to a show with her, as friends. Lauren wasn't quite ready financially to splurge on Broadway tickets, even the discounted kind. But soon.

"So, raviolis, hm?" Mia said as they closed the café together that evening.

"The fresh kind, not frozen," Lauren told her.

"Sounds great. It won't shock you to know my pantry is again bare."

Lauren grinned. Mia was so competent at work, but she was terrible about remembering to feed herself, and it brought Lauren entirely too much joy to cook for her. And spend time with her. And have access to a kitchen so she didn't have to eat another granola bar for dinner. For all those reasons, the evenings when she cooked for Mia had become her favorite.

They walked upstairs to Mia's apartment together. She unlocked the door and gestured Lauren in ahead of her.

"Hey, remember the fic that you beta read for me a few weeks ago?" Lauren asked. "*Kiss Me Slowly*?"

"Of course." Mia set down her purse and bent to pet Lola.

"It just hit three thousand views, which is so crazy. I've never had one gain that much traction so quickly." Lauren walked into the kitchen and set her insulated bag on the counter. She got right to work, familiar with where Mia kept her pans and utensils now.

"Well, it's an excellent fic," Mia said. "And I imagine the Clairantha fandom has grown since that onscreen kiss."

"You're probably right about that."

"Speaking of your writing, how's the book coming along?"

"Slowly," Lauren told her as she pulled out a pot and began to fill it with water to heat the ravioli. "It's tedious writing on my phone. Once I've found a room to rent, my next focus will be a laptop."

"Still no luck finding a room?"

"Nope." Lauren tried to keep her tone light, but she wasn't sure she succeeded, if the sympathetic look on Mia's face was any indication.

"Hopefully soon. I'll be right back." Mia headed for her bedroom.

Lauren loved that Mia felt comfortable changing into her lounge clothes while she was here. As much as she loved the stylish clothes Mia wore to work, she'd also developed a bit of an obsession with the way Mia looked in sweatpants, relaxed and casual.

When the water boiled, Lauren added the ravioli. Then she took out the jar of sauce she'd bought and began to heat that too, stirring in some extra seasonings from Mia's spice rack. Her phone dinged with a new email while she cooked, and she slid it out of her back pocket.

IMPORTANT: Your upcoming court appearance has been rescheduled.

Lauren stared at the email as her stomach plummeted. She tapped the message to open it, revealing a new court date of October 21st. As much as Lauren had been anxious about going to court on Wednesday, this felt worse, because now she'd have to wait another month to learn her fate. And *why* had it been postponed? Was this bad news? Was the State of New York building a case against her?

Mia came out of the bedroom, wearing blue cotton pants and a long-sleeved tee from NYU School of Law.

Lauren held up her phone. "Should I panic about this?"

Mia's eyebrows rose. "About what?"

Lauren slid her phone across the counter to Mia with the email illuminated on the screen. Mia read quietly then shook her head. "This is just administrative. Court dates get bumped all the time."

"Okay." Lauren exhaled, endlessly thankful she had a lawyer to set her mind at ease.

"Nothing to worry about," Mia said.

"Really wish I could just get this over with," she admitted. "I feel like my whole life is in limbo in the meantime."

"I know. Unfortunately, there's no rushing the courts." Mia handed Lauren's phone back. "Dinner smells great."

"Even though it's from a package?" Lauren asked with a smile.

"What my father doesn't know can't hurt him."

"Are you close?" Lauren asked, trying to put the court date out of her mind.

A soft smile touched Mia's lips. She stepped into the kitchen beside Lauren and reached for an open bottle of wine. "Yes. He's pretty great, even if he is particular about his food."

"I'm glad," Lauren said. "Does he live nearby?"

Mia poured two glasses of wine and handed one to Lauren. "Right here in Brooklyn. I see him a few times a month. It's nice to have him so close."

"I bet." Lauren didn't ask about Mia's mother. She hadn't mentioned her, which seemed to tell a story in itself. Lauren had lost enough people to know when not to pry. "Siblings?"

"Spoiled only child. Can't you tell?" Mia grinned as she lifted her wineglass for a sip.

"I don't know about spoiled, but you do have a bit of an only-child vibe, I guess. You're very driven and conscientious."

"I'm both of those things," Mia agreed. "To my own detriment sometimes. I'm not very good at relaxing. Now that I'm divorced, I'm finding that I don't know what to do with myself when I get home in the evenings."

"You could try grocery shopping." Lauren couldn't resist the jab.

Mia snorted with laughter, nearly spilling her wine all over the counter. "I could," she said. "I definitely should."

"But I'm happy to monopolize your kitchen in the meantime," Lauren said, sipping the wine Mia had given her. It was rich and a little bit spicy, but smooth as it went down her throat. When Lauren drank wine, she generally bought the cheap stuff. This was undoubtedly not cheap, and now Lauren had a new appreciation for fine wine.

"You must be wasting so much money staying in those hostels," Mia said, staring at Lauren over the rim of her wineglass.

Lauren sighed. "Yeah, it's not ideal, but it's my cheapest option right now."

"I might know of something cheaper."

Lauren perked up. "Really? You know someone who needs a roommate?"

Mia shook her head, and a wavy lock of hair fell across her eyes. She blew it away, still watching Lauren closely. "My couch pulls out if you want to crash here until you find something more permanent."

LAUREN GAPED at Mia like she'd lost her mind, and maybe she had. It wasn't as if she was looking for a roommate, but she liked Lauren. They got along well, and Mia wouldn't mind having Lauren on her couch for a few weeks until she found a place of her own. When Lauren was here, Mia tended to take better care of herself. She laughed more. She wasn't lonely.

"That's really generous of you, but I don't want to impose," Lauren said, her cheeks pink as she stared at her hands.

"You can pay rent, if it makes you feel better," Mia said.

"Oh, I would never...I would never freeload." Lauren looked more flustered than Mia had ever seen her, and she wasn't quite sure why.

"I know you wouldn't. And the truth is, this apartment is starting to feel lonely. I've never lived alone before, believe it or not, and I'm not sure I like it." That was more honesty than she'd meant to share, but Lauren had been vulnerable with her enough times that she felt she owed her a bit of uncomfortable truth in return, especially if it helped Lauren feel more comfortable with the idea.

"Really?" Lauren asked, her eyes darting up to meet Mia's. "I mean, I haven't either. I've rarely even had my own bedroom."

"Then my couch will feel like an upgrade for you."

"It definitely will." Lauren turned to stir the pasta. "Are you sure? Because I can keep hopping between hostels until I find a place."

"Hopping between hostels is no way to live. I wouldn't want you on my couch forever, but let's try it for now. I think I'd like the company," Mia told her, surprised by how much she meant it.

Lauren turned off the burner and moved to the sink to drain the pasta. She set the pot back on the stove and turned to face Mia. "You're placing a lot of trust in me, offering me a key to your apartment."

Mia heard what she wasn't saying. She knew Lauren's

criminal history was the reason she hadn't been able to find a place of her own yet. "I do trust you, Lauren."

"Don't get me wrong, I love the idea of staying with you. I just don't want to impose."

"You're not imposing," Mia said. "What sounds fair for rent? Fifty a week?"

"That sounds more than fair, and a lot less than I'm paying at the hostel."

"Plus, not to brag, but I have my own laundry room."

Lauren groaned. "Oh my God. I would sell my soul for laundry facilities about now. And a kitchen!"

Mia straightened. That groan had done funny things to her pulse, which was now hurtling through her veins with entirely too much enthusiasm. Okay, so having Lauren on her couch might put a crimp in her plans to start dating, but she hadn't made any progress on that front yet anyway. At least now, she wouldn't be lonely at home until she was ready to put herself out there.

"It's settled, then," Mia said. "You can go get your things from the hostel and stay here tonight, if you like."

"I like," Lauren said softly. "Thank you."

"You're welcome. Now let's eat this clearance pasta of yours before it gets cold."

10

Lauren let herself into her room at the hostel, offering a polite smile to the two women on the bunk across from hers. Beer bottles were scattered around them, and they were huddled together over their phones, talking in snide tones. Was Lauren observing internet trolls in action? She was so grateful to leave this place behind. She emptied her locker and grabbed her duffel bag, waving to the women as she left the room.

She stopped at the front desk to check out, and then she was on her way back to Mia's apartment. As she walked, she took in the strand of orange lights strung across a nearby awning, reminding her that September was half over. The evening air was cool and crisp. She loved fall, if only it didn't mean winter was on the way.

Winter meant she'd need to invest in warmer clothes, as she'd had to leave most of her belongings behind when she fled New York last year, and again when she left Rhode Island. She couldn't afford a storage unit, so she could only bring with her what she could carry. But for now, her jacket would do. She had two steady jobs and an affordable place to sleep for the next few weeks. She was doing okay. She was doing better than okay.

When she reached Mia's building, she unlocked the door with the key Mia had given her and headed for the stairs. She could hardly fathom the depth of trust Mia had placed in her with this key. Lauren wouldn't let her down.

She unlocked the door to the apartment and let herself inside. Mia looked up from the couch, paperback in hand. Lauren grinned when she saw that Mia was reading a sapphic romance by one of her favorite authors.

"Liking it so far?" she asked, gesturing to the book.

"Loving it," Mia replied, her gaze taking in Lauren's bags. "You checked out of the hostel?"

Lauren nodded. "I did, but if you end up missing your couch, I can go back anytime."

"You'll only be on it while I'm asleep in my own bed, so it should be fine."

But it wasn't time for bed yet, so Lauren sat beside her and pulled up an e-book on her phone while Mia read her paperback. Later, Mia helped Lauren unfold the couch and make it up as a bed, and then she said good night. Mia went into her room and closed the door while Lauren went into the bathroom to change into her pajamas and wash up.

When she climbed between the sheets a few minutes later, she exhaled into the darkness. Mia's apartment was quiet and peaceful. Her sheets smelled fresh and vaguely like Mia herself, as if she'd slept on them, when Lauren knew they'd come from the linen closet. Maybe it was the scent of Mia's laundry detergent.

Smiling, she rolled onto her side, already halfway asleep when she heard a scratching sound. Lauren's eyes popped open. What was that? *Rats*, her brain supplied oh-so-helpfully, and she instinctively tucked her feet against her body.

She'd lived in enough rat-infested apartments to know the sound, but this was different. Louder? As if a bigger animal was scratching.

She sat up, blinking as her eyes adjusted to the low lighting. The glow from the street provided enough illumination for her to make out the shape of various furniture in the room. Mia's bedroom door opened with a click, and Lola meowed loudly.

"Sorry," Mia whispered. She wore a light-colored robe, and Lauren's brain short-circuited at the thought of what might—or might *not*—be beneath it. "I don't usually close my bedroom door. Apparently, she doesn't like it."

"Oh," Lauren breathed as she realized Lola had been the source of the scratching sound. She'd been pawing at Mia's door.

"I'm afraid to shut her in with me, in case she needs her litter box, so I'll just leave the door cracked." Mia spoke quietly as Lola twined herself around her legs, her white fur gleaming in the reflection of the window.

"Sure. That's fine with me," Lauren said.

"Okay. Good night, Lauren."

"Night." She watched as Mia stepped backward, pushing the door so that it was only open a few inches. Lola followed her in. Lucky cat.

As Lauren lay back down, her mind drifted to Mia in her bedroom. Surely she wouldn't leave her door open if she was sleeping in the nude, so she'd probably had on some sort of pajamas under that robe. Before Lauren could ponder too much about what those pajamas might look like, she slipped into a deep, dreamless sleep.

When she woke, the room around her was bathed in early morning light and Mia was walking through the room in yoga pants and a light jacket.

"Sorry if I woke you," she said quietly. "I'm on my way to the gym."

"Have fun," Lauren murmured, still half asleep as Mia went out the door, and then she rolled her eyes at herself. Have fun? No one had fun at the gym. As Lauren came to her senses, she became aware of something warm pressed against her legs. What in the world? She pushed herself up on one elbow to find Lola curled in a tight ball in the curve of her knees. "Oh. Morning, Lola."

The cat looked up at her with big amber eyes, and Lauren smiled. She could get used to waking with a cat snuggled against her. It was kind of nice, actually. Since Lauren didn't have to work until ten—and the clock currently read 6:05—she closed her eyes and drifted back to sleep.

The sound of the apartment door woke her. Mia stepped inside, her hair pulled back in a ponytail. Several strands had escaped to frame her face, damp with sweat, and her jacket was unzipped to reveal an aqua sports bra. *Collarbones. Cleavage.* Lauren yanked her gaze back to Mia's face.

"Sleep okay?" Mia asked.

"So good," Lauren confirmed. "And I have a new friend." She gestured to Lola.

Mia gave her cat an exasperated look. "Traitor. Demanding that I open my door, and then she slept with you."

"She just wanted to keep her options open."

"Typical Lola," Mia said. "Do you need the bathroom before I shower?"

"Actually, yes." Now that she was awake, her bladder was complaining pretty urgently. "I'll be quick."

"No rush." Mia walked into the kitchen to pour herself a glass of water.

Lauren went into the bathroom to freshen up, glad she slept in a baggy T-shirt and boxer shorts so she didn't feel self-conscious in front of Mia. Lauren had never owned lingerie or skimpy pajamas since she'd never had her own private space to wear them.

When she came out of the bathroom, Mia was in her bedroom, which was probably for the best, since Lauren didn't need another peek at that sports bra, not when she was desperately trying to get over this attraction.

Instead, she went into the kitchen to start some coffee and peruse her breakfast options. There was a carton of eggs in Mia's fridge that Lauren had left there earlier in the week, and she grabbed it. Scrambled eggs had been a staple of her childhood cooking repertoire. She had a pan of fluffy eggs ready by the time Mia came out, showered and dressed for work.

"Oh my God, you cooked me breakfast?" she asked, eyes rounded.

"Just scrambled eggs," Lauren said. "But I'll bring home more groceries, as long as you don't mind me stocking your fridge."

"Stock away, but you don't have to feed me, you know." Mia moved to pour herself a cup of coffee, standing beside Lauren. Her perfume was stronger first thing in the morning right after she'd applied it, something fresh and vaguely citrusy.

"Maybe I like feeding you," Lauren said, and shit, that sounded flirtier than she'd intended, especially while she was standing in Mia's kitchen wearing pajamas. She did like feeding Mia, though. It made her feel useful. She loved that Mia—successful, competent Mia—was so helpless when it came to caring for herself.

"I certainly enjoy your cooking, but I didn't offer my

couch so you could be my housekeeper." Mia touched her shoulder, a smile curving her lips.

"That's good, because I'd probably be a lousy housekeeper," Lauren joked, scooping the eggs onto two plates. In truth, Mia had a point. Lauren had often been expected to earn her keep in the various group homes she'd lived in, and she'd carried that habit into her adult life. Her roommates liked it when she did more than her fair share of cooking and cleaning, and when she had to scrape together rent money each month, it was helpful to be liked for the months when she fell short. But she didn't need to do that with Mia...unless she wanted to. And right now, she did.

They ate breakfast together, and then Mia headed down to open the café. Lauren took a shower, and *oh*, Mia's shower was amazing. The showers at her most recent hostel had such low water pressure, she'd spent ages trying to rinse the soap from her body. She borrowed a bit of Mia's shampoo, reasoning that she'd pick up a new bottle at the market to make up for it, but as she stood in front of the mirror ten minutes later, fixing her hair, she realized she smelled like Mia. And *that* was going to be distracting today.

She sighed, rolling her eyes at herself. She hadn't dated since before she robbed the bar. Sex had been the last thing on her mind the past year and a half, and this was a hell of an inconvenient time for her libido to wake up. Sleeping on Mia's couch meant she couldn't exactly bring a woman home with her, even if she met someone.

All the more reason to hurry up and find her own place, because honestly, having Lauren on her couch was going to cramp Mia's dating life too.

Lauren turned to find Lola sitting in the doorway to the bathroom, watching her. "Not used to having someone else around?"

The cat just stared at her.

Lauren went into the living room and folded up her bed, leaving Mia's couch the way it usually looked. She hesitated, not sure where to put her bags. Mia's apartment was so neat, she didn't want to leave her stuff all over the place. And now that Mia had left, Lauren felt vaguely uncomfortable being in her apartment alone, a sentiment Lola seemed to share as she tailed Lauren around the room, giving her suspicious looks.

She remembered the hall closet where Mia had gotten Lauren's bedding last night and peeked inside. There was just enough space on the floor for Lauren's duffel bag, so she tucked it inside and closed the door.

When she turned around, her gaze caught on the urn sitting discreetly on a shelf in the corner. "Back together again," she whispered as she crossed the room and pressed her fingers against the cold metal. In that moment, she would have given anything to wrap her arms around her brother. She took several slow breaths, pushing past the threat of tears.

"You'd be giving me such shit about my crush on Mia if you were here," she told Craig with a laugh that was dangerously close to a sob. "And you'd be right. I really miss you, you know that?"

Someday soon, she needed to get his urn off Mia's shelf and scatter Craig's ashes, but that day wasn't today.

WHEN MIA GOT HOME that evening, she paused in the living room. Lauren's things were gone. There was no sign of her anywhere, except for the urn that had been on the shelf in the corner for weeks now, so long that Mia had almost forgotten it was there. Had Lauren changed her mind and moved out?

Mia was surprised by the disappointment that settled in her gut at the possibility that Lauren had left. Logically, she ought to be relieved. It wasn't ideal to have someone sleeping on her couch. And yet, last night Mia hadn't felt lonely.

Now what was she supposed to do with her evening? She brought her laptop to the couch to answer a few emails she hadn't gotten to during the workday. It had been busy in the café today, and Jordy had needed to leave early for an appointment, so Mia had worked the counter alone for the last few hours before closing.

She lost herself in work emails with Lola curled at her side. A new foster cat was arriving in the morning, which meant she'd have to go down early to get him situated.

A key turned in the lock, and Mia looked up as Lauren stepped through the door, her arms laden with brown paper grocery bags. "Hi," she said breathlessly as she bent to set them on the floor.

"Hi yourself," Mia said. "I thought you might have left. Where are all your things?"

"I put them in your linen closet. I don't like to leave a mess. Why did you think I'd left?"

"Your bags were gone," Mia said, realizing how silly that sounded. Of course Lauren had put her bags away.

Lauren gave her a quizzical look. "Is it okay that I put them in the closet?"

"Totally fine. Make yourself at home." Mia gestured around the room, her spirits already boosted now that Lauren was here.

"Behold," Lauren said with a smile, gesturing to the grocery bags. "You're about to have food in your pantry. And

I brought home a chicken we can roast in the oven for dinner, if that sounds good."

"That sounds great, but you really don't have to stock my kitchen for me."

Lauren waved a hand. "I get an employee discount, and most of this stuff was on clearance, so it didn't cost much. I'm an excellent bargain shopper."

"I'd say so." Mia set her laptop on the table and got up to help her put everything away, feeling vaguely frivolous that she'd never paid much attention to the price of her food. She tended to look for what was quick and easy to prepare.

Once the groceries were put away, Lauren took out a bowl and mixed several spices together with some olive oil, which she rubbed on the chicken. Next she prepared two potatoes, and then she put it all in the oven. The sight of so much food made Mia's stomach rumble, reminding her that she'd only had a protein bar for lunch.

"Anything exciting happen at the café today?" Lauren asked as she worked.

"Not especially. It was busy, but uneventful."

Lauren gave her a knowing look. "Doesn't Beth usually come in on Tuesdays?"

"I didn't see her today," Mia said. "And honestly, what am I doing? I don't think she's interested."

"I disagree," Lauren said as she wiped down the counter. "She doesn't seem interested in adopting a cat, so I suspect she's visiting for an entirely different reason. But maybe it would be easier for you to start with a dating app?"

"Maybe," Mia agreed, but she heard the skepticism in her voice. "I know it's time for me to start dating. I'm just so intimidated by the process."

"Let's set up a profile for you while the chicken cooks," Lauren suggested with an eager smile. "It'll be fun. The app gives you control. You don't have to say yes to anyone if you don't want to, but it can be fun to browse profiles and see who's out there."

"Well, okay." Mia had been putting this off for weeks now, and she really did need to take the plunge. She wasn't getting any younger, and she didn't want to be alone. "Can we make an account for you too? Or do you already have one?"

Lauren's expression became hesitant. "I do have one, but it's been deactivated for a *long* time."

"Let's reactivate it. Then we can browse women together." Mia glanced at Lauren over her shoulder as they walked toward the couch. "Or do you date other genders as well?"

"I dated a few men when I was younger," Lauren said as she sat beside Mia. "I guess that makes me bi or pan, but lately, I only seem to be interested in women." She shrugged. "I don't really put a label on myself."

"No reason you should have to." Mia reached for her phone.

"I usually just call myself queer."

"See, that word had a different connotation when I was younger," Mia said. "I heard it used as a slur, and now I have a hard time using it to describe myself."

Lauren nodded. "I get that, although I'm glad my generation has reclaimed it as an empowering word instead of a slur."

"Your generation." Mia groaned, elbowing her playfully. "Way to make me feel old."

"Oh my God, you know that's not what I meant." Lauren looked horrified. "You're not old at all, and I'm just going to shut up now."

Mia arched an eyebrow at her. "Out of curiosity, how old do you think I am?"

Lauren's mouth fell open, and then she gave her head a quick shake. "Oh, nope. I'm not going there. There's no right answer to that question. Suffice it to say, I find you very sophisticated and beautiful and not even remotely old."

"Sophisticated and beautiful?" Mia was still teasing, but now her heart was racing. Lauren's cheeks were pink, and the energy between them felt charged with something Mia was trying very hard not to define. When she started dating, she would need to dip her toes in slowly. More than likely, she needed a rebound relationship, someone casual and insignificant while she found her footing. Not Lauren. She was *not* going to rebound with a friend.

Lauren was staring at Mia as if she wasn't sure whether to be embarrassed or enamored, and this conversation had gone off the rails with record speed.

"I'm forty-two," Mia said, hoping to steer them back on track. "Now tell me how much younger you are." Maybe they both needed to hear it.

"Thirteen years," Lauren murmured.

"Jesus." Mia rubbed her forehead.

"That's not...I mean, I've dated older women." Lauren's cheeks were still pink. "I'd totally date someone who's forty-two."

Mia wasn't sure what to say to that. It was on the tip of her tongue to say she'd never date a twenty-nine-year-old, but that felt insulting to Lauren somehow. And anyway, when she looked at Lauren, while she was aware of their age difference, she still saw a peer. "We're off topic again," she said instead. "Which app should I download?"

11

L auren scrolled through the photo roll on Mia's
phone. "No offense, Mia, but where are your selfies?"
"I look like an idiot in selfies." Mia gave her an
aggrieved look.

"I doubt it, but I can't confirm or deny because there are
literally no selfies here," Lauren said with a giggle.

Mia huffed, crossing her arms over her chest, and
Lauren laughed harder.

"Seriously, though, you have almost no recent photos of
yourself. How are we supposed to convince the single ladies
in Brooklyn to date you?" The photos on Mia's phone were
mostly shots of the café, pictures of Lola, and random snaps
around Brooklyn.

"Why can't I just use this one?" Mia pointed to a shot of
herself behind the counter in the café.

"Because you look like a barista, not a business owner,
not to mention your logo is all over the place. You don't want
everyone on the internet to know where you work."

Mia flinched. "You're right. No logos."

"Let's take some new photos of you," Lauren suggested.

"Right now?"

"Why not? You haven't changed out of your work clothes yet. Go touch up your lipstick, and I'll snap some pictures." Lauren resisted the urge to point out that Mia looked amazing just as she was. She'd already called her beautiful once tonight. No need to make things awkward by pointing it out again.

Mia rolled her eyes, but she got up and went into the bathroom. When she returned, her lips were glossy with a dusky rose hue. "Better?"

"Yep," Lauren said, somehow managing not to stare at those perfectly kissable lips. She was committed to her mission to get Mia on a date. If Mia met someone, that might be the easiest way for Lauren to get over her infatuation, because she didn't tend to lust after people who were with someone else.

"Where do you want me?" Mia asked, one hand on her hip as she glanced around her living room.

"Let's try the couch," Lauren said, trying and failing not to hear sexual innuendo in everything they said. She picked up Mia's phone.

"All right." Mia sat and faced Lauren with a forced-looking smile.

Lauren took a few pictures, but they were lacking Mia's natural charisma. They looked staged. "Hey, did I tell you about the time I sat on a chocolate truffle while I was on a first date, and it looked like...well, I'm sure you can guess."

Mia snorted with laughter, and Lauren snapped several pictures of her. "How did you sit on a chocolate?"

"The person who sat at that table before me must have left it? I don't know, but by the time I realized, it had melted into the back of my skirt. A total mess. My date was so embarrassed."

Mia's lips pursed. "If they didn't offer you their jacket to protect your dignity, then they weren't worth dating."

"She didn't, and she wasn't, but I just got some great photos of you." Lauren turned Mia's phone so she could see the photos Lauren had snapped while she wasn't paying attention. "My favorite is the last one."

Mia took her phone, squinting at the photos. "Oh, these are kind of nice."

"Candid laughter for the win," Lauren said. "Just put a filter on it to brighten the lighting, and you're good to go."

Mia tapped at her phone for a few minutes, her brow furrowed in concentration. She was indeed using only one finger, and it was as cute as Lauren had anticipated. Then Mia looked up at her. "Well, it's official. I just switched my profile to active."

"Success." Lauren fist-pumped the air. "Now let's browse some available women for you."

Mia shook her head. "You first. Let's get your profile set up too."

"I'll update my profile, but I'm not sure I'm ready to make it active," Lauren said. "I have to get my shit together before I start dating."

Mia's face fell. "Sorry for pushing."

"You didn't, and it doesn't hurt to see who's out there, right? I just need to take my time." Lauren reached for her own phone and opened her photo roll. She wouldn't go on any dates until after her court date, but a little online flirting might help to distract her from Mia. "Luckily, I have plenty of selfies to choose from."

"Let's see." Mia extended a hand, and Lauren passed her the phone. Mia scrolled for a minute in silence, smiling periodically as she looked at Lauren's photos. "Okay, definitely this selfie you took the weekend of our *In Her Defense* marathon. You look adorable."

Lauren beamed at the compliment. "Okay."

"And this one in the park. That top looks great on you. Just enough cleavage to catch a lady's eye." Mia handed the phone back.

Lauren felt slightly dizzy at the thought of Mia looking at her cleavage. "Thanks." She updated her photos, and what the hell, she set her profile to active. "All right. We're both officially on the market, although I'm more interested in looking than dating."

Mia grinned at her. "Nothing wrong with looking."

Lauren scrolled through the list of compatible women the site had compiled for her. The fifth profile on the list made her freeze, nervous laughter bubbling in her throat.

"What?" Mia asked, glancing at Lauren's phone, and then she froze too.

The site had matched Lauren with Mia.

"I'M NOT SURE ABOUT THIS," Mia lamented three days later. She was in her office, staring apprehensively at the message she'd just received from a woman on the dating app. Since activating her profile, she'd received a *lot* of messages. Most of them were blatant attempts at hooking up, but while Mia wasn't looking for anything serious, at least not yet, she really wasn't the one-night-stand type either.

"Oh, come on. She's pretty, and she invited you to get a coffee. That seems like a good place to start, doesn't it?" Lauren sat across from her, eating a chicken wrap while they shared their lunch break.

"I suppose." Mia studied the woman's profile picture. Joy was a few years older than Mia, with bits of silver sprinkled through her dark hair and a warm smile. She was a stockbroker, a career woman like Mia.

"Do it." Lauren's eyes sparkled mischievously. "You smile whenever you message Joy, so why not have coffee with her?"

"Fine." Mia knew her hesitation was mostly rooted in her own insecurities. It had been *so long* since she'd been on a date. She needed to rip off the Band-Aid and get the first date over with, and, as Lauren said, Joy seemed as good a place to start as any. She tapped out a quick reply, letting Joy know she was free tomorrow afternoon. Tomorrow was Saturday, so Joy shouldn't have to work. "Done."

"Yay," Lauren said. "You may have to go on a lot of first dates before you make it to a second, so be prepared for that, but I think that might be exactly what you need, anyway."

"I need a lot of bad dates?" Mia twisted her lips to the side as she picked up her own wrap.

"Not bad dates, but you need some experience under your belt," Lauren said. "You were off the market a long time. I think you'll feel a lot more confident once you've been on a few first dates."

"I hope you're right."

"Maybe you'll even get the courage to ask Beth out," Lauren said with a smirk. "The flirting's getting pretty heated these days."

Mia wanted to scoff at that, because it was embarrassing that Lauren had seen her flirting with Beth, but earlier this week, Mia had sat at Beth's table while they shared a cup of coffee, and it had been...nice. She felt like a schoolgirl with a crush when they talked, the way she remembered feeling when she and Kristin first met. Maybe Mia would ask her out.

But first...Joy.

At three o'clock the next day, Mia sat in a coffee shop in Queens, one foot tapping restlessly against the floor and an uncomfortable ache in her stomach. It would be a damn shame if dating caused her ulcer to flare up.

The door opened, and Joy walked in. Mia recognized her easily from her profile pictures. She waved to catch Joy's attention, hoping she was as easily recognizable.

"Mia, hi." Joy approached the table and took her hand. Her grip was warm and firm, and Mia relaxed a little bit. This was okay. Just coffee.

"Hi," she said. "You look great." Why had she said that? Was that too forward? Mia wanted to slap herself on the forehead.

Joy's smile widened. "Thank you. You look pretty nice yourself. What can I get you?" She gestured to the counter.

"Oh, I can get my own," Mia said automatically.

"Nonsense. I invited you here. My treat."

Mia nodded. It would be silly to argue about money when they both had careers that brought in plenty of it. "A nonfat cappuccino. Thank you."

"My pleasure." Joy moved to the line at the counter.

Mia took the opportunity to observe her while she waited. Joy wore a floor-length, loose-fitting black dress. Not Mia's style, but it seemed to suit Joy. She was an attractive woman, and she seemed as confident and friendly in person as she had online. Mia had a sudden urge to text Lauren and tell her about her date so far, which was silly since it had barely begun. Mia settled in her seat and tried to relax.

"So," Joy said when she returned with their drinks a few minutes later. She slid a cup in front of Mia. "Tell me more about yourself. You mentioned that you used to practice law?"

Mia told her all about her former career, which Joy seemed much more interested in than Mia's current work at the café. Joy then told her about her work as a stockbroker, including an offer to take a look at Mia's investments, to which Mia could only feign a sudden interest in her coffee. She'd prepared herself to be propositioned on the first date, but not for someone to request access to her financial information.

She found herself tuning out as Joy detailed all the ways she'd diversified her own investment portfolio. When Mia's phone chimed with an incoming message, she ought to have been embarrassed for forgetting to silence it, but instead she felt relieved for the interruption.

The text was from Wendy, letting her know they'd received an adoption application for one of the café cats. It wasn't urgent, but Joy didn't know that.

"I'm sorry," Mia said. "Something's come up at work. I'm afraid I need to head back."

"Oh, no problem. I understand all about having a demanding job," she said, as if Mia was still a high-powered lawyer and not a café owner. "I enjoyed meeting you, Mia. Maybe we could try dinner next time?"

Mia hesitated, debating whether to turn her down here or later via email, but she'd always believe in being direct, so there was no time like the present. "I don't think this is going to work for me, but thank you again for the coffee. It was nice to meet you too."

Joy blinked, then nodded. "I understand."

Mia said goodbye and got the hell out of there. She walked to the nearest subway station and rode the train back to her café, exhaling in relief as she stepped inside.

"How was it?" Lauren asked, peeking out from the cat enclosure.

"I think she was more interested in diversifying my investment portfolio than dating me." Mia couldn't quite contain her laughter at the ridiculousness of what she'd just said. "It wasn't horrible, but I'm not going to see her again."

Lauren gave her a sympathetic smile. "Sorry, but I'm glad it wasn't terrible. Hopefully you'll have better luck next time."

"Hopefully," Mia agreed, although the last thing she wanted to think about right now was going on another awkward date. "In the meantime, I need a drink. Want to stop by Dragonfly after we leave here tonight?"

Lauren pressed her lips together. "Josie told me I was welcome to come in, but do you think she really meant it?"

"I wouldn't have asked if I didn't," Mia said. "So what do you say?"

Lauren nodded, still looking somewhat hesitant. "Okay. A drink to celebrate you putting yourself out there."

"There's the spirit," Mia said. "All right. I need to catch up on some paperwork. Jordy's closing tonight, so just stop by my office when your shift's over."

Mia walked to her office and sat, surprised to realize how disappointed she felt. Apparently, some small part of her had hoped she would get lucky on the first try, that she and Joy would hit it off and that would be that. She sighed as she opened QuickBooks, smirking as she imagined what Joy would think if she saw the café's modest income.

Her first date had been a bust, but Mia was looking forward to going out for drinks with Lauren later. She and Lauren always had fun together, and Mia was eager to catch up with Josie, hoping for a happy update to the news Josie had shared the last time she saw her.

Mia had just finished reconciling her budget for the month when Lauren tapped on the open door to her office. "Closing time already?" Mia asked in surprise.

Lauren nodded. "I've already cleaned up and gotten the cats squared away for the night."

"Let's get out of here, then." Mia stood and reached for her purse.

"So Joy really asked about your money?" Lauren asked as they went out through the back door together.

"About ten minutes after we met," Mia said, lips curving in amusement. "I think she'd have liked me more if I were still practicing law, to be honest."

"Then she wasn't the right woman for you."

"No, definitely not." Mia inhaled the fresh fall air. "And what about you? Has anyone caught your eye yet?"

Lauren gave her a sheepish look. "I set my profile back to inactive for now. I need to find my own place and get this court date behind me before I start dating."

"Fair enough." Mia understood her reasons for waiting, as much as it might have been fun for them to compare dating stories. She didn't want to think about why she felt relieved at Lauren's news, that maybe she didn't like the idea of seeing Lauren with another woman, because that was absurd.

They boarded the subway together, falling to lighter topics as they rode. Mia really wasn't in the mood to talk about Joy anymore this evening. Ten minutes later, she held the door to Dragonfly open for Lauren, who stepped through with a slightly apprehensive smile.

"No one's going to be upset to see you, I promise," Mia told her as she scanned the bar, disappointed that Josie didn't seem to be working tonight. She didn't recognize either of the women behind the bar.

"I'd be upset to see me if I were Josie," Lauren said quietly.

"She said you're good, so you're good." Mia led the way to a table for two along the back wall, the only empty table in the place. She'd almost forgotten this was a Saturday night, and Dragonfly was packed. "What are you in the mood for tonight?"

"Just a beer." Lauren picked up the purple drink menu on the table. "But you should get one of these." She tapped her finger against the top of the menu, giving Mia a silly smile.

"The Midnight in Manhattan?" Mia said. "I've had it before. It's good."

Lauren tapped the menu again, drawing Mia's attention to the italicized words under the drink description. *Rumor has it, if you drink one at midnight, you'll fall in love before the end of the year.* "This could be your lucky drink, Mia."

"The end of the year is only three months away," Mia said. "Not sure I want to fall in love again *that* quickly, but I'll have one all the same."

"There's the spirit," Lauren said. "I'll get our drinks."

Mia smiled as she watched her walk away, noting the parallel to her date with Joy. This was already so much better than her date. In fact...*shit*. She'd been mentally comparing Joy to Lauren all day. Actually, if she was perfectly honest with herself, she'd compared every woman who'd contacted her through the app to Lauren. None of them seemed remotely as interesting or funny or beautiful. The realization almost knocked her off her stool.

Oh, this could be a problem. Mia had been put off by Lauren's age at first, thinking she couldn't possibly have anything in common with a woman in her twenties, but Lauren was wiser than her years, maybe because of the way she'd grown up. There was just something about her, something Mia couldn't seem to get enough of.

It didn't change the fact that Mia wasn't going to date her. She needed a rebound fling, maybe more than one of them, after spending so many years with Kristin. Despite Lauren's maturity, she was vulnerable right now. Mia was *not* going to rebound with her. It had the potential to be disastrous for both of them.

She couldn't look at Lauren as anything but a friend, not even when her heart leaped as Lauren smiled at her from the bar. To distract herself, she pulled out her phone and sent Josie a quick text. *I'm at Dragonfly with Lauren. Was hoping to see you!*

Oh, yay! I'll come down and say hi, Josie replied almost immediately.

Mia set her phone down, glad she'd get to see Josie after all, and maybe a little bit relieved to have someone else at their table so this evening didn't start to feel like a date. Mia gave her head a quick shake. What was the matter with her tonight?

Josie came through the back door a minute later, grinning widely as she approached Mia's table. "Hey, lady. What's new?"

"Well, I went on a date this afternoon, and it was a total bust."

"Bummer." Josie slid into the chair across from her. "I don't miss it. Where's Lauren?"

"Getting our drinks." Mia nodded toward the bar.

Josie followed her gaze, giving Lauren a friendly wave. "You two have been spending a lot of time together."

"She's crashing on my couch for a few weeks until she finds something more permanent," Mia told her. "She's having a hard time finding someone who'll rent to her."

Josie flinched. "Yeah, I can imagine. But you two are just friends?"

"Just friends," Mia told her. "Anything new with you?"

"Nope." Josie's cheerful expression dimmed. "No luck yet, but we're trying again this month."

"I'm sorry," Mia said.

"Thanks," Josie said. "Probably too much to hope for on the first try, right?"

"Right," Mia agreed. "That was my takeaway from today's date too."

Josie laughed, lifting her hand to give Mia a high five. "Here's hoping we both have better luck next time."

12

Lauren's chest tightened as she approached the table, because Josie was there, chatting with Mia. Despite everything, she half expected Josie to ask her to leave. But Josie only smiled as Lauren set her and Mia's drinks on the table and pulled over an extra chair.

"Hi, Josie," Lauren said as she sat.

"Hi." Josie's expression was open and warm, no trace of hurt or anger remaining, at least not that Lauren could see. "So how do you like working with cats?"

"Oh, I love it," Lauren said, picking up her beer. "They're so much fun, and it's so satisfying to see them get adopted."

"It is," Josie agreed. "People always ask me how I'm able to let them go, why I don't keep them all, but to me, there's nothing more rewarding than finding them the perfect home. If I kept them, I wouldn't be able to save more."

Lauren smiled, relaxing in her seat. She'd missed Josie. They had gotten along so well for the few weeks Lauren had worked for her. "Yes. I totally agree."

"One's enough for me," Mia said. "I love having Lola around, but I'll leave the rest in the café."

"Did Lola start out in the café?" Lauren asked.

Mia nodded. "I knew I wanted to adopt one, so I figured I'd wait until the perfect cat came along, but I fell in love with Lola right away. The café hadn't been open a week before I brought her upstairs."

"Aww." Lauren grinned. "I love that."

"I admit, when you adopted her so fast, I thought you might turn into a cat lady," Josie said with a teasing smile. "I was worried you weren't cut out for rescue."

Mia shook her head. "Just the one. I haven't been tempted to bring anyone else home."

"Except Lauren," Josie said, still with the teasing tone, and Lauren almost choked on her beer. She spluttered as she set it down, drawing an amused glance from Josie.

"Well, she hasn't adopted *me*," Lauren managed. "I'm hoping to find someplace more permanent soon."

"I'm sure you will," Josie said. "All right, ladies, I need to get back upstairs. Eve should be home by now. Enjoy the rest of your night." With a wave, she slipped off her stool and headed toward the hallway in back.

"They are so disgustingly in love," Lauren said as she picked up her beer.

"They are." Mia was already halfway through her drink and looking much more relaxed.

"Tell me more about Joy. You must have talked about something other than financial planning?"

Mia laughed softly. "No, that was pretty much the extent of our conversation. Then I got a text from Wendy, pretended it was a work emergency, and bolted."

"At least you got your first date under your belt." Lauren took a drink of her beer.

"I did," Mia agreed. "My first 'first date' in eighteen years."

"Sounds like a big deal to me. Kudos to you. Any other prospects?"

"A few." Mia gestured for Lauren to move her stool closer.

Lauren scooted over so she could look at Mia's phone with her. "Ooh, she's pretty," she said as Mia showed her a photo of a brunette named Diana.

"We've exchanged a few messages. I might meet her for a drink next week."

"Drinks are good," Lauren said. "Much easier to make a quick exit than if you have to sit through a whole meal, as you found out today."

Mia smirked. "Yes. God help me if I'd had to sit through a whole meal with Joy. This seems like a good way to maximize my time while still putting myself out there."

"Good for you," Lauren said.

Mia showed her a few more profiles, and Lauren's cheeks flushed when she saw her own photo in Mia's list of potential matches. Mia hadn't commented on it—or removed it—so Lauren was just going to quietly enjoy that the app thought they made a nice couple.

Mia polished off her drink and gestured toward Lauren's beer, which was almost empty too. "Want another? I'll get this round."

"Sure." Lauren kept her stool near Mia's, sipping her beer as Mia made her way to the counter. Lauren had never expected to find herself in this bar again, let alone sharing a table with Josie. As she gazed around the room, so warm and welcoming with twinkling fairy lights overhead and a variety of LGBTQIA flags displayed behind the bar, her eyes welled with tears of gratitude.

She would never forget Josie's kindness or the trust Mia had placed in her. She'd been offered a second chance that not everyone was lucky enough to receive, and she would forever be thankful for it. With her income from the café and the market, she was able to afford the occasional night out like this one without having to dip into the money she was saving for an apartment of her own.

At the bar, Mia was talking to the woman standing beside her. As Lauren watched, Mia laughed, and the other woman brushed her hand against Mia's. She was beautiful, with golden brown skin and curly black hair, and she was definitely flirting. Mia was flirting right back.

Lauren stared into what remained of her beer. She was glad Mia seemed to be making the most of her foray back into the dating world. This was good. This was what they both wanted, because once Mia found someone, Lauren would have to move on. But watching Mia flirt with someone else didn't feel great. It made Lauren's chest ache and a heaviness settle in her stomach.

When she looked back up, Mia and the woman at the bar were doing shots together. Lauren pulled out her phone to distract herself. She had a new comment on her latest fic, which made her smile. She missed writing. Since she'd come back to the city, she'd only written that one little fic. She also been editing her book, but she hadn't spent nearly enough time on it.

Mia was accomplishing her goals, getting back into the dating world, and Lauren needed to do the same. She needed to do the legwork to become a published author. She'd decided on Lauren White as her pen name, a play on Sam's last name Whitaker, in honor of the fictional character who'd inspired her to write in the first place.

Just when she'd started to wonder if she should head out and leave Mia to her own devices, a beer landed on the table in front of her, and she looked up to see Mia sliding onto the stool beside her with a fresh cocktail in hand. Her cheeks were flushed, and there was a happy sparkle in her eyes.

"You two seemed to be hitting it off," Lauren commented. "I can make myself scarce if you want to keep talking to her."

"She just left, actually, but...I got her number." Mia grinned. "Her name's Kat, and we're going to meet here for a drink next weekend."

"Look at you." Lauren tapped her glass against Mia's. "The ladies are lining up to date you. Kat's gorgeous, and it sure didn't look like you two were talking about finance."

"We weren't. I think I prefer connecting with people in person rather than online," Mia mused as she sipped her Midnight in Manhattan. "Maybe I should come in here and hang out at the bar more often, see what happens."

"Totally," Lauren agreed.

"That was fun." Mia was still smiling. There was a new confidence in her posture, as if tonight had eased her dating fears, and Lauren felt like she'd been punched in the gut.

"Now that you're dating, just text me any time you want me to clear out of your apartment for the night."

Mia's eyes rounded. "Oh God, I'm nowhere near bringing any of these women home with me."

"Well, whenever you are, just say the word, and I'll crash at the hostel for a night."

Mia's cheeks were pink as she lifted her drink, taking a hearty gulp. "As much as I want to get laid, and believe me, I *do*, it's fucking intimidating to think about going home with someone new after being with the same woman for so long. I think I'm going to need to take it slow on that front."

Lauren wasn't sure what to say. She'd never had a relationship that lasted longer than a few months. She had no idea what it was like to be married, to come home to the same woman for eighteen years the way Mia had with Kristin. Certainly it must be daunting to start over after something like that.

"I miss it, though," Mia said so quietly Lauren could barely hear her over the noise of the bar. "Not just sex, but intimacy, you know? Kissing, touching, waking up next to someone in the morning."

"I bet," Lauren said, trying not to notice the huskiness in Mia's voice when she lowered it like that. Also, she was slurring a bit now. That shot seemed to be hitting her hard.

"This drink is really good." Mia gazed into its opaque depths, and yep, she was definitely drunk.

Lauren sipped her beer, trying to think of a new conversation topic that didn't involve dating or sex. Her phone chimed almost in unison with Mia's, and they reached for them, their hands brushing in the process. Lauren saw a new message from their WhatsApp group chat.

Ashleigh: OMGGGGGGGGGG did you see the new pic Piper posted? I AM DECEASED.

She followed the message with a flame emoji and a face with X's for eyes. Lauren opened Twitter to find the photo in question. Piper had tweeted a selfie a few minutes ago, auburn hair billowing behind her as she stood on a beach. She wore a lowcut blue top that showed off her cleavage, and *oof*, she looked good. She was so gorgeous, Lauren forgot all about her infatuation with Mia for several precious seconds.

"Okay, I get it now," Mia said as she stared at her phone, and Lauren could see the same photo of Piper on her screen. "I mean, I've always thought she was beautiful, but she seemed too young for me to be swooning over the way the rest of you do. But okay, I'm swooning." She fanned her face dramatically.

Lauren's heart lurched, because she and Piper were roughly the same age, and if Mia no longer thought Piper was too young...

"Yep, she's hot," Mia proclaimed with a little giggle.

"That might be the alcohol talking," Lauren teased. "But I'm glad you've finally seen the light, because she is *so* hot."

"Agreed." Mia took another gulp of her drink, setting the glass down hard on the table.

"Want to head out when you finish that one?" Lauren asked before Mia got any bright ideas about ordering another round. "I've got a frozen pizza I can pop in the oven for us when we get home."

"Mm, pizza," Mia said with a dreamy smile.

Lauren couldn't help laughing, because she'd never seen Mia drunk before. Their phones were going off like crazy now as the group squealed about the new photo of Piper, speculating that she was still in LA filming her new movie. Lauren and Mia chimed in to share their excitement, even taking a selfie together with their drinks, which they shared to the group.

In the selfie, Mia looked happier and more carefree than Lauren had ever seen her. And she needed to call it a night before she became any more smitten with Mia than she already was. That warmth in the pit of her stomach every time she met Mia's gaze said it might already be too late.

Lauren excused herself to visit the bathroom, and when she made it back to their table, Mia's glass was empty. "Ready to head out?"

Mia nodded. She slid off her stool, swaying when her feet hit the floor. "Whoa."

Lauren extended a hand, and Mia gripped it to steady

herself. They put on their jackets and walked outside, but Lauren was starting to wonder if Mia would be able to walk to the subway on her own, because she was alarmingly wobbly in her heels. She'd had two cocktails and a shot—or had it been two shots?—while Lauren nursed two beers. Neither of them had eaten dinner yet, but if Lauren had to guess, Mia had probably only eaten a protein bar for lunch, so she'd been drinking on a totally empty stomach.

"Want me to call an Uber?" Lauren asked.

Mia waved a hand. "I'm fine."

"Okay. Let me know if you change your mind."

They kept walking.

"Investment portfolios," Mia said, laughing quietly to herself.

Lauren just smiled. Drunk Mia was funny.

"She wanted to diversify my—" Mia's heel caught in in a crack in the sidewalk, and she pitched forward. "Fuck!"

Lauren grabbed her before she went down, sliding an arm around Mia's waist. She had lightning-fast reflexes for inebriated people after looking after her mother and Craig. Mia swayed against her. Her gaze dropped to Lauren's lips, and the hunger in her eyes sent Lauren's pulse whirling, because *oh my God.*

"You smell good," Mia murmured.

"Um, thanks?" Lauren could hardly breathe with Mia looking at her like that. Warmth flooded her system, centered low in her belly, and her heart was beating so fast, she felt dizzy.

Mia leaned in. Her lips parted, and what the fuck was happening right now? Arousal swept through Lauren in a dizzying wave as Mia's lips drew closer to hers, but...no. This couldn't happen, not like this.

She tapped the tip of Mia's nose with her index finger, smiling gently. "You're drunk."

It had the desired effect. Mia dropped her head against Lauren's shoulder with a laugh. "I am."

"Let's get you home."

"Mm," Mia murmured as they started walking again.

Lauren kept her hand on Mia's waist to steady her, trying not to notice how warm she felt pressed against Lauren, even through the layers of their clothes, or the way the side of her breast rubbed against Lauren as they walked. Nope. Definitely not thinking about it.

"You take such good care of me," Mia mumbled when Lauren's hand tightened around her waist, saving her from yet another stumble.

"Just being a good friend," Lauren deflected, because she couldn't think straight while Mia was pressed so close. The look in her eye when Lauren had thought she was about to kiss her... *Fuck.* She'd never dared to imagine Mia looking at her that way, especially after she'd flirted her way all over Brooklyn today.

In fact, that was probably why she'd looked at Lauren like that. She'd been on her first date today. She'd flirted with a woman at the bar and gotten her number, and she was on a high from it. Not to mention, she was completely trashed.

Lauren guided her down the stairs to the subway, grateful to find an empty seat, because there was no way Mia would be able to stand on a moving train right now. Lauren stood over her, keeping her safe until they'd exited at their stop. She exhaled in relief when Mia's building came into view, because the journey had done nothing to sober Mia up. If anything, she was sloppier than ever as Lauren half carried her down the street.

Without warning, Mia lifted her hand, extending her middle finger toward the building next to hers. "Fucking lawyers."

"What?" Lauren looked from Mia to the building. There was a sign in the front window for a law office. Did Mia know the lawyers who worked there? Thankfully, the office was empty due to the late hour, because whoever they were, they probably wouldn't appreciate Mia flipping them off, drunk or not.

"Can't get away from them," Mia said. "Lawyers *everywhere*."

"Okay." Lauren laughed as she pushed her key into the door. She held it open for Mia, who somehow managed to crush herself against Lauren in the doorway as she tried to walk past her. Their breasts pressed together, and she could feel Mia's heart pounding. Mia could probably feel hers too, because Lauren's heart felt like it was about to burst out of her chest.

Mia's eyes met Lauren's, blazing with heat, and a faint whimper escaped her lips. It was all Lauren could do not to kiss her. Seriously, *what* had gotten into Mia tonight? Did she always fling herself at whoever she was with when she got drunk? Well, until recently, that would have probably been her wife, so maybe she did. Either way, Lauren needed to get her sobered up ASAP for the sake of their friendship.

Lauren tugged her up the stairs to her apartment, where Lola greeted them at the door with a loud meow. "Were we late with your dinner, spoiled girl?" Lauren asked the cat, hating how breathless she sounded, but she'd lost the ability to breathe properly the moment Mia looked at her like *that*.

Mia bent to pet Lola and keeled over in the process. She landed on her butt on the floor, staring up at Lauren with a stricken expression. "I don't feel s'good."

"I bet you don't." Lauren managed a laugh, because at least they weren't in danger of kissing anymore. "Let's get some water and pizza into you."

Mia closed her eyes, swaying slightly. "The room's spinning."

"Yep. Come on. Let's get you off the floor." Lauren took Mia's hands and hauled her to her feet.

"Shit." Mia pressed her lips together and bolted toward the bathroom. The door slammed behind her, and Lauren could only hope she made it to the toilet before she puked.

Well, this evening had taken a turn. Several of them, actually. Now that Mia had looked at her out of lust-glazed eyes, had stared at Lauren's lips like she was dying to kiss them...Lauren could never unsee it. She'd never forget that for a moment, Mia had felt *something* for her. She would always wonder if Mia still wanted her. Oh God, how was Lauren supposed to get over her infatuation now?

She walked to the kitchen and poured them both a glass of water, pondering their dinner options. Pizza probably wasn't the best choice for Mia's stomach at this point. After drinking her water, Lauren rummaged through the pantry, deciding French toast might be a better idea. She'd wait to start cooking it until Mia was ready to eat.

In the meantime, Lauren fed Lola, who rubbed herself enthusiastically against Lauren's legs while she scooped cat food onto a plate. The Solano girls were extremely amorous tonight. Lauren rolled her eyes at herself for the thought.

She heard the sink running in the bathroom and then the sound of Mia moving around in her bedroom. Probably, she was changing out of her work clothes, and Lauren sent up a silent prayer that she wouldn't need help, because that might be more than she could handle right now.

Mia emerged from her bedroom a few minutes later,

face scrubbed free of makeup and dressed in lounge pants and a long-sleeved T-shirt. At least she looked steadier on her feet now. She plopped onto the couch with a grimace. "Remind me to never drink this much again." She looked up, wearing a hilariously tragic expression. "*Ever.*"

Lauren smiled as she took the glass of water she'd poured for Mia and brought it to her. "You didn't really have that much, but I'm guessing you were drinking on an empty stomach, and it's still more than you usually drink."

"Guilty." Mia took the glass and dutifully gulped down about half of it, grimacing again. "God, my stomach hurts."

Lauren sat in the chair across from her. "The ulcer?"

Mia nodded. She closed her eyes and then opened them again quickly. "Room still spins if I close them."

"Those Midnight in Manhattans are pretty sour, if memory serves. Lots of lemon juice. That probably made it worse."

"Learned my lesson," Mia said, her words still slightly slurred.

Lauren pointed to the glass. "You finish that, and I'm going to make us some French toast."

"Mm, no." Mia shook her head, and several unruly blonde strands fell across her face. "Not hungry."

"But you need to eat anyway. You'll feel better afterward, trust me."

Mia didn't respond to that, so Lauren went into the kitchen and started cooking. A few minutes later, she had two plates of French toast ready, which she brought to the living room. Mia hadn't moved. She sat on the couch with her feet tucked underneath herself, staring blankly at the window to her left.

"Dinner's served," Lauren announced as she handed her a plate.

Mia picked at her food, but Lauren was starving. She inhaled hers, pleased to see that Mia picked up speed after her first few bites too. In fact, by the time Lauren had taken her empty plate to the kitchen and brought Mia a refill on her water, she'd cleaned her plate.

"You're right. I do feel better," she said, as quiet now as she'd been flirty earlier.

"I'm glad. Drink another glass of water. You'll thank me for it in the morning."

Mia took it and sipped. Then she leaned back on the couch and closed her eyes. She was quiet for long enough that Lauren wondered if she'd passed out, but then her eyes opened sluggishly. "Not spinning anymore, which means... I'm going to bed."

Lauren nodded. "Take that water with you."

Mia stood, picking up the glass. "Good night, Lauren."

"Night."

As she reached the doorway to her bedroom, Mia glanced at Lauren over her shoulder, and if she didn't know better, she'd swear the look on her face was regret.

13

Mia swatted at the alarm on her phone with a groan. Her head throbbed, and her stomach ached. Actually, everything hurt. For the first time in who knew how long, she was hungover, and *oh*, it sucked. She managed to silence her alarm and then sat up in bed, relieved that at least she didn't feel like she was going to be sick again.

A vague memory of hunching over the toilet surfaced, and she grimaced. She remembered being at Dragonfly, flirting with Kat at the bar and then Lauren bringing her home. She vividly remembered staring at Lauren's lips and how badly she'd wanted to kiss them.

Oh God. She hadn't...had she?

She remembered Lauren's arm around her, holding her upright, Lauren's breasts pressed against hers in the doorway to her building, Lauren cooking her French toast. Mia's gaze darted to the door, which stood slightly open for Lola's benefit. Lauren was asleep on the other side of that door, and Mia hoped with every fiber of her being that she hadn't done anything inappropriate or overstepped any bounds with her last night.

Lauren had taken such good care of her while she was drunk. Vaguely, she remembered telling her so, and that memory, unlike the others, brought a smile to her lips.

Mia slid out of bed and went into the bathroom for a shower. She felt marginally better as she headed toward the kitchen thirty minutes later, dressed for work. Lauren was still asleep, brown hair spread across the pillow behind her. Lola was curled up in the bend of her knees. She hardly ever slept with Mia anymore. Traitor.

In the kitchen, Mia started the coffeepot and fixed herself some toast, which seemed like the best option for her stomach. No more shots for her, although the memory of Kat was a pleasant one. Despite her hangover, Mia felt slightly more optimistic about the prospect of dating than she had yesterday.

"Morning," Lauren mumbled from the living room.

Mia's pulse jumped, and the tingle in her belly had nothing to do with her ulcer or a hangover. *Oh.* "Morning."

Lauren sat up, swiping hair out of her face. "How are you feeling?"

"Hungover," Mia answered, hands fidgeting against the kitchen counter. "And embarrassed. I'm sorry for being such a mess last night." And for whatever led to those confusing moments still spinning through Mia's brain, Lauren's lips so tantalizingly close...

Lauren gave her a lazy smile. "Even the flawless Mia Solano deserves to be a sloppy drunk from time to time. No worries."

"Ugh." Mia rubbed her pounding head, hating that she'd been a sloppy drunk even once. That was so unlike her. And why couldn't she stop thinking about Lauren's lips?

Lauren went into the bathroom, and Mia poured herself a cup of coffee, which she brought to the table with her toast. She sipped, wishing she could bypass her queasy stomach and inject the caffeine directly into her veins. Today was going to be a struggle.

As she ate her toast, Lauren came out of the bathroom dressed for her job at the market and started folding up the couch. She seemed her usual self this morning, but Mia couldn't even look at her without remembering how badly she'd wanted to kiss her last night, how Lauren's body felt pressed against hers. And...she couldn't shake the feeling she needed to apologize for the way she'd acted, even if she couldn't quite remember what had happened.

She finished her coffee and toast, relieved to feel more alert now. "Hey, Lauren?"

"Yeah?" She straightened, pillow in hand.

"I'm sorry for my behavior last night."

Lauren smiled, making a dismissive gesture with her hand. "You have nothing to apologize for."

"I do if I made you feel uncomfortable."

"Well, you didn't." Lauren touched her shoulder as she walked past Mia to pour herself some coffee.

"Are you sure? Because my memory is a bit murky, so I really need you to tell me."

"I'm sure," Lauren said as she filled her coffee mug.

In Mia's alcohol-soaked memories of last night, Lauren had looked at her as if she'd wanted to kiss Mia just as badly, but that couldn't be right, could it? Surely Lauren would rather date someone her own age, or was it possible she felt this too? Mia was too out of sorts to even think about it right now.

Lauren sat across from her at the table. "You did do one strange thing last night."

Mia's skin flushed so hot, she knew her cheeks must be bright red. "Oh?"

"When we walked past the law firm next door, you flipped off their office. What's that about? Do you know them?" Lauren lifted her mug for a sip, eyes locked on Mia's.

She exhaled as nervous laughter threatened to escape her throat. That was a lot more innocent than she'd feared. "No, I don't know them. I was just irrationally annoyed when a law firm moved in next door. I don't even know why." She pushed a hand through her hair. "Pettiness, I guess?"

"Pettiness?" Lauren gave her a look of pure confusion. "About what?"

"Because..." This sounded even pettier when she admitted it out loud. "I walked away from that life, and lately, it just feels like everywhere I turn, there are lawyers."

"Why does that bother you?" Lauren asked. "Do you miss being a lawyer?"

Mia exhaled. She hadn't admitted this yet, even to herself, but... "I guess I must, on some level."

"Do you regret leaving?"

She shook her head. "No, I don't." No regrets, and that was her final answer on the subject. She put her empty plate and mug in the sink and started gathering her things to head downstairs to the café, having decided to forego the gym this morning. "I'm having dinner with my dad after work, so I won't be home until later."

"Okay," Lauren said. "Have fun."

"Thanks." Mia paused at the door. "I meant to offer... Feel free to use my laptop if you want to work on your book."

"Oh." Lauren blinked at her. "Really?"

"Yes. I don't use it much these days, mostly just to answer

emails, since as you know, I'm painfully slow on my phone. Anyway, there's a guest login option, so help yourself."

"Thank you. I really appreciate that."

"No problem." Mia caught herself staring at Lauren's mouth, alarmed to realize she wanted to kiss her as much right now as she had last night. She yanked her gaze back to Lauren's eyes, desperately hoping this attraction would fade before she damaged their friendship...if she hadn't already. "See you later."

LAUREN SAT in Mia's living room, laptop on her knees and a giddy smile on her face. She didn't have to leave for her shift at the market for two hours, and that meant she had a rare opportunity to work on her book. It was incredibly generous of Mia to let Lauren use her laptop.

She'd been so adorably embarrassed this morning, and Lauren wondered how much of last night she remembered. Did she know she'd tried to kiss Lauren? And even more importantly...was she attracted to Lauren, or had it just been the alcohol talking? After all, Mia had been making heart eyes at Piper's photo last night, and she didn't usually go for her either.

Either way, Lauren needed to be careful. At this point, her feelings for Mia went so far beyond friendship or even a simple crush. If she closed her eyes and thought about the kind of person she could see herself falling in love with, well...she looked a lot like Mia.

Lauren's idea of love felt like what she and Mia had shared since Lauren moved into her apartment: laughter at the dinner table, a shared appreciation of each other's interests, and the kind of friendship where they had each other's backs. Of course, the chemistry was there, at least for Lauren. She had no doubt sex with Mia would be amazing, but she was just as enamored with their emotional connection.

When she was with Mia, Lauren felt safe. She felt important and worthy of her goals, and comfortable and free to be herself. She didn't take any of that for granted. Mia was arguably the best friend she'd ever had, and if Lauren ever did have sex with her? Well, she'd almost certainly fall head over heels in love.

And that meant it was going to be more painful than ever to watch Mia keep dating other women. Lauren needed to figure out where they stood and take an emotional step back if necessary to keep herself from getting hurt.

Pushing Mia from her mind, she logged into her Google account and opened the draft of her book. It was a romance, tentatively titled *Meet Me at Midnight*, about two women who met on the subway after late-night shifts at very different jobs. The first draft was finished, but it still had a few missing scenes and needed several rounds of revisions. As she placed her fingers on the keyboard, a thrill raced through her.

An hour and a half later, she'd added over a thousand new words, and maybe even more importantly, she'd fallen in love with the story and her characters all over again. She'd been so invested in this book when she first started writing it, and then her life had gone to hell, and she hadn't had the means or the motivation to keep writing.

Now...she was back, and nothing was going to stop her from achieving her dream. She had messaged with another fanfic author last year who'd self-published a book. She'd given Lauren some publishing advice and the name of her editor. Lauren could do this. The thought was thrilling. A little bit terrifying too, but mostly thrilling.

She shut down the laptop and stood, stretching. It was time to get ready for work. Her gaze caught on the urn in the corner, and before she knew it, she'd crossed the room. Her fingers rested against its cold, smooth surface. "I miss you every day. You know that, right? I can't even tell you how much I wish you were here, making a new life in Brooklyn with me."

Tears welled in her eyes and spilled over her cheeks. It hurt so much that she'd never get to introduce Craig to Mia or show him the first printed copy of her book. Oh, how she missed his smile and the sound of his laugh. She'd never get to see the man he might have become. At twenty-three, he'd had his whole life ahead of him.

"Anyway, I'm doing okay," she whispered. "Better than okay. I just wish you were here to see it."

She touched her fingers to her lips and then pressed them against the urn. Soon, she needed to let go of this last tangible piece of her brother. Surely Mia didn't love having an urn in her apartment, the remains of a man she'd never even met. Soon.

MIA WAS FEELING MOSTLY RECOVERED from her hangover by the time she arrived at her dad's house that evening. She was glad to be here, not only to see her dad, but also to *not* see Lauren. Mia's mind was still whirling with confusing memories and feelings about last night. She needed to sort herself out and find a way to stop lusting after her friend before they shared another quiet evening at home together.

Because every evening with Lauren was lovely. Maybe

too lovely. Mia sighed as she climbed the front steps of her father's Brooklyn brownstone and pressed the buzzer.

The door swung open a few seconds later to reveal his wife, Addie, standing there with a warm smile. "Come in, Mia. How are you?"

"Fine, Addie, and you?"

"My sciatica's acting up this week," she said, rubbing her hip, "but other than that, I really can't complain."

Addie had married Mia's dad about ten years ago. People sometimes gave her an odd look when she referred to Addie as her dad's wife. They'd say, "You mean your stepmother?" But Mia had been in her thirties when they married. She thought Addie was wonderful and was glad her dad had found her, but Addie wasn't her mother.

Mia had a mother. She hadn't seen or spoken to her in twenty years, but she had one.

"Is that new?" she asked, gesturing to Addie's scarf.

"It is." Addie beamed. "Your father gave it to me."

"Dad has great taste," Mia said with a smile as she stepped inside. The blue and green patterned scarf looked fantastic against Addie's silver hair. Addie had always been a fashionable woman, and Mia's dad loved to spoil her with gifts. It seemed to make him as happy as it made Addie. They were adorable together.

"Mia!" Her dad's booming voice reached her from the kitchen. "Come in and taste the sauce."

"Happily." She followed the savory scent of marsala sauce into the kitchen, where her father stood in his red apron, sweat beading on his brow as he stood before several sizzling pans on the stove. "Chicken marsala?" she asked, peering over his shoulder.

"Your favorite," he confirmed, turning to give her a quick kiss on the cheek.

"Yum." She smiled as she watched him stir the pot of sauce. Chicken sizzled in the pan beside it. She'd offer to help if she didn't know how territorial her father was while he was cooking. He didn't want—or need—help.

"I think this is one of my best batches." He dipped a spoon into the sauce and held it toward her. His voice held just a hint of an Italian accent, much less pronounced than it had been when she was a girl.

She took the spoon, blowing on the sauce until it had quit steaming before tasting. Flavor exploded on her tongue, rich with garlic and herbs. "Mm. Amazing as always, Dad."

He beamed at her. "You're too kind, *cara mia*." It had been his pet name for her since she was little, an Italian phrase that meant "my beloved," made more special to him because it contained her name. "Does the sauce need more salt?"

"No, it's perfect," she assured him.

"Wine?" Addie asked.

Mia grimaced. "Actually, I had a bit too much to drink last night, so I think I'll stick with water tonight."

"Who were you out drinking with?" Addie asked as she began filling a glass of water for Mia. "Did you have a date?"

"Is there a new woman in your life?" Her dad glanced over his shoulder at her as he cooked, eyes bright with interest.

"No, not yet," Mia said, thanking Addie as she took the glass of water and sat with her at the kitchen table. "I did have a date yesterday, but it was for coffee, and it was a dud. I went out for drinks with a friend after."

"Just a friend?" Addie asked, her expression hopeful.

"Just a friend," Mia confirmed, even as her stubborn brain replayed the image of Lauren's lips, looking more tempting than a whole buffet of her father's cooking. "She helped me set up an online dating profile, though, so I'm getting out there. I'm trying."

"Good," her father said, and the sizzling on the stove intensified as he combined the chicken with the sauce. "I want you to be happy, *cara*. I want you to have what Addie and I have. Maybe we'll both get it right with the second marriage, *si*?"

"Mm," she agreed, although she couldn't imagine herself married again...yet. She did want it eventually. The longer she was single, the more she missed being in a relationship.

Her father gave Addie a quick kiss as he passed her at the counter, and Mia smiled. She'd harbored a lot of guilt over the demise of her parents' marriage. It had taken years —a lot of years and a lot of therapy—for her to finally accept that it wasn't her fault. Seeing her dad so blissfully happy with Addie helped.

And hopefully, he was right. Hopefully Mia would find that kind of happiness again too. She imagined Lauren here in the kitchen with them. Her dad and Addie would adore Lauren. And obviously Mia's head was still a mess where Lauren was concerned.

She didn't even know if Lauren was attracted to her, but she *did* know taking that step risked their friendship. It would be so much easier and safer to rebound with someone else. She'd keep dating until she found that some-one. She could do it. She would.

14

As September became October, Lauren settled into her new routines, working at the café and the market. She was still staying with Mia, and it had been pretty seamless so far. Mia had gone on a *lot* of first dates, but only two second dates, and she'd maintained that she wasn't ready to bring anyone home with her, even if Lauren hadn't been there.

Lauren couldn't help her relief each time Mia came home to relate yet another boring or disastrous date. She knew she should be rooting for Mia to find someone, both because Mia deserved it and because it would help Lauren get over her. But it hadn't happened—yet—and Lauren wasn't exactly sad about it.

Mia hadn't shown any interest in her since that one night when she got drunk, but Lauren's infatuation seemed to grow by the day, and it was getting harder to ignore. Sooner or later, something would have to give. She had an appointment to see a room for rent tonight, and if it worked out, it might solve at least one problem for her.

Lauren's court date had been bumped again, now scheduled for November 18th. It felt like a storm cloud looming on the horizon, a constant threat that never seemed to arrive. She couldn't fully move forward with her life until the charges against her were dropped or she served her time, and she hated being stuck in this limbo, especially as she watched Mia move forward without her.

"Hi, Lauren."

She spun at the now-familiar voice to find Darius entering the cat enclosure with a coffee cup in his right hand. "Darius, how are you?"

"Good, good." He sat at the table nearest to the cat tree where Gilbert was napping. He snapped his fingers, and the cat lifted his head. "I think today's the day when you get to say, 'I told you so.'"

"Really?" Lauren nearly clapped her hands with glee. Over the last month, she'd watched Darius and Gilbert bond, but he hadn't been ready to make it official, until today...hopefully.

Darius nodded as Gilbert hopped down and walked over to rub his head against Darius's hand. "You were right. He's the one. I'm glad I got the chance to spend time and get to know him here at the café. I think that will make it easier for both of us once I bring him home."

Now Lauren did clap her hands together. "This is the best news. Oh, I'm so thrilled for you both."

"Thanks." He smiled, looking at his soon-to-be cat. "What's the next step? I need to fill out an application, right?"

"Yes, and it won't be official until your application is approved, but I can tell you unofficially that we don't have any other applications pending for Gilbert. As long as your information checks out, there shouldn't be any problems."

"Perfect."

Lauren fetched the tablet that they kept in back so he could submit his application directly to the rescue. "You should hear back in a day or two, and if all goes smoothly, you could bring Gilbert home by the end of the week."

"Sounds like it's time to go shopping for cat supplies," Darius told her.

"Yep. Kelsey's going to be so surprised."

Darius smiled broadly. "I can't wait to see her face when she meets him."

After his application had been submitted, he stayed to visit with Gilbert for a little longer while Lauren rushed back to Mia's office. She found her tapping away at her computer, lips pursed in concentration and looking ridiculously sexy in the process.

"Darius decided to adopt Gilbert," Lauren blurted breathlessly.

Mia looked up, smiling. "Oh good. Gilbert's been here longer than any of our other cats."

"I'm so happy for him." Lauren pressed a hand to her chest, tears welling in her eyes.

"You're going to miss him, aren't you?" Mia's tone was sympathetic. "It's hard when they get adopted."

"No, that's not it." Lauren swiped at her eyes. "I'm glad to see him go home with Darius. I just—" She cut herself off, not wanting to ruin the moment by unloading her messy emotions all over Mia.

"You what?" Mia pressed. "Talk to me."

Lauren blew out a breath, wiping away a tear that had escaped her overflowing eyes. "I think...as a foster kid who never got adopted, it just really fills my heart when they go home, especially the ones who were hard to place."

"Oh, Lauren." Mia stood and came around her desk, wrapping Lauren in a warm hug.

Lauren held on to her, breathing in Mia's scent as her tears receded. "I'd never thought about working in animal rescue before I took this job, but it's such a good fit for me."

"Seems like it." One of Mia's hands rubbed up and down her back. Her hair was soft against Lauren's cheek, and she wanted the moment to last forever. "I hadn't made the connection between your work here and your history as a foster child, but I'm glad it's been a positive experience for you."

"So positive," Lauren agreed. "Like, I feel like dancing around your office right now."

Mia pulled back, meeting Lauren's eyes with a smile. "That's a good thing. You looked so sad, so lost when we first met. I'm glad to see you looking happy." Her hands were on Lauren's elbows now, and Lauren's heart was pounding to be this close to her, close enough to see the way Mia's gaze drifted—just briefly—to Lauren's lips.

Her pulse kicked up another notch. "I'm much happier these days."

"I'm glad." Mia released her and took a step back.

"You seem happier too," Lauren said.

Mia leaned her hip against the desk. "I am. I feel more settled in my post-divorce life now. Even though dating has been a frustrating experience so far, I'm still glad I'm putting myself out there."

"You'll find someone soon." Lauren hoped she sounded sincere. She *was* sincere. She wanted Mia to be happy, even if she was also hopelessly smitten with her.

"I hope so," Mia said.

"I have a good feeling about it," Lauren said with a nod.

Mia held up her hand, showing that her fingers were crossed, and then she walked behind her desk and sat. Lauren took that as her cue to get back to work. With a wave, she headed back to the café. She freshened up the cats' food and water and began to sweep the seating area. Beth was here, the businesswoman who Mia had been flirting with for as long as Lauren had been working here.

Lauren gave her a friendly smile as she passed her table, sweeping her way toward the back of the room. The cats shed a truly incredible amount of hair. When she'd finished, she put the broom away and headed out to see if anyone wanted anything from the café.

Mia stood at Beth's table, one hand resting against its surface. As Lauren watched, Beth reached for her phone and typed something in, and if Lauren wasn't mistaken, Mia was giving Beth her number. Lauren turned her back so she didn't have to watch.

A minute later, Mia was at her side, her giddy expression all but confirming Lauren's suspicion. "I did it," Mia whispered. "I asked her out...and she said yes."

"Yay," Lauren whispered back. "I'm so proud of you. Maybe all these other dates were just a warmup so you'd be ready for Beth."

"Maybe." Mia looked thoughtful. "Either that, or I've built her up in my mind and the date will be a bust. But I'm glad I finally asked."

"I am too. I can't wait to hear about it."

"Thanks, Lauren." Mia squeezed her hand before she headed to the counter to help with the afternoon rush.

Lauren finished her shift feeling vaguely melancholy about Mia's upcoming date, but she was on her way to look at an apartment, and it was a really promising lead. If it worked out, it could be perfect timing, because obviously, her feelings for Mia were getting out of hand. It would be torture to share her apartment while she dated Beth.

Several years ago, Lauren had worked a bartending job

with a man named Eliot Faraday, so when she'd seen his name listed on a rental application she was filling out, she'd added a little note to say hi and remind him how they knew each other. And she'd gotten an appointment to view the room he was offering for rent.

Butterflies flapped in her stomach as she boarded the subway. This was only the second time she'd made it as far as an appointment to view an apartment in person. She and Eliot had already had a lengthy phone conversation about her felony charge, and he seemed understanding, but she was terrified he would decide to rent to someone less risky.

Since she'd been back in Brooklyn, she'd tried to reconnect with her old friends. She'd had to cut ties when she fled last year with Craig, and it had been devastating to realize that the people who'd once been important to her had moved on without her. Apparently, a felony charge was too much for a lot of people to move past.

It made her even more thankful for Mia, but all the same, it was time for Lauren to find her own place. As she pressed the buzzer on Eliot's building, she hoped she had found it. He came to the door looking much the same as she remembered, with short brown hair and a goatee, his expression friendly.

"Hi, Lauren. Small world, huh?"

"It sure is," she agreed.

"Come on up." He motioned her inside. The building was fairly run-down, and the hallway was dark and musty smelling, but it was affordable. Eliot showed her into an apartment on the third floor, where a tall Black man with dreadlocks stood to greet her.

He extended a hand. "Tariq."

"I'm Lauren. Nice to meet you," she told him. Eliot had told her that he and his boyfriend held the lease for this apartment. They rented out the two spare rooms to help afford the rent, something many New Yorkers did in this notoriously overpriced market.

Eliot showed her around the main living space, which was honestly much nicer than she'd been expecting, with bright white walls and wood floors. The room he was looking to rent was barely larger than a closet, but it would be hers, and that was all that mattered.

"What do you think?" he asked.

"I think it's perfect," she told him earnestly. "If you decide to rent to me, I'll be the most unobtrusive roommate you ever had. Seriously, Eliot, I really appreciate you being willing to take a chance on me, and I'll make sure you don't regret it."

He nodded. "Look, there are some things in my past that I'm not too proud of either. I do have two or three other people coming to see the room, but I'll let you know in the next few days, okay?"

They talked for a little while longer, and when she left, she felt cautiously hopeful. And she wasn't quite ready to go home yet, probably because she dreaded hearing more about Mia's upcoming date with Beth. Lauren boarded the subway and rode to Prospect Park, making her way to her and Craig's oak tree—the tree where they would meet after they'd been separated in foster care—as darkness fell over the city

"I might have found a new apartment tonight," she whispered, feeling almost as close to him here as she did when she talked to his urn. "Which is perfect timing since I'm in way over my head with Mia."

She rested her forehead against the tree's cold, rough bark. "I know what you'd say. I need to get over her. It's silly to fawn over her this way when I'm pretty sure she doesn't feel the same way about me."

The wind whispered through the branches overhead. The oak tree's leaves were dry and brown now, still clinging stubbornly to its branches as winter approached. Lauren shivered. Her jacket was getting too thin for the weather. She'd have to invest in a coat soon. At least she'd been able to save up some money while she was staying with Mia so she could afford one.

Lauren stood, giving the tree an affectionate pat before she walked away. As she left the park, she became aware of a man behind her on the sidewalk, the steady thump of his shoes against the concrete seeming to follow her down the street. When she darted a glance over her shoulder, she saw the outline of a hoodie over his head and a hard, stubbly jaw.

Fear slid down her spine. Probably, he was harmless. She'd lived in Brooklyn almost her entire life, and while she'd had her fair share of experiences with men making unwanted advances or gestures, nothing worse than that had ever happened to her. But still, it was dark, and she couldn't shake the feeling that he was following too close.

She turned left a block early, hoping to lose him, but he turned too. He was walking more quietly now, as if he hoped she wouldn't notice him. Or maybe she was just being paranoid. She picked up her pace, and as a bodega came into view at the end of the block, she darted toward it and dashed inside the well-lit space. The man kept walking.

Lauren exhaled in relief. Her knees were shaking, which was silly since nothing had actually happened. She hated feeling helpless, and she especially hated when men made her feel that way. Maybe she should look into taking self-defense classes once she could afford it.

Since she was in the bodega, she wandered the aisles and picked out a couple of sandwiches to bring home. If she and Mia didn't eat them tonight, they could have them for lunch tomorrow. Mia still had a tendency to skip meals if Lauren didn't remind her to eat.

Lauren paid for her purchases and headed out, grateful to see no sign of the man who'd tailed her earlier. She boarded the subway, headed home.

MIA STOOD in front of a pot bubbling on the stove as her favorite playlist streamed through the speakers in the living room. The scent of tomatoes and herbs filled the air, and she smiled, adjusting the apron her father had given her years ago. This was the first time she'd worn it. She felt so domestic, and that felt surprisingly good.

She hummed along with the music as she stirred the soup. Garlic bread rested on a tray to her left, ready for her to pop in the oven as soon as Lauren got home. As if Mia had summoned her with her thoughts, a key turned in the lock, and Lauren walked into the apartment carrying a plastic grocery bag.

"Hi," Mia called from the kitchen.

Lauren turned, eyes widening when she saw Mia. "Are you cooking?"

She grinned. "I am. Minestrone soup."

"It smells amazing." Lauren walked into the kitchen and put her shopping bag in the refrigerator. "Sandwiches for lunch tomorrow. What inspired you to cook?"

"You," Mia said. "You've cooked so many meals for me, and I wanted to return the favor. I never used to cook because I was working such long hours. It felt like a chore, but maybe I'll enjoy it more now that I have the time. Anyway, it's nothing fancy, just soup."

"I love minestrone," Lauren said, "and it's perfect soup weather out there."

"How was the apartment?" she asked.

"Good. The room is the size of a closet, and they'd want me to pay cash so they don't have to officially add another person to the lease, but it's fine. I can't be choosy with my record." She scrunched her nose.

Mia frowned. She didn't like the sound of any of that. "You need to make sure you still sign some kind of official lease paperwork to give yourself legal recourse. Otherwise, they could raise your rent any time they feel like it or kick you out without notice. It's not legal. If they aren't adding you to the official lease, the building management could have you evicted if they found out."

Lauren patted her shoulder. "I know your lawyer brain rejects it, but people do this kind of thing all the time."

"And tenants get screwed by these types of agreements all the time," Mia countered. "I don't want that to happen to you."

"I have a felony charge pending, Mia. For robbery, of all things. Most reputable landlords don't want anything to do with me, but I know Eliot. I think he'll be fair."

Mia wanted to argue with that, but she couldn't. "Just... be careful." She bent to put the garlic bread in the oven.

"I will," Lauren said. "He's seeing a few more prospective tenants before he decides, but for the record, you didn't have me sign an official lease agreement either, so it's not necessarily a red flag."

"I'm your friend," Mia said, but dammit, Lauren had a point. "And I'm not in a hurry to kick you out, so please don't take this room if it's sketchy."

"It's not sketchy," Lauren insisted.

Mia still didn't like it, but Lauren couldn't stay on her couch forever, no matter how much Mia was enjoying having her here. And she *really* liked having her here, which was a red flag in itself. Mia was painfully aware that her feelings for Lauren weren't platonic anymore.

She should be encouraging Lauren to move out, because surely it was harder for Mia to experience a connection with the women she'd dated when she was distractingly infatuated with the off-limits woman sharing her apartment. The truth was, Mia would always rather be with Lauren, and she was starting to wonder why she kept fighting it.

Was there a rule that said all rebound relationships ended in disaster? And did Lauren like her the same way? Mia thought she did, but what if that was wishful thinking on her part? The stakes were too high. She had to be sure before she even considered starting anything with Lauren.

"Tell me more about this closet-sized bedroom." She kept her tone light as she dished up two bowls of soup.

"It's got a twin-sized bed and a little window that faces the building next door, but I think it might have a cool view at night when you can see the lights of the city gleaming. I've always loved to see that. It's not much bigger than the bed, but honestly, that's fine. It would be one of the only times in my life I've actually had my own room." Lauren sounded so hopeful about this room that Mia felt herself warming to the idea.

"Just make sure you sign something, okay?"

"I will."

"Wine?" Mia asked, lifting a bottle she'd picked up when she went shopping earlier.

"Sure," Lauren agreed. "Between my apartment news

and Darius deciding to adopt Gilbert, today was a good one."

Mia smiled as she opened the bottle and poured two glasses. "I'm glad. And I meant to tell you, Wendy confirmed that Darius's application went through, so that's official."

Lauren's whole face seemed to light up. "Oh my God, I'm so happy. Can you try to make sure I'm working when he goes home? I want to be there."

"I'll make sure." Mia would make sure she was there too, so she could watch Lauren send Gilbert on his way. It was going to be beautiful. She cut the garlic bread, and Lauren helped her carry everything to the table.

Lauren sat across from her with a blissed-out smile on her face. "An apartment, Gilbert getting adopted, *and* you cooked for me. Oh, and let's not forget, you asked Beth out."

"I did." Mia sipped her wine. "Hopefully, she'll help me break my streak of bad dates."

"I have a good feeling about it," Lauren said. "You two have been flirting for a while, so you know there's a spark."

"Mm." But she wasn't as excited about this date as she should be, and while she'd been attracted to Beth in the beginning, the only spark she felt at the moment was for the woman sitting in front from her. Mia didn't even want to think about Beth, not while Lauren was here, looking so pretty and happy and generally lovely that it was all Mia could do not to lean across the table and kiss her right in the middle of dinner.

"The soup is delicious," Lauren said.

"My dad's recipe," Mia told her. "Although don't tell him I used pasta from a box. Oh, you know what? I should send him a picture. He loves to tease me that I don't cook."

"You totally should," Lauren agreed. "He'll be thrilled."

Mia reached for her phone and snapped a picture of the bowl in front of her, which she texted to her dad.

"He loves to cook, huh?" Lauren said.

"Yes. I was spoiled with homecooked meals every night growing up."

"Did he do all the cooking for your family?"

Mia nodded. "Pretty much. My mom cooked sometimes, but she didn't enjoy it, not like he does."

Lauren looked up. "That's the first time I've heard you mention your mom," she said quietly.

"I don't talk about her often," Mia admitted.

Lauren's expression was sympathetic. "I'm sorry for whatever happened. You don't have tell me."

Mia rarely shared this story. It made her feel awful, even now, but she knew so many painful things about Lauren's past, and she was surprised to realize she wanted Lauren to know some of hers too. "I came out to my parents when I was twenty-one, the summer before my senior year of college. My mom told me to pack my bags and not come back until I'd straightened myself out...pun intended."

"Oh, Mia. I'm so sorry." Lauren reached out to cover Mia's hand with hers.

"My dad was so angry...at her, not at me. He packed his bags too. We both moved out. He divorced her, and neither of us has spoken to her since."

Lauren blinked. "That's so sad, and also, your dad sounds amazing."

"He is," Mia said. "He's the best."

"I'm so glad you have him."

"Me too, although I spent years feeling like I broke up their marriage. I had so much guilt about it. Somewhere deep down, I think I still do." She flinched at the admission, reaching for her wine.

Lauren shook her head, eyes blazing. "You're not responsible for their divorce. Put yourself in your dad's shoes. Imagine that your spouse turned their back on your child. Wouldn't you do what he did? It wouldn't even be a choice."

"No," Mia said softly. "It wouldn't. I'd never turn my back on my child."

"Exactly. And from what you've told me about him, I'm sure he doesn't want you to feel guilty about it. Their marriage couldn't have been that solid anyway, for it to fall apart so easily."

"He's told me all those things," Mia said, surprised to feel a smile on her lips. "And he's remarried now. Addie, his new wife, is amazing. They're so happy together."

"I'm glad," Lauren said.

"And speaking of my dad..." Mia held up her phone so they could both read the text he'd sent in response to her soup photo.

Che bella zuppa!! Looks just as good as mine. Does this mean you'll cook for us the next time Addie and I visit? Oh, and of course I see the store-bought pasta in there, cara mia, but I'll forgive you for it this time. Love you!!

He followed it with a string of emojis, everything from a bowl of soup to a heart to a hand that looked alarmingly like it was flipping her off, although she figured he had mistaken it for a thumbs-up. Without warning, she burst out laughing.

"Not to be dramatic, but I think I love your dad," Lauren said, grinning.

"It's the only proper response to a text like that," Mia agreed.

They laughed through the rest of their meal. In fact, Mia was still smiling as she put away the leftovers. She, Lauren, and Lola settled on the couch to watch TV together, and

Mia couldn't help hoping they got at least a few more evenings like this before things changed.

When Mia went to bed that night, she curled under the covers and fell asleep almost immediately, exhausted but happy.

Lauren's blood curdling scream jolted her awake some-time later.

15

The door to the apartment was wide open. Lauren lurched upright in bed, blinking into the darkness as terror squeezed the air from her lungs. Footsteps. She heard footsteps, someone shuffling across the hardwood floors. Her heart pounded, goose bumps pebbling her skin, and there was a shadow...

The silhouette of a man. She saw the hoodie, just like the man who'd followed her earlier, and now he was in her apartment. In Mia's apartment. Mia...

Lauren sat there, helpless, frozen, as he advanced toward her. She couldn't move, couldn't scream. Why couldn't she scream?

"Lauren..."

She whimpered, striking out with her hands.

"Lauren, wake up."

Her eyes popped open, and she bolted upright in bed, slamming into a body. Before she could panic further, she realized it was Mia, leaning over her. Lauren gulped air, grabbing frantically at Mia. Her hands fisted in the soft cotton of Mia's shirt.

"Hey," Mia said softly. "You had a bad dream."

"Oh," Lauren mumbled. Her heart was pounding, and she was still irrationally terrified even though the door—when she craned her head around Mia to look—was shut. No one was in the apartment. No one but Mia.

Mia, who was bent over her in a white, vee-necked tee that was currently giving Lauren a perfect view down the front of her shirt. She glimpsed the shadow beneath Mia's collarbones and the curve of her breasts, and if it hadn't been so dark, she probably could have seen everything. Lauren dropped her gaze, only to be faced with Mia's bare legs, and *oof*.

Lauren squeezed her eyes shut, taking several deep breaths until she'd calmed down. "Sorry for waking you," she whispered.

"It's fine." Mia's hand brushed against her arm. "You screamed. I was worried."

"Just a bad dream." Lauren opened her eyes to see that Mia was sitting on the edge of the bed beside her, and thank God the T-shirt covered her panties or Lauren's brain might have seriously melted down.

"Want to talk about it?"

"When I was walking home earlier, I thought a man was following me," she whispered.

Mia sucked in a breath, moving closer so that her arm pressed against Lauren's.

"It was nothing." Lauren shook her head. "I ducked into a bodega, and he kept walking. Just me being paranoid."

"It's never paranoid to be vigilant of your surroundings. You did the right thing going inside the bodega."

"Anyway, it freaked me out for a minute, but I forgot all about it once I got home and you'd cooked for me." She smiled into the darkness. "But then I dreamed that I'd woken up, and the door to the apartment was standing open, and he was in the room with me."

"Shit." Mia gripped Lauren's hand. "I'm sorry."

"It's a recurrent nightmare I've had since I was a girl," she admitted quietly. "Waking up to find the door open and someone in the apartment. It happened to me for real once when I was little. It was just my mom's boyfriend, rummaging around looking for drugs, but it scared the life out of me, waking to see the door open and a man creeping through the room."

"That must have been terrifying." Mia's arm came around her, drawing her against the warmth of her body.

"It'd been a while since I had that dream. I guess the man tonight triggered it."

"Sounds like it," Mia agreed. "Are you okay now, or do you want to sit up for a bit?"

"I'll be okay," Lauren told her, but she didn't let go of Mia, and Mia made no effort to free herself. On the contrary, she tightened her arm around Lauren's waist, holding her close. So close Lauren could feel the side of her breast pressed against her arm through that T-shirt.

Mia turned her head, and their gazes locked. Their faces were entirely too close to each other, and maybe it was the dim lighting or Lauren's rampaging emotions, but she could swear she saw longing on Mia's face. Hunger. Desire.

She'd only have to lean forward a few inches...

For a moment, she was sure it was going to happen, that Mia *wanted* it to happen.

Lauren's heart pounded against her ribs until she could hardly breathe. She wanted to kiss Mia more than she'd ever wanted anything, and despite what she'd told her, she wasn't entirely fine. When she closed her eyes, she still saw the shadow of that man in the living room. She felt the chilling fear of the open door. Her pulse raced impossibly faster.

"Lie down," Mia whispered.

Lauren obeyed, not quite sure what was happening, but eager to find out. She settled against the mattress, and Mia lay behind her, one hand resting on Lauren's waist as if she'd known she was still scared and that she needed her touch.

"I'll stay while you fall asleep," Mia murmured, her breath warm against Lauren's neck, raising goose bumps on her skin.

Lauren closed her eyes, wondering if anyone had ever held her like this before, providing comfort after she'd had a bad dream. Lauren had been a caretaker for most of her life, but she'd rarely received caretaking in return. Tears burned behind her eyelids, but they were the good kind this time. She'd never felt more safe or cherished than she did right now.

With Mia's hand resting on her hip, Lauren slipped into a deep, peaceful sleep. When she woke, that hand was gone, and she was alone in bed. Mia stood in the kitchen, dressed for the gym in a black sports bra and leggings, displaying entirely too much skin for Lauren's sleep and lust-muddled brain to process.

Not when her mind was still replaying the vision of Mia last night in that tee...bent over Lauren and looking at her like she was desperate to kiss her.

"Morning," Mia said as she zipped her jacket.

"Morning." Lauren studied her, looking for any trace of the heat she thought she'd seen in Mia's eyes last night, but in the morning light, she looked as impenetrable as ever. This was the Mia who was about to go on a date with Beth, not the Mia who'd come to Lauren's bed after she had a bad dream.

"I'm on my way to the gym." Mia picked up her water bottle and her keys and headed for the door. So they weren't going to discuss last night, not that there was technically anything to discuss. Nothing had happened.

Still, Lauren felt a gut punch of disappointment. She hugged her knees and nodded.

"See you at the café later." With a wave, Mia was gone.

MIA DIDN'T GET nervous very often, so the jittery feeling in the pit of her stomach on Friday night as she approached the restaurant where she was meeting Beth for dinner caught her off guard. And when her hands started fidgeting while she stood at the hostess desk, the realization that she was nervous only served to make her even more jumpy.

She'd been on a lot of dates over the last month, but this felt different because she and Beth had been flirting for months at the café. Mia really wanted tonight to go well. She was tired of first dates. She was ready to take the next step with someone. Surely she was at least ready for a kiss. God, it had been so long since she'd been kissed...

Her mind flashed to an image of Lauren, bare faced and rumpled after her nightmare. She remembered how good it felt to hold Lauren in her arms, the yearning in Lauren's eyes when she'd looked at Mia, and how badly Mia had wanted to kiss her.

She'd promised herself that she'd get through this date with Beth before she addressed her feelings for Lauren. She had to be able to at least say she'd tried, because if she and Beth hit it off, well, that would be so much less complicated than starting something with Lauren. Mia exhaled, smoothing a hand over the front of her dress.

Lauren would like this restaurant, though. In fact—

"Mia."

She turned, and Beth stood there in an emerald-green jacket over black slacks. Her dark hair was carefully styled, sleek and glossy. Mia smiled, unsure how to greet her, and those nerves reappeared, tightening her stomach. "Beth, you look amazing."

"Thanks. I was going to say the same to you." Beth leaned in, and they gave each other an awkward little half hug.

"Shall we?" Mia gestured to the hostess desk.

They were shown to a table in the middle of the dining room. Mia shrugged out of her jacket and hung it over the back of her chair before she sat, fiddling with the hem of her dress. Why was she so fidgety tonight? It was entirely unlike her.

"So, Mia," Beth said as she sat across from her. "I'm curious. How did you go from being a lawyer to owning a cat café?"

"I guess you could say I burnt myself out," Mia told her. "My wife and I worked for the same law firm, and we were extremely competitive with each other because of it, to the point where it made our entire relationship toxic. I landed in the ER with a bleeding ulcer, and it was a pretty harsh wake-up call."

"I bet." Beth's tone was sympathetic.

"One day not long after that, I jokingly said to a friend that I wished I could just run away from my life and drink coffee and play with cats all day, and she suggested I open a cat café. She wasn't serious, but I realized I was. I was ready for a change." Mia smiled at the memory. It seemed fitting that it had been Lauren who gave her the nudge in this direction. Everything in her life seemed to circle back to Lauren these days.

"It must have been a pretty big adjustment," Beth said.

"Huge," Mia confirmed. "I'm still adjusting, really. Some days, I feel like I'm about to jump out of my own skin because the café is so quiet. I miss the thrill of being in the courtroom, but I couldn't go back to that lifestyle."

"Sounds like a good change, then."

"Yes. Did you always want to work in advertising?" Mia asked, steering the conversation away from herself.

"Actually, no." Beth's lips curved in a small smile. "I wanted to be a television reporter."

"You certainly have the face for it," Mia said, meeting Beth's gaze.

"I lasted two weeks reporting on traffic accidents and unruly shoppers in freezing, soggy weather before I realized it wasn't for me. I'm much happier in an office."

The waiter arrived to take their drink orders, and they ordered a bottle of wine to share. The conversation stayed lively as they sipped wine and ordered their entrees. Beth was smart and funny, exactly the kind of woman Mia had hoped to find, and yet, she couldn't stop her mind from wandering as she ate.

Lauren was at home, working on her book, probably wearing the gray pajama pants with little kittens on them that Mia had given her last week. She'd seen them when she was shopping and couldn't resist getting them for her. Lauren looked unfairly adorable in them. And...this wasn't working.

Mia had assumed her attraction to Lauren was some-thing she could move past, something she *should* move past. She didn't want to rebound from her marriage with a friend, certainly not with a friend she valued as much as Lauren. If they crashed and burned, it could destroy their friendship, and she couldn't bear the thought of that.

And yet, as Mia sat here, feigning interest in Beth's tale about a difficult client, she wished she was with Lauren. She would be having so much more fun right now. She couldn't seem to get Lauren out of her head, no matter where she was.

"I had a really nice time tonight," Beth said after they'd settled the check.

"So did I," Mia said, wishing she meant it.

They put their jackets on and walked outside, pausing on the sidewalk in front of the restaurant. Beth moved closer, her intention clear on her face, and Mia took an involuntary step back. The thought of kissing Beth made her stomach clench, and not in a good way. Beth's brow knitted, but she didn't make another move to kiss her.

"I'd like to see you again," Beth said. "Do you enjoy theater? Maybe we could see a show together."

"I do." Mia hated herself for what she was about to say. "But I think...maybe I'm not as ready to date as I'd hoped. I'm so sorry. It's nothing to do with you. If I weren't so recently divorced..." Or so completely infatuated with Lauren, but that seemed unfair to say.

"I understand," Beth said. "If you change your mind, you've got my number. And you'll see me at the café regardless." She gave Mia the kind of flirty smile that had caught her attention in the first place.

"I will." Mia squeezed her hand before she walked away.

Her apartment was only six blocks from here, so she decided to walk. She needed to clear her head, because right now, her thoughts were in chaos. She'd just walked away from the perfect rebound relationship. *Ugh.* Why was she self-sabotaging herself like this?

By the time she reached her building, she was angry. Frustrated. Both, probably. Irrationally, she wished Lauren wouldn't be waiting in the living room, because she'd want to hear all about Mia's date, and what could she possibly tell her?

She pushed her key into the door, shoving with more force than necessary as she let herself into the building. Her heart was pounding, and her stomach felt jittery again. She understood why people called it butterflies, because there was definitely a fluttery sensation beneath her ribs. But why was she nervous now, walking into her own damn apartment?

She got her answer when she pushed the door open and saw Lauren sitting on the couch in her kitten pajamas with Mia's laptop balanced on her knees, typing away. She looked up with a bright smile, and Mia lost her breath. Her pulse raced, and the butterflies in her stomach took flight, sending a jolt of something heady and warm through her system.

Lauren closed the laptop, gesturing for Mia to sit beside her on the couch. "How was your date with Beth? I want to hear everything."

Mia sat, her mouth suddenly dry. "It was...under-whelming."

"Oh, no." Lauren turned those big brown eyes on her, and Mia lost what little common sense she had left. "What happened?"

"She..." Mia could hear herself breathing, ragged as if she'd just left the gym. Her gaze dropped to Lauren's lips, and they seemed closer now. Had Lauren leaned in, or had she? Mia knew what she'd seen on Lauren's face that night after her nightmare, and she saw it again now. Yearning. Desire.

Mia had needed to be sure that Lauren felt it too, and she had her answer. She couldn't keep fighting this. As heat flared in the pit of her stomach, burning away her self-control, she couldn't remember a single reason why she'd ever thought kissing Lauren was a bad idea.

"She what?" Lauren whispered.

"She wasn't you."

Lauren blinked, inhaling sharply. "Oh."

"Right," Mia croaked. She knew she leaned forward then, close enough to smell her own shampoo in Lauren's hair and feel the warmth of Lauren's breath on her cheeks. Close enough for Lauren to realize what was happening. Mia paused there, giving Lauren a chance to stop this if she didn't want it to happen, giving them both one last chance to put on the brakes before they crossed the point of no return.

But Lauren just stared at her out of big hopeful eyes. Her lips parted.

Mia couldn't think, couldn't breathe. She was helpless to fight the current drawing her in. Her lips brushed Lauren's, and she moaned in relief.

Because this...this was right. This was wonderful. This was *everything*.

16

"Oh," Lauren gasped as Mia's lips met hers. Oh *yes*. Mia's lips were hesitant at first, so soft, so gentle. Her eyes were shut, her features a mixture of desire and confusion, as if she wasn't sure what she was doing, and that made two of them. Lauren had never expected Mia to come home from her date and kiss her, but she had, and talk about a happy surprise...

"I'm sorry," Mia whispered against her lips. "I don't know what—"

"Shh, I don't either, but I want it. I want it so much, Mia."

Mia's exhale was a whimper. Her hands cupped Lauren's cheeks, cool from the outside air and yet somehow also warm. "The entire time I was with Beth, I couldn't stop thinking about you."

Her lips pressed more insistently against Lauren's as the kiss went from tender to urgent. Mia's tongue traced the seam of Lauren's lips, and she opened to her, tasting red wine in the heat of her mouth. Lauren leaned forward, resting a hand on Mia's thigh, realizing with a shocked inhale that Mia wasn't wearing tights beneath her dress despite the chill outside.

Lauren's pulse kicked as her fingers met Mia's bare skin, an insistent ache building low in her belly. There was something vaguely desperate about their kiss now, hands grasping, lips moving messily, both of them pausing sporadically to gasp for air. It was hot and heady, maybe the hottest kiss of Lauren's life. One of Mia's hands had wandered down to settle against the curve of Lauren's waist, fingers fisted in the fabric of her T-shirt.

Beautiful, sophisticated Mia—who'd just come from a date with a woman who should have been everything she wanted—was kissing Lauren like she couldn't get enough, like she never wanted to stop, like she'd been fantasizing about this as much as Lauren had.

When they finally broke apart, Mia's lips were slightly swollen, and her eyes were dazed. There was a hunger gleaming in their mocha depths that only added to the arousal already blazing inside Lauren. Mia's chest rose and fell rapidly, drawing Lauren's attention to the way that dress highlighted her collarbones and the swell of her breasts.

And she could look. She could look because Mia had kissed her, and now Lauren didn't have to hide her attraction anymore. She dragged her gaze slowly back to Mia's eyes, giddy to let her see Lauren checking her out.

Mia blinked at her, seemingly at a loss for words. Her hand was still on Lauren's waist, and they were leaned in close, so close Lauren could smell the soft scent of Mia's perfume and feel the warmth of her breath as she exhaled.

"That was...amazing," Lauren whispered.

And Mia broke into the most luminous smile. "It was, wasn't it?"

Lauren nodded breathlessly.

"I tried so hard to fight it," Mia murmured.

"Why?"

"Because I haven't been with anyone since my divorce. You're the first new person I've kissed in eighteen fucking years. Everyone says to start casual, that rebounds don't last. And you're so important to me, Lauren. I don't want to hurt you or damage our friendship."

Lauren gulped at the honesty in her words. "I hear you. I was fighting it too. I need to get my life back on track before I can even think about dating anyone. I mean, I still have this felony charge looming over me."

Mia's gaze was steady. "You know that doesn't bother me, as your friend or...if I'm more than a friend."

Lauren did know that, but it didn't make all her troubles magically disappear either. "Eliot called while you were out. The room is officially mine. I move in next weekend."

Mia's eyes shut, and she gave her head a little shake that made a strand of hair fall across her face. "I don't want to talk about you moving out right now."

Lauren grinned as she reached out to push Mia's hair behind her ear. "Okay."

"But we probably should talk." Mia sucked in a breath, meeting Lauren's gaze.

"Yeah, because I have an important question." Lauren cocked an eyebrow. "What was it like, kissing someone new after so long?"

Mia groaned, and the sound seemed to reverberate in Lauren's overheated body. "It was...different. Exciting. To be perfectly honest, it made me question whether I've been missing out, like maybe I should have kissed you a long time ago."

Lauren gulped, momentarily rendered speechless.

Mia straightened, taking Lauren's hands in hers. "I'm so

conflicted. I want you so much. I can't even look at other women lately because the only woman I want to look at is you. And that kiss...well, it was exceptional, and now all I can think about is kissing you again. But I can't help feeling that I'm putting our friendship at risk if we take this any further."

"It's a risk," Lauren agreed. "But I think it's a risk we've already taken. It seems like we both tried our best to ignore the chemistry, and we failed. Honestly, part of me can't even believe we're sitting here having this conversation, that you actually came home and kissed me tonight. You've totally blown my mind here."

Mia's expression turned coy. "Had you thought about it, then? Kissing me?"

"God, so many times. I'm embarrassed to tell you how many."

Mia exhaled, her gaze dipping to Lauren's lips. "I refused to let myself look at you that way for a long time. I was too aware of our age difference and feeling like I needed someone casual—temporary—for my first relationship after Kristin."

"Age isn't an issue, at least not for me," Lauren told her. "I'm pushing thirty, hardly robbing the cradle."

"And wise beyond your years." Mia brushed a hand against Lauren's cheek.

"There's probably some truth to that," Lauren agreed. "I had to grow up fast for Craig's sake."

"Yes, you did."

"The rebound thing isn't ideal," Lauren admitted. "I think the percentage of rebound relationships that go sour is pretty high."

Mia's expression fell, and she nodded. "Probably."

"But statistics aren't people. They aren't us. Real life is

messy and complicated, and I think you and I could be wonderful together." She'd halfway talked herself into a relationship with Mia before reality came crashing back in. "But...what if I go to jail?"

Mia shook her head. "You aren't going to jail."

"But—"

Mia pressed a finger against Lauren's lips. "You won't, but *if* you did, I would wait for you, okay? I'm here for you, whether we're in a relationship or not, whether you go to jail or not. I'm here."

She sounded so calm, so sure, and Lauren couldn't breathe, because no one had ever said anything like that to her before. No one had been there for her, not even Craig, because he'd been too busy fighting his own demons. She exhaled roughly as tears spilled over her cheeks. "Mia..."

"I've got you." Mia brushed her tears away, her fingers warm and soft on Lauren's skin. "No matter what happens."

And maybe Lauren fell in love with her right then and there, but she couldn't think about that yet. "I've got your back too," she managed to whisper.

"I know." Mia's smile said she *did* know. She knew Lauren, and Lauren knew Mia, and how had they ever thought they wouldn't end up here, tumbling over the line from friends to lovers?

"So we're doing this, then?"

"Yes, but I think we need to take it slow," Mia said, "for the sake of our friendship and because we both have some pretty serious baggage."

Lauren nodded. Her head was in full agreement with Mia, but when she slid her gaze over that slinky black dress, it was all she could do not to run her hands over it, to haul Mia into her lap and indulge all the delicious chemistry that had been building between them. Right now, she was all too aware of just how long it had been since she'd had sex, and perhaps even more importantly, how long she'd been lusting after Mia.

"Don't look at me like that," Mia whispered. "That look is the opposite of taking things slow."

Lauren gave her a wicked grin. She felt slightly dizzy, like she'd blinked and entered an alternate reality where she and Mia kissed and flirted and confessed their feelings. "You can't wear a dress like that and not expect me to appreciate it, not now that you've kissed me."

Mia sucked in a breath, and the look on her face wasn't very innocent either. She looked like she wanted to press Lauren into the couch and fuck her senseless.

Lauren reached out and traced her fingers over the neckline of Mia's dress. It was made of a soft, stretchy material, probably very comfortable to wear, but right now, Lauren was more interested in how it felt beneath her fingers. "For the record, I'm in full agreement on taking things slow."

"Your fingers are not in agreement with your words." Mia's chest heaved beneath Lauren's roaming touch, and her nipples were hard beneath the shell of her bra.

"My fingers really want to get better acquainted with this dress. I'm not going to take it off you." She traced a line down the front of the dress, loving the warmth of Mia's skin beneath it, and then cupped Mia's breast over the fabric.

"Killing me," Mia breathed, arching her back to press herself more firmly into Lauren's touch.

"Remember how the dating site matched us?" Lauren asked as she circled Mia's nipple with her fingertips.

Mia nodded as her eyes slid shut. "I was frustrated by it at the time, when I was trying so hard not to be attracted to you. And you're outside the age range I'd selected."

"I told it I prefer older women," Lauren said. "Might be why."

"Might be," Mia agreed. "That site knew me better than I knew myself." She reached down and gripped Lauren's wandering hand. Before Lauren could protest, Mia tugged, pulling Lauren into her lap. "That's better," she murmured, sliding her hands around Lauren's waist.

"Much better." Lauren dipped her head and kissed her, spending several luxurious minutes in the pleasure of Mia's mouth before she pulled back. "I was secretly thrilled when it matched us, because I was already pretty smitten with you."

Mia smiled against her lips. "You hid it well."

"So did you. I really wasn't sure for the longest time."

"Until the night I got drunk at Dragonfly?" Mia cocked her head.

"You really don't remember, do you?"

Mia closed her eyes and drew in a slow breath. "I remember your lips and how much I wanted to kiss them, and I remember your breasts pressed against mine in the doorway. I was so afraid I'd done something inappropriate or made you feel uncomfortable."

Lauren traced Mia's lips as her own curved in a smile. "Oh, you did try to kiss me, but it didn't make me uncomfortable."

Mia frowned. "I'm still sorry. I shouldn't have done that."

"It's fine. You leaned in like you were going to kiss me, and when I interrupted you, you stopped. For the record, I only stopped you because you were drunk."

"I'm glad you did. It would have been a disaster if I'd kissed you that night, but speaking of the dating site, what do you say if we try to play this like we met on the site?"

"How so?" Lauren asked.

"Well, for starters, I'd like to take you on a date."

"Yes," Lauren whispered, leaning in for another kiss.

"Good." Mia's hands tightened on Lauren's waist, drawing her in until their breasts pressed together, much like they had that night in the doorway. And then she kissed her, slow and thorough, until Lauren could barely form coherent thoughts. Nothing existed but the pleasure of Mia's mouth and the need blazing in her core, heightened with every shift of her hips over Mia's.

Lauren took the opportunity to run her fingers through Mia's hair, familiarizing herself with its soft depths. She reveled in the way Mia whimpered when Lauren kissed the tender skin below her ear. She loved that Mia's gasping breaths sounded increasingly desperate and the way her fingers gripped Lauren's hips, dragging her ever closer.

"Okay, okay," Mia gasped as she broke the kiss. Her lips were puffy and pink, and a hot flush had spread over her chest. "This isn't taking it slow."

"Right." Regretfully, Lauren slid out of her lap. As much as she wanted to keep going, Mia was right to slow them down. Not even an hour ago, she'd been on a date with another woman.

"I…" Mia blinked at her out of lust-drunk eyes. "I should get changed out of this dress. Actually, I think I need a shower to cool off first." She leaned over to give Lauren another quick kiss, and then she stood and went into her bedroom, closing the door behind her.

Lauren just sat there, her body thrumming with desire and grinning so wide her cheeks hurt, because yeah, that really happened.

~

MIA STRIPPED out of her clothes, leaving her dress on the bathroom floor. Her fingers shook as she twisted the knob to turn on the shower. Her evening had taken a most unexpected—and *hot*—detour. She'd had such high hopes for her date with Beth, and it had been nothing but a disappointment. Now, here she was, so turned on, she could hardly think straight because of Lauren.

God, Lauren could kiss. Mia touched her lips. They were tender beneath her fingers, bruised from the intensity of what she and Lauren had shared. Deep down, Mia had worried her first kiss after Kristin might be awkward or even lackluster. After eighteen years, it was hard to remember what a first kiss even felt like.

She remembered now, and...well, she was pretty sure she'd never had a first kiss as intense or wonderful as this one. She stepped into the shower, exhaling as hot water rushed over her body. She'd intended to use the shower to cool off, but as the water teased her hypersensitive nipples, it only stoked the fire blazing inside her.

The ache in her core was unrelenting. Not only had it been over a year since she'd had sex, but she hadn't even had an orgasm since Lauren moved in. Lola was still demanding that Mia leave her bedroom door open at night, and she couldn't masturbate without privacy. Consequently, her make-out session with Lauren had left her desperate for release. Generally, she depended on her vibrator when she was alone, but right now, she was so worked up that her fingers should be more than enough to get the job done.

She slid her right hand between her thighs, bracing her left against the wall of the shower. A surge of electricity jolted her system as she made contact with her clit, and she barely held in a groan. Pressing her lips firmly together to keep herself quiet, she rubbed frantically, eager for relief and also to keep this quick so Lauren didn't realize what she was doing.

She luxuriated in the memory of their kiss, of Lauren's fingers on her skin and how it might feel if Lauren was touching her now. In minutes, Mia was gasping, hips jerking against her fingers as her orgasm rushed through her.

It wasn't that powerful, partly because she'd rushed things and partly because it had been a while. Still, she felt boneless with relief, hands braced against the tiles as muscles that had been coiled with tension finally relaxed. She could breathe freely now. She could think clearly. And she was grinning like an idiot.

Once she'd caught her breath, she rinsed off and stepped out of the shower. She dressed in lounge pants and a long-sleeved tee and towel-dried her hair. Then she went into the living room. Lauren sat where she'd left her, reading something on her phone.

"Better?" she asked.

Mia's cheeks burned before she realized Lauren was asking if she'd cooled off in the shower. She nodded, dropping onto the couch beside her. This was the potentially awkward part of dating a friend who was currently sharing her apartment. There was no separation, no chance to go home and decompress.

But she didn't want space right now. She was glad Lauren was here. It seemed Mia never got tired of spending time with her, although now she was hyperaware of the current running between them. It made her body hum as she sat beside her.

"Were you working on your book when I came in earlier?" she asked.

Lauren nodded. "I'm almost ready to send it to the editor

I hired. And Quinn offered to make me a cover. Shit's getting real."

"That's wonderful," Mia said. "Have you decided on a release date?"

Lauren shook her head. "I don't want to commit to anything until after my court date. Since I don't really have a following yet or anything, I think I'll just upload it when it's ready and see what happens."

"You do have a following," Mia countered. "You have so many readers from your fanfic, and I'm sure they'll want to support you as a published author too."

"You think?" Lauren asked, looking hesitant. "I wasn't sure whether to connect my published work to my fandom accounts."

"You can have separate social media accounts. I'm sure it's smart to brand everything to your pen name, but then you should share it on your fandom accounts so people can follow you and support your published work."

"I don't want to feel like I'm pressuring people to buy my book."

"You aren't," Mia assured her. "You're just letting them know about your book so they can buy it if they want. And I bet they will."

"Okay. Maybe you're right."

"I usually am." She nudged her elbow against Lauren's. "So how are you feeling about things? About going on a date with me?"

Lauren's smile was both bashful and joyous. "Pretty damn excited."

"Good. Me too." Mia realized she was smiling back at her. "Tomorrow night? We can celebrate Gilbert's adoption."

Now Lauren was beaming. "Yes. That sounds perfect."

17

Lauren sat with her back against the wall. Gilbert had curled himself in her lap, purring quietly as she stroked him below his chin. Darius would be here any minute to take him home. "You don't know it yet, but this is going to be a huge day for you."

Gilbert flicked an ear, watching her out of slitted eyes. She would miss seeing him here at the café, but mostly, she was just so thrilled that he'd found his forever home. She'd only been peripherally aware of the ins and outs of animal rescue before she started working here. Now she knew it was something she wanted to stay involved with.

"Ready?"

Lauren looked up to see Mia walking toward her. "So ready."

"Good." Mia sat at the table closest to where Lauren was sitting on the floor, looking absolutely stunning in a knee-length gray dress and black tights.

"How do you manage to wear clothes like that in here without the cats ruining them?"

Mia looked down, flicking cat hair from her dress. "For

starters, I don't sit on the floor. And I keep a stash of lint rollers in my desk."

"Still seems like they'd pull strings." Lauren patted one of Gilbert's paws, which was currently hooked into her jeans. All her pants had claw picks in them since she'd started working here.

"Oh, they do," Mia said. "I try not to let them sit in my lap if I'm wearing anything I'm particularly attached to, but I have a lot of business clothes from my days as a lawyer, so I figured I might as well wear them. Also, I guess I just like getting dressed for work. Makes me feel like I'm doing something worthwhile."

"Dressing like that is definitely worthwhile as far as I'm concerned," Lauren said, thrilled with the freedom to flirt with her. Sitting here in the café, it was almost surreal that she and Mia had made out on her couch last night, that they'd decided to give this thing between them a real try.

Mia smirked. "I know a good dim sum place nearby, if that sounds good for tonight."

"Sounds great." Lauren enjoyed most cuisines, and sharing small plates with Mia sounded fun and romantic.

"Perfect. I'll make a reservation."

"I can't wait," Lauren told her.

Mia had been a bright spot in her life for a while now, even before they'd met in person, and Lauren could hardly wait to see what would happen now that they were dating. Maybe it would blow up in their faces. But as she stared giddily into Mia's eyes, she couldn't feel anything but happy, excited, and hopeful. It had been so long since she'd felt any of those things that she wasn't going to second-guess a moment of this new step in their relationship.

The bell over the door chimed. Mia glanced in that

direction, then stood. "Darius is here, and it looks like his daughter is with him."

"It's your big moment, Gilbert." Lauren glanced at the cat curled in her lap, and then she looked toward the door to see Darius approaching with a little girl at his side. She had curly black hair and pink-rimmed glasses, and she was grinning from ear to ear. "You must be Kelsey," Lauren said as they approached. "I'm Lauren. I've heard so much about you. Sorry, I'd stand to greet you, but Gilbert's made himself comfortable on me."

Kelsey knelt beside Lauren. "He's so beautiful. Oh wow, look at his eyes."

The cat peered at her out of wide yellow eyes.

"They're really something, aren't they?" Lauren said.

"Yeah." Kelsey reached a tentative hand toward Gilbert. He sniffed her fingers, watching quietly as she gave him a rub. "He's so soft. Hi, Gilbert."

"I was planning to surprise her with him the next time she visited." Darius knelt beside Kelsey. "But my excitement got the better of me."

"And I'm glad, because I got to help my dad pick out all of Gilbert's new things," Kelsey said, still petting her new cat. She was as gentle as her dad said she would be. Gilbert licked her finger, and she giggled. "Plus, I get to be here to bring him home."

"I've got your copy of the adoption paperwork right here." Mia gestured to a folder on the table. "Everything's already settled with the rescue, so he's ready to go home."

Darius nodded. "Perfect."

"Do you mind if I take a photo of you with him for the adoption page?" Mia asked.

"Sure, that's fine," Darius agreed.

"Want me to hand him to you for the photo?" Lauren asked Kelsey.

"Yes." Kelsey sat cross-legged beside her, smiling so widely that Lauren could see the gap where she must have recently lost a tooth.

"Let's take one like this first," Darius said. "I think we'd like to remember the woman who helped us find our new cat."

Lauren's heart seemed to swell in her chest, and she knew her smile was beyond ridiculous when Mia aimed her phone at them. She was so happy, she was bursting with it. Darius crouched behind her while Kelsey leaned in close, one hand on Gilbert's back as she smiled for the camera.

After Mia had snapped a few pictures, Lauren lifted Gilbert and placed him in Kelsey's lap. He wasn't too thrilled about being moved without his permission, but Kelsey managed to hold on to him long enough for Mia to take a photo.

Then Mia lifted him into a cardboard carrier and secured the top. "He's all yours," she told Darius and Kelsey. "Send us some photos to let us know how he's settling in, and if you have any questions or concerns, just reach out to me here at the café or Wendy at the rescue."

"We'll do that." Darius reached for the crate, but Kelsey beat him to it.

She lifted it carefully before making a dramatic face. "He's heavy. You can carry him, Dad."

Everyone laughed, and then Darius and Kelsey were on their way. Lauren watched them go with happy tears in her eyes and warmth in her heart. As the door closed behind them, she was jolted out of her reverie by a hand on her arm.

"Come with me," Mia whispered in her ear. She took

Lauren's hand and led the way briskly down the hall to her office.

MIA SHUT the door to her office behind them before she pulled Lauren into her arms. They stood like that for several seconds while Mia breathed in the scent of her shampoo in Lauren's hair. Then Lauren tipped her face toward Mia's, and they were kissing.

Toward the end of their marriage, Mia and Kristin hadn't done much kissing. She couldn't remember the last time she made out with someone the way she and Lauren had done last night and again right now, but *God*, she should have been doing more of this.

She feathered her fingers over Lauren's cheeks as she explored her mouth, marveling at the way her body came alive every time they kissed. Her blood pumped hot and fast through her veins, and a warm ache grew between her thighs. Honestly, it was overwhelming how much she wanted Lauren. How had she gone so long without kissing her?

Lauren's hands were on Mia's waist, and even that simple touch lit her on fire. Mia pressed closer so that her breasts met Lauren's. In her heels, they were about the same height, and she loved it. She could kiss Lauren like this all day, but eventually, a need for oxygen drove them apart.

Mia rested her forehead against Lauren's as they both gasped for breath. She slid her hands down Lauren's back and held her close.

"Is this what you brought me into your office for?" Lauren asked breathlessly.

"Actually, I just wanted a minute alone to tell you how

amazing you were with Darius and Kelsey, but apparently, now that we've started kissing, I can't stop."

"I can't either." Lauren's cheeks were flushed, and her smile was radiant.

"You're a natural, both with the cats and with the adopters. That's what I brought you in here to tell you."

"I love working with them," Lauren said. "I want to get more involved in animal rescue."

"You should," Mia agreed. "You may have found your calling, or do you miss bartending?"

Lauren shrugged. "I enjoy interacting with customers, but I do that as much here as I did when I was tending bar, and now I get to work with the animals too. It's more rewarding."

Mia clasped her hands behind Lauren's back, holding her close. "I'm glad."

"I'm so happy," Lauren whispered, and when she tipped her face toward Mia's, tears glistened in her eyes.

Mia felt a jolt in the pit of her stomach at the raw honesty in Lauren's words. "Me too. I've been happy since you moved into my apartment."

"Really?" Lauren asked.

Mia nodded. "It should be annoying, having someone sleep on my couch, but it hasn't been, not for a single moment."

"I'll be off your couch next week," Lauren reminded her.

Mia's arms tightened around her. "And I'm not entirely happy about that."

"Well, I am. Not that I haven't enjoyed sharing your apartment, because I have, *so* much, but I need to do this for myself. I need to stand on my own two feet again. It's important to me, and it's probably good for us too. It might be a strain on our relationship if we were working *and* living together. It'll be good to have a little separation."

"It could be a strain. It *should* be, but somehow I haven't gotten sick of you yet," Mia said, dipping her head to give Lauren another kiss.

"And this way, you still won't."

"Still won't like it either." Mia kept kissing her, drunk off the feel of Lauren's lips on hers and the way her whole body rejoiced every time they touched.

"It'll be good for us. I promise," Lauren insisted.

If Mia had been able to think logically right now, she knew she would agree. It was important for Lauren to have equal footing in their relationship, for her to achieve the goals she'd set for herself when she came back to Brooklyn.

Mia had never experienced anything like this before. She and Lauren just seemed perfectly in sync. They worked well together. They lived well together. And if their kisses were any indication, they were going to be pretty damn compatible in the bedroom too. How could they possibly not be?

"I really need to get back out there," Lauren murmured against her lips. "There isn't an employee in the cat enclosure right now."

"So responsible." Mia gave her one more indulgent kiss before she released her and took a step back. "Fine, you get back to work, and I'm going to make our dinner reservations."

"You got it, Boss Lady." Lauren gave her a goofy smile.

Mia flinched. "Is that weird? Me being your boss? I didn't really think about that in terms of our relationship."

"Nah. I'm only working here part-time, and I've always been looking for a full-time job somewhere else. I think of you more as a friend than my boss."

"Well, for the record, I'll do my best to make sure nothing to do with our relationship affects your job, and if you ever feel like it is, please tell me."

"I will, but I just can't see it being a problem. I mean, I'm only here a few afternoons a week. You don't hold my career in your hands or anything. Now, I'm off to hang with the cats." She pressed her lips against Mia's, and then she left her office.

Mia walked around behind her desk and sat. Her head was spinning in the most wonderful way. This thing with Lauren had knocked her sideways, but it didn't feel like she was off track. Instead, it felt like she'd been spinning in circles and now she was finally moving in the right direction.

LAUREN DISCOVERED one downside of living with the woman she was dating when she went upstairs to get dressed for dinner that night. She and Mia would have to get ready for their date together in the same apartment, which took some of the mystery out of things, but honestly, she didn't really care, because she was *that* excited for their date.

She spent a lot more time than usual in the bathroom, getting ready. She didn't have many wardrobe choices right now, so she put on her nicest black pants with a gray top that plunged in the front, accenting it with a simple silver necklace. She fussed with her hair, touched up her makeup, and then she headed back into the living room.

Mia was in her bedroom with the door closed, so Lauren sat on the couch and picked up her phone. And then she gasped because she had an email from Quinn with the subject "Cover concept — I hope you love it!" Lauren stared at her phone, heart pounding in anticipation of seeing her first book cover. She didn't open the email yet, though. Instinctively, she wanted to wait and share the moment with Mia.

Lauren's knees bounced with nervous excitement as she waited for her. A few minutes later, the bedroom door opened, and Mia stepped out, wearing a sapphire-blue dress that draped elegantly over her curves. Her hair was pulled back from her face, emphasizing her cheekbones and her pink lips, and *wow*.

"I'm so glad you saved that dress for our date, because I don't know how I would have possibly hidden how much I love it if you'd been wearing it for someone else. Seriously, you look so gorgeous," Lauren gushed as she stood. She'd had to hide her feelings while Mia dressed up for so many other dates, and it was unbelievably freeing to be able to tell her how beautiful she looked tonight.

"Thank you." Mia's eyes sparkled as she walked toward her.

Lauren didn't even notice Mia had a hand behind her back until she brought it forward, holding out a bouquet of flowers.

"Oh," Lauren gasped as she stared at the flowers, a mixture of fall colors with some greenery mixed in. They were so pretty, and the woman holding them was even prettier, and Lauren had completely lost the ability to form words.

"You look fantastic," Mia said as she gave Lauren the flowers.

Lauren closed her fingers around the paper sheath surrounding the bouquet. There were red roses and orange flowers that might be lilies and several others she couldn't identify by name. She bent her head and inhaled, intoxi-cated by their scent.

"Do you like them?" Mia asked, reminding Lauren she still hadn't said anything.

She looked up, blinking away the moisture in her eyes. "I love them. They're...they're so beautiful. No one's ever given me flowers before. Thank you."

Mia reached out to touch Lauren's necklace, her fingers brushing against the delicate skin of her neck. "In that case, I might have to find more excuses to buy them for you."

"When did you get them?" Lauren asked, cradling the flowers in her arms.

"I snuck out for a few minutes this afternoon."

"That's so romantic." She stepped forward to press a kiss against Mia's lips, the scent of fresh flowers mixing with Mia's freshly applied perfume. Here she'd been worried that getting ready together in the same apartment would take something away from their date, and Mia had still managed to surprise her in the most wonderful way. "You really made my night with these flowers, Mia. I love them so much."

"I'm glad," Mia said, looking awfully pleased with herself.

Tonight could have been weird or awkward. Their friendship had undergone a monumental shift since Mia went out with Beth last night. But it didn't feel weird or awkward at all. On the contrary, neither of them seemed to be able to stop smiling.

"Here, I'll get you a vase." Mia walked to the kitchen and pulled a slender glass vase out of one of the top cabinets. She filled it halfway with water and showed Lauren how to mix in the packet of plant food that had been tucked in among the stems.

Lauren snipped the stems and spent a few minutes

arranging the flowers in the vase, adjusting them this way and that. She was mesmerized by how pretty they looked. "Gorgeous," she said as she carried the vase to the kitchen table.

Mia smiled. "Ready?"

"Yes." Lauren looked around for her jacket, then froze. "Wait! I almost forgot. Quinn sent me a cover concept, but I was waiting for you so we could look together."

"Oh, exciting! Let's see it." Mia moved to stand beside her.

Lauren pulled out her phone and clicked on the email, and then she held her breath as the image loaded. This was a moment. Her first book cover. Her first bouquet of flowers. Her first date with Mia. So many firsts tonight, Lauren's head was spinning.

The cover showed a woman's silhouette from behind, backlit by the glow of the city. Her hair billowed behind her, and a crescent moon and a canopy of stars lit the night sky above her. The title, *Meet Me at Midnight*, was overlaid in a swirly font. And there was Lauren's pen name at the bottom of the cover. Lauren White. Her breath caught in her throat.

"It's beautiful," Mia said. "It fits the tone of the book perfectly, and the image is so eye-catching."

"Yes," Lauren whispered. "I love it."

Mia wrapped an arm around her shoulders. "How does it feel, seeing your cover?"

"Big," Lauren said. "Like a 'remember when' moment. I think it feels a little more real now that I'm going to be a published author."

"And soon," Mia said.

Lauren nodded, still staring at the cover. She hadn't had a clear idea of what she wanted when she started chatting with Quinn about it, but Quinn had come through in amazing fashion. This was perfect. Lauren wouldn't change a thing. "Let me just send Quinn a quick text to tell her how much I love it, and then we'll go."

"Sure. No rush."

Lauren sat on the couch, tears in her eyes as she texted Quinn, using an abundance of exclamation points and emojis. Once she'd sent the text, she looked up to a most distracting view of Mia's ass as she bent to fill Lola's food dish.

"I'm ready," Lauren said.

Mia straightened, turning to face her. "Let's go, then."

Lauren zipped her jacket while Mia put on a black coat that belted at the waist. Then she extended her arm. Lauren hooked her arm through Mia's like it was the most natural thing in the world, like she'd done it a million times, and together, they headed out on their first date.

18

Mia tapped her wineglass against Lauren's. "To our first date and your first book cover."

Lauren was luminous tonight. With the added effect of the candle flickering on the table between them, she seemed to glow with happiness, and Mia couldn't look away. How had she ever thought she'd find someone more interesting, more beautiful, more *anything* than Lauren?

Mia had been so afraid of damaging their friendship that she'd ignored what was right in front of her. Already, she was having a better time than she'd had on any of her other dates.

"The first of many," Lauren said. "Many dates and many books. I'm calling it right now."

"Agreed." Mia tasted her wine. They'd chosen a bottle of rosé to share, and it was good, crisp and fruity. "Any idea what you'll write next?"

"I have a few ideas," Lauren told her. "I've got notes in my phone, random thoughts I've jotted down over the years when something inspired me. All sapphic romance, all set here in the city. I'd love to do an enemies-to-lovers romance next, or maybe rivals-to-lovers between two lawyers, sort of vaguely inspired by *In Her Defense*."

"I'll read anything you write, but I really like that second idea. Plus, you've got me as your legal expert."

Lauren grinned. "That *is* handy."

The waiter brought out their first few dishes: mooncakes, Sichuan cucumber salad, and edamame ginger dumplings, along with dumpling sauce and a red pepper paste. Mia's stomach rumbled as the savory scent of the food reached her.

"Oh, wow," Lauren said. "This looks amazing."

"And it tastes just as good as it looks," Mia told her. "I've been coming here for years."

"How spicy is this pepper paste?" Lauren asked as she dabbed some of it onto her plate.

"Very spicy. Proceed with caution," Mia told her with a laugh.

"I like it hot," Lauren said, then blushed, probably having realized how that sounded.

Warmth spread through Mia's belly, and she hadn't even touched the pepper sauce yet. "Good to know."

Lauren darted a glance at Mia as she reached for a dumpling. "Sometimes it hits me, you know? That I'm flirting with *you*."

"Yes, we've undergone a seismic shift in twenty-four hours. It's jarring sometimes, but maybe not as often as it should be? Mostly, it just feels right." Mia unwrapped her chopsticks and added some of the cucumber salad to her plate.

"Yeah. Exactly that." Lauren nodded emphatically. "I mean, I'd been fighting my feelings for a while, so maybe that's why. It's like *phew*, I can finally just feel what I feel."

"How long?" Mia asked, suddenly curious. She'd been in such denial about the whole thing that she hadn't even picked up on whatever signals Lauren had apparently been sending.

"Um." A red flush spread over Lauren's chest, and she hadn't eaten any of the pepper sauce yet either. "All my cards on the table?"

"Yes," Mia responded immediately.

"The day we met," Lauren admitted. "I was walking behind you on the way to the Airbnb, and I was checking you out, before I knew who you were. You'd cut your hair, and I didn't recognize you from behind."

"Oh." Mia blinked, reaching for her wine. "Really? That night?"

Lauren nodded, looking embarrassed. "That night, it was more like 'wow, she's hotter in person than I expected,' but yeah, there was an attraction for me right from the start."

"Wow." Mia let that sink in for a moment. She'd had no idea, and she certainly hadn't been looking at Lauren as anything but a friend that weekend.

"Now your turn. Lay it on me."

"There wasn't a definitive moment for me," Mia told her. "It was more of a gradual realization, and one that I tried very hard not to acknowledge, because I was afraid of the ramifications. I think the moment of no return was the night I got drunk at Dragonfly. I woke up the next morning, and I couldn't even look at you without wanting to kiss you."

As she looked at Lauren now, she felt the same damn way.

"Yeah, you were pretty blatant about wanting to kiss me that night," Lauren said with a giggle. "It was the first time

I'd ever imagined you might feel that way about me, but I wasn't sure if it was just the alcohol talking."

"Now you know." Mia picked up a bite of salad with her chopsticks.

"Now I know," Lauren agreed with a grin as she smeared pepper paste on her dumpling. She took a bite, seeming unaffected by the heat. Interesting.

Mia took a dumpling for herself. "So you're moving next weekend?"

Lauren nodded. "Saturday, so yeah, a week from today. I'm working at the café until two, and then I'll go pick up my keys. I need to do a little apartment shopping between now and then. I don't need much since it's furnished, probably just bedding and towels and maybe some decorative accents."

"That's the fun part of moving." Mia tamped down her discomfort about Lauren's new rental arrangement or how much she inherently disliked the idea of Lauren leaving her apartment at all. "Picking out new things."

"Yes," Lauren agreed. "I can't have pets, but maybe I can get a plant or something. I've always wanted one of those cute little plants that come in the decorative pots."

"A bonsai?" Mia asked.

"No," Lauren said with a contemplative look. "The ones that look...squishy?"

"A succulent?"

"Yes!" Lauren exclaimed. "One of those."

Mia smiled as she bit into her dumpling, picturing Lauren in her new room with a little succulent on the table by her bed. Maybe she'd give her one as a housewarming gift. She'd seen them in the flower shop around the corner where she'd bought Lauren's bouquet earlier.

They polished off their food and ordered a few more

small plates to share while they chatted about everything from Lauren's book to the new foster cat who'd be arriving at the café tomorrow. Mia loved the constant influx of new cats, watching them blossom and find their forever homes, and Lauren seemed to feel the same way.

Not everyone was cut out for fostering. It required a certain level of detachment from the animals, or at least it did for Mia. She never thought of them as hers or allowed herself to bond with them on more than a superficial level. Nothing like her bond with Lola. But Lauren seemed to get attached, especially to Gilbert, and yet she was always overjoyed when one of the cats went home with their new family.

Mia was endlessly impressed with her, and not just at the café. Lauren had worked hard to get her life back on track, and she was succeeding. She was thriving, and Mia loved watching it happen. They made their way through shrimp dumplings and sticky rice balls, and then Mia insisted on paying the check since she'd been the one to invite Lauren to dinner.

As they walked outside, she turned to Lauren with a coy smile. "Forgive me if this is too forward for a first date, but... would you like to come back to my place for a drink?"

Lauren gave her an incredulous look, and then she burst out laughing. "I don't know, Mia, I'd have *such* a long walk home afterward."

LAUREN WALKED beside Mia as they headed back to her apartment. The night had grown unexpectedly cold while they were inside the restaurant, and she shivered, stuffing her hands into her pockets. The street glowed with lights from surrounding businesses. Here and there, people had strung orange lights to celebrate the season, and pumpkins adorned their doorways.

Mia hooked her arm through Lauren's as they walked. "I had a really nice time tonight."

"Me too." Lauren stepped to the side, bumping her shoulder against Mia's.

"Best date I've had all month."

"Same," Lauren told her with a cheeky smile.

Mia raised her eyebrows. "It's the *only* date you've been on this month."

"Doesn't matter. Even if I'd been on as many dates as you have, this would still be my favorite."

Mia leaned in, brushing her lips against Lauren's. "You know just what to say to make a lady swoon."

"Still pretty giddy about being able to kiss you like this," Lauren murmured against her lips. They stumbled to a stop on the sidewalk, stepping out of the way as they kissed. Mia's hands framed her face, a habit of hers that Lauren was starting to notice, and she loved that she'd kissed her enough times now to know these things.

"You can kiss me any time you like," Mia said, "because I can't seem to get enough."

"That's lucky since I feel the same way."

Mia groaned as her tongue delved into Lauren's mouth. She was a passionate kisser, a woman who kissed like she enjoyed the act of kissing itself and not just as a precursor to sex. Lauren wasn't sure she'd ever experienced that before.

They kissed for long minutes, until Lauren had forgotten the chill of the October air, and honestly, she wasn't sure she remembered anything but the magic of Mia's mouth. How did she do that? How did she make every kiss the best kiss

Lauren had ever experienced? Or was this what it felt like to kiss someone you really cared about?

Mia lifted her head, giving Lauren a dazed smile as the breeze whipped wayward blonde strands across her face. "Come on, let's go home."

"Yes," Lauren agreed, and although she was glad "home" meant Mia's apartment for both of them tonight, she was also glad she was moving into her own place soon. It would put them on more equal footing as they took this step in their relationship.

Mia slipped a hand in hers, and they started to walk. "I'm still thinking about that book cover of yours. Quinn is really talented."

"She is. I'm so lucky to know her."

"And I think she feels the same way about you. It's great to see you all sharing your creative talents with each other. I for one can't wait to have a copy of *Meet Me at Midnight* on my bookshelf."

Lauren's head was spinning from a combination of their kisses and the thought of releasing her first book. Last year this time, she'd been hiding in Rhode Island with Craig as her life fell apart. Now, Craig was gone, but in so many other ways, Lauren's life was finally coming together. It was so unfair that he hadn't gotten the same chance.

Tears blurred her vision, and the breath whooshed from her lungs as grief wrapped itself tightly around her chest.

"Hey, what just happened?" Mia stopped walking, again tugging her to the edge of the sidewalk.

"It just hit me that Craig won't be here to see my book release." She swiped at the dampness under her eyes. "I've got a new apartment, a new girlfriend, my book's about to be published...all these amazing things, and he's not here."

"Oh, Lauren." Mia wrapped her arms around her. "I'm so sorry. You're right. It's not fair."

"I miss him so much." She pressed her face against Mia's jacket and hugged her back.

"Of course you do. I've heard you talk to his urn. Does that help?"

"Sometimes." Lauren exhaled into Mia's jacket, closing her eyes. "I'm not religious, so I don't really know where I think he is now, but talking to him does seem to help me feel closer to him."

"I have pretty complicated views on religion," Mia said, stroking her fingers through Lauren's hair. "I was raised Catholic, but then Catholicism cost me my relationship with my mother. I do like to think Craig hears you, though, wherever he is, and that he knows about these positive things going on in your life."

"It's a nice thought," Lauren whispered.

"It is." Mia's fingers kept stroking her hair, and it was so soothing.

"Sorry for ruining the mood on our first date."

Mia's arms tightened around her. "You haven't ruined anything. Are you kidding me? There's nowhere I'd rather be than right here with you, tears and all. This is what real life looks like, and I'm glad to share it with you."

Warmth filled Lauren's chest, and she lifted her head, peering at Mia through damp eyes. "You always know just what to say."

"I'm not feeding you a line," Mia said, her gaze unflinchingly direct and sincere.

"I know. I feel the same way about you." Deep thoughts for a first date, but everything about her relationship with Mia just felt like *more*.

"Come on. Let's go home." Mia tucked her arm around

Lauren's waist as they started walking again. "What do you want to do this evening? I feel like we need plans before we just make out on the couch all night...not that I don't enjoy making out with you."

"But it gets frustrating after a while."

"Exactly," Mia said with a laugh that was almost a groan. "Remember when you offered to clear out of the apartment so I could bring women home with me, and I told you I wasn't ready for that? I wasn't kidding. My body is very, *very* ready to have you in my bed, but my head's not."

"Honestly, we only kissed for the first time yesterday," Lauren said. "Sleeping together tonight would be moving super fast. Not to mention, you were on a date with someone else yesterday. We need time to adjust to this, I think."

"Yes," Mia agreed.

"I've had casual hookups before, but that's not what I want with you."

"I'm not a hookup kind of woman, sorry to say," Mia said.

"And this isn't a hookup kind of relationship." She gave Mia's fingers a squeeze.

They turned the corner onto Mia's street, walking quietly for the last few minutes of their journey. Upstairs, they took turns in the bathroom, washing up and changing into more comfortable clothes.

"Have you seen Piper Sheridan's new movie?" Lauren asked when Mia joined her on the couch, face damp and wearing her favorite lounge pants. "*Tempted*. It's a romcom with Landon Wilkes."

"Nope." Mia leaned in to give her a kiss. "Is it good?"

"So good," Lauren confirmed. "And she looks super hot in it. Want to watch it tonight?"

"I'd love to." Mia gestured for Lauren to move closer, so they were snuggled against each other on the couch. Then she picked up the remote control and tabbed through screens until she'd rented the movie.

Lauren turned sideways, her head resting against Mia's chest. Lola hopped up to join them, curling herself into the bend of Lauren's legs. She sighed in contentment, smiling as Piper appeared on the screen with all those glossy red curls.

"Should I be jealous of the way you're looking at Piper Sheridan right now?" Mia asked as she wrapped an arm around Lauren, drawing her closer.

"Nope. My celebrity crushes are more of a fantasy, if that makes sense. I think she's beautiful and talented, and I have a lot of respect for her as a person, but I don't really know her. You're the person I want to kiss and be with."

"I've always wondered about that," Mia said. "The way some of you guys talk about Piper in our chat, I feel like you'd fling yourselves at her if you ever had the chance."

"More like grovel at her feet," Lauren said. "I just want to tell her how much I admire her as an actress, and how I appreciate seeing her being out and proud and kissing women onscreen."

"She must live here in New York, right? Don't they film *In Her Defense* here?"

"She does, but so do a lot of celebrities, and I've never bumped into any of them on the street," Lauren said. "Have you?"

Mia chuckled. "I probably wouldn't know if I did. Looking for celebrities is the furthest thing from my mind when I'm walking."

"I wonder how many celebrities I've walked right by and just didn't notice. I mean, if they're in jeans and sunglasses, I probably wouldn't give them a second glance. I feel like I'd recognize Piper, though. That red hair is awfully distinctive."

"It is," Mia agreed.

Lauren relaxed against her with a smile. Her gaze caught on Craig's urn on the shelf, and a pang of her earlier sadness returned, but it was dulled now by her overall sense of contentment, cuddled up with Mia and watching one of her favorite movies. This time, her eyes stayed dry.

On the screen, Piper's character was relating a terrible first date to her best friend, the man she'd realize she was in love with before the end of the movie. Mia laughed, and Lauren turned her head to watch her, mesmerized by how pretty she looked in these unguarded moments, at home on the couch in her pajamas.

"Friends to lovers, hm?" Mia said. "Sounds familiar."

Lauren grinned, because yeah, she'd listened to Mia tell her about plenty of terrible first dates recently. "I wasn't even thinking about that when I suggested the movie, but yep."

Mia's hand slid beneath Lauren's top, resting against the bare skin above her leggings. As they watched the movie, her fingers rubbed gently back and forth, exploring Lauren's skin in a most deliciously distracting way. Her hand gradually roamed farther until she brushed against the underside of Lauren's bare breast.

Lauren's libido jumped for joy, a hot thrill racing over her skin, and Mia sucked in a breath. She lingered there for a moment before cupping Lauren's breast in her hand.

"Not playing fair, going braless when I'm trying to resist you," Mia said, her voice low and rough.

"We're basically in our pajamas. You mean to tell me you're wearing a bra right now?" Lauren asked, rolling toward her, but careful not to displace her hand.

Mia cocked an eyebrow at her. "Wouldn't you like to know?"

"Yep, I would." Lauren's gaze dropped to Mia's breasts, hidden beneath her oversized T-shirt. She slid a hand up Mia's side, encountering a soft cotton band against her ribs, like a sports bra. She gave it a gentle tug. "I honestly can't believe you're wearing this to watch a movie on the couch with me."

Mia groaned. She shifted to lie on her back, drawing Lauren on top of her. She landed with her legs threaded between Mia's, and oh yes, this was a nice development. As she brought her lips to Mia's, she slipped one of her hands under Mia's shirt to explore her breasts over that cotton bra.

"Killing me," Mia murmured as her hands slid down Lauren's back to her ass, pressing her closer.

"Hey, you started it." Lauren had been minding her business, watching the movie until Mia felt her up, and now... now her pulse was skipping happily through her veins, and warmth bloomed everywhere her body touched Mia's.

"Guilty," Mia whispered before crushing her lips against Lauren's. Her nipples had tightened beneath Lauren's touch, and her chest heaved as she lost herself in the kiss.

They kissed as the movie carried on without them, laughter and conversation from the television mixed with their gasps and giggles and the wet sound of their kisses. Lauren's heart felt full, her body flushed with heat, and when tears filled her eyes this time, they were the happy kind. Mia's fingers brushed them gently from her cheeks.

"You okay?" she asked, wrapping Lauren in a warm hug.

"I'm wonderful," she whispered, pressing her face against Mia's neck so she could breathe her in while she got her emotions—and her libido—under control. She rolled to the side, and they lay like that for what remained of the movie, holding each other close, content even if they weren't entirely relaxed due to the unspent desire charging the air between them.

When the movie ended, Mia shut off the TV. "I might need to watch it again when I'm not so distracted."

"True, although I might just distract you again."

19

On the following Saturday morning, Lauren moved into her new apartment. It was bittersweet as she packed her things to leave Mia's, but she knew she needed to do this for herself, even if she ended up moving back at some point in the future.

"Leave a few things here?" Mia had asked as she packed. "In case you want to spend the night sometime."

Lauren had agreed, and now she had a few clothes tucked into one of Mia's drawers and a toothbrush in the bathroom...just in case. But this morning was all about making her new room *hers*. She started with the bed, putting on the sheets she'd purchased yesterday, which were a vibrant aqua that matched the stripes on her new blanket.

"Can you believe it?" she whispered, her gaze darting to the urn on the dresser. "My own room. I'm winning at adulting this month, Craig." She knew it was time to let him go, but with November only a few days away, she'd made the unofficial decision to wait until spring. She'd spread his ashes in their favorite park among green leaves and flowers, not in the barren cold of winter. In the meantime, he'd stay with her in her new apartment.

Once the bed was made, she put her clothes in the dresser. She didn't have a closet, but she didn't have anything that needed to be hung anyway. There was a hook on the wall for her coat, and that was enough. She hung her new curtains, filled every inch of every drawer, stuffed a few things under the bed, and voila...her room was complete.

She sat on the bed and looked around. The bare white walls could use some art. She'd work on that next. A few inexpensive prints ought to brighten the place up. The room might be small, but it already felt warm and inviting, and once she added a few accents, it would really feel like hers. She lay back on the bed and closed her eyes.

She'd shared a room most of her life. Even last year in Rhode Island, she and Craig had shared a studio apartment. It hadn't been ideal, but they'd made it work for the sake of their limited budget. There had been so many moments over the years when she'd yearned for the ability to close a door and be alone. Now she had it.

Lauren took several luxurious minutes just lying in bed, listening to the world around her. She could hear cars driving by outside and the occasional blast of a horn. Water ran through a pipe somewhere overhead, and the rhythmic beat of music thumped softly through the walls. Her roommates moved about on the other side of her door, laughing and talking.

She'd go out and join them in a minute, but first, she needed to revel in this moment by herself. She bounced lightly, testing the mattress. It was surprisingly comfortable, a lot more comfortable than Mia's couch, although she'd loved every moment she spent on it, because it meant being near Mia. Also, it had been a safe, dependable place to sleep, and that was never something she'd taken for granted.

She missed Mia already, and more than that, she missed the comfort of sharing the apartment with her. But she'd be back to visit soon enough, and in the meantime, Mia was stopping by this morning to see Lauren's new place.

After a few minutes of happy daydreaming, she got up and opened her door. She followed the sound of voices to the living room, where she found Tariq and Eliot on the couch together, watching the *Great British Baking Show* or something similar. Lauren wasn't familiar enough with the show to be sure.

"All settled?" Tariq asked when he saw her.

"Yep. I didn't have much to unpack."

"Did we show you the color-coding system for the fridge?" Eliot asked, glancing at her before returning his attention to the contestant painstakingly decorating a cake.

"Yeah, briefly when I came to look at the place," she said.

He nodded. "There's a chart on the fridge door, but basically we each have a color. You're purple. Put one of those little stickers on everything that's yours. Anything without a sticker is fair game for anyone who wants it."

"Got it," she said. "How do you usually handle meals?"

Tariq shrugged. "We fend for ourselves mostly. Eliot and I cook together a lot, but Harmony mostly keeps to herself."

"Would I be stepping on any toes if I cooked something for the whole apartment tonight?" Lauren asked. "Nothing fancy. I was thinking about lasagna."

Tariq grinned at her. "I don't think anyone would complain about that."

"Great." She returned his smile. She wanted to make a good first impression on her new roommates, and this would be a chance to get to know them too.

"Harmony's a vegetarian, FYI," Eliot told her.

"Good to know. But she does eat cheese?"

"Might want to check," Eliot said.

"I'll do that. Thanks." She went down the hall to Harmony's room. The door was closed. Soft music came from behind it, probably the source of the beat Lauren had heard in her own room. She knocked.

The music got quieter, and a few moments later, the door opened a crack. Harmony peered out. Her hair was hidden under an orange beanie. "Yeah?"

"Hi," Lauren said. "I was thinking about making lasagna for dinner, but Eliot mentioned you're a vegetarian, so I just wanted to check on dietary restrictions."

Harmony's brow furrowed. "You're making dinner for all of us? Why?"

Lauren shrugged. "Just a way to get to know my new roommates. I'm not much of a cook, but I enjoy making simple things. Comfort food."

"Cool. I like lasagna, as long as it doesn't have meat in it."

"Cheese is okay, though?"

"Yep." Harmony stepped back as if she was about to close the door in Lauren's face, pausing at the last moment. "Thanks for checking."

"Welcome." Lauren smiled as she headed down the hall. Harmony's abruptness didn't bother her. She didn't seem rude, probably just shy or cynical of others. Lauren sat in a chair at the kitchen table and started putting together a shopping list using the notes app in her phone.

Mia should be here soon, and when she left, Lauren would go pick up some groceries. As if she'd summoned her with her thoughts, the buzzer rang, and Lauren leaped up to answer it. She pressed the button on the intercom.

"Hi," she said. "Mia, is that you?"

"It's me," Mia's voice came through the intercom.

"Come on up. 3B is at the end of the hall when you come off the stairs," Lauren told her before pushing the button to unlock the front door.

"Having friends over already?" Eliot asked. "Remember the rules about parties and quiet hours."

"Oh, I'm not a partier, and I won't have many people over at all, I promise. My girlfriend just wanted to stop by and see the place."

"That's fine." Eliot returned his attention to the show.

Lauren hadn't lived anywhere with as many rules as this apartment, but she welcomed it. She would be glad to keep things orderly and respectful here, and after her experience at the hostel earlier this fall, the promise of quiet when she was trying to sleep sounded amazing.

She heard Mia's shoes on the stairs and pulled the door open to greet her just as Mia was coming down the hall toward the apartment. She wore her burgundy jacket over black pants and was carrying a pink gift bag, which immediately had Lauren's heart doing all kinds of lovestruck cartwheels in her chest. "Hi. Long time, no see."

"It's been *hours*," Mia said with a dramatic sigh, her lips curving in a smile. "I miss you already."

"You'll see me tomorrow at the café, and maybe I can cook dinner at your place after work?" Lauren said, motioning her into the apartment.

"Yes," Mia agreed, smiling politely at Lauren's roommates.

"That's Tariq and Eliot," Lauren said. "Guys, this is my girlfriend, Mia."

"Hi, Mia," Tariq called. "Nice to meet you." Eliot echoed the sentiment.

"It's their apartment, but they rent out their spare rooms

to help with the rent. Mine's the first one here on the left," Lauren explained as she led the way down the hall. "Harmony's room is on the other side of mine." She opened the door to her room. "What do you think?"

Mia stepped into her room, turning in a full circle to take it in. "As small as you'd described, but nicer than I was expecting."

"I'm glad," Lauren said. "And Tariq and Eliot seem really serious about their rules, so I don't think you have to worry about me here."

"Good." Mia held out the gift bag. "A little housewarming gift."

"Thank you." Lauren accepted it as warmth flooded her cheeks. She'd never had a girlfriend give her random "just because" gifts the way Mia did, and it felt impossibly good. She sat on the bed to open it, patting the blanket beside her.

Mia sat as Lauren tugged at the tissue paper to reveal a brown paper box inside, the kind that might contain a cake or pastry. Intrigued, she lifted it out of the gift bag and unfolded the top. A small plant with perfect squishy leaves was nestled inside, held in place by a cardboard piece with a round cutout in the center to keep it from sliding around in the box.

"Oh," Lauren gasped as she reached down and touched the plant with her fingertips. The leaves were just as soft and smooth as she'd imagined they would be. "The little squishy plant I wanted."

"A succulent," Mia said with an amused smile. "This one is called echeveria, but the variety is called Lola, which seemed kind of fitting."

"My very own Lola." Lauren carefully removed the plant from the box, revealing the dark purple pot that housed it. Its leaves were arranged in a neat circular pattern, radiating out from the center of the plant, almost like a flower. It was a pale green, but some of the leaves took on a lavender hue. "Mia, I love it."

"I'm glad. It should be an extremely low maintenance first pet."

Lauren grinned. "Just what I need. I'm going to put Lola on the windowsill. Does she like sunshine?"

"I think she does." Mia waited until she'd set the plant by the window, then reached for Lauren, pulling her into a leisurely kiss. Lauren scooted closer, resting a hand on Mia's thigh.

When they came up for air, Lauren couldn't contain her smile.

"Hey, I have a question for you," Mia said. "I know it's a bit early, but do you have plans for Thanksgiving?"

"I usually volunteer at the shelter and eat there afterward." Lauren felt her smile fade. This would be her first holiday since losing Craig, and it was going to be hard. Christmas would be even harder. They hadn't always seen each other on holidays, and even when they had, the situation had often sucked. But still, she'd known he was out there, and they had snuck out to meet each other at their oak tree when they could. This year...

"Would you like to come to my dad's with me?" Mia asked. "And before you say I'm moving too fast, I was going to ask you as a friend before we were dating. He and Addie have always welcomed anyone and everyone to their house at Thanksgiving."

"Oh, I don't know." Lauren dropped her gaze to her lap, skin prickling with a confusing mix of emotions. "I like volunteering at the shelter."

"What if I volunteer there with you, and then we go to my dad's together after?"

"I..." Lauren pursed her lips, still not meeting Mia's eyes.

"It's fine if you don't want to. I just wanted to ask. My dad called this morning and started talking about Thanksgiving, and he asked if I would be bringing anyone." Mia paused. "Although we don't have to tell him we're dating. You could just come as my friend if that takes some of the pressure off."

"Maybe." Lauren finally looked up. "Look, the truth is that I've never really done a family Thanksgiving before. We had turkey when I was a kid if my mom was sober enough to remember to buy one, but it was never anything like those scenes you see on TV."

"Then you should definitely come." Mia reached out and covered Lauren's hand in hers. "My dad and Addie do a TV-worthy spread, but it's all very casual. Lots of food. Lots of laughter. Lots of people. Absolutely no expectations. Plus, it means you get to spend the holiday with me."

"Well, I don't see how I could possibly say no to that."

Mia spent a restless night at her apartment without Lauren, and consequently, she wasn't in the best mood as she opened the café on Sunday morning. It was silly how much she missed Lauren already, even though she knew logically that this was a good move for them both. Lauren needed her own space, and it was healthy to have a certain amount of separation as they settled into a relationship together.

If they'd kept on as they were, working and living together while newly dating, it might have blown up in their faces. Not to mention, it was awkward relationship-wise for Lauren to be sleeping on the couch. If—or hopefully *when* —Lauren moved back in, she'd be sharing Mia's bed.

Mia grumbled under her breath as she cleaned up after the cats, freshened their food, water, and litter, and swept the café area before she opened it to customers. This was one of her least favorite parts of the job and one she passed off to her employees whenever possible.

When Lauren opened with her, she always seemed so cheerful as she greeted the cats and cleaned up whatever messes they'd made overnight. She seemed to genuinely love every moment she spent here in the café...maybe more than Mia did.

Cleo, a new cat who'd arrived a few days ago, trotted over to greet Mia with a loud meow.

"You've certainly settled right in, haven't you?" Mia said as she gave her a chin rub. Cleo purred, tail stuck straight up in the air as she twined herself around Mia's legs. "You won't be here long."

Mia gave her another pet and then went down the hall to the bathroom to wash her hands before she prepared the café counter for opening. Jordy was there when Mia came back out, warming up the espresso machine. "Morning," Mia said.

"Morning." Jordy tied their apron around their waist and began unboxing today's selection of pastries from the bakery down the street.

The morning passed in a blur, busy with the usual Sunday crowd, a steady stream of customers at the counter and nearly all the café tables occupied. Mia found herself checking the clock more often than usual, waiting for Lauren to arrive for her shift at eleven.

"Mia."

She was jolted out of her thoughts by the unexpected voice, every muscle in her body involuntarily tensing as she focused on the woman standing at the counter in front of her. For a moment, Mia just stared. "Kristin? What are you doing here?"

Kristin had cut her hair since the last time Mia saw her. It was neatly styled in a layered bob. Mia didn't recognize her charcoal-gray suit either. "As cliché as it sounds, I was in the neighborhood."

"Oh?" Mia's brain was misfiring at the sight of her ex-wife here in her café. They hadn't seen each other since the divorce was finalized in January, and Mia wasn't sure how to feel about seeing her now. It was unsettling to see Kristin with a new haircut and clothes, visual evidence that Mia didn't know her anymore. When you spent eighteen years of your life with someone, that felt...strange.

"I met with a client a few blocks over, and I decided to stop in and say hi, see how you are," Kristin said. There was something hesitant in her demeanor, and that threw Mia as much as her appearance, because Kristin was *never* hesitant. She was as brash and outspoken as anyone Mia had ever met.

"It's good to see you," Mia said, surprised to realize she meant it. Despite everything that had happened, she didn't hate Kristin. Their marriage had grown toxic as the years passed, but they bore equal blame for how it had ended. Maybe now that some time had passed, they could be civil to each other.

"You too," Kristin said. "You look good. Love the haircut."

Mia raised a hand absentmindedly to touch her hair, because yes, she'd changed hers since she last saw Kristin too. "Thanks. I was thinking the same about yours."

"Well, this is awkward, isn't it?" Kristin said with her trademark hearty laugh. "Look at us, complimenting each other's hair. What's next, we start talking about the weather?"

Mia chuckled. "If there's a guide for this kind of conversation, I didn't get a copy."

"Neither did I, but would you be able to take a break and share a cup of coffee with me?"

"I should be able to manage that," Mia said. "Your usual?"

Kristin nodded and headed toward an empty table near the front of the café. Mia fixed their drinks, made sure Jordy and Mateo were set to cover the counter, and brought both cups with her to Kristin's table.

"The café seems like it's doing well," Kristin commented as Mia sat across from her. "Are you loving it?"

Was she? The answer wasn't as quick or as easy for her as it probably should have been. "It's been a nice change," she said instead.

Kristin nodded. "You were looking for a slower pace. Seems like you've found it."

"I have." Mia took a sip of her cappuccino. "And you? How are things at the firm?"

"Oh, same as ever." Kristin spent the next ten minutes regaling Mia with tales from court, and she felt an unexpected twinge of nostalgia. That life had nearly wrecked her, and yet, she missed the thrill of standing in front of a jury, making her case. To some extent, she missed the long hours, coming home too tired to do anything but fall straight into bed.

It had been overwhelming while she was in it, a kind of all-consuming madness that had been equal parts exhilarating and devastating. She couldn't go back. But as Kristin described the malpractice lawsuit she'd just won for a client who'd been left disfigured after a botched surgery, Mia felt wistful for what she'd left behind.

"But enough about work," Kristin said finally. "What else is new with you? Enjoying the single life? Met anyone?"

"Yes." Mia felt undeniably pleased to be able to say so. "I'm seeing someone. You?"

Kristin reached for her coffee, but Mia caught the momentary surprise on her face. "Oh, you know how it is. I downloaded a few dating apps, but I've been so caught up in work..."

Yes, Mia did know how it was, or at least, how it had been before she left that life behind. "I doubt I'd have found time to date if I was still working at Gonzalez & Warren either."

"Tell me about her." There was an edge in Kristin's tone now, as if she disliked that Mia had moved on before she had. It fit the theme of their relationship perfectly. Of course, even post-divorce dating would be a competitive sport. "How long have you been dating?"

"It's really new, so I don't want to say much, but I like her a lot." So much more than she was willing to admit to her ex-wife. She looked up and saw Lauren watching her from the other side of the room, and her cheeks heated, although she wasn't sure why.

"What does she do?" Kristin asked.

"She's a writer." Mia smiled into her cappuccino as she thought of the fan fiction that had brought them together. She'd been messaging with Lauren long before she left Kristin, but that didn't feel like a detail to mention now, no matter how innocent it had been.

"A writer, huh? Books or what?"

"She's about to publish her first book. It's amazing. I'm so proud of her."

Kristin sipped her coffee. "I can't picture you with a

writer, but then again, I can't picture you owning a cat café either, even though I'm sitting in it."

"Why not?" Anger began to prickle under Mia's skin because this was exactly what happened every time she and Kristin attempted to have a conversation. Why had she thought it would get better after their divorce?

"This place just doesn't seem to suit you, that's all." Kristin's tone was every bit as condescending as Mia remembered from the last years of their marriage.

She narrowed her eyes at her ex-wife. "Maybe you don't know me as well as you thought you did."

20

L auren had planned to cook dinner for Mia tonight, but Mia left the café at lunchtime and didn't return, leaving Lauren to wonder. She'd been wondering ever since she saw Mia sharing a coffee with a brunette that she was pretty sure was Mia's ex-wife, according to the gossip Jordy had passed along.

The conversation had looked intense, but not unfriendly. On the contrary, Mia had worn such a wistful expression a few times that Lauren felt an awful sinking feeling in the pit of her stomach. And then, shortly after Kristin left, so did Mia.

Now Lauren didn't know what to do. Nothing in her dating history gave her any frame of reference for how to deal with her girlfriend's ex-wife, or perhaps more accurately, how to deal with her girlfriend's reaction to seeing her ex-wife. But she knew Mia shouldn't look at Kristin like *that*. Lauren wasn't a jealous person by nature, but her mood was uncharacteristically dark as she finished her shift.

Seeing Kristin today had made Lauren feel small somehow. Kristin was beautiful in the same sophisticated way as Mia. They were the same age and dressed in the same classy style. Successful. Confident. They looked good together. And here was Lauren in her threadbare jeans, a thief barely holding her life together.

Just before she clocked out, she received a text from Mia. *Come up when you're finished!*

I need to pick up a few things for dinner first, Lauren replied, wondering if Mia was going to mention that she'd seen her ex-wife today or why she'd left the café afterward.

Nope. I've got it covered. Come on up.

Well, okay then. Lauren wasn't sure if that was reassuring or worrisome. Did Mia have something to feel guilty about? Should Lauren be upset about this? Only one way to find out. She cleaned up and headed upstairs to Mia's apartment. She still had a key, but using it now that she'd moved out felt awkward, especially after what she'd seen earlier. She knocked.

"It's open," Mia called from inside.

Lauren opened the door and stepped inside, surprised to see Mia in the kitchen, stirring something that smelled delicious.

"You don't have to knock, you know," Mia told her, and she seemed like her usual self, but Lauren still felt uneasy.

"Feels like I should," Lauren said. "How are you?"

Mia gave her a cautious look. "Kristin came in today."

"I saw," Lauren said, relieved that Mia had brought it up so she didn't have to. "What was that about?"

"She just wanted to say hello." Mia shrugged as she began to dish up two plates of food. "Chicken cacciatore."

"I've never had it before, but it smells delicious." Lauren walked to the cabinet and pulled out two glasses, which she filled with water. "So how did it go with Kristin?"

"It was fine but also...strange." Mia made a face as she carried their plates to the table.

Lauren followed with the glasses of water. She sat, deciding to let Mia lead this conversation.

"Caught me off guard more than anything," Mia said before taking a sip of her water.

"I wondered where you disappeared to after she left," Lauren admitted.

"I needed to clear my head." She poked at her chicken with a fork. "So I went for a walk and then decided to shop and cook for you. Didn't really feel like going back to work, and Jordy and Mateo had the counter covered today."

Lauren leaned back in her seat, too anxious to eat until this conversation was over. "Did it bring up a lot of emotions for you when you saw her?" *Do you miss her? Do you want to go back to her?*

"Yes, but..." Mia looked up, and her eyes widened as she saw Lauren's face. "Not like whatever you're thinking, Lauren. I'm not in love with her anymore, but...I don't know. It was good to see her and catch up, I guess, or at least it started out that way. It didn't take long for us to start sniping at each other the way we used to."

"You looked at her like you miss her, like maybe you regret leaving her." There. She'd said it.

Mia shook her head. "No. Absolutely not."

"Maybe you don't realize it, but I know what I saw." Lauren dropped her gaze to the plate in front of her, chunks of chicken in a red sauce with tomatoes and peppers, steaming as hot as the hurt flaming in Lauren's cheeks.

Mia reached across the table to grip Lauren's hand. "I don't know what you saw on my face, but I promise you none of those things were in my head, not for a single moment."

"Then what?" What else could it be?

Mia's expression hardened. She looked defensive, and that hard knot was back in Lauren's stomach. "Obviously, you misread me."

"I don't think I did," Lauren said quietly.

"I haven't *ever* regretted leaving Kristin, and that's the damn truth."

"Your face said differently," Lauren insisted, and for the first time, she had an idea of what it must have been like to go up against Mia in court, because her expression was truly intimidating right now.

Mia's lips pressed into a harsh line, and for a moment, Lauren feared they were about to really fight, but then Mia sighed. "If you saw something wistful on my face when I was with Kristin, it was probably while she was telling me about her recent cases."

"I don't understand."

"If I miss anything, it's practicing law. Not Kristin." Mia met her gaze, looking vaguely uncomfortable, but not insincere.

"Oh." Lauren stared at her for a moment, absorbing her words. "You regret leaving your law firm?"

"No," Mia said. "I don't."

"Then what?"

"Then nothing," Mia said with a stiff shrug. "I miss being a lawyer, but I also *don't* miss it. Do you know, Kristin hasn't found the time to go on a single date? I don't want that. I love that I'm here with you."

The vehemence in her voice sent something warm through Lauren's system. "Surely there are lawyers who don't work themselves to the bone."

"There are absolutely lawyers with a better work-life

balance than I had. I could have chosen that route. I could have gone into private practice or something similar, but I was so miserable and sick and worn out at the time, I threw in the towel and bought a cat café."

Lauren flinched, remembering that the café had been her idea, even though she'd only meant it as a joke when she'd suggested it. "Do you regret buying the café?"

Mia scrubbed a hand over her face. "No. I'm just...I don't know. I'm out of sorts today."

"Because you saw Kristin." Lauren poked at her food. Neither of them had eaten a single bite, which was a shame after how much effort Mia had put into cooking it.

"Because I saw Kristin, but not because I want to *be* with Kristin."

"Are you sure? Because you keep telling me you're not ready to take things further, and maybe it's because...maybe you're not over her."

"Stop that. There's not any part of me that wants to be with Kristin." Mia sounded harsher now, almost angry. Abruptly, she stood from the table and held out a hand to Lauren. "Come here. Obviously, we need to talk this through before we eat."

Lauren stood and faced her. "I'm sorry for pushing."

"Don't apologize for voicing your concerns." Mia's hands came to rest on Lauren's hips. "Never apologize for that. I have baggage to work through, but none of it affects my commitment to you. My relationship with Kristin wasn't healthy, and I'm glad to be out of it. You and I...we're good together. We're so good together that I don't want to rush in and mess it up."

"Are you sure?" Lauren asked, and she could hear her voice waver.

Mia drew her closer, wrapping her arms around Lauren. "Positive. You're the only person I want to be with. I was so lonely here last night without you, and I...I think I'm falling for you, despite how much that scares me, because I *am* trying to take things slow."

"Oh," Lauren whispered as tears spilled over her cheeks, because she could hear the sincerity in Mia's voice, and she was falling for her too. The truth was, Lauren had already fallen, although she didn't want to say the words for the first time after a fight about Mia's ex-wife.

"I've been divorced less than a year. I'm still figuring out who I am in this new chapter of my life, but I'm going to get there, so just be patient with me, okay?"

Lauren nodded with tear-filled eyes. "I can be patient."

"Are you okay? Are *we* okay?" Mia pulled back so she could meet Lauren's eyes.

"Yeah, we're okay. I got worried when you ran off after Kristin's visit. I guess I got a little insecure and...and jealous, which isn't like me at all. I've never been in a relationship like this before, and today, I got scared."

"Like what?" Mia asked, still holding her close. "You've never been in a relationship like what?"

"The kind where I have someone worth feeling jealous about. Serious. Committed. Hopefully long-term. Any of those things."

Mia slid a hand up to cup Lauren's cheek, her expression tender. "We're quite a pair. You've never had a serious relationship before, and I just came out of a decades-long one."

"And yet, we're making it work."

"We're doing better than that," Mia said. "Because nothing about being with you feels like work."

"Yes," Lauren agreed breathlessly, and then they were kissing. She clutched Mia against her, hands fisted in the back of her blouse as she let her insecurities melt away beneath the heat of her kiss.

After a minute, Mia pulled back. "Come on. Let's warm up our supper."

NOVEMBER ARRIVED with a cold snap that forced Lauren to spend some of her hard-earned money on warmer clothes and a new coat. Mia went shopping with her, and they had a fun afternoon together. On the one hand, Lauren felt like they'd settled seamlessly into their new relationship, but at the same time, she sometimes sensed a restlessness in Mia that she wasn't sure how to interpret.

Whatever it was, it seemed to have started around the time Kristin visited the café. On her more confident days, Lauren wondered if Mia still missed practicing law, if she was unfulfilled at the café. And when her late-night insecurities crept in, Lauren wondered if Mia was unfulfilled by Lauren herself.

And then there was the date looming on the calendar: November 18th. The court date that had already been rescheduled twice. Maybe that was why she spent less time worrying about it now than she had the first two times. Surely, the courts would be busy the week before Thanksgiving. She'd probably get bumped until after the new year. Would she ever get out of this legal limbo?

In the meantime, she and Mia settled into a routine where they had dinner together most nights, but Lauren always returned to her apartment to sleep at night. Their relationship seemed to be in limbo too, neither of them sure how or when to take that next step.

Lauren's new space was working out well, though. She

got along with her roommates, and she'd spent a lot of time making her little room *hers*. Lola the succulent was thriving, and Lauren smiled every time she looked at the cheerful little plant. She spent most of her free time working on edits for her book, although she was still reluctant to set a release date until she learned her fate with the felony charge.

She'd been so caught up in this feeling of limbo, so sure her court date would be postponed, that she was completely unprepared when it wasn't. On the morning of the eighteenth, she dressed in a blazer she'd borrowed from Mia and her best black slacks, hands shaking so badly, she had trouble buttoning her shirt. This was it, her day of reckoning.

After today, she'd either go to jail or...she'd be free to move on with her life.

She met Mia on the steps of the courthouse, and they walked inside together. Mia had on a black skirt suit with a cranberry-colored blouse underneath, her hair swept back in a neat twist, and she looked gorgeous, but more than that, she looked like a lawyer. As she led the way through the lobby, her heels clicking against the marble floors, Lauren couldn't help feeling that Mia looked in her element here in a way she didn't at the café.

Then they were standing at the doors to the courtroom, and Lauren couldn't breathe. She hugged her coat around herself as something cold slithered over her skin. "Mia, I..." She broke off as her chest constricted, squeezing the air from her lungs.

Mia rested a hand against Lauren's back, rubbing up and down over her blazer. "It's going to be okay. I know the judge and the ADA, and they're both reasonable. We have Josie's statement from when she came to the station with us. There shouldn't be any surprises."

"What if…" She gave Mia helpless look.

"I never make promises when it comes to legal cases, because nothing's ever definite, and in the end, it's up to the judge, not me," Mia said, and did that sound ominous? Lauren's head went fuzzy. "But you're going to walk out of here a free woman, Lauren. I wouldn't say that if I didn't believe it."

Lauren dragged a desperate breath into her lungs. She knew she'd make it through a prison sentence if it came to that, but right here, right now, it felt so overwhelming. She'd have to leave her apartment and her job at the café. Mia had said she'd wait for her, but it would be *hard*. Tears burned her eyes.

"Mia Solano, as I live and breathe," a deep voice called.

Mia turned with a smile as a man in a gray suit approached.

"Didn't think I'd see you walking these halls again." He stuck out a hand, and they shook.

"I'm just here today as a favor for a friend," she told him, then glanced at Lauren. "Lauren, this is ADA Benny Ramirez. Benny, Lauren Booker."

Lauren might have been insulted that Mia had introduced her as a friend, but she knew it was probably because of the circumstances. Was Mia even allowed to represent her girlfriend in court? Lauren had no idea, and her brain wasn't exactly functioning right now. "Hi," she managed. "Nice to meet you."

"You too, Lauren. You've got yourself a top-notch lawyer here," Benny said. With a wave, he headed inside the courtroom.

"Is he the ADA on my case?" Lauren asked.

Mia shook her head. "No, Shia Nader is assigned to your case. She's probably already inside. Shall we?"

Lauren nodded. She'd been cold before, but now she was hot, sweat causing her shirt to stick to her skin beneath the borrowed blazer. Her stomach felt like she'd eaten rocks for breakfast.

Mia pulled open the heavy wooden door in front of them, leading the way into the courtroom. It didn't look quite like Lauren had expected, but then again, her only frame of reference was *Law & Order*. This room was relatively small, with bright white walls and windows to the left. Neat rows of chairs faced the area at the front of the room where the judge sat.

Mia led the way toward a pair of empty seats, and there was a swagger in her stride that Lauren hadn't seen before. She looked calm and confident, Lauren's exact opposite.

"They'll call your name soon," she told Lauren as they sat.

"Okay," Lauren mumbled, trying not to hyperventilate. First, she hadn't been able to breathe, and now she was gasping for air like she'd just gone for a run.

"That's ADA Nader," Mia murmured, gesturing to a woman near the front of the courtroom. She wore a beige suit, her black hair pulled back in a tight bun. She looked serious, but if anything, Mia looked more intimidating than the ADA.

Lauren had never been more glad for *anything* than she was that Mia would be standing beside her when she faced the judge. As she waited, she watched a man sentenced for selling drugs and another whose charges were dismissed because the prosecution's witness didn't show up. All the while, Lauren became increasingly agitated while Mia watched the proceedings with laser sharp interest, looking cool as a cucumber.

"Lauren Booker, docket number 22 Cr 4502 GL."

Lauren bolted to her feet on wobbly knees. Mia gave her a confident smile before she led the way to the front of the courtroom.

21

"These charges are dismissed." The judge banged his gavel.

Mia pushed her shoulders back as the all-too-familiar thrill of victory raced through her system, something she hadn't felt in damn close to a year. She nodded briskly. "Thank you, Your Honor."

Beside her, Lauren looked like she might cry with relief. She'd been heartbreakingly anxious this morning, when Mia had known it would end like this. The ADA hadn't even put up a fight when Mia made her case. Thanks to Josie's sworn statement and Lauren's otherwise spotless record, this had been a no-brainer.

Mia turned to thank ADA Nader, and then she led the way out of the courtroom with Lauren at her heels. She kept walking until they'd made it outside. Then, as she stood on the front steps of the courthouse with crisp November sunshine glinting off Lauren's glossy brown hair, Mia pulled her in for a hug. "See? I told you it would be okay."

"I'm so relieved," Lauren murmured against Mia's jacket. "I can't quite believe it's over."

"Believe it. If a future employer does a background check on you, they could still see that these charges were filed, but since you weren't convicted, you should have a much easier time going forward."

"Good." Lauren stepped back, tucking her hair behind her ears. "I think it's going to take some time to really sink in, but I feel like that cliché about a weight being lifted. This had been looming over me for so long, and I couldn't really let myself make plans for the future until it was behind me. I didn't want to commit to a publication date for my book or get too serious with you...just in case."

"Now you can." Mia leaned in to press her lips against Lauren's. "And for the record, I am wholeheartedly in support of both of those things."

Lauren's lips curved, and her eyes sparkled. She *did* look like a weight had been lifted. There was something about her, a lightness, a radiance that hadn't been there before, and it thrilled Mia to see it.

"You're working at the market this afternoon, right?"

Lauren nodded. "I'm off at six."

"Come over after? We can grab something for dinner... maybe some champagne too. We ought to celebrate your freedom."

Lauren's smile was luminous. "Yes to all of that."

"Perfect."

"Also..." Lauren's brown eyes met hers. "Mia, you need to be a lawyer again."

"What?" She straightened, feeling suddenly off balance.

"You came alive in there," Lauren said. "I've never seen you like that before."

"I..." She pressed her lips together in frustration because she knew exactly what Lauren meant. She felt it too, but she'd stuffed that uncomfortable realization into the back of her mind because she wasn't a lawyer anymore. She owned a cat café. She couldn't just give that up, even if—for a moment in that courtroom—she'd wanted to.

"Maybe you could give yourself an extra day off from the café and volunteer somewhere or *something*," Lauren said, her voice earnest. "I've noticed lately that you don't seem entirely happy at work, and I think this might be why."

Mia's fists clenched, her entire body bristling against the truth of Lauren's words. She'd been fighting this knowledge for a while now. It was the reason she'd been so unsettled after Kristin's visit. Seeing her ex-wife had been less upsetting than the yearning she'd felt when Kristin shared tales from the courtroom, the realization of how much Mia missed it.

"Just think about it," Lauren said. "You were really something in there."

Mia shook her head. "There's not much to think about. I'm not going to close the café."

"I'm sure you can find a solution if you put your mind to it." Lauren took Mia's fists in her hands and carefully unfurled her fingers, then leaned in for a kiss. "I have faith in you."

"Hm," Mia said noncommittally.

"In the meantime, thank you again for everything this morning. Having you there made it so much less scary, and honestly, the ADA might not have been as nice if you hadn't been there, looking so fierce and competent and amazing. I just...really appreciate it."

"It was my absolute pleasure," Mia told her. That much she was sure of.

"I'll see you later for dinner."

"Yes, you will."

They parted ways on the courthouse steps. Mia wasn't

working at the café until later, and she made the split-second decision to go home and change for the gym. She needed to burn off some of her frustration before she saw Lauren again tonight.

AFTER WORK THAT EVENING, Lauren went home for a quick shower to rinse off the stress of the day. On her way to Mia's, she stopped for takeout from the Thai restaurant on the corner and then she stopped in the café for Mia herself, who was just closing up for the night.

As they climbed the steps to Mia's apartment together, Lauren reached for her keys to open the door for her. She felt as much at home at Mia's as she did at her own apartment, and when had that ever been the case for her before? She'd rarely felt at home anywhere in her life, let alone in two places at once.

"I feel like taking on the world," Lauren said as she set the bag of takeout on the table. "It hadn't really sunk in when we talked outside the courthouse earlier. I was still in shock, and now I feel so overwhelmingly relieved. I feel like a whole new woman."

"I'm glad." Mia stooped to pet Lola as she strutted toward her, meowing her greetings.

"Sorry if I overstepped earlier about your career." It had been weighing on her since, although she stood by what she'd said. Mia came alive in a courtroom. She oozed confidence and competence, but she'd chosen to give up that life, and maybe Lauren shouldn't have pressed her about it.

"You didn't overstep." Mia had been defensive earlier, almost angry, but she didn't seem that way now. "You forced me to face an uncomfortable truth."

"I did?"

Mia nodded. She exhaled, her features a mixture of frustration and something that looked an awful lot like vulnerability. "You've been brutally honest with me since we met, and now it's my turn."

"Okay." Lauren stepped closer, and that tingling feeling in the pit of her stomach said she wasn't sure whether this truth was going to be good or bad.

"Remember after Kristin's visit, you were upset because you thought I had looked at her like I missed her?" Mia's brown eyes met Lauren's, and her stomach dipped, because oh yeah, she remembered that, and she still felt a little bit insecure about it.

Lauren nodded, waiting for Mia to say what she needed to say.

"The truth is, I wasn't missing Kristin that day. I was missing my old career, and I wasn't ready to admit it, not even to myself." Mia stood with her hands clasped in front of herself, head bowed as if she were making a confession.

Lauren closed the gap between them, resting her hands on Mia's waist. "And this morning in court?"

"Like you said, I felt more like myself this morning than I have all year." Mia sighed. "And I don't know what to do about it...if anything."

"I really think that if you look around, you could find something to fulfill that part of yourself, Mia, even if it's just some volunteer work when you have the time."

"I don't entirely trust myself to do that." Mia settled closer in Lauren's arms. "I didn't balance work and life well before when I was a lawyer. My ulcer is still healing. What if I fall back into old habits?"

Lauren's heart melted at her honesty. "I don't think you necessarily would. It seems like you and Kristin brought out that unhealthy side of each other, and maybe toward the end, you were burying yourself in work because your marriage was falling apart. You're in a happy, stable place now. You have me and Lola and the café. It might be an entirely different experience if you gave it another try."

Mia's lips curved in a smile. "It sounds so possible when you put it like that, but I don't know. I need to give it some thought, and I don't even know what I'd do if I did go back. I can't just give up the café."

"You'll figure it out," Lauren said. "I'm sure of it."

"I hate being indecisive," Mia said with a huff of annoyance. "I'm committed to the café."

"I know."

She wrapped her arms around Mia and held her tight. If it was possible, Lauren felt even lighter than she had after she left the courthouse that morning. This conversation had alleviated her insecurities about their relationship, and she had every confidence that Mia would sort herself out professionally. In the meantime, Lauren would be here for her every step of the way.

When they parted, they were both smiling.

Mia held on to one of Lauren's hands. "Stay here tonight?"

Lauren inhaled sharply. "Are you sure?"

Mia nodded, and there was no mistaking the heat—or the affection—gleaming in her eyes. "And to be clear, I want you in my bed, not on the couch."

Lauren let out a laugh that sounded more like a giggle. "Well, I was certainly hoping."

Then she was back in Mia's arms, and there was nothing tender about this kiss. It was ravenous, fueled by weeks—months—of pent-up sexual tension. Mia's lips met hers with bruising force, awakening something inside Lauren that she hadn't felt in a long time, an urgent kind of arousal that made her feel like she might come out of her own skin if she didn't satisfy it.

She groaned, gripping Mia's ass through her pants as she hauled her closer, loving the way Mia's breath hitched and her eyes fluttered shut as her hips pressed against Lauren's. She was a few inches taller than Mia, but when Mia wore heels, everything lined up perfectly.

Mia's hand slid beneath Lauren's shirt, skimming up her back to release the clasp of her bra. Those rich brown eyes glinted into Lauren's as she took Lauren's breasts in her hands. Her fingers were soft and warm, and Lauren could hardly breathe because it felt *so good*. The next thing she knew, Mia had wedged a thigh between her own, and they were moving together, and damn, Mia was a force to be reckoned with when she made her mind up about something.

Right now, Lauren's thoughts were a hazy mixture of *yes* and *please* and *more…*

"Hey, Lauren?" Mia asked as she slowly dragged one of her hands down Lauren's stomach to the waistband of her jeans.

"Yeah?" she managed through ragged breaths as her core clenched in anticipation of Mia's touch.

"How do you feel about postponing dinner?" She tilted her head in the direction of the takeout bag on the table.

Lauren had forgotten it even existed. "I'm totally in favor of it," she gasped.

"Good." Without breaking the contact between them, Mia stepped her backward into her bedroom and pushed Lauren onto the bed.

22

Mia exhaled roughly as she followed Lauren onto the bed. One of her legs slid between Lauren's, and Mia's mind was spinning with a combination of arousal and anticipation. She'd waited so long for this moment. Warmth swept over her skin, need pulsed in her core, and her heart felt full, bursting with affection for the woman beneath her.

Lauren gazed up at her out of lust-drunk eyes, her cheeks flushed pink and her chest heaving just as rapidly as Mia's. For a moment, they just smiled at each other, and then Mia dipped her head, bringing their lips together. It should have been a simple kiss, but there was nothing simple about it. This kiss was fire. It was passion. It was two women who had to have each other...*right now*.

Lauren nipped at her lower lip, and that was all it took for Mia's restraint to snap. Her hips bucked against Lauren's as she drowned herself in the pleasure of her kiss. She and Lauren had been dancing around each other for weeks while they built the foundation of their relationship, bridging the gap from friends to lovers.

Mia would have needed to take this slow no matter who she was dating. It had felt like a monumental step to give herself to someone new after being with the same person for so long, but as she pressed her body against Lauren's, she wasn't sure anything had ever felt so *right*. She and Lauren just seemed to fit.

As much as Mia was desperate for relief from the need blazing inside her, she also wanted to take her time and cherish every moment. She wanted to explore every inch of Lauren's body. She wanted to know everything Lauren liked and didn't like. She wanted to feel their bare skin pressed together and look into Lauren's eyes as she came.

Lauren looked so beautiful with her dark hair spread beneath her, a perfect contrast to Mia's light-blue bedspread. Mia stared at her for a long moment, loving the dazed look on her face and how warm her body felt beneath Mia's. Then she slid a hand beneath Lauren's shirt, palming her breast and drawing the loveliest little whimper from her throat.

"I've been tested since my divorce," Mia told her before she got too carried away. "All clear. And as you know, there hasn't been anyone since."

Lauren nodded. "I don't have health insurance, but I got a checkup at Planned Parenthood before I left Brooklyn last year, and there hasn't been anyone for me since then either."

"Now that that's out of the way..." Mia pushed Lauren's shirt and bra up, baring her breasts. They were fuller than Mia's, the nipples already drawn into tight buds. Mia dipped her head and took one of those nipples into her mouth, grazing Lauren's skin with her teeth. Vaguely, she was aware of Lauren's hands grasping at her and her moans of pleasure.

"More. Mia, please."

She didn't need to be asked twice. Mia slid a hand between them and popped the button on Lauren's jeans. She pushed down the zipper and slid a hand inside, cupping Lauren over her panties. The contact made them both gasp and sent a sharp bolt of need to Mia's clit. She pressed her hips against Lauren's thigh as she stroked her over her underwear.

Lauren's hands fumbled against Mia's hips. For a moment, she thought Lauren was pushing her away, but then she realized Lauren was struggling with the clasp on Mia's pants. She sat up to help her out, eager to be rid of her clothes.

But as she untucked her blouse from her pants, she hesitated, suddenly aware of her age. Mia had never been with a younger woman before, and while she was generally confident about her body, she apparently harbored a small amount of insecurity there too.

"You okay?" Lauren asked, intuitive as ever.

"Yeah, just..." She sighed. "I was younger than you are now the last time I got naked with someone for the first time. God knows my body doesn't look the same as it did in my twenties."

Lauren cocked her head to the side. "I was attracted to you from the first moment I laid eyes on you. You know that, right? Whatever you look like under your clothes, I'm going to think you're beautiful because I'm interested in so much more than your skin...although I happen to think your skin is pretty beautiful too." She gave Mia a cheeky grin.

Mia felt herself relaxing, and she gave her head a shake, laughing under her breath. "When you put it like that..."

"Do you want me to undress first so you can see the cellulite on my thighs and the stretch marks on my hips?" Lauren asked teasingly.

"No, but thank you for humoring my insecurities." Mia reached for the button on her pants.

"I meant every word." Lauren was already unfastening the buttons on Mia's shirt, her fingers hot as they brushed Mia's skin, almost as hot as the look in her eyes. Mia's shirt gaped open, revealing the flesh-toned bra she wore beneath.

"So pretty," Lauren said reverently as she took Mia's breasts in her hands.

Mia could feel the warmth of her fingers through her bra, and it fueled the heat burning inside her. To hell with her vanity. She needed to feel Lauren's fingers on her bare skin. She slipped her shirt over her shoulders and tossed it on the floor, then popped the clasp on her bra and sent it after her shirt. "Your turn."

Lauren nodded, and Mia helped her slide out of her shirt and bra. They stared at each other for a moment, and then they were scrambling out of their pants, laughter mixing with kisses as they scooted and kicked their pants to the floor.

"May I?" Mia asked as she slipped a finger under the waistband of Lauren's panties and gave a gentle tug.

"Yes," Lauren panted. "And take yours off too."

Mia's fingers were impatient as she tugged Lauren's panties down her legs, and then she swept her gaze over Lauren's naked body, feeling drunk off the sight of her. Lauren's cheeks were flushed, hair wild and messy around her face. Mia took in her full breasts, the crimson birthmark below her rib cage, and the soft curve of her hips.

"Beautiful," Mia murmured as she traced her fingers over those curves, making Lauren sigh with pleasure, even as her fingers pushed at Mia's panties. She lifted her hips, helping Lauren slide her out of them.

Finally naked, she pressed her body against Lauren's. All

the air whooshed from her lungs as their bare skin met, because *yes*, this was what she needed, what she'd been craving for so long. Somehow, it felt even better than she'd anticipated.

"Mia..." Lauren shifted restlessly beneath her, and Mia was glad she wasn't the only one having trouble going slow.

She brought their lips together as she slipped a hand between Lauren's thighs. Her fingers slid through Lauren's wetness, and she whimpered beneath Mia, hips arching to meet her touch. Lauren moaned into her mouth, and the sensation only increased the pulsing ache in Mia's core.

"I can't get enough of you," Mia gasped into her mouth.

"Same." Lauren rolled Mia onto her side so they were facing each other, and then her hand was between Mia's thighs, and *poof*, Mia's brain went up in smoke.

She moaned in relief as Lauren's fingers stroked her clit, because *God*, how did it feel so much more wonderful when someone else touched her than when she touched herself? The intimacy of sex always seemed to heighten the pleasure.

Her hips moved with Lauren's fingers, and Lauren seemed to mimic that rhythm with her own hips so that they thrust against each other in a perfectly orchestrated dance, fingers swirling and plunging as their hips rocked together.

Mia pressed her face against Lauren's neck, kissing the delicate skin there, breathing her in, loving the way their sweat-damp skin slipped as they moved together and the weight of Lauren's breasts against hers. Mia savored the impossibly wonderful pressure building inside her as Lauren stroked her closer to her release.

Lauren's fingers seemed to dance against her skin, never quite where Mia expected them to be, and somehow that made it even more erotic. She couldn't help the gasps and moans spilling from her lips, but Lauren was making just as much noise, and her sexy sounds only turned Mia on even more.

"Mia," Lauren mumbled, hips grinding steadily to the rhythm of Mia's fingers.

"Mm?"

"Are you close? Because…" She whimpered, hips moving even faster.

"Oh yeah. I'm with you," Mia whispered, and a tremor raced through her as she felt the urgency in Lauren's words. "Come for me, Lauren."

Lauren cried out, her movements becoming erratic as she chased her orgasm. Mia pushed two fingers inside her, curving them forward to hit her G-spot.

"Oh God," Lauren gasped as her body clenched around Mia's fingers. "Oh…yes!"

The sound of her orgasm was all it took to push Mia over the edge, pleasure radiating from her core, flooding her with sensation.

When she regained her senses, she was wrapped in Lauren's arms, their bodies slick with sweat, both of them gasping for breath. Mia's body tingled with the aftershocks of her orgasm, and she felt impossibly warm and languid and wonderful.

Lauren smiled at her, looking similarly blissed out, and then, without warning, she yelped, lurching against Mia. She'd barely registered alarm before Lola came scrambling over Lauren's back. She landed in between them, glared at Mia, tail twitching, and then jumped off the other side of the bed.

"Well, that was dramatic," Lauren said, and then she burst out laughing.

Mia's lips twitched, and before she knew it, she was

laughing too. "What the hell, Lola?"

"Scared the crap out of me when something sharp poked me in the back before I realized it was a claw," Lauren gasped through her laughter.

"She didn't scratch you, did she?"

"I don't think so."

Mia ran a hand through Lauren's hair. "Next time, we'll close the door."

Lauren grinned. "She must have wondered what we were doing in here."

"Well, I haven't been with anyone since I adopted her, so who knows what she thought."

"*I* thought it was amazing," Lauren said, suddenly serious. "Like really, really amazing."

"So did I." Mia brought her lips to Lauren's. "And I'm not finished with you yet."

LAUREN DRIFTED to sleep that night with Mia's arm resting over her stomach, warm and secure. When she woke the following morning, their positions were reversed. Mia slept with her back against Lauren's stomach, spooned against her with Lauren's arm wrapped snugly around her waist.

Lauren lay like that for a few minutes, watching Mia sleep until she stirred in Lauren's arms, rolling to face her. A smile touched Mia's lips before she'd even opened her eyes, and Lauren felt herself smiling right back.

"Morning," she whispered.

"It's a very good one," Mia mumbled. Those brown eyes blinked at her, less intense when they were still glazed with sleep.

Lauren had seen her in the morning before, but only

after Mia had already gotten out of bed, never the moment she woke, and she was immediately enamored with the soft, unguarded woman in front of her. "I love waking up with you."

"Same. Are you working today?"

"Not until noon, here at the café."

"Mm, that's right. I'm only doing admin things this morning. Jordy's opening, so I vote that you and I take our time getting out of bed." Mia's fingers toyed with the hem of Lauren's T-shirt.

"Sounds perfect to me, but hold that thought for one minute." Lauren gave Mia a quick peck on the lips before disentangling herself to go into the bathroom. She freshened up quickly, but when she came back into the bedroom, Mia's eyes were closed.

Lauren crawled into bed, trying not to disturb Mia if she'd fallen back to sleep, but she gripped Lauren's T-shirt and hauled her in, pausing just before their lips met.

"You brushed your teeth," Mia murmured.

"Yep."

"Well, I'm not going to be the only one with morning breath." Mia released her, then scooted backward and climbed out of bed.

Lauren watched her go, loving the way her bare ass peeked out from beneath her shirt. "Hey, do you have some lip balm I could use?"

"In the bedside table," Mia said, and then the bathroom door closed behind her.

Lauren reached over and tugged at the drawer. Inside, she found various odds and ends, including a tube of lip balm. As she applied it to her dry lips, her gaze landed on a black, wand-shaped... Was that what Lauren thought it was?

Before she could stop herself, Lauren touched it, and

wow, it was so much softer than she'd expected. The surface was almost velvety beneath her fingertips. The buttons on the base left little doubt as to its purpose, but this was fancier than she'd expected a vibrator to be. It seemed as classy as Mia herself.

Somehow, Lauren had imagined them all to be big, purple cock-shaped things, but this...this was nice. And she was totally snooping right now. She quickly withdrew her hand, only to look up and find Mia watching her with an amused smile.

"Want to use it together?" she asked.

"Oh, I don't...I've never..." Lauren spluttered.

"You've never used one with a partner?" Mia asked. "It can be a lot of fun, if you want to try."

"I've never used one at all." Lauren's face was burning, and certain other parts of her were warming up too as she imagined using the vibrator with Mia.

"Really?" Mia sat beside her and took the vibrator out of the drawer.

Lauren stared at it. Nestled against Mia's palm, it looked even more inviting. "Never, and I didn't know they looked like this either. It's so fancy."

Mia pressed one of the buttons, and it began to buzz in her hand, a low purr of a noise that immediately made Lauren wet. "Want to try it?"

"Yes," Lauren whispered. "I want to use it with you."

Mia's grin was pure sex as she slid forward, pressing Lauren against the sheets. Lauren could still hear the vibrator, but she couldn't feel it, and the sound was its own form of foreplay as she imagined what it would feel like. Mia dipped her head and kissed her, simultaneously pressing the vibrator against Lauren's inner thigh.

"Oh!" She jerked like she'd received an electric shock,

but this was a million times more pleasant. The vibrator was as warm as Mia's fingers now and just as soft where it hummed against her skin. The ache between Lauren's thighs intensified.

"You like?" Mia murmured against her lips.

"Yes." Lauren squirmed beneath her as Mia slowly slid the wand up her inner thigh.

"Ready?" Mia's eyes were scorching hot as they met Lauren's.

She could only nod, desperate to feel the vibrator against her clit. Or inside her? Maybe both. Mia brought the vibrator to the junction of Lauren's thighs, pressing it firmly against her aching flesh, and she couldn't contain the cry that burst from her lips.

"Oh," she gasped. "*Oh*. That's...that's so good." Her thighs clenched around it, and a tremor of pleasure raced through her body.

Mia angled it so it pressed against her clit, and Lauren almost levitated off the bed. Instinctively, her hips started to move, seeking more. If only those vibrations were just a little bit stronger...

"More?" Mia asked, thrusting the wand gently between Lauren's thighs, and she could feel how wet she was. She could *hear* it as the silicone slipped against her skin.

"Yes," she whimpered, not even sure what she was asking for.

The vibration intensified. *Oh.* Lauren's hips jerked in response. Already she felt a warm tingling sensation building inside her. "I didn't know it could do that," she gasped.

"It's got five speeds," Mia told her. "And patterns."

The vibrator started to pulse against her, and Lauren gripped Mia's hips, holding on to her. She'd never felt anything quite this intense. As the vibrator pulsed against her, she felt mindless with need. She whimpered, hips moving, seeking more.

"Want to feel it inside you?" Mia asked, her voice low and husky in the way Lauren was starting to realize meant she was turned on too.

"Yes," Lauren managed.

Mia positioned the wand against Lauren's entrance and slowly pushed it inside.

"Oh," Lauren gasped. She felt supercharged, as if she was vibrating with as much strength as the wand inside her. It felt good, *so* good, but... "I need it against my clit."

Mia obeyed, gently repositioning the vibrator. She changed the pattern to one that was slower, matching it with subtle rolls of her hips. Lauren fisted her hands in Mia's hair, dragging her down for a messy kiss as her body buzzed with pleasure.

"More?" Mia whispered against her lips.

Could she even handle more at this point? "Yes," she panted.

The patterns ceased, and the vibration kicked up another notch. All Lauren could do was close her eyes and hold on. Her body shook, and for a moment, she hung on the precipice, tingling in anticipation before the orgasm rushed through her in powerful waves, drawing an embarrassingly loud groan from her lips.

"Oh my God," she said when she could speak. She pushed the vibrator away from her too-sensitive flesh, but when Mia moved to turn it off, Lauren grabbed it from her instead. She rolled Mia beneath her, seeing the need blazing in her eyes. "Your turn."

"Mm," was all Mia said as she closed her eyes. Her nipples were hard beneath her T-shirt, and Lauren could feel her arousal where one of her thighs rested between Mia's.

Lauren pressed the little buttons at the base of the wand, making sure she knew how to work it. She turned it back down to its lowest setting, and then she brought it between them, pressing it against Mia. She moaned, tensing beneath Lauren.

"More," she demanded, fingers fisted in Lauren's shirt.

Lauren tapped the button to increase the vibration, moving the wand against Mia the way she'd done for Lauren. Already, she was breathless and grinding herself against it. She must have gotten pretty worked up from getting Lauren off, because...

"More," Mia moaned, and almost as soon as Lauren tapped the button, Mia arched beneath her with a cry, gasping her way through what looked like a pretty intense orgasm.

Lauren turned off the vibrator and gathered Mia in her arms. "What a way to start the day."

"YOU WANT to close for me tonight?"

Lauren looked at Mia in surprise. "Really?"

"Yes," Mia said. "I need to grocery shop—don't laugh—and then I thought I'd cook us something for dinner."

Lauren grinned at her, because Mia was adorable, but she was also getting better at these domestic things. "Sure. You think I'm ready?"

Mia nodded, looking as certain as ever. Did she even know what it felt like to be indecisive? "You've helped me close several times now. You're ready."

Lauren swallowed, because they both knew what had

happened when she closed for Josie the first time. This was a huge show of trust on Mia's part. "Okay," Lauren said, pleased with how steady she sounded.

"Great," Mia said. "I'll let Jordy know. Just come up after you're finished."

"Okay," Lauren agreed.

Mia headed out, and Lauren spent the rest of the evening moving between the cat enclosure and the counter, jumping in where she was needed. She was mellow and happy after her amazing night with Mia, feeling like she could take on the world. And she loved every moment she spent in the café, even when Mia wasn't here.

Lauren would see her later, and maybe for the first time ever, she felt confident that *later* meant more than just seeing Mia tonight. It meant lots of nights, a future full of them. Without the threat of a prison sentence hanging over her, Lauren could finally look ahead, and she liked what she saw...a lot.

At seven, she flipped the sign on the door to Closed and started cleaning up in the cat enclosure while Jordy wiped down the café counters. Lauren had just put down the cats' nighttime meal when Jordy waved from the other side of the glass.

"I'm heading out. Night!"

"Night," Lauren called after them. She smiled to herself as she watched the foster cats gather around the plates of food. She was all alone in the café for the first time. It felt peaceful, just her and the cats. Lauren took her time feeding and playing with them, and then she finished cleaning their enclosure.

"See you guys tomorrow," she told them as she closed the glass door behind her. She went to the bathroom to wash her hands and then walked behind the café counter.

Her next task was the cash register. She needed to balance its contents against today's sales and then lock the cash in the safe in Mia's office. Lauren walked to the register and punched in the code to unlock the drawer.

It slid open with a ding, revealing an empty cash compartment. For a moment, Lauren just stared, because there was no way... Every dollar, every penny, *everything* was gone.

"No," she whispered. The tremor started in her knees, racing up her body until she had to grip the counter to keep herself upright. Her stomach clenched painfully, and her head spun.

Oh God. How had this happened? Had someone at the café found out about Lauren's past and taken the cash to try to frame her? Had the café been robbed while she was in back, washing her hands? She hadn't double-checked that the front door was locked before she went to the bathroom, had she? No, she hadn't. Oh *fuck*. She'd just gotten the felony charge against her dropped. No one would believe she hadn't taken the money herself.

She'd lose her job. She'd lose her apartment. She'd lose *Mia*.

Lauren's knees gave out, and she slumped to the floor. Ice swept through her veins, and she could hear herself gasping for breath. Mia's words the day she'd hired Lauren echoed in her head. She'd told her that if Lauren ever betrayed her trust, she wouldn't be as forgiving as Josie.

What should Lauren do now? What *could* she do? She was right back where she'd started when she returned to Brooklyn a few months ago, but it was worse this time, because she had so much more to lose.

Mia...

With numb fingers, Lauren picked up her phone and dialed.

"Hi," Mia answered. "Got a question about closing?"

"No," Lauren managed. "But...you need to come downstairs."

23

Mia entered the café to find Lauren on the floor behind the counter, arms wrapped around her knees, rocking herself like a frightened child. Her eyes were wide and unfocused. Mia's pulse spiked. "Lauren? What happened?"

"The cash is gone," Lauren whispered. "It's empty... someone took it."

"What?" Mia looked at the register. The cash drawer was open. She peered inside. It was empty, like Lauren had said. Mia's stomach sank. Oh shit. She'd left Lauren to close, and now all her cash was missing? Surely Lauren hadn't taken it, but then where was it?

"I'm going to jail after all." Lauren's words sounded like a moan.

Mia lowered herself to sit beside her. "Tell me what happened. Where is the cash?"

"Gone. It's all gone."

Mia rested a hand on her shoulder, feeling Lauren tremble beneath her touch. "I don't understand. Can you start at the beginning?"

"You said...you said if I ever betrayed you...you wouldn't be as forgiving as Josie." Lauren's voice was high-pitched, bordering on hysterical.

"Have you betrayed me?" Mia asked as something heavy settled in her stomach. Why wouldn't Lauren just tell her what happened?

"I lost it," Lauren said, and even her lips were shaking now. "I lost all the cash."

When Mia gripped her hand, Lauren's fingers were ice cold. Was she in shock? Had something happened to her? "Lauren, did someone rob the café? Are you hurt? Please talk to me."

"I don't *know* what happened," Lauren practically shouted, making Mia jump. "The cash is just...gone. Everyone will think I took it, because that's what I did last time. I'm a thief."

Mia couldn't take this any longer. They were both getting upset, and she still had no idea what was going on. She gripped Lauren's shoulders, forcing her to meet Mia's eyes. "You aren't making any sense. I need you to start at the beginning and tell me what happened."

"You'd never believe me," Lauren said miserably. "This is exactly what happened when I closed for Josie for the first time. What are the chances someone other than me robbed you tonight?"

That was a good question. Mia didn't like the odds, but why would Lauren steal from her? It made no sense. And if she had, why was she curled up on Mia's floor, too hysterical to speak coherently? This wasn't the behavior of a thief.

"Look, I'm a lawyer at heart, okay? I always collect all the facts and hear both sides of the story before I make up my mind about something. So please, for the love of God, take a breath and tell me what happened."

Lauren blinked, and then she sucked in a deep breath. "I was closing up, going through the routine the way you showed me, but when I opened the register, it was empty."

"And where was Jordy?"

"They left a little while ago." Lauren glanced wildly around the café as if expecting a thief with a bag of cash to leap out from under a table.

"Did anyone come into the café while you were closing?"

Lauren shook her head. "No, but I forgot to make sure the front door was locked before I went to wash my hands. Someone could have come in, but it doesn't seem likely. I was only gone a minute. I…I'm the obvious suspect."

"Would you please stop talking like that?" Mia gave her a little shake before wrapping one of her arms around Lauren's shoulders. "Honestly, I'm offended that you didn't even give me the benefit of the doubt. After everything we've shared, it never occurred to you that I might take your side?"

"But…I'm the only one here." Lauren looked at her out of wide, terrified eyes.

"And did you take the cash?"

"No," Lauren whispered.

"Okay then." Mia exhaled harshly. "That's all you had to say."

"Really?" Lauren's face crumpled, and she burst into tears.

"Yes, really." Mia's head was spinning, because what in the world had happened down here tonight? If not Lauren, who else could have possibly emptied out the cash register? It seemed unlikely anyone could have robbed the café during the time it took Lauren to wash her hands.

"Thank you," Lauren gasped between heartbreaking sobs.

Mia tightened her arm around Lauren's shoulders. "You're welcome."

"The police will think it was me," Lauren said in a small, shaky voice, and she probably had a point there.

Perhaps, if Mia set aside her natural cool headedness and looked at the situation through Lauren's eyes, she would panic too. At worst, Mia was out a few hundred dollars tonight. Hardly a catastrophe. But Lauren...well, the stakes were much higher for her.

"I think the next step is to call Jordy." Mia tugged her phone out of her back pocket. "Let's see if they know anything."

Lauren said nothing, sobbing quietly next to Mia. She looked absolutely wrecked, like her whole world had imploded, and maybe it had, but not if Mia had anything to say about it.

"Jordy," she said when the call connected. "Did you happen to check the cash register before you left tonight?"

"Oh shit," Jordy said in her ear. "I totally forgot you said Lauren was going to close tonight. I was on autopilot while I was cleaning up, and I closed out the register myself. I hope she doesn't think I did it because I don't trust her."

Mia exhaled, holding in a hysterical laugh. Of course, this was the simplest, most logical explanation, one Mia would certainly have reached on her own if she hadn't gotten sidetracked by Lauren's meltdown. "No worries at all, Jordy. I just needed to check."

"You got it. Sorry if I caused any confusion tonight."

"It's fine, just a simple misunderstanding. I'll see you tomorrow, okay?"

"Sure thing. Good night, Mia."

"Bye." Mia set the phone on the floor and turned to face

Lauren. "No one robbed the café. Jordy forgot you were closing tonight and closed out the register themself."

"What?" Lauren gave her a blank stare. Her face was too pale, and her skin was so cold. She was probably in shock. That would also explain why she hadn't made any sense since Mia came downstairs.

"Sit tight for a minute. I'll be right back." Mia stood and went down the hall to her office. She tapped in the code to the safe and opened it. Sure enough, there was the bag with today's date on it, right on top. Just to be sure, she peeked inside. All the cash was accounted for.

Mia walked back into the café. She double-checked that the front door was locked, and then she took Lauren's hands and hauled her to her feet. "The cash is in the safe. The door is locked. Everything's fine. Come on. You're coming upstairs with me."

Lauren followed her, blank-faced and silent. Her hand trembled in Mia's. Once they were in her apartment, Mia guided Lauren to the couch. Caffeine was probably the last thing she needed right now, but a hot beverage might help warm her up. Mia turned on the coffee maker. Her kitchen was littered with the ingredients of the meal she'd been in the middle of preparing when Lauren called, and while Mia generally couldn't tolerate a mess, right now, she was more concerned about Lauren than her cluttered countertops.

Mia made a decaf coffee for Lauren and carried a steaming mug with her as she went into the living room. She handed it to Lauren. "Talk to me. Are you okay?"

Lauren shook her head. "No," she whispered.

Mia sat beside her. "It was just a misunderstanding. Jordy forgot you were going to close tonight, and they locked up the cash themself. That's all it was."

Lauren stared at her coffee mug with wild eyes. "I

thought I'd lost everything. I was going to go to jail. I'd lose my job and my apartment and...and *you*."

"But you haven't," Mia reminded her. "Everything's okay. Why didn't you think I would believe you?" That was the one thing still bothering Mia. Lauren's lack of faith in her felt like a betrayal in itself.

"I don't know," Lauren whispered. She sat there, quietly sipping her coffee, and Mia just held her, unsure what to say. As the minutes passed, Lauren's breathing became more natural, and she quit shaking. When she finished her coffee, she set the mug on the table and burrowed herself into Mia's arms.

Mia held her, feeling the warmth of Lauren's tears as they soaked through her shirt. What a night. Mia felt like she'd been through an emotional blender, and now she couldn't quite seem to settle.

Finally, Lauren straightened. When she looked at Mia this time, her eyes were clear and focused. "I'm sorry I lost it earlier."

"I don't blame you for being upset, but I wish you'd had a little faith in me."

"It's just...it looked bad. I'm a thief, and the cash was gone. You'd warned me not to betray you, and I didn't even have an explanation for what had happened."

"I barely knew you when I said that, and I also told you I had your back, no matter what. Did you not think I meant it?" Mia could hear the hurt in her words.

Lauren pushed a hand through her hair. "No...I don't know. I guess...no one's ever really had my back before. I've always had to look out for myself. When I opened that drawer, and it was empty, I panicked. I spiraled out. I couldn't even think clearly, let alone explain myself to you."

"You were in shock," Mia said, gentler this time. She had

no frame of reference for what Lauren must have felt when she saw that empty cash drawer. Given Lauren's personal history, of course she had panicked.

Lauren gripped Mia's hands. Hers still trembled slightly. "You were so amazing tonight. You were calm and rational, and you never blamed me. I wasn't even trying to defend myself. I was being a complete idiot, and you still didn't blame me."

"It didn't make sense for you to have robbed me. I was just frustrated that you wouldn't explain yourself, and I'm sorry about that, because in retrospect, it's obvious that you were in shock."

"I was afraid I'd lost everything. The thought of losing you..." Fresh tears spilled over Lauren's cheeks.

"Well, that's not going to happen." Mia drew Lauren against her, holding her tight. "And you did the right thing tonight, Lauren. Despite how scared you were, you didn't run. You called me immediately, even thinking I wouldn't believe you."

"I'm so sorry for thinking that," Lauren whispered against Mia's chest. "I won't doubt you again."

"Neither will I." Mia tucked a lock of hair behind Lauren's ear. "I already trusted you completely, but tonight proved that I was right in my trust."

Lauren lifted her head from Mia's chest to give her a shaky smile. "And you certainly proved that you meant it when you said you had my back. I can't tell you how much that means to me."

"Then maybe something positive came out of tonight after all. Now do you feel up to helping me salvage our dinner?"

～

ON THANKSGIVING MORNING, they woke together in Mia's bed. Lauren had spent several nights here over the past week, and as much as she loved her own bedroom, nothing compared to waking with Mia snuggled against her. Somehow, they stayed nestled against each other all night, and it had become one of Lauren's favorite things in the world.

Something had settled between them since the night of the "not robbery," as Lauren had started calling it. Every time she remembered the way she'd felt that night—the overwhelming fear and helplessness—she saw Mia, so calm and logical as she talked Lauren through it.

Lauren wasn't alone anymore. She had someone she could depend on, someone who would be there for her, no matter what. For the first time in her entire life, she felt truly *safe*. Not just a momentary respite between crises, but a sense of peace and security she'd never imagined possible. She snuggled closer against Mia in bed.

"Happy Thanksgiving," Mia murmured, her face half-hidden in the fabric of Lauren's T-shirt.

"Oh, yeah." Lauren felt a flutter of nerves at the reminder that she'd be meeting Mia's father and his wife later today. "Happy Thanksgiving."

Mia must have felt her tense, because she lifted her head to meet Lauren's eyes. "My dad's going to adore you. So will Addie. They're so laidback and welcoming. I promise you're going to get along."

"It's not that I'm afraid he'll dislike me. It's just...I don't know."

Mia's hands fisted in the back of Lauren's shirt, holding her close. "You're missing your family and feeling weird about spending the holiday with mine?"

"Something like that," Lauren whispered, leaning in

until her forehead rested against Mia's so she could breathe in the comfort of her scent.

"I'm sorry. I know it's hard without Craig."

"It is, but being with you makes it a little easier."

"You've made this year a lot better for me too," Mia murmured, and her lips brushed Lauren's, a gentle, comforting kiss. They held each other for several minutes, and all of Lauren's tension melted away within the warmth of Mia's embrace and the pleasure of her lips.

"I have a lot to be thankful for today," Lauren said.

"So do I, and speaking of Thanksgiving, I need to bake a pie this morning."

Lauren smiled. "Since when do you bake?"

"Only on holidays," Mia said against her lips, "which means, as much as I want to spend the morning in bed with you, I've got to get moving."

"That's a damn shame, although I can't wait to help you bake a pie."

"It can wait just a *few* minutes," Mia whispered before she disappeared beneath the sheet, kissing a hot trail down Lauren's stomach.

"Oh," Lauren gasped as Mia placed a gentle kiss against her hip.

"Yes," Mia murmured, her lips hot against Lauren's skin. She placed several kisses across Lauren's thighs while her fingers traced erotic patterns on her skin. Everything felt heightened with Mia hidden beneath the sheet, and Lauren was already intensely aroused.

And then Mia's mouth closed over her clit. Lauren moaned, long and low, her hips arching toward Mia. She closed her eyes and surrendered to the pleasure of Mia's mouth as she licked and sucked and swirled her tongue until Lauren was about to lose her mind.

She came with a cry, pleasure bursting through her system, obliterating the last remnants of sleep from her brain. Yep, she was wide-awake now, still gasping with pleasure as Mia reappeared from beneath the sheet to give her a quick kiss.

"Did I hear an offer to help me bake pie?" she asked with a cocky grin.

"Yep, but not until I have a taste of you first."

Lauren tossed the sheet aside and shimmied down Mia's body, finding her already wet. Apparently getting Lauren off turned Mia on, and she could relate. Nothing was more arousing than watching Mia come apart beneath her.

Lauren took her time, kissing and teasing until Mia was good and ready for her, and then she pressed the flat of her tongue against Mia's clit, rewarded by a harsh gasp. She coated two of her fingers in Mia's wetness before sliding them inside her. Mia's hips bucked beneath her, and she sank her hands into Lauren's hair, holding her close.

Within minutes, Lauren had Mia writhing beneath her. She came with a shout, her body tensing and then going limp against the sheet. Lauren trailed her lips over Mia's stomach and up her chest to her mouth, where they met for a passionate kiss.

"Happy Thanksgiving indeed," Mia murmured, still breathing heavily.

Lauren laughed, but yeah, she was pretty thankful for the way their morning had started too. They held each other until they'd caught their breath. Then they got up, dressed, and went into the kitchen.

"What kind of pie are we baking?"

"Chocolate cream," Mia said as she took a ball of dough out of the fridge.

"That's not what I was expecting," Lauren admitted.

Mia gave her an affectionate smile. "It was my favorite when I was growing up, and to be honest, it's the only one my dad trusts me with. I'd definitely screw up something more complicated."

"I'm not sure I've ever had a chocolate pie before, but I think I'm going to like it," Lauren said with a grin.

"Based on your coffee order, I think you agree that chocolate makes everything better?"

"I sure do."

Lauren worked side by side with Mia in the kitchen as they rolled out the dough and pressed it into a pie pan, kissing and dotting each other with flour as they worked. While the dough baked, they made the chocolate cream filling, which they poured into the crust and then placed it in the fridge to set.

"It needs to chill at least four hours, so I'll have to stop back here for it after we finish volunteering, but we'll need to get changed before we go to my dad's anyway."

They got in the shower together, which was highly distracting since Lauren was much more interested in the way the water splashed over Mia's body than in getting clean. But she managed, and they both dressed in jeans and casual shirts to go to the shelter. But first, they stopped downstairs to feed and care for the foster cats since the café was closed today.

They spent the next three hours at the shelter prepping massive amounts of food. Lauren baked rolls while Mia peeled and chopped potatoes, and they finished out their shift serving plates of food to a steady stream of people who'd come in for a hot meal. That was always Lauren's favorite part, and she left the shelter feeling tired but satisfied.

"Damn, I'm starving already," she commented as they boarded the subway.

"Tell me about it," Mia said. "We missed lunch, and being around all that food was just a tease."

"Something tells me your dad's about to make up for that," Lauren said as a hint of her earlier nervousness crept back in. She was about to meet Mia's father. She'd never played "meet the parents" before, nor did she have any context for a happy family Thanksgiving. Logically, she knew it was going to be great, but it didn't stop her from feeling out of place.

"Big time," Mia confirmed.

After a quick stop at Mia's apartment to change and pick up the pie, they were on their way to Mia's dad's house. Lauren tried not to fidget as they exited the subway at his stop, but she knew Mia could tell she was nervous. She reached over and took Lauren's hand, giving her a reassuring smile.

"Will you stay with me again tonight?" she asked.

"Oh, um, yeah I can, but I have to be up early to work at the market."

"That's fine. I'm opening the café tomorrow too."

They smiled at each other, and Lauren's chest loosened. This was going to be okay. She blew out a breath. It would take time for her to stop feeling like the other shoe was about to drop. She'd spent her entire life searching for the kind of stability she'd found in the last few months. Ironically, she'd had to hit rock bottom to get here.

Mia pointed out a brown-paneled row house ahead, and Lauren tensed again as nerves burst to life in her stomach. Mia gave her hand a squeeze before leading the way up the front steps, balancing the pie in her free hand. Before she'd even had a chance to knock, the door swung open to reveal a smiling, gray-haired man wearing a red apron.

"You must be Lauren," he said, extending his arms for a hug. "I'm Mia's father, Francisco, and I am so pleased to meet you."

24

A s she headed down to open the café, Mia was glad Black Friday was just another Friday for her. Lauren had left an hour ago to stock the shelves at the market, expecting an influx of customers looking for deals, but people didn't tend to bargain shop at a cat café.

A dull headache had wrapped itself around Mia's temples, the result of too much wine yesterday and not enough sleep, thanks to the woman in her bed. Now that they'd started, they couldn't seem to keep their hands off each other.

But Mia was dragging this morning. She was grumpy and frustrated as she cleaned up after the cats and prepared their breakfast. It wasn't the early hour or the prospect of a long day ahead that had her holding in a sigh as one of the cats stepped on the plate and tracked wet food across the floor with his dirty paw.

As a lawyer, she'd gotten up earlier than this too many times to count, eager to get a head start at the office, never tiring as she poured over briefs and depositions or prepared for a long day in court. She'd worked twelve-hour days with hardly a break and loved every moment.

Sweeping cat litter off the floor didn't provide the same thrill. Now that she'd acknowledged how much she missed practicing law, it felt like a persistent itch between her shoulder blades, out of reach but annoying enough that she couldn't quite forget it was there.

What could she do about it, though? She'd invested her savings and almost a year of her life into this café. She couldn't just abandon it. That wasn't her style. And she did love the café. She loved helping these cats get adopted and being home in time to spend lazy evenings with Lauren. But the days were starting to feel monotonous. Boring.

She let out a groan as she put the broom back into the closet. Twelve hours later, as she closed up for the night, she was still groaning. Lauren had texted earlier that she was going to her apartment for the evening to work on edits for her book and then calling it an early night. Mia went upstairs, changed into workout gear, and headed to the gym.

She did some strength training and sweated out a few miles on the treadmill before pulling on her jacket and heading out. She stopped to pick up a sandwich for dinner on the way home. As she approached her building, she noticed an Office Space Available sign in the window of the law practice next door.

Huh. She paused, staring at the sign. Would she be getting new neighbors? She felt a stab of jealousy toward the lawyers who worked inside, doing what she loved while she served coffee and scooped litter boxes next door. And then... an idea sparked. Maybe there was a way to have her cake and eat it too, so to speak.

It was something to think about, at least. Her mind was spinning with possibilities as she unlocked the door to her building and let herself inside. Upstairs, she ate her sandwich and sat down with her laptop to research a few things. And then, feeling tentatively hopeful, she showered and went to bed.

The weekend was a busy one, with Mia filling in for Jordy, who'd gone out of town for the holiday. Lauren worked both days at the market, and although they had dinner together on Saturday, that was the only time they saw each other. On Monday morning, Mia was at the café early again, but today, Lauren would be working here with her, and Mia was surprised how impatient she was to see her after spending most of the weekend apart.

"Hey," Lauren said as she came into Mia's office, bag slung over her shoulder.

"Morning." Mia felt herself smiling. "Did you get a lot of edits done this weekend?"

Lauren nodded as she tucked her bag into a cubby. "I just need another couple of days to finish, and then it'll be ready for the proofreader...which is slightly terrifying, because after that, it's done. Ready to publish."

"That's the good kind of terrifying," Mia said.

"It is." Lauren beamed at her. "Now that the felony charge is behind me, I'm really excited about publishing this book. I think I'm going to set a release date after all, maybe early spring, and give it as much of a push as I can."

"You should, and let's plan something for your release day. Maybe the ladies from our group chat would want to come into the city and have a little launch celebration for you."

Lauren flinched. "That feels like...a lot."

"Really? Why?"

"I don't know. I feel weird asking them to plan a whole trip into the city just for me?" Lauren ducked her head.

Mia tsked at that. "I think they'd love the excuse to celebrate with you, and if it's too much for anyone, they just
won't come. You aren't twisting anyone's arm if you extend
an invitation."

"I'll think about it," Lauren told her with a hesitant
smile.

"Okay. Hey, are you working at the market after you
leave here this afternoon?"

"Nope. I was going to try to work on some more edits."

"Want to do that at my place?" Mia asked. "Surely you
can work faster on my laptop than on your phone."

"Aren't you working?"

"I'm only doing admin after lunch, which means technically, I could take my work home with me."

"But then wouldn't *you* need your laptop?" Lauren asked
with a smile.

"Okay, smartass, I just want to hang out with you later.
I've missed you. I'll try to finish up early, okay?" She leaned
in and gave her a quick kiss.

"Okay," Lauren agreed. "I'll catch up with you after my
shift."

Feeling significantly better about her day, Mia headed
out to help at the counter until lunchtime. Her morning was
further brightened when Josie came in for a coffee.

"My new favorite home away from home," Josie told her.
"I'm so glad this café exists and that I have time to sit and
drink coffee while surrounded by rescue cats."

Mia laughed. "I'm glad for those things too." Although,
Josie's words made her feel guilty all over again for her
recent bitter feelings toward the café. She fixed Josie's latte
and didn't comment on the fact that she hadn't asked for
decaf. She knew better than to bring up what might be a

sensitive topic if things were taking longer than she and Eve had hoped.

Josie took her coffee and a croissant and sat in the cat enclosure, where she alternated between messing around on her phone and playing with the cats, and Mia smiled when she saw her chatting with Lauren too.

By lunchtime, Lauren joined her at the counter, and Mia retreated to her office to finish her admin work as quickly as possible so she could enjoy the afternoon with Lauren. She opened her accounting software and was hard at work when Lauren came in later to retrieve her bag.

"Still want me to come up and work at your place this afternoon?" she asked.

Mia nodded. "You go on up, and I'll be there in a half hour or so."

"'Kay." Lauren leaned over the desk and gave her a quick kiss.

Mia finished what she was doing and went down the hall to check in with Jordy, annoyed that she could feel a migraine beginning to throb behind her eyes. Maybe she'd go upstairs and take a nap while Lauren worked. But first, she had a quick—but important—errand to run.

MIA LET herself into her apartment an hour later, bubbling with nervous excitement to tell Lauren what she'd just done. But also...her migraine had fully manifested, leaving her woozy with pain. Lauren was on the couch with her laptop, hard at work. Mia exhaled, smiling. She'd missed the sight of Lauren on her couch, writing. Her apartment felt more like home when Lauren was here.

"How's it coming?" Mia asked as she walked to the kitchen to take her medication.

"I was just messaging with another author, actually," Lauren told her. "I've met a few other indie sapphic romance authors on Twitter, and they've been so helpful, showing me the ropes."

"That's wonderful." Mia poured a glass of water and swallowed her pill, and then, rubbing her forehead, she sat beside Lauren on the couch.

Lauren gave her a bashful smile. "I don't know if you saw it yet, but the ladies in our group chat are harassing me to set a release date so they can plan a trip to the city."

"See?" Mia nudged her with her elbow. "They want to support you. Can I plan a launch event for you? Maybe we can have it at Dragonfly."

Lauren hesitated for a moment and then nodded. "Yeah. Okay."

"Consider it done." Mia leaned in and kissed her. "Would you like me to let you work for a while?" Maybe she was stalling, nervous about Lauren's reaction to her news, but also, it was hard to think straight with this pain throbbing behind her eyes.

Lauren smiled against her lips. "As much as I want to be distracted, I really do need to get these edits finished."

"And I want you to finish them. Actually, I've got a migraine so I'm going to lie down for a bit while you work."

"Okay. Sorry about your migraine. Anything I can do?"

Mia shook her head. "I saw my doctor earlier this month and got a new prescription that shouldn't upset my stomach. I just took a pill, so hopefully I'll feel better soon."

Lauren's expression softened. "Look at you, taking such better care of yourself than when we first met."

"I am," Mia agreed. "Good luck with your edits."

She went into her bedroom, where she changed into comfortable clothes and climbed into bed. And then she lay there, listening to the clatter of keys from the living room. It was surprisingly soothing, or maybe that was just the knowledge that Lauren was here. She loved these quiet, domestic moments just as much as she loved the passionate ones.

The next thing she knew, she startled awake to the sound of a siren passing by on the street outside. She opened her eyes, surprised to see that her bedroom was bathed in the golden glow of the setting sun, but also relieved that her migraine seemed to be gone. Wow, those new pills really worked, but how long had she been asleep?

She rolled over, looking for her phone, but she must have left it in the living room. "Lauren?" she called.

"Hey, Sleeping Beauty," Lauren responded, appearing in the doorway. "Feeling better?"

"Much," Mia confirmed, although she didn't sit up, fearing the change in equilibrium might bring her headache roaring back to life. "Sorry for conking out on you."

"Don't be." Lauren came to sit on the bed. "I finished my edits, and you obviously needed the sleep."

"I like having you here," Mia murmured, reaching for her.

"I like being here." She lay beside Mia, rolling to face her. "And I got through my edits so much faster on your laptop."

"That's the first purchase you should make with all the money you're going to earn from your book release." Mia ran her fingers through Lauren's hair, content with the world.

"I've got to pay off my editor and all that good stuff first,"

Lauren told her. "Self-publishing is expensive when you're just getting started."

"I bet, but I predict big things for you." Mia scooted closer so she could wrap an arm around Lauren.

"Hope you're right." Lauren settled against her. "I want to be realistic, though. This first book isn't going to make me rich. From what I'm hearing from other authors, the best thing I can focus on right now is writing the next book, and then the one after that."

"Sounds smart," Mia said. "So have you? Written the next book, that is."

"I've started the outline for it. I'm learning so much from these other authors. It's exciting. I feel like I can really do this."

"I'm so proud of you." That pride filled her chest, and it spilled over into a kiss as she pulled Lauren closer. "Feel free to hang out on my couch and use my laptop anytime."

"Thanks." Lauren's cheeks were adorably pink. "You've done wonders for my self-esteem with this book."

"I'm glad, because I believe in it and you. And so do a lot of other people in the fandom community, so you can't accuse me of being biased."

"Even if you *are* biased."

"I might be now, but I read your fic before I met you, remember? And I believed in you then too. I fell in love with your words before I fell in love with *you*." They both froze as Mia's words hung in the air between them. She hadn't meant to blurt it out quite like that, but she didn't want to take it back either.

"Um." Lauren blinked at her out of watery eyes.

"You heard me," Mia whispered. "And you don't have to say it back if it's too soon."

"On the contrary." Lauren's voice wavered slightly. "I had

been looking for the right moment to tell you that I love you too."

Mia felt her whole body flush hot, joy flowing through her veins, and then unexpected tears were spilling over her cheeks. Mia was *not* a crier, but if there were ever a moment...

"This is a first," Lauren said as she wiped away her tears.

"What? Me crying?" Mia rolled her eyes playfully. "Believe it or not, it's happened before."

"No... Me falling in love," Lauren told her quietly, and the truth of her admission was written all over her face.

"Oh." Mia reached out to cup her cheek, almost overwhelmed by the emotions swirling inside her, all good ones, love and affection and gratitude that they'd found each other. "I never imagined that this was going to happen. For the longest time, I thought we were just friends. And somewhere in there, you snuck in and stole my heart."

"You've had mine almost from the moment we met."

"I'll be careful with it." Mia pressed her palm over Lauren's heart, because she knew this was a big deal for her. She'd been through so much, and Mia would happily spend the rest of her life making sure Lauren knew how much she loved her.

"Thanks," Lauren whispered with tear-filled eyes. "I know it's in good hands."

"I have something to tell you," Mia murmured, and then her heart was pounding for an entirely different reason.

"Yeah?"

"I rented the empty office next door."

"What?" Lauren's voice rose. "The law office?"

Mia nodded. "The building is leased by a group of lawyers who all practice independently, but they share a space to save on rental costs, and they have an empty office to fill, so I rented it. You were right. I need to practice law again, but not the way I was before. I'm not going to be part of a firm this time, chasing partnership and working twelve-plus hours a day. This will be just me, taking on the clients I believe in. Maybe I can channel my inner Samantha Whitaker and represent women who need someone to fight for them."

"Mia, that's beautiful," Lauren said. "Look how Sam has inspired us both, me as an author and you as a lawyer."

"Poetic, isn't it?"

Lauren nodded. "But what will happen to the café?"

"I'll hire a full-time manager, someone to run the café for me when I'm not there. In fact, I'd like it to be you."

Lauren blinked at her in surprise. "Me?"

"You love it more than I do," Mia said. "I noticed that over the last few months. It fulfills you in a way it doesn't for me. I'll still check in, and I might even work a few shifts, but I can't think of anyone more perfect to run the café than you."

"Wow," Lauren said. "Um...I don't know what to say."

"Do you want it? Because please tell me if you don't, and I'll hire someone else."

"I do." Fresh tears spilled over Lauren's cheeks. "I really do. You're right about how much I love it there. I love inter-acting with the cats and the customers and being involved with the rescue. Everything about it is perfect for me. But wait... What about Jordy? They're your assistant manager. Wouldn't they want this job?"

"Jordy is content as assistant manager while they attend college in the evenings. They're going to be a nurse."

"Oh." A smile bloomed on Lauren's face. "They'll be an awesome nurse."

"Yes, they will. If I make you the full-time manager, the

day-to-day decisions and operation of the café would fall to you. I'd be more like a silent partner, not your boss. And you'd have a steady income and all the benefits you don't have now."

"Honestly, it sounds like my dream job."

"Might cut into your writing time," Mia warned.

"It will, but I'm years away from supporting myself on the income from my books no matter what, and who knows? Maybe by then, I'll be able to afford enough staff at the café to give me more time off to write."

"I like the way you think." Mia grinned at her. "I *love* it. And I love you, and while I totally respect that you need your own place right now, please know how much I miss you every moment you're not here and that I desperately hope you'll move back in once your lease is up."

Lauren gave her a goofy smile. "Pretty sure there's a U-Haul joke in there somewhere."

"I'm a total lesbian cliché," Mia agreed.

"Better rent that U-Haul then, because in this case, I love being a cliché," Lauren whispered as she leaned in for another kiss.

Mia smiled against her lips. "Look at that, you just wrote another happy ending."

Lauren was beaming, happiness and joy seeming to radiate from her. "The most important one I'll ever write."

EPILOGUE

FIVE MONTHS LATER

Lauren clutched the backpack containing Craig's urn in her lap as the train whisked her toward her destination. The floor vibrated beneath her feet, but unlike that day last August when she'd ridden into the city with all her worldly possessions crammed into the seat with her, today she wasn't alone.

"You don't have to do this today if you're not ready, you know." Mia reached over to give Lauren's hand a squeeze. Her hair had gotten longer over the winter, curling against the collar of her shirt. It softened her look a bit, not that she needed any softening. Lauren loved all of Mia's sharp edges...as well as the soft ones.

"I'm ready," Lauren said. "Although we'll have to stop at home so I can redo my makeup before the event later, because I'm definitely going to cry."

"You'll probably cry again later too," Mia said with a gentle smile. "Happy tears."

"Very likely." Lauren tightened her grip on the backpack. She'd dreaded this day for so long, and now that it was here, she felt...okay. This wasn't a farewell. She'd said goodbye to her brother last year. She could still talk to Craig when she missed him. She didn't need his urn to do that, and Prospect Park was only a short subway ride away if she needed to feel closer to him.

The train pulled to a stop at their station, and they exited and climbed the steps to the street. Mia slipped her hand into Lauren's. Before them, Prospect Park beckoned, and Lauren was so glad she'd waited until spring to do this. The trees were lush and green, and flowers bloomed along the paths, filling the air with their fresh scent.

"Lead the way," Mia said. "You mentioned a special tree?"

"There's an oak near the lake." Lauren's voice was hoarse from the lump that had formed in her throat. "We would meet there on holidays and birthdays when we were living in different homes. We even carved our initials into the trunk to mark it as our spot."

"That's beautiful," Mia said quietly.

Hand in hand, they entered the park. They circled partway around the lake before Lauren led Mia off the path to where her oak tree awaited. Its branches sprawled overhead, providing a green canopy of leaves. The trunk was thick and gnarled, and roots jutted from it where it met the ground, smooth in places where people had used them as seats.

Lauren and Mia walked to one of those spots and sat. For a few minutes, neither of them said anything. Lauren watched people stroll by on the sidewalk, grateful no one else was sitting near the oak tree today. Birds called overhead, and the air was rich with the scent of earth and vegetation.

She unzipped her backpack and lifted the urn out before setting the empty bag on the ground. Tears spilled over her cheeks as she hugged it to her chest one last time. "I'm celebrating my book launch later today, Craig, and I'm going to miss having you there so much."

Mia's arm wrapped around her shoulders and squeezed.

Lauren rested her head on Mia's shoulder. "Craig was my first reader, technically. I used to write these silly stories for him since we didn't have many books at home. I wrote about a brave knight named Craig who fought fire-breathing dragons and evil sorcerers. His sister Lauren fought alongside him, because she'd gotten bored being the princess in the castle, waiting for the white knight to save her."

"A feminist to your core." Mia kissed the top of her head. "I wish someone had written stories like that for me when I was a little girl. I can only imagine how much it meant to Craig to have those stories—and you—in his life."

"He was my whole world," Lauren whispered as more tears splashed over her cheeks. "I don't think this ache in my chest will ever go away."

"It might not," Mia murmured, "but I do think it will get easier with time. He'll always be with you, and when you talk to him, you're keeping him alive in your heart."

"That's what I started to realize these last few months too. I don't need this urn full of ashes to feel close to him. It's time to set him free." Lauren stood and opened the urn, carefully lifting the bag of ashes out of it.

Mia picked up a leaf from the ground before standing beside Lauren. She held it up. "To see which way the wind is blowing," she said before allowing the leaf to flutter from her fingers.

They watched it drift to the ground, blowing toward the woods away from the lake. Lauren followed it and stood behind the tree, sheltered from the path and the other people exploring the park on this beautiful April day. Mia slid an arm around her waist, and Lauren leaned into her as she opened the bag and tipped it, allowing ashes to drift into the air.

"Bye, Craig," she whispered. "Be free. Be beautiful. Shine your light down on me from wherever you are up there, okay? I love you, and I'll always keep your memory alive with me."

She watched as the ashes drifted with the breeze, light and wispy, almost like smoke. It reminded her of the dragons Craig had drawn to illustrate her stories, with plumes of smoke coming from their nostrils. She waved the bag gently back and forth until all the ashes were gone, dispersed into the air.

Maybe the oak tree would absorb some of Craig's essence where bits of ash settled on its roots. In a way, that would make him as powerful as the knight in her stories. She put the empty bag back into the urn, and Mia pulled her wordlessly into her arms, holding her tight as she cried.

When she lifted her head, a ray of sunlight met her face, warm and bright, and she felt peace.

DRAGONFLY GLOWED WITH FAIRY LIGHTS, but instead of the usual white and lavender, today the lights were shaped like little golden stars to go with *Meet Me at Midnight*'s theme. Stacks of books were displayed at each end of the bar, and the room was filled with people who'd come to help Lauren celebrate. She'd changed into a shimmery aqua blouse and black jeans for the event, and she glowed almost as brightly as the fairy lights overhead.

Mia couldn't take her eyes off her. She kept her phone in

hand, snapping photos of everything so neither of them would forget a single moment of this day. Josie had opened the bar early for the party, and it was theirs for the afternoon. Quinn, Sarah, Fatima, and Ashleigh were here, as well as a number of other friends from the *In Her Defense* fandom.

Wendy and Jordy from the café had come, along with some of Josie and Eve's friends, and even a few of Mia's new clients. Since January, she'd been working at her new office Monday through Thursday, finishing out the week with Fridays at the café. Lauren had really blossomed in her role as manager, and Mia had found her passion again in private practice.

She and Lauren spent their weekends at home together and saw each other a lot during the week too. Lauren had moved back into Mia's apartment permanently last month. It was *their* apartment now. Mia was happy and fulfilled in her new law practice. Now that she had an equally satisfying life outside the office, she no longer felt driven to work herself to death.

"You're staring at Lauren with hearts in your eyes," Josie said, startling Mia out of her thoughts.

Mia smiled, watching Lauren as she chatted with several fandom friends. "I suppose I am."

"I'm happy for you," Josie said. "And I have some happy news of my own to share."

Mia whirled to face her, suddenly aware of the blush on Josie's cheeks and the extra sparkle in her eyes. "Oh my God. You're pregnant?"

"Actually, no," Josie said, and Mia's stomach dropped that she'd jumped to the wrong conclusion and blurted out something insensitive, but Josie was still beaming, gesturing toward Eve, who stood nearby, talking to her friend Kaia and her new girlfriend. "Eve is."

"Oh." Mia exhaled, excitement replacing embarrassment. "Wow...oh wow. That's wonderful news!"

Josie bounced on her toes. "We're so excited, you have no idea. Last year was really frustrating. I was inseminated five times, and it just wasn't working. Eve finally convinced me to let her try, just once...and boom, she's pregnant."

"Why did she have to convince you?" Mia asked.

"Because she's—"

"If you say I'm old..." Eve had turned to face them, eyes narrowed as she tuned into their conversation. She wore a formfitting gray dress, looking as slim as ever, but maybe there was a bit of a glow to her complexion, now that Mia was paying attention.

"You're old*er* than I am." Josie kissed her wife's cheek. "And you have fused vertebrae in your spine."

"The doctor says I'll be fine." Eve brushed a hand reflexively against her stomach.

"So...we're having a baby," Josie gushed, tears on her cheeks.

"And I'm going to be an uncle." Adam stepped between Josie and Eve and slung an arm over both of their shoulders, answering Mia's unasked question about whether he was still their donor.

But now that Eve was carrying their baby instead of Josie...Mia's lips twitched at the implication.

Eve pointed a finger in her direction, obviously having guessed the source of her amusement. "Don't you dare make an Adam and Eve joke." But she looked like she was fighting a smile too.

"I wouldn't dream of it. I'm just so happy for you both," Mia said. "Congratulations."

"Thank you." There was something different about Eve,

and it wasn't just the glow of pregnancy. She looked...radiant. Happier than Mia had ever seen her, and if anyone deserved this kind of happiness, it was Eve.

Warmth bloomed in Mia's chest, as well as a tug of longing. After her divorce, she'd thought she had missed her chance to start a family, but maybe...maybe she'd get a second chance too.

Lauren walked over to join them, looking absolutely thrilled for Josie and Eve when she heard their news. They talked for a few more minutes, and then Josie glanced at the clock. "I'd better get up there and officially start this event. Lauren, you ready?"

Lauren nodded with a nervous smile.

Josie crossed the room to stand in front of the bar and clapped her hands together, drawing everyone's attention. "It's time for our favorite new author to read us a scene from her book, and by the way, the copies you see here on the bar are available for purchase. A portion of the proceeds will benefit my kitten rescue, and Lauren will sign them for you too."

Cheeks pink, Lauren accepted the copy of *Meet Me at Midnight* that Josie held out to her, and then she hopped onto a barstool. She'd practiced her reading at home with Mia last night, trying out a few scenes until she found the right one. Mia lifted her phone and took another series of photos as Lauren opened the book and began to read.

"The stars overhead were muted by the glow of the city as Isabelle lifted her gaze to the night sky. She wondered if the woman she'd met last night was looking at them too..."

Mia's heart swelled with pride as she listened to Lauren read. She'd come so far in the last year, reclaiming her life after hitting rock bottom right here in this very bar. Now she'd realized her dream of becoming a published author.

Mia felt sure Craig was here somewhere, silently cheering for her.

After her reading, Lauren signed copies of the book while Mia took more photos. Once she had plenty of pictures of Lauren signing, Mia got drinks for them at the bar. Josie had created a new signature drink just for Lauren, a pink cocktail called Love Struck, garnished with a hibiscus bloom.

"Cheers," Mia said when Lauren was alone at last. She handed her one of the glasses, and they tapped them together.

"To the woman who inspired me to reach for the stars." Lauren's eyes glittered with happy tears.

"And to the woman who showed me love's a partnership, not a competition," Mia said.

"Aww," Lauren whispered as her tears broke free. "I'll drink to that."

Mia brushed Lauren's tears away with her fingertips. "I was a lost soul when I met you. I might have looked like I had my shit together, but as you know, I barely even remembered to feed myself."

"You were pretty bad at self-care," Lauren admitted with a grin.

"I was terrible. I'd never lived alone before, and I was hating it. I was so lonely, and I was trying so hard to pretend the café was all I needed to be fulfilled. Then you came along and showed me friendship and took care of me and made me laugh and cooked me the best damned grilled cheese I've ever had." She smiled at the memory. "You helped me realize what I truly wanted out of life."

Lauren was crying openly now, her free hand clenched in Mia's. "Maybe you should be an author too, because that's the most romantic thing I've ever heard."

"Oh please. I can write a hell of a legal brief, but my talent stops there. I'm just so glad you wrote *Skin Deep*, because that fanfic is what first brought us together."

"To Sam Whitaker and to Piper Sheridan for bringing her to life," Lauren murmured, lifting her glass to Mia's for another toast.

∾

"STICK AROUND FOR A BIT, OKAY?" Josie said. "I've got a surprise for you before you leave."

"Sure, but you didn't have to do anything else, Josie. This party was already amazing enough." Lauren felt a tug of discomfort, hoping Josie hadn't gone overboard.

"We raised a ton of money for my rescue today, so I'm calling the party a success for us both." Josie tapped her knuckles against Lauren's before she headed down the hall to her office.

Lauren rested her elbows on the bar, watching as the remaining party guests finished up their drinks. Mia was at a table along the back wall, talking to one of her clients on the phone. There was a gleam in her eye since she'd opened her new law practice, the same one Lauren had first seen the day Mia walked into the courthouse with her.

Practicing law was in her blood. Now that she'd gone into private practice, she'd chosen to represent women almost exclusively, not unlike the character who had first brought them together. Lauren was so proud of her, she could burst.

"Will you stop by the Airbnb later?" Ashleigh asked as she came over to give Lauren a hug. "We're going to do an *In Her Defense* marathon."

"Absolutely," Lauren told her. "Thanks so much for coming today."

Before she knew it, she was enveloped in hugs from Ash, Sarah, Quinn, and Fatima. They took selfies with their newly signed books, and then they headed out with promises to meet up again later.

The door closed behind them, and Lauren was alone at the bar. Well, almost alone. Mia was on her phone at a table in back, and Eve sat at the other end of the bar, talking to Adam. She wore a sleek gray dress, looking as polished and glamorous as ever. Lauren slid off her barstool, not wanting to dampen this perfect day with another uncomfortable encounter with Eve.

"You don't have to run away from me, you know."

Lauren turned to find Eve watching her, and heat rose in her cheeks. *Busted.* "Sorry."

"I don't hate you." Eve swirled the drink in her hands. It was pink—Love Struck—the drink Josie had created in Lauren's honor, but probably a virgin version of it, given her pregnancy.

"You have every right to," Lauren said. No matter how rosy her life was these days, that awful night would never leave her mind completely. She'd robbed this bar. She'd committed a felony. No, she'd never forget.

"I'd be a hypocrite to hold it against you now," Eve said. "You paid for your crime, and you've obviously worked hard to do better. Lord knows I've made mistakes myself, not criminal ones, but I hurt people when I was at my lowest. I hurt Josie too, you know."

Lauren wasn't sure what to say, so she just listened.

"I broke up with her after you robbed the bar," Eve told her. "I panicked and broke both our hearts in the process, but when I came to my senses, she forgave me, just like she forgave you. The least I can do is extend you the same courtesy."

"Thank you," Lauren said quietly.

Eve held her drink toward Lauren. "To new beginnings."

"New beginnings." Lauren lifted her own drink and took a sip.

Josie came bursting out of the back hallway. "Ready?"

"Sure," Lauren said, and there was a funny tingle in her belly, because what in the world was Josie up to?

"Is she almost done on that call?" Josie gestured to Mia, who held up a finger in acknowledgement. "When I found out about your fan fiction and how you and Mia met through the *In Her Defense* fandom, I couldn't resist." Josie's smile was pure glee.

"Resist what?" Lauren asked, drawing a blank on what Josie could possibly mean.

Mia ended her call and walked over to join them. "What's going on?"

"You're about to find out." Josie's eyes sparkled mischievously. "Come on in!" she called.

Piper Sheridan walked into the room, and Lauren slid right off her barstool. If Mia hadn't grabbed her, she'd have ended up on the floor. Piper's hair was down, glossy red waves falling over her shoulders, and *oh God*, she was so pretty, and she was here, in Dragonfly, walking toward Lauren with a wide smile on her face.

Lauren just stared. Her face was hot, and her body tingled with shock.

"Surprise," Josie said, clapping excitedly.

"Oh my God," Lauren croaked. Her heart was hammering in her chest, and there was a bubbly sensation in her stomach like it was filled with confetti.

"Hi," Piper said. "You must be Lauren."

"Hi," Lauren managed. Were her lips numb? Her lips were numb. And they were shaking. "What...how..."

"Did I not mention that I know Piper?" Josie asked, sounding absolutely delighted with herself.

Lauren shook her head, feeling a bit like she was having an out-of-body experience.

"I met my fiancée in this bar." Piper gestured to the blonde beside her, who Lauren somehow hadn't even noticed until this moment.

"I'm Chloe." She introduced herself with a friendly wave. "The fiancée."

"Hi," Lauren said, sounding embarrassingly breathless.

"When Piper and I were first dating, a friend of mine sent me the link to a Clairantha fanfic called *Skin Deep*," Chloe said. "Piper and I both read it. Well, I think she skipped some parts..."

"The sex scenes," Piper said apologetically. "Felt weird since Sam is essentially me, you know?"

"Oh," Lauren gasped, and she was *definitely* having an out-of-body experience, because Piper Sheridan was standing in front of her, telling her she'd read her fanfic, and this was *not* her real life.

"Anyway, I love that fic, and when Josie told us who you are, I asked her to set aside a copy of your new book for us," Chloe said. "Congrats on that, by the way."

"Thank you," Lauren breathed.

"She's usually a lot more eloquent than this," Mia said, giving Lauren a playful squeeze. "I think you've officially blown her fangirl mind. I'm Mia, Lauren's girlfriend."

"Nice to meet you, Mia." Piper stepped forward and shook Mia's hand.

"I'm a huge fan as well," Mia told her, as composed as

Lauren was starstruck. "In fact, your show is what brought Lauren and me together."

Piper smiled widely. "Oh, I love that."

"I'm a defense attorney, and I obviously think Sam Whitaker is a total badass," Mia told her.

"Sam's my hero," Lauren managed, trying desperately to find her composure, because Piper Sheridan was here, and Lauren was totally blowing the moment. "She—and you— got me through some hard times. I can't tell you how much it meant to see you on my TV, this out-and-proud actress playing one of the most incredible characters on TV. I'm just... This is such an honor."

"Thank you. That means a lot to hear." Piper extended her arms and pulled Lauren in for a hug, and when she released her, Lauren was crying again. Happy tears. So many happy tears.

Chloe held up a copy of *Meet Me at Midnight*. "Could you sign this to Piper and me?"

And so Lauren found herself signing a book to her idol. Her hand was shaking so badly that her handwriting looked weird. Talk about a surreal moment...

"We need pictures," Josie announced when she'd finished.

"Oh geez." Lauren wiped her cheeks, because apparently she was still crying.

"Here." Mia brushed her fingers beneath Lauren's eyes, touching her up.

They posed for pictures, one of Lauren and Piper, Lauren and Mia with Piper, and several group photos too. Chloe and Piper even posed for a picture with Lauren, holding their copy of her new book.

"Feel free to share these on your social media," Piper told her. "Just don't mention *that*"—she pointed to the diamond on Chloe's left ring finger—"until after we've made our public announcement, please."

"Oh, of course," Lauren gushed. "And congratulations. That's amazing news."

"Thank you." Piper gave Chloe an adoring smile. "We're really excited."

They shared more hugs and a few more photos, and then Piper and Chloe went out through the back, leaving Lauren and Mia alone with Josie and Eve.

"Well, this has been an eventful day," Mia said. "Josie, you know how to pull off an epic surprise."

Josie grinned. "Piper and Chloe come in here semi-regularly, so when I found out you two were mega fans of the show, I couldn't resist asking her if she'd be willing to meet you. I had a feeling she'd say yes."

"I drink at the same bar as Piper Sheridan." Lauren mimed her head exploding.

"You've *met* Piper Sheridan now," Mia said with a laugh. "The rest of the gang's going to lose it when they find out."

Lauren turned and flung her arms around Mia. "This day... Mia, I don't even know what to say."

"You don't have to say a word, because I see it all on your face," Mia murmured, bringing their lips together for a kiss. "Now, what do you say we head home for a little private celebration before we go to the Airbnb later?"

Lauren nodded, feeling suddenly overwhelmed. A little quiet time with Mia was exactly what she needed before she celebrated with her friends again later.

They said goodbye to Josie and Eve, thanking them profusely before they walked outside together. Lauren could hardly feel her feet on the pavement. She was literally walking on air. "I can't believe I signed books today. I met Piper Sheridan. Piper and Chloe are *engaged*."

"And Josie and Eve are having a baby. So much good news."

"So much," Lauren echoed.

"Remember the first time we went for drinks together at Dragonfly?" Mia asked.

"The night you got drunk," Lauren said, grinning.

Mia rolled her eyes. "Never going to live that down, but yes. I was drinking a Midnight in Manhattan, and you reminded me about the myth."

"If you drink one at midnight, you'll fall in love before the end of the year," Lauren said breathlessly. Oh yeah, she remembered.

"At the time, I thought there was no way I'd fall in love that quickly, and yet barely a month later, I was head over heels for you."

"The drink works. Josie always said so."

"I'm a believer." Mia's thumb brushed against Lauren's ring finger, and Lauren forgot to breathe, because Mia had stopped walking, and she was looking at Lauren like...like... "Marry me," Mia blurted, gripping Lauren's hand in hers.

"Yes," Lauren gasped. "Really? But yes!"

"Really." Tears shimmered in Mia's eyes. "I know this isn't the most romantic proposal, but I just love you so much, and there was so much happy news today, and I just... I want that for us. I want all of it."

"A family?" Lauren's heart clenched as tears rolled over her cheeks. She'd barely dared to dream of having a family of her own when her life was such a mess, but now...

Mia nodded. "If you want that too. I'd love to start a family with you."

"Yes." Lauren nodded, crying in earnest now. "I want that so much."

Mia cupped her cheeks, drawing her in for a kiss, and

then she dropped to one knee. A woman passing by on the sidewalk exclaimed, "Oh my God. Congratulations!"

"Lauren Booker, you are the love of my life. Because of you, I feel content and fulfilled and so excited about everything the future will bring. I promise to take you ring shopping tomorrow, but until then, please accept this kiss as a token of my love." She pressed her lips against Lauren's ring finger.

"Oh my God, Mia..." Lauren rested her free hand against her heart. "You're wrong. That was the most romantic proposal ever. I can't wait to marry you. We're going to be so freaking happy."

Mia looked up at her with a radiant smile. "We already are."

ACKNOWLEDGMENTS

This book has been a long time coming. As I was writing *Don't Cry for Me* back in 2019, Lauren was supposed to be the villain, a throwaway character who would never be seen again, but she caught my attention. I could see her back-story, and I knew I wanted to redeem her, but I'd already plotted *It's in Her Kiss* and was ready to write it, so I decided I'd tell Lauren's story in book 3.

Originally, it was going to be a cop-thief dynamic in which Mia would be the detective assigned to Lauren's case. They would be online fandom friends but enemies in real life, and I was pretty excited about that concept. I'd always wanted to write an online friends/real life enemies book, vaguely inspired by the dynamic in *You've Got Mail*, after all.

Then covid happened, along with a lot of unrest in the United States about police brutality and institutionalized racism. For many reasons, it wasn't the right time to write a book about an NYPD detective...or a book as emotionally dark as what I had originally planned. I put Lauren's book on hold while I decided how to move forward.

In the meantime, I had the opportunity to pitch a book to Montlake, and on a whim, I pitched a sapphic *You've Got Mail*, which became *Read Between the Lines*, so...there went the online friends/real life enemies aspect of Lauren's book. I had no idea if I could make a new book out of what was left. I began to wonder if I should just shelve Lauren's book.

As a longtime fangirl myself, I'd always envisioned that

Lauren and Mia would be online fandom friends before they met in real life, brought together by their love of a television show. I also knew that I might later write the story of the actress who starred in that show, so that I could tie in Lauren's fanfic.

As I scrambled to write my first book during lockdown, I decided to flip the order and write Piper's story first. While I was writing *Come Away with Me*, I knew they were reading Lauren's fanfic. And through that process, I discovered what Lauren and Mia's new story would be. And you know what? I love it so much more than all the other versions I had considered along the way! This is how their story was meant to be. It's so much softer, and they just make me so happy.

As you probably know by now, I often let readers choose and name the pets in my books. For *She'll Steal Your Heart*, I owe thanks to Jennifer Kridler who allowed me to honor her late cat, Gilbert, with a storyline in this book. Jennifer, I hope you enjoyed seeing the fictionalized version of Gilbert on the page. Thanks also to Nancy Holten for naming Chaos and Mayhem – they were a blast to write!

Thanks as always to my family for being so supportive of my often unpredictable and demanding schedule. Also thank you to my critique partner, Annie Rains, for providing invaluable insight during an early draft of this book, and to my editor, Linda Ingmanson, for bringing it all together.

I am endlessly grateful to every reader, blogger, reviewer, and friend who has supported me along the way, whether it's by reading one of my books, leaving a review, following me on social media, or sending me a Tweet or an email. Your support means more to me than you know!

xoxo

Rachel

KEEP READING

Have you read my standalone, stranded sapphic romance, *Lost in Paradise*? Turn the page to read the first chapter...

LOST IN PARADISE

CHAPTER 1

Nicole Morella rested a hand on the doorway as the floor shifted beneath her feet. It had been eight hours since they set sail from Naples in southern Italy, and she hadn't found her sea legs yet. Was it called setting sail on a modern-day, engine-powered boat? Nicole steadied herself as she took in the lounge before her. Couples and groups lingered over drinks at the various tables and sofas filling the room. Laughter and conversation drifted on the air, undercut by gentle strains of jazz music.

Her gaze wandered to the bar, which was just as crowded. A man sat alone at the near end, watching her as he sipped from his drink. She looked away, determined not to lose her nerve and retreat to her cabin on her first night at sea. This trip was her post-divorce gift to herself, and she was going to make the most of it. Tonight, she was going to enjoy a drink at the bar—alone—and she was going to have fun doing it.

About halfway down the bar, a blonde in a red dress sat talking to the man beside her. The seat to her right was empty, and Nicole decided to take it. She crossed the room and slid onto the empty stool, setting her black clutch on the polished wood in front of her. Keeping her back angled slightly toward the man on her other side, who had already begun to eye her with curiosity, she held the bartender's gaze as he sidled over. "Do you have a house red?"

"Yes, ma'am. It's a cabernet blend from Veneto. Very smooth. Would you like to try it?"

"If you like red, you should try the Petit Verdot," a husky British voice said. "It's from Bordeaux, very full-bodied, with just a hint of berries."

Nicole turned to find the woman to her left watching her out of sky-blue eyes as she swirled the contents of her wineglass. "The Petit Verdot?"

"It's excellent." The blonde swiveled to face her, tucking an unruly strand of thick, wavy hair away from her face. She looked to be about Nicole's age—mid-thirties. Light freckles spattered her forehead and chest that, combined with her wild hair and direct stare, lent her a sort of unconventional beauty that Nicole found it difficult to look away from.

"I'll, um, I'll try a glass of that," Nicole told the bartender.

He nodded, moving down the bar to pour her drink.

"American, hm?" the blonde said, still watching her.

Nicole nodded, inexplicably flushed and tongue-twisted when she herself hadn't had even a sip of alcohol yet tonight. She'd booked herself a private Mediterranean cruise to find her footing after the divorce, and she had every intention of doing it alone. Yet, here she was, heart racing for a total stranger. It had been a long time since she'd felt this kind of attraction and even longer since she'd felt it for a woman. "I'm from New York. And you?"

The blonde swirled her wineglass again before taking a

sip. "I live just outside Nice, along the southern coast of France."

"Oh, I thought you were..." Nicole fumbled, grateful as the bartender interrupted to hand her a glass of wine identical to the one the woman beside her held.

"I'm an expat," the blonde said, tossing an amused glance over her shoulder at Nicole. "Born and raised in London."

"Right." Nicole lifted the glass and took a sip. The wine was rich, spicy but fruity. It tasted expensive. And exotic. A lot like the woman next to her. "It's good."

"Glad you think so," she said.

Nicole couldn't figure why the blonde was still talking to her, why she'd basically turned her back to her date when Nicole sat down. But then again, maybe he wasn't her date at all, because he was sitting there now, looking annoyed but also interested, his gaze flicking between the blonde and Nicole. Maybe he was just a random guy hitting on a single woman in a bar, and that woman was now giving him the cold shoulder.

Nicole found her spirits buoyed at the good fortune to have sat next to another single woman...for casual conversation purposes, anyway, not because she was ridiculously attracted to her. "I'm Nicole," she said.

"Fiona," the blonde replied. "Are you here alone, Nicole?"

She nodded. "You?"

"Unfortunately, yes." Fiona dropped her gaze to her wineglass, and Nicole couldn't help admiring the swell of her breasts beneath the formfitting bodice of her dress. Every inch of her was foreign and beautiful, dangerous for a woman committed to a week of solo soul-searching. "I was supposed to meet someone on the boat...a man."

"Oh." Nicole went for casual and hoped she succeeded. It was a good thing if Fiona was straight. It meant Nicole could sit and chat with her harmlessly. Safe.

"He stood me up," Fiona continued, a sharp bite to her tone. "The bastard."

"Aren't they all?" Nicole mumbled, reaching for her wine.

"Indeed," Fiona agreed. "I thought this one was an exception, at least good for a week of sex on the high seas."

The man on the other side of her choked on his drink, and Fiona cast a disapproving glance in his direction at his blatant eavesdropping. Nicole swallowed her laugh with another sip of the luxuriously rich wine Fiona had recommended. So much better than the house red she would have gotten otherwise.

"It's why I generally prefer women to men," Fiona said, a bit louder, and her would-be paramour's cheeks darkened before he turned away.

It was Nicole's turn to choke on her drink. She coughed and spluttered as wine burned its way down her esophagus while Fiona gave her a knowing look that said she'd read her interest and—God, was it possible she returned the feeling?

"So that's my sad story," Fiona said, still holding Nicole in her intense stare. "Why are you all alone on this lovely, romantic boat?"

"It's my post-divorce splurge for myself," Nicole said, clearing her throat and wishing she had a cup of water to cool the burning sensation from inhaling her wine. "I came here to rediscover my sense of adventure or find myself... something like that."

Fiona's eyes crinkled in a warm smile. "I must say I

prefer your story to mine. Not the divorce, but making your own adventure. I like that."

"Thanks." Her cheeks were burning. They were probably as red as Fiona's dress. She really needed to get a grip. Her fingers tightened around the stem of her wineglass. "I'd always wanted to visit the Mediterranean—my family's from Italy originally—and I'd always wanted to take a cruise. So, here I am."

"Ballsy of you," Fiona said, her gaze sliding to the simple gray knit dress that Nicole wore.

She crossed her legs involuntarily. "Do you know this area pretty well, then?"

"I do. It's lovely," Fiona said, tossing her hair over her shoulder as she returned her attention to the wineglass in front of her, leaving Nicole feeling somewhat bereft after the intensity and heat of her gaze. "Although I prefer the French Riviera to Italy or Greece."

"Is that why you moved there?"

"Mm. My favorite place in the world."

"I was in Paris once, for business," Nicole said, remembering that she'd been somewhat lonely and off-balance on that trip too. That was two years ago, when she'd first begun to realize how unhappy she'd become in her marriage. If only she'd known then just how much worse things would get.

"Paris is charming, but if you really want to get the flavor of France, you've got to visit the countryside," Fiona said, swirling her wine.

"I'll have to visit sometime." Nicole felt a tingle in the pit of her stomach, as if she'd somehow accepted an invitation to visit her, when in reality, Fiona was just making idle conversation. Likely, the attraction was entirely one-sided. After all, it had been an eternity since Nicole had flirted with anyone, gone on a date, done anything but steel herself for another battle of the wills with Brandon. She wasn't sure she even remembered how to flirt at this point...

"And what is it that you do for work?" Fiona asked.

"I'm the senior marketing manager for an investment firm in Manhattan."

"Sounds very...corporate."

"It is." Nicole released a sigh that seemed to reach all the way to her soul. "I've been so caught up in work, I'm embarrassed to tell you how long it's been since I took a vacation."

"I'd say you needed this one, then," Fiona said.

"I did. I really did."

The man on the other side of Fiona was watching them again. She gave him an irritated look before her gaze darted back to Nicole. "Care to go for a walk?"

"Um, sure."

"I could use some air." Fiona stood, reaching for her wineglass and a small white purse that she slung over her shoulder.

Nicole followed, bringing her own wine and her black clutch. Alcohol hadn't improved her seaworthiness, though, and she stumbled as they reached the doorway.

"Careful," Fiona murmured, the "r" lost to the cadence of her accent as her free hand grasped Nicole's elbow. Her fingers were warm, her grip surprisingly strong, and Nicole was almost positive that Fiona lingered several moments longer than was strictly necessary.

FIONA BOONE LED the way onto the deck, dotted here and there with couples in search of fresh air and darkness to cover their actions. She'd thought this cruise was going to be dreadfully dull after Dimitris stood her up. That was before she met Nicole.

She led Nicole toward the rear of the boat to a quiet spot she'd discovered earlier. The curve of the deck hid them from view, but the protruding hulk of one of the lifeboats kept it from being a popular spot...unless one was looking for a place to hide from prying eyes, and right now, that was exactly what Fiona was going for. She leaned her elbows on the railing, taking in the glittering lights of the Italian coastline in the distance. "Beautiful, isn't it?"

"Yeah." Nicole's voice was softer now, as if hushed by the night.

The ship's engine hummed beneath them, accentuated by the splash of water against the hull. Rhythmic and soothing. Fiona had always loved the sea, although she preferred to enjoy it with her feet on dry land. She dangled the wineglass in her left hand, watching the play of white against black as water sprayed out of the darkness below. "I like places like this...out of the way, private. I'm not much for crowds."

"You seem like you could handle just about anything." Amusement laced Nicole's tone.

"I didn't say I couldn't handle them. I just prefer solitude, that's all."

"And here I had you pegged as a social butterfly."

Fiona turned her head, meeting Nicole's gaze in the near darkness. "Is that how you had me pegged?"

"Among other things." Nicole licked her lips, and they glistened in the moonlight, driving Fiona to distraction.

"Good, because I'm many things."

"Tell me a few of them. What do you do for work?"

"I'm an artist." Fiona watched the lights bobbing on the horizon, twinkling like fallen stars.

"Oh, really? What kind of art? Do you paint?"

"Digital mostly, but yes, I do paint." She slid her gaze to Nicole, who was watching her intently. They stood close enough that Fiona could inch her elbow to the right and bump Nicole's. Could have, but she didn't. Not yet, anyway. "Graphic design pays the bills. I paint mostly for myself, although I sell some locally."

"Landscapes or people?"

"Both." She let her gaze drop from Nicole's face to her body, endless curves highlighted by her formfitting dress. Brown hair, hazel eyes, olive-tinted skin. Earth tones. She'd look so much more vibrant in a mossy-green dress than this gray one. "I could paint you, but I'd use brighter colors."

"Like Jack draws Rose in *Titanic*?" Nicole's voice had dropped an octave or two, into the timbre of Fiona's lusty daydreams.

She scoffed. "Hardly. That's a rubbish movie. The ship sinks, and they all die, even poor Jack because Rose's too selfish to share her bit of wood with him."

"Why, Fiona, are you a romantic at heart?" Nicole asked, shifting subtly closer.

"I can be romantic." She lifted her right hand from the railing and brushed it against the curve of Nicole's waist, lingering for a moment there. An innocent enough gesture if Nicole didn't want this to happen, but Fiona had pretty good radar about these things, and she was confident she hadn't read her wrong. Nicole wanted her as badly as she wanted Nicole.

She sucked in a breath at the contact, her eyes finding Fiona's in the dark. Fiona was fairly sure Nicole's interest had more to do with avoiding memories of her ex-husband than Fiona herself, but she didn't mind. She was only looking for a distraction, someone to pass a lonely night or two with here on the ship. It had been months since she'd had sex, too many months, and she was ridiculously horny, an itch she'd been counting on Dimitris to scratch. But now, she found herself even more excited by the prospect of it being Nicole.

In the distance, another boat motored in their direction, engine rumbling in the night. Fiona reached out, sweeping the dark curtain of Nicole's hair over her shoulder. Her fingers brushed Nicole's neck, and she felt goose bumps rise beneath her touch. Fiona leaned in, her pulse going haywire the closer her lips got to Nicole's. They met in a rush of hot breath, noses bumping as their lips pressed together. Nicole let out a hum of pleasure, her eyes sliding shut as Fiona pressed a light kiss against her cheek before bringing their mouths back into alignment.

This time, Nicole opened to her, and Fiona slipped her tongue into her mouth, tasting the same wine she herself had been drinking. Somehow, it tasted sweeter in the hidden pleasure of Nicole's kiss, heady and lush as the Italian countryside they'd left behind that morning. Fiona slid her free hand to the hollow of Nicole's back, pressing her closer, kissing her deeper, drinking her in, suddenly certain this kiss was a hundred times better than anything she would have shared with Dimitris this week.

"Whoa," Nicole whispered as she lifted her head.

"Is that a good thing?" she asked, feathering a hand through Nicole's hair.

She nodded, her face bobbing in Fiona's vision as a shy smile played around her lips. "Better than good."

"I thought so too." Fiona brushed her fingers over the soft fabric of Nicole's dress, smoothing it over the dip of her waist. "In fact, I'm very glad to have been stood up."

"Is he your boyfriend?" There was something hesitant in Nicole's voice now.

Fiona was a lot of things, but she wasn't a cheat, and she wouldn't have Nicole feeling any guilt over Dimitris. "No. He's my... Even lover is too familiar a term. He's a businessman who travels almost exclusively. Occasionally, maybe once or twice a year, if he's in town and we're both currently unattached, we'll get together for a few nights. It's just sex, and in this case, he was called away on business last minute, so I wound up all alone on this lovely boat."

"That's..." Nicole's brow furrowed. "I was married for so long, I don't have any experience with an arrangement like that."

"It's the only kind of relationship I have experience with," Fiona said, a warning in case Nicole wasn't interested in a night of casual sex.

"Oh," she said quietly.

"Your divorce is recent?" Fiona asked.

"Three months. I'm supposed to be using this trip to figure things out by myself."

Fiona sipped her wine, feeling slightly desperate at the thought of having to let her go. She so rarely experienced such an instant connection with someone, let alone this kind of sizzling chemistry. "Would you like me to leave you to it, then?"

"No," Nicole answered quickly, stepping closer.

Fiona met her gaze. "Good."

The other boat had drawn closer, its engine obnoxiously loud. It seemed like their boat, the *Cyprus Star*, had picked up speed, perhaps trying to put more space between itself and its new neighbor. Fiona wished for a table so she could set down her wine. Nicole was stuck carrying wine in one hand and her clutch in the other, no free hands for touching, and maybe Fiona hadn't planned this little rendezvous as well as she'd thought.

"Do they seem too close to you?" Nicole asked, turning her attention to the approaching boat. It seemed to be heading straight for them.

"Mm," Fiona agreed, annoyed at the interruption.

"Maybe it's the Coast Guard?"

"Could be." But the other boat had drawn close enough now that its outline was visible in the night, and it didn't look like an official vessel. There were no identifying marks she could see, no maritime flag or police lights. Instinctively, she stepped into the shadows, drawing Nicole with her.

The approaching boat drew alongside the *Cyprus Star*, and with a horrible screech, their hulls bumped and rubbed, sending a shudder through the deck beneath her feet.

"Oh my God," Nicole whispered.

Almost immediately, men dressed in black tossed ropes to secure their vessel to the *Cyprus Star*. The engine roared belowdecks, an apparent attempt by the captain to shake free, but it was too late. The marauders threw a ladder that hooked onto the *Cyprus Star*'s railing and began scaling it one after another.

"Fuck," Fiona mumbled. She tossed her wineglass into the seething depths of the Mediterranean, then grabbed Nicole's and sent it after hers. She crouched, drawing Nicole down with her, and they pressed themselves into a darkened recess in the side of the ship.

"What's going on?" Nicole whispered. Her hand, still clutched in Fiona's, shook.

"Shh. I don't know, but I don't think it's anything good."

Men's voices shouted in Greek, too jumbled for Fiona to pick out more than the fact that they'd just been boarded by some kind of maritime pirates, and *fuck*, this was bad. She wrapped her arms around Nicole, who promptly buried her face against Fiona's chest, something she would have appreciated a lot more five minutes ago. Now, her heart was about to burst out of her chest, and she wasn't the least bit aroused.

"Everyone listen to me!" a man shouted, followed by the *pop pop pop* of gunfire, and Fiona recoiled. A shaft of moonlight passed overhead, illuminating her red dress like a beacon in the night.

ALSO BY RACHEL LACEY

Ms. Right Series

Read Between the Lines

No Rings Attached

Midnight in Manhattan Series

Don't Cry for Me

It's in Her Kiss

Come Away with Me

She'll Steal Your Heart

Standalone Books

Stars Collide

Lost in Paradise

Hideaway

Off the Rails

ABOUT THE AUTHOR

 Rachel Lacey is a contemporary romance author and semi-reformed travel junkie. She's been climbed by a monkey on a mountain in Japan, gone scuba diving on the Great Barrier Reef, and camped out overnight in New York City for a chance to be an extra in a movie. These days, the majority of her adventures take place on the pages of the books she writes. She lives in the mountains of Vermont with her family and a variety of rescue pets.

facebook.com/RachelLaceyAuthor

twitter.com/rachelslacey

instagram.com/rachelslacey

amazon.com/author/rachellacey

bookbub.com/authors/rachel-lacey